Z-ROD

Part 2: Heirs of Promise

A Celtic saga of warriors and saints

However long the day, the evening will come
Celtic proverb

Martin C. Haworth

To Naomi –
Hoping you'll engage again with these familiar
characters. Very Best Wishes,

Martin Haworth

malcolm down

PUBLISHING

First published 2022 by Malcolm Down Publishing Ltd.

British Library Cataloguing in Publication Data
A catalogue record for this book is available from the British Library.

ISBN 978-1-915046-08-6

Cover design and Celtic geometrical designs by Meg Daniels:
https://www.bergamotbrown.com/

The maps and Pictish images are drawn by the author and most
of the remaining sketches are by Avril and Karyn Priestley.

Art direction by Sarah Grace

Printed in the UK

Commendations

"A compelling saga of Picts and Gaels in sixth-century Scotland. Martin C. Haworth is a gifted writer with the imagination to make the past live. The writing is vivid, at times poetic, with many memorable scenes. Characters are credible – both male and female – and all of life is here: birth, love, marriage, death, fear, challenge, ecstasy, and human strength and weakness.

Martin's deep love of the hills and wildlands is palpable in these pages, as is the depth of his knowledge of tribal lifestyles and customs.

The Z-rod trilogy contrasts two belief systems and is as much about a clash of ideologies as about skirmishes in pursuit of political power: on the one hand, the old faith of Scotland, on the other the new Christian beliefs.

These two ways of being are embodied by cousins Taran and Oengus. *Heirs of Promise* depicts Oengus's growth as a warrior leader, nurtured by the wisdom of Conchen and Alpia, and following druidic teaching to placate the Bulàch.

In parallel, we follow the growth in maturity of Taran as a Christian saint. He is disciplined by the wisdom of Fillan, a monk from Ireland, by the prophecies of Ossian, and the testing challenges of his 'white martyrdom' which leads him to renounce marriage – for the moment – and to encounter a wonder and love beyond all understanding.

But the Z-rod symbol, denoting leadership of the Ce tribe, is still on Taran's back, which haunts Oengus. What will its significance be in Taran's mission to bear *fire to the north*?

Readers of *Heirs of Promise* will await the final volume in the trilogy with immense anticipation."

Dr John Dempster, Highland News columnist

"Immediately I became involved with these characters, immersed in their world and caring about their struggles. This is a confident and impressive piece of writing. The vivid scenes are of long-ago Scotland, but the uncertainties and sure things of life are just as now."

Andy Raine, Northumbria Community

Contents

Characters featured in the story

(arranged in alphabetical order)

Aleine Brona – crippled girl on Inis Kayru.

Alma – Aleine Brona's mother.

Alpia – Conchen's great-niece.

Aniel – monk at Dindurn.

Brude – warlord of the Fortriu Picts and overlord of the northern Picts.

Caltram – Oengus' son.

Carvorst – the ferryman.

Castantin – monk at Dindurn.

Coblaith & Elpin – Ce peasants who provided refuge for Taran.

Conchen – wife to the former warlord, Talorgen, and great aunt to Alpia and Oengus.

Cynbel – warlord of the Circinn Picts.

Derile – Oengus' sister and wife to Cynbel, the Circinn warlord.

Domech – warlord of the Fotla Picts with seat of power at Dindurn.

Drostan – Taran's undercover name.

Drest – one of Domech's guards.

Drust – Oengus' deputy commander.

Drusticc – Oengus' mother.

Eithni – Oengus' wife.

Fillan – abbot of Dindurn.

Fionnoula – wet nurse at Rhynie.

Gabran – king of Dal Riata.

Gest – assistant to the chief druid, Maelchon.

Girom – father of Aleine Brona.

Kessog – Fillan's martyred mentor.

Maelchon – chief druid at Rhynie.

Maevis – chief priestess of the Bulàch.

Nechtan – Taran's father.

Nola – midwife in Rhynie.

Oengus – warlord of the Ce Picts.

Ossian – itinerant bard.

Taran – exiled prince and pilgrim (also known as Drostan).

Talorgen – former warlord of the Ce Picts, featured in Part 1.

Map of 'Scotland' in the 6th century AD

The journey of Taran's White Martyrdom

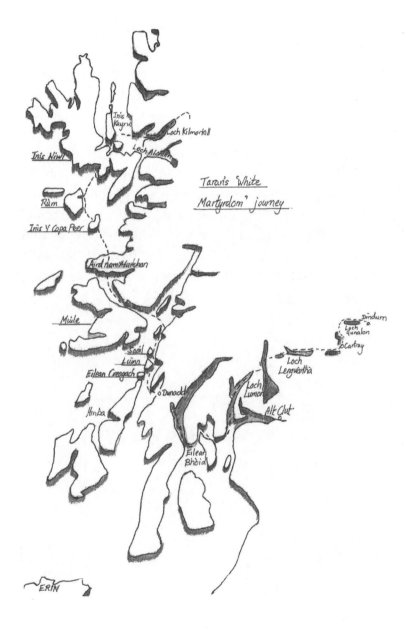

Taran's 'White Martyrdom' journey

Acknowledgements

The enthusiasm of friends and strangers who have left reviews on the first book in this series have encouraged me to further develop this trilogy. Writing fulfils the creative urge and there is great satisfaction in that alone, but the warm reception means the writing has connected with like-minded individuals in appreciating this fascinating fusion of Picts and early Celtic saints.

A very special thanks to Andy Raine for all his proofreading at short notice, for his warm support and in providing an endorsement, along with Dr John Dempster. Also, a hearty thanks to Karyn and Avril Priestley for their contribution of chapter heading sketches. Finally, a big appreciation again to Meg Daniels in creating another iconic cover image for this series.

Dedication

To the Buhid tribe of Mindoro, the Philippines who took us under their wing, showing how community and lifestyle operate at the level described in this trilogy.

Synopsis of Part 1: Chosen Wanderers

This is the second part of the Z-rod trilogy. The first book, 'Chosen Wanderers', tells how cousins, Taran and Oengus, are driven apart by the marking of the Z-rod on Taran's back, a mysterious Pictish power symbol, reserved exclusively for the warlord. After the loss of lives in an ambush, a council is convened at which Oengus' dying father names Taran as a traitor. The chief druid leads the main characters to his mentor's crannog to determine a dire remedy. Sensing that he is to be sacrificed, Taran makes good his escape despite his cousin's efforts to kill him.

Running parallel to the main drama, Fillan's story begins with his leaving Erin (Ireland) with an older monk, Kessog, and of their establishing a *muintir* – a Christian monastic community – on Loch Lumon on the borders of the Pictish world. Their island fastness acts as a springboard for forays into the territory of the Fotla Picts, one of which is detailed as they confront the powers of pagandom and Domech, the unpredictable warlord of the Fotla. After a contest of spiritual knowledge and strength, Fillan is invited to establish a *muintir* at the seat of the warlord's power at Dindurn.

With Taran out of the way, Oengus is frustrated in his plans to reform his tribe by his revitalised great-uncle, the existing warlord, Talorgen. The mounting tension between the two ends with Talorgen's mysterious death, and Oengus sweeps to power unopposed. His headstrong ways are typified by rejecting Eithni, who is carrying his child, but is checked by the outspoken and powerful chief priestess of the Bulàch, the mother-earth goddess. Increasing alienation and lack of popularity lead Oengus to follow the advice of his Aunt Conchen, a fount of homely wisdom, resulting in him bringing Eithni back to their community as his wife. Overshadowing his rule is the unknown whereabouts of his missing cousin and the hostility of Taran's family and Taran's former girlfriend, Alpia.

Nurtured by a peasant couple in an obscure place in the mountains, Taran begins to recall the prophecies surrounding the Z-rod in a bid to take revenge on his cousin, reclaim his right to become warlord and be reunited with Alpia. His onward adventure leads to a surprise meeting under the Stone of Refuge with Ossian, the bard who had uttered prophetic words determining Taran's mysterious destiny. At Ossian's injunction, Taran goes south to Dindurn to find sanctuary in Fillan's *muintir.* The abbot prophetically reveals how Taran could move beyond his fallen status and remake himself as a warrior-saint by acquiring nine graces through undertaking a series of quests to enable him in the ultimate challenge of *bearing fire to the north.*

The Ossian Prophecy

Make great haste when you leave. Be cunning, be brave, be humble. Your surrender will be in the south; your transformation in the isles of the west; your fulfilment coincides with the anticipation of the learned ones far to the north, before you return east with great peace.

Before that peace blossoms, there will come much strife, like a blight threatening to consume. Heartache and anguish lie before you. Many a journey awaits, full of ordeals that you consider will be your undoing, though these are in truth, rites of passage for your own preparation. You will be the doer of mighty deeds and the acts will be the making of the man. Take heart, my son, through one you will overcome the world.

Fillan's prophetic prayer

*The nine graces for a warrior saint to withstand
the powers of this world.*

*May these be acquired:
mercy to confound the foe,
and to bind up the injured;
humility and perseverance as characteristics
to be known by and be outstanding in.
Render your sword in surrender
so that obedience to the King will be complete
and thereby, to be rid of all pride so as to love totally.
May valour, to champion the oppressed, be for your renown;
and peace abundant when considering apparent failure;
hope to prove firm in the face of despair;
and faithfulness to lead to the very ends of the earth.
Where there is loss, may gain be known;
with ill-repute, the High King's approval;
where there is disgust, the favour of the Almighty;
and when in poverty to perceive the riches of the
Everlasting's glory.*

Chapter One

Uncertain Imbolc

556 AD   Rhynie

"I have brought you a gift," Gest, the druid's assistant, presented a folded-up pig's hide with a flourish, suggesting to Oengus a good deal of satisfaction on the part of the giver concerning his handiwork.

What could his friend have prepared? he thought, as he took the gift. What piece of artistry was he to receive?

"Open it out," Gest instructed eagerly, shifting weight to his other leg.

He tried to shake out the folds, but being so stiff, the parchment required another hand to open the folds. He held it at arm's length, admiring a large tattoo. "The boar's head!" he pronounced with wonder and admiration.

"I thought you would like it!"

He could see from the corner of his eye that Gest was beaming.

"I mind you telling me, after returning from Brude's court, how you would like the boar's head to represent the new Rhynie you intend to build to rival Y Broch with its bull figures!"

"Well remembered! Thank you — I shall prize this, and hang it in my new home."

"It looks finished," Gest nodded in the direction of the hut.

"Almost. Come inside and look." They stepped over the threshold. "It is not as large as Eithni and I had at first intended, but that means it was finished sooner."

"Good morning, Eithni!" the druid greeted. "It looks like you have received many gifts already."

"Folk have been kind," she replied, arranging some sheepskins around a seating place. "We have received deer pelts, woven lengths, cooking pots, baskets, vessels and more besides."

Oengus grunted with satisfaction. "The main thing is we now have a place of our own. It was grim staying with my mother still mourning father's death."

"Preparing a home in readiness for parenthood," observed Gest agreeably. "I will leave you two to get on with things. I just called by to see how you were doing and bring a gift for the new home."

"Thanks, Gest, especially for this fine gift. I shall hang it now." He felt slightly flustered as he wished his friend to remain longer, and found himself poised indecisively between the wall, where he thought of hanging the gift, and barring the doorway to prevent his friend's premature departure.

"It would be better if you were to place it under your bedding for a few days to flatten. That way, it will hang better."

"I shall do that. But why the haste? Must you leave so soon!"

"I did not wish to intrude!"

"Intrude! A friend can never intrude! You have been absent from Rhynie for weeks ..."

"I was back home by the sea. Having not seen my family in over a year, they pressed me to stay longer than I had intended and it did not take much persuading." In his

18

amiable way, Gest spoke at length about people Oengus did not know, or would ever likely to meet, which would have been tedious were it not for his friend's enthusiastic manner. He made these people of the coast seem the most pleasant characters one could ever wish to meet.

Pulling himself upright, Gest paused thoughtfully and asked with slightly knitted brows, "Tell me, how have things been with you, Oengus? You appear more settled. Does a new home have that effect on a person?"

"Oh, yes – at least in part! It is most decidedly a joy to have your own home; something that should have happened earlier were it not for the whirlwind of events that swept us all along!" He looked upon his own hut, as he was in the habit of doing frequently, and his heart swelled with an unfamiliar gratitude. "Here, I can breathe easily and be my own person."

"And completed at a crucial time for Eithni too!" The young druid shifted his eyes momentarily to Eithni's belly, now most swollen with child.

"Indeed," he smiled easily and with good humour. "Eithni has been like a swallow in late spring, flitting here and there, making mud in her beak, eager to build her nest!"

"And you have been like a swallow yourself!" retorted Eithni, eager to put the record straight.

"Well, this is grander than a home built of mud," observed the young druid, seeming eager to pay them both a compliment.

Oengus was glad of his friend's approval. The home represented the reconciliation with Eithni who he had spurned, marking the huge turning point following the rebuff from the high priestess of the Bulàch. Their new start together was full of possibilities, combined with the joy of anticipated parenthood.

"So," the young druid turned to Eithni, "how have you been keeping?"

"Well!" she replied almost evasively.

Gest held her in his gaze, awaiting her elaboration.

"I feel extremely heavy, tired, unbalanced." She raised both arms, hunching her shoulders. "Aside from that, I have kept as well as any mother-to-be could hope for. I am looking forward to seeing this child come safely into this world."

"This time last year," continued Gest, "you were both just lone individuals, and then you became two! And now, look at you, you are soon to become three!" Gest smiled, shaking his head with a little incredulity.

"Aye, it is yet another part of feeling propelled forward." He felt the ordeal of keeping his head above the sudden flood of events, which like a river in spate, had swept him forward. He had known that inexorable sense of being swept along by an impetuous and unstoppable force. Where others may have succumbed and been dashed and drowned, he had held his own, going with the current, making the most of its unanticipated progress.

"So, you are enjoying the domestic progress common to mankind. But you have not spoken about your responsibilities as ruler over your people and how people are responding to you."

"Things feel more established now that Talorgen has been buried. It seems that his rule has been finally put behind us! People are coming around to accepting peace with the Circinn, welcoming a cessation to the age-old conflict that was a thorn in our side. Without that distraction, the Ce can take a new trail for us to ascend to the heights."

Gest looked at him good-naturedly. "You sound inspired, my friend, intent to make your mark on the world!"

Oengus was glad of Gest's friendship, forged on that unforgettable morning when they rode together on horseback in pursuit of his cousin, Taran, following his rival's escape from the crannog. Most welcome was Gest's support, coming at a pivotal time, when others had been unsure and had judged critically. Moreover, Gest was a crucial ally from among the fraternity of druids, a peer who he trusted and understood, different from the morose-mannered chief druid, Maelchon, who was hard to read and easy to cross. Maelchon was forever associated with Talorgen, of the same generation and both taciturn.

"Well, I must be on my way – Maelchon is expecting me." Gest turned to leave and Oengus accompanied him beyond the threshold, walking to the gateway to their modest citadel. He could sense that his good friend had something on his mind when he slowed, looking thoughtfully at the ground. "Are things well now between you and Eithni?"

"Poof! What is well?" he uttered evasively.

"Then, I take it that things could be better?"

"That is one way of putting it." He felt awkward talking, and thought of dismissing the subject, until he reminded himself that Gest was his confidant in whom his secrets were secure. Besides, his friend knew him well – and what was left unsaid would be given its own interpretation. "Things are not what they were before I abandoned Eithni. We make the best of things. Who knows? In the passing of time, with the coming of parenthood, we shall perhaps move on and find a fresh delight in being together."

"And Taran?"

He has saved his pithy questions to the end, he thought, biting his lip. "I should like to forget Taran and believe that he has met some untimely end, perished in the hills, or at the hand of man. But Maevis revealed otherwise."

"That was back last autumn. Maybe, since then, he has perished."

"I do not feel that he has, but that he is still at large, awaiting his moment to pounce. I feel his shadow at times at my back, haunting, seething with indignation, biding his time for his moment to take his revenge."

"It is not healthy to think like that, my friend!"

"Well, I am just being honest, as I only can be with you."

Gest reached out an arm and placed his hand firmly upon his shoulder. "You shall rise, Oengus; you will grow in stature and fulfil your ambitions."

"Are you speaking prophetically like a druid, or saying things to make me feel better about my situation?"

"I do believe that it is not of my own accord. Ambition is a creative force, and you are not the man to leave things undone. Your boldness will bring things into being – and the Bulàch will strengthen your arm if you continue to pay her homage."

He felt warmed by his druid's words of hope.

Gest turned to go. "Oh, I almost forgot!" he said, turning in his tracks. "Maelchon said that we will celebrate Imbolc tomorrow, just before sunset, here at the threshold stone." With that he left.

The following day, when Gest had concluded a formal prayer around the salmon and beast stone, Maelchon came to the fore, raising his voice to be heard by those standing at the back of a deep gathering.

"Today, is a marker, the first of three. Imbolc precedes Ostara and Beltane, stating the ascendancy of the light." A gust of wind plastered the side of his hair and beard with icy sleet. He stopped to scrape it away. "Winter is being banished as spring is anticipated." Even the morose chief druid, detecting the irony of his words, smiled. "On this day, the Bulàch has journeyed to the bubbling spring of youth to drink of that elixir, and the old hag shall be born again as the youthful maiden, the fecund Brigantia."

Oengus mused that these truths had to be taken in trust, irrespective of weather. He felt encouraged regarding the ascendancy of the sun, believing a significant corner had been turned on this journey out of winter. He further considered his own position as warlord, with the way cleared for him to progress and begin the reforms that were fermenting in his mind.

The chief druid nodded to Gest who carried a broad basin in one hand and a ewer in the other. Placing the basin right at the foot of the standing stone, he filled the container with water, and taking a wooden vessel from his bag, laid it down beside the basin alongside eight candles. Maelchon brought over a smouldering brazier suspended from a pole. The two druids crouched on either side of the large monolith, leaning against its bulk to shield the brazier from the strong gusts of wind. A kindling ball of straw and wood shavings were placed on the charcoal's glowing embers which combusted almost instantly. The two druids lit the candles, dripping wax onto the wooden base of the vessel to secure them in place. Then, they floated the vessel in the basin.

Straightening himself, Maelchon addressed his audience. Oengus noticed a veil of dark vapour, full of moisture, move towards them, outlined against the tattered grey of an overcast sky.

"The candles burn anew, one for each of the eight stages of the year. Light emerges in our dim, winter world; the old hag is transformed into the beauty of the young maiden who becomes our mother. Be respectful to her, for she looks upon you."

Just then, a strong gust came and extinguished half the candles. Maelchon paused whilst Gest relit them. "The light burns above the cleansing waters from which Brigantia emerges in her transformation. Friends, this is a time to recall our infancy, nurtured by a mother's love, she, who sings over us as we descend into the safety of rest beneath her gaze."

After the ceremony, he took Eithni home. She had grown cold.

"I did not like the candles being blown out!" she remarked oddly, warming her hands at the hearth.

"Oh, that is just the wind; it is usually blustery at this time of year. It is winter after all, even though the druids will insist on saying it is the first day of spring!" His glib response, though, sounded slightly hollow, for Eithni's words brought a momentary chill down his spine. However, not one for superstitious premonitions, he deliberately passed on to consider other matters.

Chapter Two

An Opportunity

558AD Dindurn

As Taran crossed the meadow, his attention was captured by a murmuration of starlings, wheeling about in a dense column, changing shape yet maintaining a distinctive series of forms in a group orchestration. As the flock whirled around in perfect unison, the light caught the underside of their wings, changing their previously heavy dark formation into something almost transparent and insubstantial that made him think his eyes were playing tricks. Filled with a deepening sense of wonder, he watched this shifting cloud of wings descend from the heavens. Then, something exceedingly odd happened, a sight he had never seen before, or would have given credence to ever occurring. Several of the starlings broke rank from the shifting rhomboid to alight on a fellow standing beneath their formation. Being at a distance, he had not noticed the man's arms outstretched in a cruciform manner.

What strange apparition is this? he thought as he briskly crossed the field, the hairs on the back of his neck bristling with that peculiar sensation of awe. Once he drew near enough to see the man's features, he recognised Aniel, the monk whose company he particularly enjoyed. He half raised a hand in a questioning gesture, not daring to speak, less he disturbed this spectacle.

Noticing his approach, Aniel looked up with a face full of the sublime quietude of a man who had been deep in prayer. For an instant his features were expressionless, then in that moment of recognition, Aniel's face blossomed into a warm grin.

Not daring to venture further, and noticing a nearby boulder, he slowly sat down with the kind of reverence shown when monks entered the oratory. He watched, enthralled by this strange spectacle, as the rhomboid continued to spiral above his friend like some heavenly sign indicating a chosen one. He observed more birds descending from the spiralling mass to alight upon his fellow pilgrim, replacing their companions who ascended back into the whirling column. Had Aniel been praying like that when the starlings had gathered above him, or had he opened out his arms in this welcoming gesture, inviting them to perch? Transfixed by the scene, he wondered what manner of spirituality set his friend apart. He had observed, from previous occasions, that animals had a special affinity with his friend, seemingly recognising a gentleness of character that posed no threat. These birds showed such confidence, as if intent on including a human in their exuberant display . . . could it be some kind of mystical celebration?

The spectacle lasted briefly, for the starlings suddenly moved on, like a fast flow of water that had been abruptly poured out, streaming through the air swiftly above the meadow, disappearing over the treetops.

"That was truly incredible!" he remarked, approaching his friend.

Again, Aniel just smiled broadly, like a child lost in his own world, in no haste to emerge into the ordinary world of man. He considered Aniel's silence was something especially hallowed, aware that speech would break the euphoria of what had taken place. Aniel came to meet him with slow steps.

"Has a flock of birds alighted upon you before?" he pursued.

"No, I cannot say that one ever has." Aniel lowered his face in a modest gesture as if to say that he was no one special.

"You do not sound surprised!"

"Why should I be?" Aniel lifted his eyes to meet Taran's in a good-natured look that this time lingered, indicating that he was now ready to converse freely.

"What is it about you and animals? They seem to relate to you and you have the ability to make them trust you."

He tilted his head reflectively to one side, in no hurry to respond. "It is an attitude, I suppose!"

"How do you mean? Tell me, I am eager to learn!"

He noticed Aniel's jaw move slowly as though he were chewing on something. "It is rather like praying, but it is focussed on the animal; communicating, sometimes audibly, or by gesture, or sometimes just within myself, willing. I often pray for animals not to be afraid of me."

"Why do more people not have this ability?"

Aniel appeared to consider the question.

"If you want to connect with animals, you need to make time, to observe and be still. Show that you are a friend and are approachable."

"You make it sound simple! I had a strong connection with a dog once. But then that is a common for man, is it not?"

"Ah, dogs! They are much easier to train. But the principles are the same. If you observe the animals, they have their own way of communicating and you can learn what they are feeling. The other consideration is to be careful what we communicate with our gestures, the tone of our voices. Usually, people are too much in a hurry to even notice animals, too consumed with their own world."

"I should try to make connection, then, with other animals! That would help break up the pattern of our days in the muintir!"

"Oh, are you bored with our ways?"

"I feel restless," he found himself unexpectedly confessing. "I am not really suited to this quiet and predictable pattern of prayer and reading, working and worship. I was raised to be a warrior!"

"Are you missing adventure?"

"It would be welcome if adventure presented itself!"

Aniel sat thoughtfully, seemingly pondering the progress of a cloud over the rugged ridge above them. "Drostan – worship is an attitude. It has to be developed. It is not naturally there."

"Do you mean, rather like developing the attitude to notice and relate to the animals?"

Aniel nodded slowly. "I presume it is harder for the man of action, for you are trained to respond immediately to the need of the moment and do not have the inclination to consult with the High King."

"That is helpful. I am aware there is a God. But just as man is aware of the presence of the animals and does not give them much time, so am I lacking in my ability to communicate with God . . ."

"But life in the muintir is all about making time to connect with the heavenly King!" he protested mildly.

"Yes; but it is by means of a liturgy in complicated Latin and forcibly done at set times, day and night, depriving us of sleep and half starving the body! It feels alien and contrived!"

"Do you suppose, then, that the High King is some distant being, beyond our reach?"

"Well, is he not?"

"He may be mighty and elevated, far above all mankind, but he is also as close as that flock of starlings."

"Maybe I have yet to learn how to be attuned to the Presence in a similar manner that you have demonstrated earlier with the starlings!"

The two did not converse further, as Taran reflected on how two years had passed since his arrival at the muintir. Although grateful for being rescued from the life of a vagrant, provided with shelter and nurtured to read and write, he became disturbed by wondering how much of his life was to pass in this alien world of too much silence.

Whilst Taran was mending a wattle fence, a youth from the citadel on the rock came alongside. Noting his jaunty air, then the mischievous grin, he kept him surreptitiously in sight from beneath his brows. The youth stepped over the fence and, seizing a kid goat, ran off. So that was his intention! I was right to have been suspicious.

He went in pursuit and soon caught up with the thief.

"What is this to you, holy man?" The youth drew his dagger.

"I demand you return what is rightfully not your own."

"Then come and reclaim it."

"You have a dagger!" Noting that the youth was trembling, he felt more the master of the situation. His own voice struck him as sounding particularly calm.

The young man smiled, taunting him with the dagger in a menacing manner.

"Let us fight, sword to sword, and the winner keeps the kid," proposed Taran.

For a moment. the youth seemed taken aback. Looking at him curiously, he spoke derisory, "I thought you soldiers of Christ do not fight with the weapons of this world? You will regret that you crossed my path, for I am a warrior. What hope do you have in fighting me? I might take your life for challenging me, and I will keep this kid."

"Give me a sword and let that determine the outcome." He quelled the sensation of feeling aroused, keen to control his faculties.

"Come to the citadel and we shall have some sport, although I fear it will soon be over."

He noticed that the youthful warrior was grinning as they walked in silence to the great rock. He felt indignant about this brazen theft and the presumption arising from the youth's privileged arrogance that he could seize whatever he wanted. Passing beneath the ramparts, they walked across the upper courtyard and stopped outside a larger hut. Beneath the thatch were a row of shields daubed with colourful Pictish symbols. The kid, which had been clutched under the youth's arm, was passed to a girl. He watched the thief enter the hut to emerge a short while later with another youth bearing two swords.

"Give this soldier of Christ a sword," he said in a mocking tone. "Let us return to the courtyard."

He faced his combatant in the square. There were not many people about at that time of day, but those present, mostly women, bairns and old men, turned to watch. It appeared to him that seeing one of Fillan's monks tucking up his long garment into his belt to bare his knees, aroused their curiosity.

"I am going to teach you a lesson, not to meddle in things too great for you holy peasants who live down below." The youth spat his words with disdain. "Know your position and I will have you soon pleading for your life, which I do not know whether I will grant or not."

"Cease your prattle and let our swords do the talking!" he returned, now feeling impatient.

The young warrior came upon him, bearing his sword with both hands above his head. Taran did not move until the other, bearing down his sword with all his might, was almost upon him. He parried the blow with composure and noted that his adversary looked surprised. The loud clash of iron that rang around the courtyard roused those who had been indifferent on the periphery to move into the ring of the human arena forming around them.

He deems he can intimidate me, and assumes that I am just a simple pilgrim from a peasant's background.

The youth pursued the combat with much noise and aggression as he slashed and lunged. By maintaining my own composure, thought Taran, the youth is the more provoked. He is spirited and does not exhibit much training. How natural, it felt, to take up arms again!

Perhaps on realising the futility of his attacks, the young man spoke. "Come on, you do not really fight, but merely fend off. Show me your attack!"

The small crowd parted slightly, allowing the entry of two grim warriors, each brandishing hefty axes. He recognised the Lord Domech behind these two henchmen. Domech wore a slight smile as he weighed up the scene with keen eyes. The warlord stopped within the rim of the human circle and said nothing whilst keenly observing.

"It seems that you bear out the proverb well," Taran addressed the youth. "*Never give a sword to a person who cannot dance.*"

"What do you mean?" responded the youth, realising an affront, yet not comprehending the proverb.

"Have you not been taught anything?" he goaded. "Perhaps you did not heed your foster parent's instruction in swordplay. Before wielding a weapon, you first need to master your footwork. Once you have mastered the basics, your skill with the sword will improve!"

"How dare you assume to be my teacher!"

"One moment!" The Lord Domech's voice spoke in a manner that was used to inciting respect and even fear within the crowd. "Soldier of Christ, you have taken on my son!"

Taran was a little taken aback by this disclosure. Domech's son's behaviour was not surprising, for he exhibited the arrogance of a privileged youth.

Domech grimly pronounced, "Be sure no harm befalls him, otherwise I shall have your life."

He bowed, showing respect and compliance. "Lord, you give your son an unfair advantage. Your son has the will to take what he pleases and the notion to take my life."

"No one shall take a life," decreed the warlord. "Fight on."

He came towards the warlord's son in a calculating manner. Their long swords crossed as they met in an exchange. Stooping low, Taran swivelled round quickly on an axis, and when semi-rotated, he sprung into the air, bringing down the flat of his sword on the other. The blow was parried, although whilst absorbing its force, it caused the youth to stagger. Seeing him stumble, he followed swiftly with a forceful blow to the body with the flat of the blade, bringing his elbow full force into his adversary's face. With a twisting lunge of the sword, he caused his opponent's sword to fall.

"We have done our talking with swords. As your father has decreed, there will be no bloodshed, although I see I have bloodied your nose." He picked up the other's sword and returned it gallantly, which the defeated one took, crestfallen. *"Many a time, a man's mouth broke his nose,"* he said, quoting a favourite proverb as he walked over to reclaim the kid goat from the girl.

Pulling himself together, Domech's son advanced stealthily from behind with raised sword, and in an instant, bore his weapon down in a deadly manner upon Taran's head. Taran swiftly sidestepped the blow, causing the assailant to be unbalanced. Taran exploited the situation to the full, pushing him to the ground with his foot. With two brisk strides, his foot pinned the young man's arm to the ground and, stamping on the hand clenching his sword, dislodged the weapon from its grasp.

Domech stepped before him. "Young man, brave warrior, come with me!"

With no choice in the matter, Taran followed the warlord into the gatehouse.

"Who are you?" demanded the ruler. "You are no soldier of Christ!"

"I am a soldier of Christ, my lord. I was merely defending our community's property. Your son stole a kid goat."

Domech looked at him with a cold, searching stare before he unexpectedly smiled. "It is obvious that you have been trained in combat, and to a very high standard. You have considerable skill," he said, then added with a tone of disdain, "soldier of Christ." The warlord continued to interrogate, giving no pause, raising his voice as his anger grew.

Taran remained stubbornly quiet.

"I could have you tortured – then you would speak!" Abruptly he rose, as if to carry out this threat, his face flushed with excitement contrasting lividly against the whiteness of his beard. Although an old man, he stood impressively upright with the bearing of one long used to having his way. "If I were you, young man, I would talk!"

Taran held his silence. His mouth grew dry, realising the gravity of his situation, but maintaining the composure of one justified in his actions.

The silence seemed to have an effect on Domech. As his features softened, he adopted a calmer tone. "You are brave and composed – you need not be afraid. Tell me, who are you? I could use a man like you in my retinue. Why, think upon it, you could be my bodyguard! Imagine that, humble man! I have the power to elevate your position, lift you from your poverty and the restricting rule of Fillan's muintir. I could have you sat at my table to dine off the choicest things, drink dark wine, wear the best armour and become a man of special note in my court."

Domech was on his feet, slowly pacing about him, observing him with much curiosity.

"Or perhaps I owe you even more respect? Come, tell me what manner of people you hail from, you are a true Pict, but not of the Fotla, nor of the Circinn, for your accent belies that you come from the north. From the Fortriu perhaps? Has the Lord Brude usurped your rightful place? What led you to Fillan's muintir? I sense some misfortune, uh? Come, tell me, for I have the power to reverse things. I would help a noble-born to stand proud once more and reclaim his inheritance and his reputation."

He felt seduced by the flattery. This was the talk that he had been brought up on; a warlord speaking the words to his own kind, in a customary manner that was intelligible. It felt like a breath of fresh air after all the humiliation and loss endured. Had he not smarted from his plummeting descent, from being a prince on the brink of becoming the warlord of the Ce, to then being made a peasant in Elpin's household? Did he not feel uncomfortably humbled under the austere practices of the muintir?

Domech had recognised his nobility, had admired his swordsmanship, and it pleased him to be considered among the warrior aristocracy. His whole upbringing, until the last three years, had been built upon this premise, sealed by the Z-rod tattoo decreed by the gods.

Domech continued unabated, with patient and consummate skill, bringing about his design. This he pursued, with a doggedness not reducing the pressure, nor wearying. Taran was conscious of his need to remain alert, astute, not to be easily won over. The learned diplomacy, the silvery speech, he likened to the wooing of a maiden, who at first resistant to any advance, had then revealed a glimpse of interest. The words of recognition and approval were affirming, something he had wished Talorgen might have stated.

The warlord artfully elaborated, creating a picture of what he could become in his court, turning his floundered fortunes about. A warlord's sumptuous table appealed a great deal compared to the meagre fare at the muintir. Could a flattered maiden resist the unremitting advances? He felt the swollen pride, was softened by the courtesy extended towards his identity. Here was a fellow noble, who had recognised that he was not some ordinary monk, nor a swordsman, but perceived that he was destined to rule. If he were to win back his position, he needed a powerful ally. Was Domech not the man? The resurgent vengeance that had lain dormant all this while flooded his mind with outrage over his cousin's treachery. Insult had been added to injury when Oengus swooped in to take Alpia too. For nearly three years, he had been rendered powerless, alone, without either strategy or resources to reclaim his birthright. Now the possibility of a reversal to his low fortunes had unexpectedly presented itself. The outrage of being made a fugitive called for cunning strategy.

Finally, he raised his hand to indicate that the Lord Domech need not continue with his wooing. "I am whom you presume me to be – Taran – heir to the lordship over the Ce!" It felt liberating to proudly state this disclosure. He began to tell his story, encouraged by Domech's engaging manner who patiently and skilfully extracted the truth.

"Well, you are like my very own son, Taran. You should have said who you were from the beginning! We can make an alliance that will serve us both. Now let me see, just give me pause to consider." Domech's features ruffled as he grew pensive.

Perhaps he is thinking how he can take advantage of my vulnerability, Taran reflected with unease, alarmed now to have rashly revealed himself. To counter the disquiet, his own thoughts turned to his status of monk. Humble though it may be, it was better than being destitute as a homeless wanderer. Did he not approve of the muintir's peaceful ways, of the sense of equality in having all things in common as brothers? He had been encouraged to learn Latin, enabled to form letters to document all manner of things and to read about past events, broadening his knowledge extensively. Fillan had prophesied about a different path ahead in which he would persevere to eventually win through to achieve his destiny. But it was an unclear destiny, full of contradictions and fraught with frustration and hardship. Did Ossian not say that the Z-rod had a bearing on who he would become – a ruler over men? That was all shadowy. Domech's talk was the straightforward, practical speak of a ruler who knew how to achieve what he set his mind upon. That appeared the pragmatic option, a certain thing to help realise his ambition and destiny. How could he pass over this unexpected opportunity of having a strategy and the resources to accomplish it?

"Our best option would be to take a band of our finest men through the lands of the Circinn," said Domech, as he began to unveil his plan. "I would go first to speak with the Circinn warlord, the ancient Cynbel – with whom I am on good terms, and explain things so that he would permit untroubled passage for our warband to reach their far border along the flowing Dee. We will choose our moment to rid your people of this accursed cousin of yours. Surprise will be everything, and having you as a scout with local knowledge will be of great gain. With word of Oengus' movements, his downfall will come about and you shall be instated in your rightful place."

He smiled at the plan. It appeared bold, although dependent upon sound alliances . . . but such is the nature of risk. "Are you sure Cynbel would allow our warband to pass through? I understand that he has married Oengus's sister."

"Oh that!" Domech cast his hand to one side. "That is just a gesture of accord which will not alter a long-standing animosity. The far stronger alliance is with ourselves, which has been in place since I came to power and brought the Circinn to acknowledge my overlordship. "He leant forward, and in a lower voice, remarked, "I once had their nobles in chains!" Domech paused, waiting to see the effect his words would have, as though courting respect. "I could have taken their heads from off their shoulders, but it is better to be wise in these matters. Better, I thought, to have their nobles indebted to me by my showing clemency and thus gain an ally than to be o'er hasty. They have since grown soft, abandoning their warrior ways, as some now follow Christ, including Cynbel himself."

"Good. But, tell me, how are you to gain?"

"How would I gain?" Domech repeated slowly, looking slightly taken aback for just a moment. "This is how I would gain and how the people of the Fotla should profit. Such a plan, successfully executed, with you rightfully instated as warlord of the Ce, could forge an alliance between three peoples: the Ce, the Circinn and the Fotla. With our two peoples united, it would discourage the Circinn from any conceivable thought of rebellion to break their alliance, knowing that they are caught between us two. The consequences of suffering simultaneous attacks on borders at the opposite ends of their lands, will keep them in place." Domech wore the self-satisfied smile of the artful master of events. "Are you with me in this, Taran? I need your oath of allegiance as your overlord, if I am to help you."

"Aye, you do." His throat felt dry and the words came out abrasively. "I can see how such a triple alliance could be advantageous for you, now that Brude's star is gaining ascendancy in the north. It is said that he has ambitions to be overlord of all the Picts. Our alliance, though, will be like a rope of three strands that will not be easily broken!"

"Spoken like a veritable warlord. You have an old head on young shoulders. But this is much more than just a strategic move with fellow Picts, for it will strengthen the Folta's reputation to counter any potential ambition from Alt Clud, Dal Riata and the Manau, all of whom have borders with us."

After a brief silence, Domech eyed him shrewdly. "Let us lose no time. Come and kneel before me and make your allegiance."

Hesitating slightly, he detected a tightening in Domech's lips. He slipped to his knees before the man who promised much, without whom he was nothing. "I pledge my allegiance to you, Lord Domech, as my overlord, and to the people of the Fotla." Wondering whether this would suffice, he suddenly added, "In exchange for your might to return me as lord over the Ce."

"But breathe no word of this to Fillan. Continue as you are – a soldier of Christ – and I will send for you once everything is in place. Dindurn shall equip you for the overthrow of your cousin."

They clasped hands. He descended the hill towards the muintir with both a spring in his step, and yet with a nagging sensation of apprehension over the enormity of what lay ahead. He rationalised that the stress felt was natural, for his undertaking with Domech was audacious.

Chapter Three

Eithni's Baby

556AD Rhynie

On the night of Imbolc, Eithni woke Oengus with her sobbing.

"What is wrong?" he asked groggily.

"I have been bleeding and lots. Feel the bedding!"

"How do you know it is blood?"

"It is sticky!" she answered, distraught and tetchy.

He went over to the hearth and, finding some embers glowing beneath the ash, lit a candle and brought it over. The lower part of Eithni's smock was drenched in blood and the bedding was much soiled. He set the candle up on a table.

"Will you bring me a basin of water?" she asked with a waiver in her voice.

After bringing her the basin, he fastened his boots and said, "I will fetch Nola." He looked across the room as she had made no reply. She was trembling, seemingly finding her task of cleaning herself more difficult than expected.

"I am continuing to bleed!" she said shakily.

"I am on my way," he replied, throwing a plaid around him.

With the solid snow cover, there was enough light to see his way without need of a firebrand. As Nola's house lay a short way beyond Gest's, he decided to awake his friend as soon as he had roused the midwife. He could do with the intercession of a druid and the companionship of a friend.

Nola was quick in gathering what she needed. They went to Gest's hut.

"Gest, wake up! Can you hear me?" he shouted and rattled the door. A sound came from within. "Come as soon as you can. Eithni is bleeding heavily and we fear for the baby."

"I am coming!"

"We are going on ahead." He felt a rising anxiety.

Being an older woman and overweight, Nola was slow climbing the brae up to the palisaded village. He so frequently offered her a steadying hand on the icy slope that eventually she did not let go. The nearing conical roofs of Rhynie stood out clear on the skyline along with the corners of the high stockade. It felt a long time to reach the standing stone incised with the salmon and the beast, which he touched briefly, invoking Brigantia's help.

"How are you faring?" he asked Eithni on entering the hut.

"Much the same," she said flatly.

He reached out and touched her cheek tenderly.

"Oh!" she flinched, involuntarily, moving her face away from his hand.

He was reminded of the smouldering animosity that lurked behind her front of trying to behave otherwise.

"You are cold," she expanded with a faint smile.

Taking hold of the candle, Nola asked, "When did you start bleeding?"

"I am not sure. I woke up feeling wet and sticky."

"Just move over on to your side," Nola instructed, as she pulled the blanket and bear pelt back to disturb the straw base on which she lay.

"My, oh my! You have lost much blood! You can move back again; make yourself comfortable. Oengus mentioned that you are still bleeding?"

"Yes. I am using a cloth to stem the flow."

The midwife froze in thought for a moment. "I need to see whether the flow is just a slow seepage or something more."

Nola examined Eithni who was trembling.

There was a cough at the door before Gest emerged, lifting and sliding the door ajar before putting it back in place. "How are things?" he enquired.

Oengus went over all the details.

"Light a fire!" Nola ordered with a touch of impatience in her voice. "It is freezing in here." To prove it, she breathed slowly before the candle, which illuminated a voluminous cloud of air. She turned to Eithni and said with a degree of gravity, "You are bleeding steadily."

"Will I lose the baby?" Eithni sounded frightened.

"How long have you been with child?"

"A good while now – since the beginning of summer."

"So you conceived around Beltane?"

"No, it was after Beltane for sure. Sometime around the summer solstice – that was the time when I noticed my monthly bleeding had stopped."

Feeling Eithni's swollen abdomen, Nola seemed in no hurry to speak, evading Eithni's question. "If you had conceived around Beltane, then this would be the time for birth; but this is sooner than what is normal." She felt around her abdomen at length, before straightening herself. "It is too soon for the baby's head to have turned." She seemed preoccupied and turning to him, said, "I need you to heat water for me to clean Eithni. It is hopeless trying to clean away blood with cold water. Also, bring cloths."

Having resurrected the fire, he was glad to have another practical task. With that amount of blood loss, he sensed matters were far from good. A knot formed in his throat and tightened.

Meanwhile, Gest had positioned himself near the door, with his back to the women, mindful of the intimate examinations taking place. His lips started moving and a barely audible mumbling could be detected as he petitioned the Bulàch. Although the hut was warming up, Oengus noticed his wife was the only one still shivering.

By daybreak, there was little change.

Eithni called him over. "Ask Alpia to come – I could do with a female friend."

"Aye, I will get her straight away." Turning at the door, he stopped, "And what about your own family?"

"Call them too."

As the settlement came to life under the gradual brightening of an overcast sky, a bitter wind whistled mournfully against the pointed stake ends of the palisade. He went to Aunt Conchen's hut where Alpia was busying herself with kindling a fire.

"Eithni is losing a lot of blood and has asked for you!" He could hear his voice sounding unfamiliar, speaking with the urgency of one who felt out of his depth.

Alpia stopped blowing a petal of flame into life.

"You should go immediately," advised Aunt Conchen. Turning to him, she asked, "Have her waters broken?"

"No, they have not . . . at least, not that I am aware of! Nola is with her, and Gest too."

"I will come as soon as I can get myself ready."

He dawdled uncertainly by the door. "I had better return." Looking back, he added, "I am supposed, though, to get Eithni's mother and family . . ."

"Just go to Eithni," Aunt Conchen said calmly, "I will tell them."

"Will you also tell Mother what is happening – she ought to know." He felt flushed.

"Yes, yes, I will make sure everyone knows who needs to. Now, go."

He returned and saw Eithni faintly smiling. Alpia was kneeling beside the bedding holding her hand. Gest joined him by the fire, taking a pause from his intercessions. They exchanged glances, looks laden with the tension within the home. He stirred the porridge, staring thoughtfully at its thickening consistency, then rummaged about. "There is some honey somewhere," he mumbled, looking into various containers. "A little honey would be good to restore some strength." Finding some, he added a laden spoonful to a bowl of porridge and placed it down beside the bedding. Alpia helped Eithni to sit up against an upright house support, placing some straw to cushion her back. He came over with a thick plaid and wrapped it around her shoulders.

"There is plenty more porridge in the pot," he encouraged, passing her a bowl. She shook her head. He offered porridge to everyone in the room. Gest found more bowls and served out portions.

"No, I do not want any!" he said when Gest offered him a serving.

"You should eat," replied Gest, placing a bowl beside him.

He did not touch it. His eyes were dry and prickly and he rubbed them until they were sore.

Aunt Conchen was not long in joining them, accompanied by Drusticc, his mother. Soon after, Eithni's mother and two sisters appeared. All asked questions of the midwife, who by this time looked tired and drawn. He noticed Eithni's pallor and how still she lay. He felt for her in her suffering, for the one undertaking this mysterious process of bearing their child.

Gest came over to him, putting on his jacket. "I will let Maelchon know what is happening and then shall return."

"Very well."

Drusticc and Eithni's mother started making a fresh batch of porridge together after the first pot had been consumed. During this silence, Eithni, who appeared to have been asleep, stirred, looking a good deal flustered.

"What is the matter?" asked Alpia. Nola, who had her eyes closed at that moment, became alert.

"There has been a sudden rush of blood," Eithni said with some panic. "I can feel my thighs all wet!"

Nola discreetly lifted the bed coverings. "It is your waters, my dear, not bleeding."

"Well, that is good, is it not?" he asked, looking to the women for clarification.

"Better than a bursting of blood, for sure," said the midwife, but without the assurance he was hoping for. He scanned everyone's faces in search of some kind of explanation.

"It means the baby will soon be on its way," explained his mother, putting a hand upon his shoulder.

Nola and Alpia both busied themselves in cleaning and drying Eithni. He brought over a bundle of fresh straw to place over the soiled bedding.

"We need more cloths," ordered the midwife, a tad impatiently.

"I am not sure if there are anymore."

"I will fetch some," said Alpia rising. He took her place at the bedside and brushed Eithni's hair away from her forehead. She flinched.

"I am sorry!" he uttered subdued with a sense of rejection.

She reached out her hand to him. "It is not you." She looked as if she would explain, but instead, nodded in the direction of the midwife. He observed Nola massaging Eithni's belly quite forcibly.

"What are you doing?" he asked Nola, hearing the consternation in his own voice.

"I am trying to turn the baby!".

Eithni grimaced several times, gripping his hand forcibly. The heavy massaging continued, inducing Eithni to vomit up the little porridge she had managed to consume.

Alpia shortly returned with a good supply of rags.

Nola ceased the massaging. "It is no good; I cannot turn the baby!"

Aunt Conchen and Drusticc glanced with concern at one another, an exchange that he noted. He stopped himself from asking what the significance might be, deciding instead to think through the implications without unduly alarming Eithni. He concluded that it would be a feet-first delivery, and knowing that was not normal understood that it could lead to complications. He felt sick. Already weak from the loss of blood, he wondered how Eithni could endure even a normal birth. He felt responsible for her suffering and looked at her with a tenderness he had not felt for a long time. At least she was not enduring this ordeal among strangers, he told himself, thankful to have brought Eithni back to Rhynie. The repulsion over his callous rejection appalled once again. Was this concern an expression of love, he asked himself? If there was some genuine love, then somehow . . . it might exonerate his past rejection and see her through this ordeal.

Contractions started later that morning, bringing Eithni's suffering to a new level, intensifying as they became more frequent. Maelchon appeared with Gest. The two druids performed some rite, involving burning a slightly acrid smelling offering near the doorway. No one took much notice of them; yet at the same time all were thankful for their presence to help bring Eithni safely through this ordeal. As the strong scent of the offering that masked the smell of blood and uncleanness began to wane, Oengus threw some resinous pine logs on the open hearth.

Nola called for another candle to aid her examination of how far Eithni was opening. Afterwards, she tried to turn the baby.

"Please, stop!" Eithni sobbed.

"It will be much better for you and the baby if I can turn it," reasoned Nola.

"No, no more," he interjected coming over to Eithni's side. "It seems the baby is intent to come into the world feet-first!" Turning to Nola, he said firmly, "You have done what you can."

Nola sat back with a resigned air, wiping her glowing brow. Rising to her feet, she took a ewer of water and washed her bloodied hands just beyond the threshold.

The birth pains came with increased regularity. He overheard Aunt Conchen's remark to his mother, "It seems Eithni has lost the fighting spirit!"

"I was thinking the same myself," his mother replied in an undertone. "She has nothing left."

He noticed Eithni's brow that had been wet with perspiration was now dry, not due to Alpia's attention at dabbing it, but because she no longer seemed to be sweating. Aside from her moans, his wife spoke no word: her eyes had been closed a long while now, alone in her combat with forces unencountered before. When she did open them, he and Alpia lent forward.

"How much longer?" she mumbled.

Turning to the midwife, he relayed the question, and she not so discreetly pulled aside the blanket to peer with candle in hand.

"She is opening well," she confirmed with a hint of renewed enthusiasm. Leaning forward she commanded, "I want you to start pushing when the birth pains come again!" He thought she spoke louder than seemed necessary, but at least there was no mistaking her instructions.

"I am scared," Eithni said, looking at him and Alpia in turn. The expression was pitiful, like an injured rabbit trapped in a corner, without the will nor the opportunity to escape. She emitted a long groan from deep within – a sound that was haunting and unnatural.

"Come on, you need to push," ordered Nola with a note of impatience. "Push harder!"

He watched Eithni's body contort, her shoulder braced against the wooden roof support. Again, she emitted that deep groan, followed by a desperate growl that he found unsettling. What pain to have to go through, he thought, as he looked helplessly on.

"You are doing well. Just a little while longer," comforted Alpia, patting Eithni's hand that had drained white with the effort of pushing. He noticed a slight colour return to Eithni's hand as it relaxed its grim grip, but returning slower than usual. The mounting concern reached a sense of impending doom, which he was unable to rid himself of – despite his efforts to think of a positive outcome. Placing his hand upon Eithni's shoulder, he clasped it, willing to impart some strength.

When the next series of birth pangs came, Nola brushed him, along with Alpia, aside with a vague apology and spoke almost into Eithni's face, "You need to push really hard with the birth pain – your baby is ready to come."

He stood back, feeling useless.

Again, that strong force of nature wracked Eithni's abdomen, causing the unnatural growl to sound, like an injured beast defending its lair. The inhuman noise, more prolonged than before, filled the hut with its dread. Not caring whether Nola objected or not, he stepped around Eithni's head and knelt on the other side, gently massaging her shoulder. Alpia followed his lead and knelt beside Eithni opposite, taking up her friend's hand as before.

"I have hold of both of the baby's feet!" announced the midwife hopefully. He looked and saw Nola pulling gently, but firmly, to reveal legs and then its waist. "It is a boy!"

He was shocked at how tiny the baby was. I have a son, he thought to himself, with a flicker of delight – a joy that briefly fluttered through the room.

"Eithni, you need to give another big push with the next birth pains, bigger than you have done before."

Eithni vaguely shook her head, her eyes tightly closed with the pain. When she opened them, she looked distraught and fearful, her eyes momentarily fixing on Alpia and then upon himself. She looked out of her depth, drowning under the waves of pain engulfing her. As he moved in closer to Eithni, Alpia's hair swept his cheek, who likewise had the same impulse to lean forward.

Eithni's breathing had grown shallow. She seemed incapable of speaking.

"Do not give up the fight!" urged Alpia.

"Only the baby's head remains to be born – you are almost there!" he encouraged.

"A boy?" Eithni whispered with the slightest hint of a smile at she looked upon Alpia.

"Yes, it is a boy!" Alpia returned warmly. He could see her squeezing Eithni's hand.

"I am here," he spoke reassuringly, unsure why Eithni was only looking at Alpia. Eithni took hold of his hand, and thinking at first that she was just squeezing it, he realised that she had a different intention. He allowed her to direct his hand across her upper abdomen. Was she wanting to lay his hand there? he thought. She continued to bring his hand to the far side where her other hand was clasped by Alpia. Oengus and Alpia briefly exchanged dismayed looks as their hands unexpectedly touched.

Alpia retracted her hand whilst still holding onto Eithni.

Eithni deliberately pushed Alpia's hand back to his own and tried to speak but only incoherent sounds were uttered. His wife opened her eyes with some effort, and grimacing in a way that found the light hard to bear, she looked at him meaningfully. She then turned to Alpia. What did she mean by that look? he thought. Alpia's eyes briefly met his own with a glance that conveyed she had understood. Alpia seemed to slightly recoil from the suggestion, whatever it was.

With the next birth pang registering vaguely on Eithni's face, it was apparent that she had no strength left to push.

"Come on, Eithni, push!" Nola spoke, holding on to the son who was not completely delivered.

"O Brigantia, help Eithni in her great need," he muttered under his breath.

He felt Eithni's hold on his hand suddenly slacken.

Nola fidgeted uneasily, making careful observations. She uttered under her breath, "She has stopped bleeding!" Nola took one look at Eithni's face before reverting her attention to the baby.

The hut was filled with a tense silence that he found almost unbearable.

"Drusticc," Nola commanded. "Take hold of the baby like this." She demonstrated the hold that she had on the infant. As soon as Drusticc had hold of the baby, Nola brushed Alpia aside and placed her cheek next to Eithni's mouth whilst looking down to the mother's abdomen.

What was she doing? he thought, finding her behaviour most strange.

"She has died!" uttered Nola, before announcing with some urgency, "I must deliver the baby." Turning to Alpia, she said testily, "Stand back and give me room to finish my task."

Alpia dutifully rose and stood back, putting her hand to her mouth. He had not comprehended Nola's words and only now, recalling what she had declared, felt a tremor pass through him.

Nola shifted position as she knelt and laid both her chubby hands on Eithni's belly. She looked up at Drusticc. "When I push, I want you to gently draw the baby towards you."

What followed appalled him as he watched her heave with considerable force into Eithni's belly. Though he understood that she was trying to save the baby, the actions looked brutal and abhorrent as Eithni's dead body writhed upon the bedding in a macabre manner.

His mother, tensely maintaining her hold around the baby's hips, eased the tiny body towards her. His new-born son's head then appeared, dirty and gory. Nola grabbed the infant from Drusticc's hands, and holding him by his feet, slapped the baby's back three times. The body swayed inertly.

"Oh, he is so small!" observed Drusticc.

"Not my son, as well!" he muttered, horrified by the thought of a double death. Drusticc came over, her face quite distraught and placed her bloodied hands about him. He slightly flinched, unused to her affection. He watched

Nola unceremoniously poke a forefinger into the infant's mouth and scoop out some matter that she flicked onto the floor. Again, she smacked the body.

A cry, thin and rather desperate, filled the room, a sound that was greeted with an audible gasp.

"Our baby is born!" he uttered, turning automatically to Eithni. Her eyes stared vacantly at the roof, reminding him, without doubt, that this birth had cost her life. How odd, he thought, to feel both new joy and great sorrow at the same moment.

He watched Nola wrap the baby in an unused rag and then in another.

"Fetch a woollen wrap," Nola ordered. One was produced and she bound it around the premature baby several times. Looking up, she presented him the infant which he received uncertainly. The child's torso nestled completely within the palms of his outstretched hands. The baby's face was red, screwed up as though objecting to the light of day. Looking as though he had emerged from a fight, beaten and swollen, even somewhat disfigured, the baby protested.

"Oh, what a beautiful boy!" crooned his mother, stooping over the child.

There is little beauty about him, he thought, looking at this frail life that clearly exhibited the ordeal he had been through.

"Keep him warm!" Nola barked, flustered. Then more in an undertone, she exclaimed, "I do not see how he can survive, though, born so small! I have seen larger babies perish."

He looked at the midwife starkly, fearing for the life that was so helpless in his own hands. He was afraid of the responsibility, lacking the knowledge to preserve this pitiful life. Aware of Alpia sidling up to view the new-born, he looked up and noted her compressed lips lengthening into an uncertain smile. He offered her the child which she took without hesitation. He felt relieved to be eased of the responsibility, believing women instinctively knew better what to do in such circumstances.

Moving over to the bedside, he knelt beside Eithni, uttering, "No!" involuntarily under his breath. Leaning forward, until his chest overshadowed her, he passed an arm underneath her shoulders and tenderly drew her towards him and whispered her name. Her corpse felt light in his grasp. With his other hand, he stroked her long, fair hair.

"Oh Eithni — I had not been good to you!" he whispered intimately into her ear. "But we made things good again, had we not? We have a wee lad now! We are parents! Will you not come back — the boy needs a mother . . ." He paused, loosening his grip to see her face and felt the tears form heavy in his eyes. "We have lost time to recover, Eithni. Come back to rebuild a life now that we shall be three and all will be well."

Eithni's eyes stared vacantly into his face in an horrific manner, not quite meeting his own gaze. It was brazenly apparent that life had departed, robbing from this body, her one-time playfulness. Unable to endure the death stare longer, he closed her eyelids.

She has been taken to the land beyond the sea, he told himself, unable to bide longer and be my woman. We will not grow fat and grey together. We will not have opportunity to be happy and defy all expectations after our troubles.

Cradling her one more time in his arms, she hung limp with arms that swayed as he gently caressed her.

The baby started to cry, Alpia went over to Nola. Their exchange caught his attention.

"A wet nurse will have to be found, but I doubt it will be for long!" remarked Nola ominously.

"What do I need to do to ensure this bairn has the best chance to survive?" Alpia asked earnestly.

Nola looked at her thoughtfully, pursing her lips. "Keep the baby next to your chest and make sure he is always kept warm from your own body warmth. But really, I do not see how one so small can possibly survive!" She made for the door.

Aunt Conchen stepped around Alpia and Drusticc and he felt her place her hand on his shoulder. "Oengus my dear, let me embrace you."

He saw his aunt's eyes filled with tears. Laying Eithni down, he rose into her embrace.

"It is hard to accept! She is only young." He stared upon Eithni, hoping to see her chest rise, or to detect even the slightest twitch of movement to contradict this news. Taking hold of his arm, Aunt Conchen drew him gently away. "She was so spirited too, until I broke it!"

"Come, do not dwell upon that. You mended things," she comforted.

Gest came over and placed an arm about him and held him silently.

"You know, Eithni had a premonition that something bad would happen! I had tried to dismiss it at the time, for it seemed commonplace that the wind would blow out some of the candles during yesterday's ceremony."

"What can be commonplace to one, is significant to another! The Bulàch had something to convey to her concerning her impending fate and she was receptive to it!"

He fell silent, wrestling with signs and fate when he believed force of will could push through and bring about what was required. After a while, he asked, "What do we do with Eithni?"

"Leave that to us." Gest went over to Maelchon who directed him to one of the women in the room. After speaking with her, Gest returned. "We will take Eithni to a place to prepare her." Gest covered the corpse with a blanket she had been lying on, and together with the woman, they carried her out of the hut.

"I will name the child Caltram, after Father," he announced resolutely, trying to grapple with how life would be from now on. "And can someone find a wet nurse for him?"

"Nola is already seeing to that," replied Aunt Conchen. "Fionnoula is close to weaning her child."

"Will that mean Caltram going to live with Fionnoula if she agrees to suckle the babe?" He was not keen on the idea.

"She stays close by," Aunt Conchen replied.

"Caltram should remain with us," he said emphatically.

There was a slight pause whilst those present considered the best arrangement.

"I should like to fulfil Eithni's wishes," spoke Alpia, "to raise this child." She added with an emphatic ring that made clear no one was to contest, "I should like to do this for her sake."

What Eithni had indicated earlier when bringing his hand to Alpia's, then made sense to him.

"Then it would be best for all concerned that Caltram is raised in my home," said Aunt Conchen with a slight smile. "You heard what Nola said! The bairn will need all the love and care we can give him if he is to survive. Raised in my home, you can come and go, like you usually do; only, Alpia, if you are serious about your intention, you will need to stay with the bairn all the time. He is so tiny!"

He felt distressed, and although not naturally a religious man, he recognised the real threat to the life of his newborn son. He vowed to Brigantia that he would be in earnest in observing all the festivals if only she would spare this child. He was pleased with Aunt Conchen's suggested arrangements, knowing that it took away any awkwardness for Alpia to be in a home where she already passed most of her time.

Nola soon returned with Fionnoula alongside.

"Oengus, I am so sorry for your loss!" the young mother said. After a respectful pause, she added, "I should be pleased to be a wet nurse for your son. I have been of a mind to wean my own bairn these past days."

Chapter Four

Disciplined

558AD   Dindurn

News of the armed combat between a soldier of Christ and Domech's son inevitably leaked, for tongues were wagging. It came to Fillan's attention and provoked a tense exchange.

Taran observed a flush of anger in the old abbot's face who complained, "A soldier of Christ does not take up arms!"

"But I was protecting our property!" he protested, genuinely taken aback by the absence of gratitude.

"Did our King not say that *if someone takes your cloak, do not stop him from taking your tunic?* As for crossing swords – that is not the action of a saint! You bring shame upon our whole community! You cannot behave independently and think it does not affect us all. Your conduct reflects our King and he does not resort to violence."

He had nothing to say, understanding Fillan's point of view. He was indebted to the kindness of the muintir, giving him opportunity to consider his future step.

The abbot paused to take breath, perhaps conscious of the flush of anger that had come over him. "I heard it reported that you admonished Domech's son with the proverb, *never give a sword to a person who cannot dance.* But you, my son, need to master yourself, to exercise self-control to keep you from futile scrapes. Self-control is vital if you are to overcome the passions of the flesh."

The abbot gave him a stiff penance of solitary confinement and additional prayer and fasting.

He did not protest, accepting the punishment, which Fillan maintained would be 'good for his soul'. He determined to work the discipline to his own advantage, to fashion himself into a warrior, steadfast in his purpose. If he aspired to become the warlord, this discipline would steel him to be a ruler who would not be bent by the wind.

Keeping true to his conviction, he applied himself to his devotions, which were rather mechanical. When praying, he recognised the contradiction between his intention to forcibly overthrow his cousin and what he understood about the character of Christ.

How can I ask the Lord of peace to bring ruin upon my cousin? He felt convicted, ashamed to have reverted to using worldly means, and repented. His peace was short-lived, though. Forgiveness of my cousin is required from me! But, I do not have that capacity, nor the will to forgive that snake. Can I deny my birthright? Do I stand aside and not redress the wrongs of having my woman taken and my status removed? Can I reject perhaps this one opportunity of claiming back the lordship over the Ce?

This internal battle brought about a crisis. Believing his life as a monk to be a sham, he resolved to renew his commitment to the Bulàch. Strong feelings of vengeance and worldly ambition were not incompatible with the worship of the goddess. She was the rightful heavenly sovereign over the Picts, suited for their warrior struggles and ambitions. Had she not looked over him in the wilds, keeping him safe from bears and wolves, protecting him from the gaze of the gods from the duns on high? Had she not permitted him taking a deer with a single arrow? The muintir had taught him the need to be rigorous in worship – a rule he needed – but from now on, he would apply this commitment to venerating the goddess of his people.

Outwardly, he continued with his penitential routine, bearing it with humility and without complaint. In his times of mentoring with Fillan, though, it was a challenge to conceal his duplicity. If his anam cara had been another man, his task would have been easier, but Fillan's reputation as a seer made him fear his pretence could be seen through. He felt resentful, experiencing guilt twice over, begrudging the one who meant him well and regarded him as a son.

One day Fillan remarked with a perceptive gaze in his eyes, "You have not given up faith in the Bulàch have you?"

He replied, eventually, with a silent nod. The indignation of having his innermost thoughts searched and exposed riled him. He surprised even himself when he said with some passion, "And why should I abandon her? She has led me safe this far! She provided for my needs in the wilds and sustained me from harm."

The older man met his rather petulant defence with thoughtful silence. Eventually, he remarked, "God's goodness extends to all, even to those who do not acknowledge him."

Fillan brought their discourse to a close and concluded with a customary prayer. The abbot smiled tentatively, but with his customary kindness of spirit, as he rose to leave the cell.

When his period of penance was completed, Taran maintained a low profile so as not to draw attention to himself, continuing to engage in the daily rhythm of rising early to sing psalms and to pray, followed by domestic and field duties, punctuated by, and concluded with, scripture reading and prayers. Before others, it was not difficult to present himself as an uncomplaining, hard-working and punctual brother, for he had no complaint with his fellows. But within his heart, he longed to be freed from this pretension, impatient for his fate to propel him forward to reclaim his inheritance and to exact vengeance upon his cousin. When he heard that Domech had set off on a tour which included visiting the Circinnian lord, Cynbel, at Migdele, he knew his time was about to come, and his impatience took on a new form of agitation, eager to realise the plan hatched with the Lord Domech. It was only a matter of time now before he would leave the muintir and become the prince raising his sword in his ascension to the warlordship, fulfilling what the Z-rod had destined him for.

Meanwhile, he had to endure the regular sessions with Fillan, which had now increased in frequency as well as in length. Before his anam cara he felt exposed; the abbot's eye having that keen glint, penetrating through to the core of his thoughts.

"My dear son, commit yourself wholeheartedly to Christ in whom there is no disappointment. His plans are to prosper you, to bring you into a place of fullness and contentment in his presence," began the familiar exhortation of the old saint. His smile waned and, narrowing his eyes, he pronounced in a tone that conveyed genuine concern, "I detect ambition smouldering in your heart, and a vengeance that wars with your soul. It will only lead to calamity – do not pursue that way."

He chose not to reply, as though through his silence, he not only denied the truth of the old man's insights, but somehow also hoped it would act as a screen to conceal his soul. The warnings arose every session, with much earnestness. "Drostan, I implore you to turn back, to repent and embrace a new life beyond revenge."

Fillan's loving-concern made him feel guilty, for the old man expressed a genuine affection, wishing him peace in his soul.

"I learned *the way* of the High King from my anam cara, Father Kessog," continued the abbot, in a tone that indicated he was about to recount a treasured memory. "When I was a youth, much as yourself, I had only ever known *the way*, for, as I have previously told you, I was literally brought up in the muintir from the cradle. It would be fair to say that I accepted everything I was taught without question."

Fillan paused, his lips registering a slight smile perhaps on noting that he had gained the younger man's curiosity. "My youth, though, was marked with impatience over the slow progress of events and dissatisfaction with who I was. An inner restlessness compelled me to be on the move, often out of frustration over the low ebb of my spiritual life."

Fillan rolled a long sleeve up to his elbow, revealing a forearm still strong from manual work. He noticed how the abbot's skin was speckled in places by the darker discolouration that age brings. "But, the thing I learned from Kessog is that when we give ourselves wholeheartedly to the King, a power and a peace that is not from us guards and shapes our lives. Then, all worries and stratagems are yielded before the King. It is better not to make our own plans . . . for to follow the King is better by far."

He felt Fillan's endearing warmth and admired his ability to be humble and transparent, although this revealed his own shortcomings. He understood the lesson was intended to encourage him back to his faith, but found the predictable talk, always pointing to Christ, wearisome.

"Kessog impressed the heroic hearts of the Picts through his courageous, and sometime outspoken, example. His occasional forthright talk was surprising for he was known as a man of diplomacy, adept at the ways of court, always maintaining right speech that was full of dignity and respect. In his final year, though, it seemed a cloak of protection was wrapped around him so that the envy of the druids and the murderous intent of man could not touch him . . ." His speech tailed off. He then added, with levity, "until his time came."

"How did his life end?" he asked curiously.

A stillness came into the eyes of the old abbot. "Our work at Cartray had been contested by Phelan, the druid there, and by his daughter Beatha, the sorceress. Both had been seriously crossed when their old order was challenged. Beatha lost her ability to speak after a curse she uttered upon our heads was countered by Kessog. He spoke a word of authority with an abrupt severity that was surprising to observe by all who knew his gentle and noble ways."

Fillan wiped the moisture from his lips with the back of his hand. "Our visit to Cartray had aroused the open interest of two people during our overnight stay. By the time Kessog returned that way with Ronan weeks later, about eight people were already gathering, keen for instruction and anxious to be prayed for. Kessog demonstrated great mildness of character by laying hands on Beatha, fulfilling the promise, that once he had come that way again, her power of speech would be restored."

He listened, intrigued by the unfolding of these events.

"Beatha, though, was unchanged. Far from being thankful, as soon as she discovered her tongue again, she was full of spite, chastising Kessog to his face. She uttered curses, which made others flinch and take particular note, awaiting Kessog's demise. Her spoken threats, far from doing the harm they intended, served not only as a reminder to the community of the generosity of the saint in giving her voice back again, but demonstrated moreover the power of the King to protect him from the malevolence of one they knew held virulent, dark powers. Now it was Kessog, rather than the sorceress, of whom they were in awe. Such admiration led immediately to further curiosity about the teachings of *the way*, and many of those who filled Irb's home on the night of Kessog's return visit, continued to meet after the abbot had gone home to Inis y Mynachon – our founding muintir on Loch Lumon."

Fillan beamed brightly with the memory. The smile began to fade as his eyes grew lustrous with moisture. "As you can imagine, events only rankled Phelan and Beatha the more, for they saw power and respect withdrawn from them and transferred to the soldiers of Christ. Their status in the community was undermined." Fillan shook his head and, after a pause, lent forward slightly and spoke in a lower voice. "They hatched their plans. In that same year, before the autumn had come, a small band of hired brigands who waited for Kessog to come off Inis y Mynachon, set upon him, carrying out their murderous intent on the shores of Loch Lumon."

"So, he was killed? he clarified with a sense of disappointment.

"We all must die – that is inevitable!" Fillan responded to his line of thought. "But what is death? Is it not to exchange this shadowy world for the splendour of the court of the King? Yes, it is an end: a cessation of all trials, suffering and temptations."

"But Phelan had triumphed in his intent to silence Kessog!"

"That is one view," he conceded quietly, not appearing in the least ruffled. "Consider, though, Kessog's legacy. Colonies of heaven now stretch from Alt Clud, past Inis y Mynachon, through the regions of the Fotla. I was assigned to here at Dindurn, Ronan was instated at Cartray and another was placed at Ucheldi Ucha. Kessog was not a man in a hurry, nor one full of ambition to leave his mark. He was a quiet, noble man, noted for his princely bearing and godliness in his steadfast devotion to the King."

As Fillan continued to reflect upon Kessog's life, a distant look came into his eye. "In his final year, he shone like a star blazing through the heavens. The dangers and the uncertainties made him especially prayerful, resulting in a heightened intimacy with the King. In his pursuit of seeing the Fotla enter into Christ's peace, the High King enabled him in extraordinary ways never exhibited before in his life. His final year was greater by far than all the preceding years put together. Kessog's example inspired other pilgrims to bring news of the King to the Circinn and to the Fib."

Taran was not inclined to be dismissive, for he genuinely respected their learning and wholehearted commitment to their cause. He could learn from their example and apply it to his own ends, and like Kessog, rise to fulfil what was on his heart with a burning determination. However, he foresaw no martyr's end for himself.

He began having unsettling dreams, often beyond recall, yet leaving him wide awake, too troubled to sleep. One recurrent theme emerged. He repeatedly saw Domech smiling, almost father-like, and then, with only the slightest change of expression, the warlord was grinning gleefully, gazing just beyond him. He interpreted this as a sign, alerting him not to trust the sincerity of Domech's affections. The warlord was, after all, a man of power, serving his own ends. Did he not know that already? He would not be deluded, and recognised the need to go cautiously. And yet he still maintained that Domech was the only one who could serve his destiny.

As the brethren were filing out from their oratory at the close of prayers one evening in spring, he noticed Fillan was standing beside the doorway, his eyes shining with a strange lustre as though something of great importance had been entrusted to him. As he approached, the abbot's attention suddenly fixed upon him, gesturing impatiently concerning some pressing matter.

When he reached the door, Fillan pressed a hand behind his shoulder and ushered him aside, scanning the way ahead with urgency. "We must not tarry another moment here," he said under his breath.

Fillan led the way briskly, without greeting those he passed. They crossed over the western extent of the vallum where he stooped to pick up a coracle placed there which he handed to him. He took up a leather satchel, also lying among the stones of the wall. Still the abbot did not speak, but looked about warily. Taran was compliant with the apparent need for secrecy and did not question, understanding that his anam cara would disclose the reason in due course.

Moving out into the darkness of the fields beyond, Fillan explained, "Domech has returned from his tour just earlier and is sending a guard to your cell as we speak now."

His heart pounded, knowing the abbot with his abilities as a seer, must have already discerned his intentions. But his intuition told him that he seemed to know more. "The Spirit has alerted me to a plot. Domech will claim from the Circinnian warlord the blood-money upon your head."

"What!" he uttered dismayed.

"There is no time for discussion – Domech's men are after us. Am I not correct – you have an agreement with Domech?"

"Y-yes," he confessed reluctantly.

Lengthening his strides, Fillan moved with an alacrity surprising for his age. He spoke with his head half-turned towards him in a subdued tone directed towards the ground.

"Domech gave you the pretext of taking a small warband through the lands of the Circinn to win back your lost inheritance, right?"

He grunted with increased consternation, dismayed that his plan had been revealed, and feeling increasingly alarmed by this treacherous disclosure.

"Are you with me?" the abbot asked with urgency. It seemed that the question was not just asking whether he was comprehending unfolding events, but more probed as to whose side he was looking to.

"Yes, I am." Crestfallen, it felt like suddenly awakening from a dream to see all the insubstantial fabric de-materialise that had once appeared so real. How foolish he felt, so easily deluded in his desperation. The seer's ability was beyond question, so ably had it been demonstrated.

He became aware of a shadowy form following them. He looked back and saw the large bulk of a person running towards them.

"It is Aniel with another coracle," enlightened the abbot. "Go! Run, for you are quicker than me, and wait for me at the edge of the woods on the southern corner of the loch."

He ran briskly. A three-quarter moon emerged from behind a cloud, illuminating the meadow as he made towards a dark line of tall trees along the edge of the pasture. Looking back, he noted the far-off muintir gathered in darkness. A strong breeze blowing down the strath turned back the new leaves and made the branches clatter vigorously. Shadows stirred fleetingly, and imagining Domech's men closing in on him, he ran in earnest. He reached the woods above the loch, and waited. His laboured breathing began to subside. Aniel then arrived, followed not that long after by Fillan.

"Take both coracles close to the water, but wait concealed among the shrubs," the abbot instructed. Aniel left.

"Here is a satchel full of provisions for your journey, complete with knife, tinder, flint, food and clothes from your cell." The abbot passed him the leather bag. "I have been concerned for your salvation, even before you confessed to worshipping the Bulàch. I have often wondered what the outcome would be and have been confused by the premonition about your coming, suggesting you would be a great soldier of Christ." Fillan fixed him earnestly with his gentle eyes. "I still choose to believe this will become true. But you need to rid yourself of this destructive revenge and give up all hope of regaining your lost rights. You are an intelligent man, although I do not fully understand how you could have been taken in by Domech!"

"I was flattered and therefore duped. Domech made it sound plausible, with him being in effect, master over the Circinn . . ."

The old saint interrupted. "Domech is no master over the Circinn!"

"But he told me of a great victory won when the Circinnian nobles were in chains and Domech could have had them all decapitated."

"No such thing happened. The Circinnian power is at least equal to that of the Fotla, if not greater. You were told what you wanted to hear and were gullible enough to believe. Anyway, no time for recriminations now. Relinquish all thought about becoming warlord over the Ce. It is not to be – do you hear? Yours is a higher calling!"

"What could be a higher calling?"

"That will become clear once you have seen the King in all his glory. Such a vision will strip away all worldly ambition and give you a heart for greater things." He passed his hand slowly across his face as though removing a beatific smile that had softened his features. "Listen carefully, we have so little time and you must be away!" Fillan's tone was clipped, making it the more surprising when he added, "But first, I will pray." He did not pray for long and his prayer showed as much concern for Taran's spiritual salvation as for physical safety.

"I have an instruction for you," added Fillan, placing a hand upon his shoulder. "You are to take the course of *white martyrdom.*"

"What is that?" he asked dubiously, fearing adventures involving tribulation were about to recommence.

White martyrdom is what I undertook along with Kessog. It is a leaving of home, of all that is familiar, forsaking all security, in an abandonment to the will of the High King. At its heart is a pursuit to know him profoundly. Your *white martyrdom* will take you west to Dal Riata. Make for Dunadd and present this message to the king."

He took a small roll of parchment from the abbot.

"He will assist you in your quest. At the earliest opportunity, take a boat north along the coast, to territories beyond Dal Riata, to a Pictish place of pilgrimage. In a picture, I saw a conical shaped peak rising from a whale back of a hill that forms an island. The conical peak is distinctive, looking like its top has been sliced at an angle by a giant sword. Make for the peak which, I hope, is to become the place of your renewal."

He listened with incredulity, marking all his words, keen not to forget any detail.

"The purpose of your pilgrimage is different from that of the Picts. This is your opportunity to know the King and to pursue your destiny. That destiny has something about . . ." He paused. A puzzled expression came across his face as he pronounced, "something about *bearing fire to the far north.*"

The hairs on the back of Taran's neck stood on end, making him suddenly declare, "I do not dismiss any of what you are saying." He stopped involuntary, choked by emotion. "I have been slow to learn, unwilling to walk the path of obedience. Please forgive me!"

"Seek the forgiveness of the King who has a significant purpose for you to fulfil. Now make all haste – you will reach Cartray tomorrow where Ronan will help send you on your way with fresh provisions. Aniel knows the way west, a journey that goes by a hamlet of believers near the great Loch Lengwartha. They too will supply your needs for your journey westward to Loch Lumon and from there over the narrow neck of land that will lead to the sea loch on the other side. There, take a boat bound for Dal Riata. Do not overnight in any of these places because Domech will have his men on your trail and will guess this course."

"Is there no alternative route?"

"There is, but it is wild and we do not have friends to help you that way. But remember however far the journey may be that *two people shorten the road* and an unseen third will make it safe. Go with all haste and you will outrun Domech's men – they will not pursue beyond their own territory because you do not mean that great a deal to

Domech – you were only good for acquiring him silver and gaining the favour of the Circinn and the Ce."

"Will I see you again?" For the first time, he was afraid to lose the abbot's friendship.

"God willing."

Fillan embraced him and they descended to where Aniel was concealed. The thick shadows of the woods heaved under the strength of the wind as they placed their coracles onto the lighter coloured waters.

Paddling a coracle was difficult into the force of a substantial wind blowing down the loch. The great peaks, rising straight up from the south shore of the loch, loomed dark under the clouds which the moon barely broke through.

"West," he muttered under his breath. "Was it not in the isles of the west that Ossian had prophesied my transformation would occur? How did it go: *Your surrender will be in the south, your transformation in the isles to the west*. He then realised that another part of the prophecy, his 'surrender' in the south, had taken place.

Chapter Five

Domech's Revenge

558 AD Dindurn

As Fillan approached the muintir, he could hear shouted threats coming from the oratory. On arriving there, he saw Lord Domech accompanied by a band of men bearing flaming torches. They had rounded up the eighty-or-so monks.

"Where have you been?" hissed Domech, as Fillan stepped into the arc of light.

"About the High King's business," he returned drily.

"Do not speak to me like that!" shouted Domech coming over to the abbot. "Where is Taran, the one who calls himself Drostan?"

"Drostan is under the governance of God . . ." he replied mildly.

Domech cut his words short, taking hold of the material of his smock and screwing it up in a clenched fist. He noticed how Domech's cheeks became an unhealthy purple hue.

He looked at the warlord passively, concealing as best he could the unease welling up from within. What could he say? He would not lie, but he needed to stall proceedings to allow Taran to gain a good start down Loch Gunalon to evade capture. He had prayed for a smooth passage, before considering deeper matters concerning Taran's true transformation. His intercessions had been lengthy, and by the time he had risen from his knees, the two coracles had become distant specks way down the loch. He had taken his way, slowly, through the woods and across the open ground before Dindurn, past the cattle and walled-in enclosures.

"Drostan is no more a part of this muintir," he replied, looking Domech square in the eye. He noticed how bloodshot the whites of the warlord's eyes were and how his mouth was grimly set. Domech's grip tightened further around his clothing, he tugged him forward then suddenly repelled him with a forceful thrust.

He staggered back, and losing his balance, fell on the ground. A gasp went up from his fellow pilgrims. One of them stepped forward. "My lord, this is one who rules peacefully . . ."

The man was cut short with a resounding slap across the face from one of the soldiers.

He looked up and identified the faithful Castantin.

Pointing at him, Domech spoke to one of his bodyguards. Pulled to his feet, he was walked over to the nearby corner of the oratory where he was pushed against the heavy supporting pillar.

"Old man, speak, if you value your life and the lives of your pilgrims." Domech's face was threateningly close to his own. "I have been patient with you, but I will not tolerate insolence. I will repeat one more time, where is Taran?"

He was truly lost for words, stunned by what was taking place. Domech took a faltering half step backwards, clutching at his chest briefly, before standing proud and in command once more. It was just a brief moment, but one that he noted. Knowing that stalling the interrogation further was not an option, nor was deceit, he simply said, "Taran has left..." He paused, considering how to continue.

"We know he is not here," shouted Domech, slapping him across the face twice before spitting onto his cheek.

His cheeks stung and he could feel the trickle of saliva.

"Will you speak or are we to kill you?" Domech stood so menacingly close to his face that Fillan could smell wine on his breath.

"Lord Domech, Taran is already a good distance from here, so that pursuit would be in vain. Besides, you are fighting against the true King, and no good will come of it if you persist. Consider how I knew about your plot to sell Taran? Was it not the Lord Himself who informed me! Even if you were to catch up with Taran, what is force against a soldier of Christ?"

"I will show you what force can do."

"Although I may perish, remember, lord, the invincibility of the one who is master over death and ruler over all the earth."

This time, Domech punched him despairingly on the cheek bone, causing his head to heavily knock against the pillar behind. He felt his knees give way and pain course through his clouding head. The next conscious moment, he was being pulled up from the ground, forced to kneel.

"Take him," ordered Domech. "Incarcerate him in the guard room."

Dragged to his feet, he stumbled forward, only managing to remain upright because he was gripped by a soldier on either side.

"Torch their meeting house!" he heard Domech ordering, followed by the protests of the monks, who, from the sounds of it, were rough handled at that moment. He heard something being smashed repeatedly by some heavy implement, followed by a crackling sound. Although forced to walk away from the oratory, and unable to turn his head about, he noticed the gathering firelight about them. That will be the thatch catching, he thought. He staggered on, supported by his two captors, following his leering shadow weaving uncertainly before him.

He had bought Taran time. Domech's short temper had got the better of him as he failed to learn about Taran's whereabouts. Their progress up to the guardhouse was slow and he could feel the bruising swell around his eye, blurring his vision. The throb in the back of his head, at the point of its impact with the pillar, was still keen, filling the rest of his head with a sickening pain that made him feel especially weary. He thought of what lay ahead. Was this his *red martyrdom*, meeting some end like Kessog had at the hand of some ruffians? He was ready to lay down his life, but feared the manner in which it would be taken.

Lord, give me strength for the ordeal ahead, he prayed in his head.

Once they reached the guardhouse, his captors did not bother to speak to him, giving him calm to prepare his spirit to meet with his Lord. What would Domech do with his brothers? The warlord's anger was unbridled, and he feared for their safety. Maybe the burning of the oratory will have satiated his appetite for violence for the night. Perhaps that had been an act to demonstrate his disregard for the muintir and all things sacred, measured to instil fear and to make men talk. Domech had to be seen to be master. But, Domech was a frustrated ruler and therefore the more unpredictable. Was Taran so important to him, he wondered? Probably it is his pride that is most at stake. Domech had chosen him to make an example of, and maybe Domech's anger would be appeased through his own death, and his fellow pilgrims would be spared.

The guard continued to ignore him whilst they regaled their fellows about firing the oratory. This news was greeted with insidious laughter. Glad of this respite, he prayed, hoping that his end would be swift and, should it not, that he would preserve some dignity and not bring dishonour.

Domech appeared later, looking gleeful, carrying the abbot's pastoral staff like a spoil of war. "Your meeting place is burned to the ground," he said, rubbing his hands. A gloating grin broadened his cheeks.

Did he think he had truly damaged their cause by burning the symbol of the muintir? A building could be re-built and the reconstruction would only strengthen their resolve to uphold their cause.

"Moreover, I have sent men in pursuit of Taran. They will bring him back."

"How do you know where he has gone?" he found himself asking, keen to maintain his composure and not feel crushed under the warlord's foot.

"A bit of deduction. Taran would not go east, would he, into the hands of the Circinn. West is the only other viable direction due to the hills north and south of us. West is where you have allies in Alt Clud and Dal Riata. You see, I did not need your compliance. It is no good resisting my will."

"You forget, Drostan is a highly trained warrior, used to living in the wilds. Going north or south into the hills would not be a concern for him."

Domech seemed to ignore the comment and asked something from one of his bodyguards. A small wooden cross was produced.

"This was taken from your meeting place before it was torched, the one piece of ornamentation. Tell me, what does it mean for it must be important to you?"

The question seemed a little odd, for he had spoken about the cross on several occasions in the early years before Domech had dismissed *the way*. He considered his reply. "It is the symbol of compassion and victory."

"How?" Domech seemed curious.

"As no man is worthy of heaven, Christ offered his life in our place as a sacrifice that whoever trusts in him may be with him in paradise."

"Yes, I remember now," he pronounced with a mischievous smile, "you worship one who was killed!" He sneered and concluded with a cold laugh. "Not a powerful High King, when it ended in death!"

"But it is a victory!" he returned. "You think like the world, that by crucifying Christ, you are rid of him! Do you not recall that the story did not end in death?" He waited for a response, but finding none, continued. "Christ was raised to life, victor over death. All who trust in him will likewise be raised when Christ shall return."

"Poof – such nonsense! This is mere wishful thinking and delusion. You believe in a story that happened long ago, in a country far away. It is a tale told by unreliable strangers to deceive you into becoming sheep. That is it – sheep! Sheep is how you refer to yourselves is it not? What are sheep other than stupid animals, fretful, who blindly run after one another."

"You did not always have such a view of us, did you? Can you recall how Kessog outwitted your best druid? Remember how water was sourced upon the rock?"

Domech waved his hand dismissively. He looked up, stony-faced, "Tell me, how does a cross kill a man?"

Instinctively understanding where this question was leading, that his death sentence was being written, he chose to be silent.

"You do not need to conceal," Domech laughed with the swagger of a bully. "Nails pierced his hands and feet." He looked satisfied.

The warlord turned to his bodyguard and announced, "Order the fashioning of a cross. It is a simple structure like this." He raised the replica that was still in his hand. Turning to him with a smile, he suddenly brought the cross down with both hands across his raised knee. The cross did not break. It took a further two attempts before it snapped in half. He tossed it at his feet. "Tomorrow, you shall have your *victory*. I have endured you for too long – what is it . . . for nearly forty years?" Turning, he walked out of the guardhouse.

He sat forlorn, a captive to be crucified. Had he not lived a full life, he thought, trying to come to terms with what starkly awaited him. He had long outlived Kessog and would, anyway, be dying a natural death soon, so what was it to hasten the inevitable end! But he thought of the suffering on the cross, not a swift death, as earlier hoped, but an execution that imitated the Lord he served. Maybe, through his death, more would be moved to come into the heavenly kingdom. That way, his death would not be in vain.

"Old man, you will have no more use of this," said one of the guards taking up the abbot's pastoral staff that Domech had left behind. It was a rather plain piece of wood, but nevertheless, the guard handled it as though it was of value. Then looking up with a gloating look, he said, "You have lived in vain! All your community will be scattered, if not slaughtered."

"Leave him be," his companion complained. "What has he ever done to you?"

"Uh, Drest! Are you a pilgrim too?"

"Of course I am not!" Drest quickly replied. "But I recognise that Fillan and his people have done us no harm. Think of the many they have helped, the sick who have been healed."

The other went over to the corner by the door and did not reply. Drest came over to him with a blanket. "Here, you will need this, that is if you can manage to sleep this night."

Taking the blanket, he thanked him. Wrapping himself in it, he lay outstretched on the wooden bench. He comforted himself with the thought of what lay beyond his suffering, beyond the current crisis; of arriving in a place he had looked towards all his life, coming to the One who would wipe away every tear, who would greet him with the words, *Well done, good and faithful servant.* He tried to pray. It felt like swimming against a current with much debris flowing against him, as disconnected thoughts and fears checked his progress, frustrating his intent to reach a point beyond the strong flow. At times, he gained brief respite, envisaging his High King's welcome.

The night was long. He slept intermittently and fitfully.

At daybreak, he heard the work of chisels and hammers outside the guardhouse, reminding him of what grimly awaited him. He roused himself to pray, feeling sick within. "O Lord, calm my fears. May you not be disgraced this day. Make me strong, holding fast to the peace of what lies beyond," He thought of Taran and Aniel, hoping they had evaded capture. By now, he reckoned, they would be nearing Cartray, where Irb would assist and speed them further west, more distant from Domech's reach, and more importantly, propelling Taran on to his *white martyrdom.* As his own life was passing, he prayed for the resurrected life of this noble warrior to begin in earnest. He envisaged a tree pushing up beside him, growing towards the light. He was to be felled, and his falling would mean light and space for the sapling hopefully to flourish. He thought of all that had been achieved over nearly forty years in Dindurn, of how the muintir had grown. Others would be capable of leading the community forward, even if for the present they should be persecuted and dispersed.

His thoughts were interrupted by a voice outside. "We want to see Fillan."

He recognised Castantin's voice.

"You are barred from the citadel. You and your monks have no welcome here," returned the guard.

"But we are family to Fillan and should be with him at this time."

"On your way," the guard said in a threatening tone. "Do you need the tip of my spear to speed you back?"

He could not hear their reply, for it seemed, judging from the scuffling sounds, they were forced back.

Drest shared some bread and water with him, ignoring the taunts of his fellow soldiers.

"Bless you," he said, looking into the guard's eyes that held his own with an engaging kindness. "No small token will go unnoticed. Do not fear for me, for I am in the High King's ranks. Fear for yourself, though, and make your peace with the High King."

"What?"

"You will understand *the way* at the muintir. Do not delay in going there. Even though you are a soldier in Domech's charge, you will be received with kindness." He was unsure how Drest received his words, for the guard turned aside without comment. He watched the soldiers outside lift the cross from the ground, inspecting their workmanship, chatting about other everyday matters as free men whose end was not in sight.

Shortly, a guard came down from the citadel. "Fillan is to be made to carry the cross up the hill to the courtyard. The Lord Domech awaits him there. There is quite a crowd gathering."

One of the soldiers came in and gruffly said, "Get up, old man!"

He rose, lifting the blanket to fold it. Grabbing him by the shoulder, the soldier turned him forcibly round to face the door. He stepped out into a day of brightness, filled with birdsong, a day when men feel good to be alive. Before him stood the cross partly raised, resting on one of its crossbeams and its base. He was motioned to pick it up. Bending down on one knee, he put his shoulder in the place where the crossbeam intersected with the main shaft and raised the cross. It was heavier than he had imagined.

"Get on your way – it would not be good to keep the warlord waiting."

"It could not be any worse than what it is," he heard Drest remarking.

He took a step forward and felt the resistance of the stump of the cross dragging with a scraping noise over the ground. He took another step and then another, gaining a steady, although crawling pace. He stopped briefly to adjust his clothing where the wood was bruising his shoulder. Moving the cross again was not so easy, so he determined after that to keep moving and not to lose momentum. The roughness of the wood cut into his shoulder, chaffing his skin, and made his joint ache severely. How like his Lord he felt, bearing this reluctant burden. But there were no crowds here jeering and shouting insults. His way was quiet, but the way was long and increasingly steep as the track climbed up to the upper gatehouse that opened into the courtyard.

How unreal it felt. How could this be happening? He had lived his life immune to this level of suffering. He recalled the bairns he used to play with on the fields behind him, when all was well, having gained the goodwill of the common people. He remembered the liberating sense of abandonment when he climbed, with the young ones, right into the treetops, hanging there, held as it were, by the wind on an extremity that could just bear his weight. The image turned into an unhappy picture of what lay ahead. Again, he prayed for strength, to endure the ordeal by visualising that it was the means to transport him from this life into paradise.

As the hill steepened, he stopped, wiping the sweat from his brow, and rubbed his sore shoulder.

"Get on with you," shouted the guard. He heard running steps behind him before feeling the full force of a kick just beneath his buttocks. Emaciated with age, his thighs no longer offered him protection and the force of the kick impacted upon his testicles. He crumpled, but stopped himself from falling by holding on to the cross. The pain coursed through his body and he wanted to vomit. Then, it passed.

Bending low, he took up the weight of the cross and tried to drag it forward up an incline that was steeper than before. Age was against him. Heaving with all his might, it would not move. The cross lurched sidewards, toppling him over with it onto the ground and wrenched his shoulder. He raised himself on to his knees and saw the guard coming swiftly over, no doubt about to kick him again. He closed his eyes, waiting for the moment of impact. But it did not come.

"What are you doing?" his assailant protested.

He saw Drest holding the other's leg.

"Leave him alone. Can you not see he is an old man? Have you no shame!" It looked like Drest might topple him over, but thinking better of it, he let go and came over to him. "Let me help you up." Feeling a hand placed under his arm, he was raised gently to his feet. Turning to his companions, Drest said, "We know Lord Domech awaits, and to avoid delay, I shall help bring the cross to the courtyard."

Drest directed him to his side and placed an arm about him. Having secured the cross upon his own shoulder, the guard commenced walking in tandem with him up the hill. In this manner, they passed through the archway and into the courtyard where the leering cheers of the crowd broke upon them. They were directed to a central place, near to *Fillan's Well*, where a small, but deep hole, had been dug. The guard lowered the cross to the ground.

Chapter Six

White Martyrdom

558 AD   West Coast

When Aniel and Taran had reached the far end of Loch Gunalon, they did not pause, but shouldering their coracles, proceeded southwards. The hills, closing in on either side, surveyed their progress, rearing up with their vast, dark mass etched on the starless night. Those ancient hills, raised at the dawn of the world, made him feel their headway was particularly slow, although he knew they were making haste. They reached the loch known as the *Bent Loch*, glad, at first, to be able to rest weary legs – until their arms began to grow tired with the paddling. A steady drizzle descended in the heavy gloom of the night that saturated their clothes and made their skin itchy before it eventually chafed. They kept looking over their shoulder for pursuers, sensitive to every sound and shadow that haunted throughout a night that felt immensely long.

They reached Cartray at first light where the community, busy with the daily chores of fetching water and lighting fires, was coming to life. They quietly entered Irb's house, hoping they had not been noticed. Irb was well advanced in years, and housebound due to his blindness.

"Aniel! I recognise your voice. Welcome. But who is with you?"

"This is . . . Drostan." He noted how his friend paused, hesitantly, in naming his identity.

"Drostan, you say?" the old man seemed to question. He turned in his direction and spoke, as it were, to someone beyond his shoulder. "And are you a follower of *the way*?"

"I believed I was until I wavered!"

"That is honest," pronounced the old man with a certain approval. "And now?"

He was lost for words, unprepared for this question.

"We cannot remain long, for we are probably being pursued by Domech's men . . ." Aniel explained their circumstances briefly.

"So, how can I be of service to you?"

"Grandfather, if you could provide us with fresh provisions, we would be most grateful, for we are weary and our journey is long."

"You need not have asked for that!" chided the old man good-naturedly, "for my simple hospitality would have extended as much." He instructed a young boy to fill one of their satchels with bannocks and cheese. "Permit me to pray for you though, whilst this is being prepared."

Without awaiting their consent, he bowed his head. "Forgive us, Father, for our foolish ways, for we err from your way and make our own crooked paths . . ."

He noted how the old saint's prayer spoke significantly into his own situation. He felt strangely encouraged that his life had been laid bare before the old man, by the all-knowing One. It served to remind that the High King was mindful of his predicament.

Their journey struck west from Cartray into remoter country, bringing an increasing sense of relief from evading capture, embracing the growing awareness that they were free men, especially when passing over the high watershed beyond Loch Lengwartha and the descent to Loch Lumon. Feeling exceedingly weary for missing a whole night's sleep, they took shelter in the thick of the forest and slept some hours until sunset. They awoke in the gathering darkness.

"How good it would be to have a fire," remarked Aniel, folding his arms about himself.

The air felt saturated with damp.

"Are we beyond the lands of the Fotla?"

"Not quite. It would not be wise to reveal our whereabouts with a fire – just in case!"

"Where, would you say, would be safe to set up camp?"

"On the far shores of Loch Lumon, in the lands of the Britons of Strath Clud."

"Oh, that is close . . ."

"Sssh!" Aniel stretched out his hand before him. "I thought I heard footsteps!"

The two stood poised, motionless. He strained his ears as best he could, "Aye, I heard something then!"

"Stay back and I will investigate," Aniel said, taking stealthy steps forwards into the dark.

"I am coming with you, for two are better than one against whoever comes against us."

Aniel did not argue. Being in the thick of a forest forced them to walk in single file. They approached a high boulder where the trees grew less densely. He noted that the ground was clear of leaves and pine needles as though someone was in the habit of walking about the boulder. His hand moved instinctively to his belt to reach for a sword, then he remembered that he was a defenceless pilgrim. He paused, sensing that someone was lurking around the boulder, and tried to tell Aniel to hold back.

It was too late. Standing before Aniel was a huge, dark figure standing a good head taller than his friend. About to join the ensuing fray, he felt himself strangely held back, a feeling he could not account for, as it was not out of self-preservation, being ready to fight, even with his bare arms. It was then that he realised that the figure was not a man but a bear standing proud on his hind legs and looking as though it had been ready to attack, but was now having second thoughts. Stranger still, was Aniel's stillness, as though mimicking the pose of the bear. His companion stood with his arms hanging limp at his side with his chin slightly turned upwards, gazing to the side of the bear's face, but presenting himself calmly as if to show the beast he meant no harm.

He is striking a non-confrontational pose, he thought.

The bear seemed to acquiesce and leaned forward to sniff Aniel's head curiously. He could hear the breathy investigation which concluded with a lick across Aniel's face. The bear backed down onto all four legs.

Aniel stepped back a single pace and still facing the beast, said, "Pass quietly behind me. The bear will not harm us."

He did as he was told. He walked on and heard Aniel following. He glanced over his shoulder and saw that it was Aniel and he alone.

"Praise the Creator for giving you such a way with animals!"

"We had better keep quiet," Aniel spoke cautiously in an undertone. "We were fortunate to only stumble across a bear and not Domech's men. Perhaps we should not have slept in the lands of the Fotla. We will not be safe until we reach the far shore of Loch Lumon."

He was amused by his friend's comment about being 'fortunate to only stumble across a bear'. He recalled his close and almost deadly encounter with a bear when with Garn crossing the Minamoyn Goch, heightening his awe of Aniel, who without the long training of a warrior, handled the situation so much better. It was apparent that Aniel walked closely with his God who enabled a protection that was now extended even to himself. It impressed that although a true saint was physically unarmed, he was a force to be reckoned with. The stories of Kessog he had so often been regaled with served as reminders of the power of the man of God over the fierce rivalry of druids and warlords. It contradicted all appearances and suppositions. And yet, he countered this line of thought, Aniel is unusual when set alongside the other pilgrims at Dindurn who mostly led unremarkable lives of quiet sanctity, presenting a different view of the world that sometimes left him feeling cold and alienated. Was he being particularly critical of the others? Was it not more the case that he did not share their desire for the quiet rhythms of a monk's discipline, set apart from the world of action and adventure?

Once they reached a clearing, they stood side by side in the gloaming, with the last of the light expiring in the west, watching the pale colour of the clouds fade and eventually extinguish, giving way to a heavy grey. The long, vast basin of the loch lay below them as a natural boundary, its waters glowing pale between the ink black folds of the hills that encompassed them. It represented freedom, but the far shore presented unknown territory, occupied by foreigners, where his next episode was about to unravel. He felt a slight unease until he chided himself for his own inconsistencies, for had he not been hungering for adventure, freed from the predictable rhythms of the muintir? He quietened his own unrest, reasoning that the muintir had prepared him for this new episode for he could now speak the tongue of the Gaels. He was encouraged to be re-entering the world, better equipped as a pilgrim, and yet mystified by the concept that the true pilgrim was not wholly protected.

The way was steep and in places, slippery, challenging balance as they carried coracles. They were glad to place their craft in the water and paddle across the divide and be received into the mysterious darkness of the far bank, thankful for its cover. They lit a fire and sat around its flames, too drowsy to talk, exhausted from the race they had won, and drained from the nagging fear that had driven them incessantly onwards. Eventually, exhaustion overcame them.

Aniel remarked the following morning, "I have never known this journey to pass so quickly." They broke camp and walked the narrow isthmus between Lumon and a deep inlet of the sea.

"And a couple of boats await on the jetty," he observed as they passed the low watershed through the clearing. On arriving at the shore, they learned that one vessel was bound, later that day, for Eilean Bhòid on the boundary between Strath Clud and Dal Riata.

"This is where we part." Aniel sounded flat.

"I am deeply indebted to you," Taran began, with feeling. "I recognise the goodness of the King, helping us to evade capture. And . . ." he paused, running his hand over the lengthening stubble of his shaved forehead, "I recognise your own goodness, Aniel, for being a brother to me from the start, helping me adjust to the strange ways of the muintir."

"We have been granted safe passage," he agreed emphatically. "Drostan . . ." he paused. "Taran, for brothers should call themselves by their true names, I am glad you came to Dindurn and that I could meet a stranger from among the Ce of the north and call him my brother. I pray that you will follow no other than the King of kings and forsake the Bulàch, as I did many years ago, when

I emerged from my stupor of unbelief and pursuit of passing pleasures."

"Be assured, I have been brought to my senses, much to my shame, for trusting Domech. And, I should add, I have been much impressed by the way you have with animals!"

They prayed, clasped one another, then parted. He watched Aniel walk up the clearing to the top of the rise above Loch Lumon, at the start of a lengthy journey back to Dindurn. He reflected on the past two years that had provided more than a safe haven for him. I have made brothers, unexpectedly, from among a people not my own, other Picts, Britons and men hailing from far-off Erin with their peculiar beliefs in the risen Christ. Have I not undergone strict disciplines, the value of which I have not despised, steeling me for my destiny?

He experienced a keen sense of loss, watching Aniel's form diminish as it passed over the near horizon; the final link to the life of the muintir being severed. With it was taken the security of a known way, the soothing familiarity of a daily rhythm – concepts which had suddenly become valued where previously he had grown weary. Uprearing in the foreground were unpredictable adventures, ominously referred to as his *white martyrdom*.

The letter to the king of Dal Riata had its desired effect, for the day after arriving at Dunadd, he was on a merchant vessel bound for Aird nam Murchan, journeying north across waters sheltered by a string of islands to the west: the three-peaked Hinba, the rocky-ribbed Eilean Creagach, and the lower-lying isles of Luinn, Saoil and Kerrera.

This was different country, so unlike where he had been raised; a land overwhelmed by water, whose long straths had been drowned, leaving only hilltops emerging from the inundation of the Great Western Sea. It stirred him to look upon the wonders of a foreign land, filled with an overwhelming sense of thankfulness to have been delivered from Domech's near fatal clutch. Rest was what he yearned for after the frantic time of fleeing, and to be reconciled with the keen disappointment he felt about himself. This voyage, on calm waters, was what his soul craved, where he might regain the capacity to contemplate what lay ahead.

Emerging from a lengthy narrow channel between Kerrera and the mainland, his boat sailed north-west towards Muile's great bulk of lofty hill ridges, onto the turbulent waters of a broad sound. The tidal flow was intense and so convulsed that the water seemed at times to boil, enabling them either to move swiftly on, or to be seriously impeded despite the wind filling the sail. Fascinating as this alien world was, it filled him with a sense of trepidation. He was pleased to reach a lengthy strait with the wild hill country of Muile to their left and the mainland on the other side.

A good while later, one of the sailors pointed towards less sheltered waters, "That is Aird nam Murchan ahead!". The few bays along its shores, sculptured by sea at the feet of the hills, provided bases for the mercantile Gaels to establish their trading posts on the extremity of Dal Riata. The interior was covered by a vast expanse of uncleared forest with rocky crags rising clear of the trees. Surprised to find himself in so wild a place, he acquiesced, knowing his destiny lay beyond the reach of the Gaels.

"The lands north of here are wild." The skipper informed him with a cautionary tone.

"Whose authority are they under?"

"The Picts!" The skipper spat into the water, implying that the Gael dismissed the notion that Picts were capable of exerting any semblance of governance.

"I am a Pict," he replied, looking the skipper in the eye.

"You do not look like one!"

"Maybe so. I am one who has learned your language, can write Latin and have adopted your ways. However, I do not forget that I am a Pict and am proud to have been raised a warrior."

"You look more like a pilgrim to me!" He turned away dismissively.

Equally keen to cut short their brief exchange, he picked up his coracle and, walking up the pebble beach to the scattering of huts, asked an old man mending a net, "I am heading north looking for an island with a conical peak that looks like it has had its top sliced off. Do you know of such a peak?"

The fisherman shrugged his shoulders. "There are many peaks north of here. Inis y Copa Peer has a peak that perhaps matches your description."

"Is it far?"

"Not so very far, two days at the most. If I were you, though, I would take the overland route and avoid the rough waters at the point. There, the tidal race can take you where you do not want to go!" His toothless mouth closed in a rather grotesque manner, cutting short any further talk of the treacheries of the ocean.

He set off with his coracle and satchel strung across his shoulders to cross the peninsula's neck. There was a kind of way to begin with, beyond the settlement, but before long it appeared to peter out, forcing him to enter forest growing dense and tall upon steep braes. Encumbered by the broad coracle upon his back, he passed through what seemed a thicket of unruly branches, relieved to eventually reach the dividing ridge of the peninsula where the trees thinned. He stopped involuntarily, stilled by the immensity of the view that suddenly opened up before him, having walked unsighted for a long while.

"This is where my *white martyrdom* begins," he said aloud. He shivered, thinking where this might lead. Studying the seascape to the north, he noted that it was quite different from what he had encountered so far on his journey. Stretching as far as his eye could see were vast expanses of sea, scattered with islands much further out from the mainland than had been the case previously along this coast. Reaching these entailed crossing vast extents of open waters.

Heavy grey curtains of rain passed in a squally series of showers over sea and island, driven by a wind unchecked by the openness of the ocean. The ruffled waters had the appearance of a much-dinted war shield, upon which the sun broke occasionally with brilliant shafts of light piercing the gloom. His eyes focussed on a solitary sunbeam probing the water with majestic sweeps of glittering radiance, as if searching for some lost soul amidst the desolation.

For the first time since his arrival at Dindurn, he was truly alone, finding himself in a world alien to all that he had previously known, with the ocean presenting an obstacle that filled him with enormous apprehension. This departure, embarking upon a new adventure, was somewhat reminiscent of setting out from Coblaith's farm, leaving the protection of home with its provision and comfort to journey through the dangers of the Minamoyn Goch. The mountains, though, were a familiar environment, where much of his training as a youth had been carried out. Familiar as they might have been, he still shuddered at the recollection of those harrowing days that eventually culminated in the killing of his faithful Garn. At least then, he had a more specific goal of reaching the strath on the far side, guided by Elpin's instructions and Coblaith's vision leading to that providential encounter with Ossian. This time, though, he was without a route description, with only Fillan's vision of a peak to somehow guide to a place of Pictish pilgrimage. Ahead rose a huge array of peaks, stretching as far as the horizon and no doubt beyond. Even across the lonely tracts of ocean, mountainous islands rose, so distant, as to be faint grey smudges on the rim of the world. It made him question whether they were figments of his imagination or impairment of sight, seeming quite unreachable by coracle.

Thankfulness over escaping Domech's evil arm began to be replaced by a growing unease at the huge odds he faced. He would prefer to pass again under the duns of the gods rather than ride in this tiny animal-hide frame on open seas.

"Why does my fate lead me to wander in perilous places?" he complained aloud. "Oh, this mysterious Z-rod has set me apart, put me on a collision course with Oengus, and once again has made me a fugitive. I would settle for a simple peasant's lot right now, digging Coblaith's field; for at least life was predictable, preferable to what lies ahead."

On that boundary between the two worlds of Dal Riata and the Picts, he railed, unable to hold back the bitterness. After a bout of fury and an impotent sense of self-pity, Fillan's paternal face came to mind. How long-suffering the old saint had been. How ungratefully he had responded to the abbot's kindly efforts to re-make the broken man he had become. He recalled their one-to-one sessions, the saint's wise and engaging efforts, doing his utmost to prepare him. His more recent indignation, suppressing the mounting resentment of being led in so alien and unsought a way, came to mind and filled him with shame.

I owe my very life to Fillan, he thought. His gratitude was checked by reliving the ignominy of so easily being duped by the wily Domech. How could I have been deceived by the flattery that fed my youthful vanity? How could I have been so naïve? How could I think I was fit to rule my people?

Recalling the time when he and Oengus had been immobilised by shock after killing the peasant couple, he had deliberately chosen, back then, to move forward and not to allow the past to incarcerate. He consciously chose to stop the futile questioning as to why these misfortunes should have singled him out. Remembering how his former state of being a peasant made him aware of his own powerlessness, without the means, nor a scheme, to regain the lordship, he reminded himself now how vital it was to rely upon higher powers and prophetic utterances.

"*Your transformation is in the isles of the west,*" he quoted Ossian's prophetic outburst three years back upon the hill above Rhynie. "Following my *surrender in the south,*" he continued, "*there will come much strife, like a blight threatening to consume*". Had his life at Dindurn not been a surrender? Had he not submitted to the ways of the muintir and embraced, for much of the time under Fillan's guidance, the ways of a soldier of Christ?

So, that part of the prophecy has come true in the same way that heeding the caution to *make great haste when you leave* had sown the idea of flight from the crannog. Following the directive, *be cunning, be brave, be humble* had also spared me from being sacrificed at Loch Kinord.

He smiled with a degree of consolation that bordered on satisfaction. Therefore, if these things came to pass because I heeded the prophecy, then surely the next part, my *transformation in the isles of the west* will also occur.

However, his solace was short-lived upon recounting what else the prophecy predicted: *heartache and anguish lie before you. Many a journey awaits, full of ordeals that you consider will be your undoing, though these are in truth, rites of passage for your own preparation.*

Heeding visions and direction was his only hope. How far north had he to voyage before he would encounter this peak? How far do the realms of the Fidach Picts extend beyond these horizons? For a good while these thoughts consumed him, stirred by that sight of white-crested seas and far-flung islands and myriad mountain peaks that mocked the chances of finding the very one referred to in Fillan's vision.

"*White martyrdom!*" he pronounced aloud with resentful resignation after a lengthy silence. The abbot had been quite specific in his choice of phrase, outlining the condition in which he would succeed and overcome. "What of my veneration of the Bulàch?" He recalled the secret supplications, the furtive oblations of milk in the dark of night within the muintir. What good had they been? Then what of the troubled dreams – where did they originate? Had the Bulàch tried to warn him, or were these indeed the work of the High King of Heaven?

"My task is assigned by a godly man in whom there is no falsehood or wickedness. I can trust him, just as I have trusted Ossian who told me to rely upon Fillan. If I am to be guided by Fillan, then surely I should also follow Fillan's God."

In their parting conversation, Fillan had spoken about his choosing to believe that Taran would become a true soldier of Christ. The abbot had also revealed that his arrival at the muintir had been predicted by Kessog decades ago, even before his birth, that he would be set aside for 'a high calling'. Fillan had concluded that the calling would become apparent 'once you have seen the King in his glory'.

Through one, you will overcome the world! had been Ossian's prophecy. It was imbued with new meaning now that he uttered it three times. "Could that 'one' be Christ?" He recalled the extraordinary meeting with the bard under the Rock of Refuge and the reminder of the missing parts of the forgotten prophecy. He knew how to persevere and how this would become *the making of the man*. Persevering had been drilled into him by his foster father during his military training and more recently at the muintir.

And then, there was that brief meeting with Irb, who aware of his duplicity, encouraged him to make right choices. He decided to say a simple prayer as he made camp in the shelter of a low ridge before the cheerful light and warmth of his campfire. It was a prayer not learned at the muintir, which so often he would say out of custom, but instead was of words filled with heartfelt conviction.

"O Great High King, may all my thoughts and actions be responsive to your prompting. Help me to see your mercies in everyday events and to know your grace, enabling me to overcome the difficulties before me. Amen."

Chapter Seven

The Toppled Stone

558 AD   Dindurn

Fillan saw Domech rising from his seat, surrounded by other dignitaries who occupied the prime place, raised upon a dais to better view the spectacle of execution. To his surprise, Drest did not leave his side, but stood with him, it seemed, in solidarity. To everyone else, though, he mused, it probably appeared that Drest was keeping guard over the condemned.

"Where is the strong man now?" jeered Domech, relishing the situation. "Your reluctance to explain how a cross kills a man set me thinking." He paused, seemingly labouring with his breathing. "I believe it would have been spikes of this size that the Romans used to carry out the execution." He brandished in the air, a lethal section of iron, half the length of his forearm, displaying it to the crowd. He then wiped his brow, which Fillan thought odd, for Domech was perspiring on a cool day. "Do you have anything to say for yourself before these spikes impale you to the cross?"

"What is your charge against me?" he found himself asking boldly.

"Aiding Taran to escape."

"You speak of him as a traitor. Taran is not of the Fotla. He belonged to the muintir, and therefore was not under your command."

"He is a wanted man."

Fillan could see Domech's colour deepening as an anger welled up to consume him.

"Taran has done you no harm."

"Taran was wasted as a pilgrim."

"What is that to you? You were to hand him over to be killed. You may despise our cause, but we do no one harm. Taran is a good man and does not deserve to be sold to the Lord Cynbel."

"What makes him good?" sneered Domech, his lips turning a purple colour.

"Good people," Fillan addressed the crowd. "you will recall how Taran fought with the warlord's son." He was encouraged by the stillness that came over the people as they fixed their attention upon him. "As a warrior, he behaved nobly, sparing the Lord Domech son's life, even though he had faced treachery. The noble warrior has renounced violence, for he has understood the futility of fighting with the weapons of this world. Taran has chosen a different course. I should say he has been chosen from some time back for a heavenly task of bearing divine fire to a distant people. He has been set aside, marked by the Z-rod, to be a prince of men and bringer of peace."

"Enough of this talk. As we speak now, Taran will be in the hands of my men who pursued him."

"How would you know that?"

"Be quiet! It is not your place to question me. You are the one on trial." He stopped, tugging at the neckline of his garment as though it were choking him.

"I have been put falsely on trial," Fillan said, defiantly. This was not his usual manner, but he felt compelled to speak the truth before he was executed. Judging from the crowd's keenness to hear what he had to say, he sensed some were with him.

"How dare you speak to me like this!" the warlord shouted, raising his fist. "You do not deny aiding his escape, so . . ." He stopped mid-sentence, clutching at his chest and staggered back into his seat.

The crowd began to stir.

"Let the holy man free!" shouted a voice from the crowd.

The soldiers scanned the crowd, trying to determine where the voice came from.

"Aye, free the soldier of Christ – he has done no one harm," protested another.

"He has healed our ailments," reminded a woman with a piercing voice.

This began a wave of protests, all crying for his release. The soldiers did not try to quell their shouting; and without orders being given, it appeared to Fillan that some even shared the sentiments. As it proved impossible to control public expression the crowd became emboldened. Moving into the vacant space of the courtyard, they came upon him, and in their human tide, bore him towards the gate. Drest placed an arm about his back to steady him amidst all the jostling. He could just make out Domech being carried away in the direction of the big hall, attended by a druid, his close bodyguard and some family members.

Some of the crowd, going only as far as the upper gate, turned aside. Fillan surmised that they had fulfilled their purpose in ensuring he was not to be executed. The more enthusiastic accompanied him all the way to the muintir, with Drest remaining at his side the whole way.

Castantin and the brothers, who were assembled by the charred remains of the oratory, greeted this spirited party with joy.

"We have been much in prayer for you," Castantin exclaimed with relief and joy. "And it would seem that the High King has answered, delivering you from the hand of evil."

"Your God seemingly listens," exclaimed Drest, who proceeded to relate all the events since Fillan had been seized on the previous evening. By the time he had finished, he announced that he should return to his duties.

"But maybe that is not such a good idea," remarked Fillan.

"Oh, why?" the soldier looked at him with some wonder. "Will your God not also help me?"

"If you are believing, then you have the Almighty with you. But, this does not mean that you will go unharmed. All the help you have shown me might be considered treason by others?"

"That may be so. But judging by the public reaction, many side with you."

"But you are a soldier – that is different, is it not?"

"Someone needs to make a stand for what is right among Domech's guard. That seems to be the bravest course of action befitting a soldier." With that, Drest left them, hailed by the brethren as a brother.

"We thought we had lost you," said Castantin. "I came to the citadel this morning with two others to make an appeal, but had been prevented by the guard at the outer gate. They were busy doing some carpentry work."

"I heard you come," returned Fillan. "That carpentry was to be the cross of my execution."

Castantin shook his head. "The High King has intervened. Now it is Domech who is in danger. What do you think shall be the outcome?"

"We should pray for him." He could see one of his fellow monks mouthing a silent 'No' in dismay. "Let us pray that he might learn his lesson before it is too late. All my time here, I have hoped to see Domech turn from his brutal ways. He has seen so much evidence, particularly in Kessog's time, so as to know *the way*, but has avoided walking in it. Now, may the Lord be gracious in giving him yet another chance before it is too late. All the anger that has consumed him, now weighs heavily in the balance. I do not know whether he shall die now, for I have not received a word of knowledge. Maybe one of you knows better though?" His neck craned to survey the faces gathered before him, but no one was any the wiser.

Later that day, Fillan and Castantin went up to the citadel, surprising the guard by their unexpected appearance. The one who had kicked Fillan gestured them through to the top gate, shaking his head in disbelief, but not with ill-will. Fillan detected that he even looked a little awkward.

At the second gate, they were told to wait whilst a guard went to enquire of Lord Domech. Their appearing in the courtyard, set up for Fillan's execution, surprised those who were there, and they could not restrain themselves from coming over.

"We are amazed that no harm befell you!" exclaimed a middle-aged woman, touching his upper arm tenderly for a moment.

"How could you face death with peace and composure, and make such a calm defence?" commented a man, shaking his head.

"It was you mentioning the noble and brave Taran that turned opinion in your favour," said another with an animated face. "We witnessed how he fought truly as a noble one without any guile."

This piece of information intrigued Fillan, recalling how he had reprimanded Taran for taking up arms for the reason that it would be a bad witness. It seems I stand corrected, he thought.

At that moment, an elderly woman pushed the others aside. "Brother Fillan, I am one of the old ones here who can remember your arriving all those years ago when we were both young and strong. You amazed us all with your secret knowledge of where the well shaft was to be sunk, we have been spared so much toil all these years. We have been slow, ever so slow, to give you credit. Earlier, we nearly witnessed you being strung up as a criminal and committed to some foreign means of execution. Thank the Bulàch that the evil plan was not carried out."

"Thank the High King," corrected Castantin.

"Well, that is what I meant," she said, slightly flustered. "I do not know who this High King is, but today I have seen your deliverance at his hand."

"Join us one day at the muintir," warmly invited Fillan. "You, and anyone else, are always welcome. Do not come because I invite you, though. Come of your own accord. I believe from those who have witnessed my deliverance earlier this day that many will question and seek."

"Why do you want to see the Lord Domech?" asked a younger man, scratching his head. "He tried to kill you!"

"But the High King constrained him. That might be for a bigger purpose than sparing me."

"Surely, it was to spare your life, solely!" he replied.

"I do not deny that, for our heavenly father is mindful of his children. But, I also believe it provides the Lord Domech with another opportunity to make his peace with the High King before he must face him to give an account for the way he has lived in this world."

"He does not deserve it," whispered the old woman, taking him by the wrist as if to restrain him. "You are too good."

"No, none of us can be too good. We can, at best, walk in the light of his mercy. and show compassion because we have been forgiven."

"What have you been forgiven for?" asked the old woman. "You have always been a mild man, full of goodness, healing us who have been short on thankfulness. Now here you are, coming to one who would kill you, to carry out, I suspect, some act of kindness."

"You suspect rightly. But I am not all good. I spent last night afraid, struggling to find peace."

"Who of us would not have been the same!" exclaimed the young man. "I would have been dragged into the courtyard, screaming and kicking, if it had been me! But no, you come in compliantly, mild as always."

"You are kind. But you should know my strength was spent. I could come no other way after bearing that heavy cross up the hill."

The guard returned. "The Lord Domech does not want to see you. If I were you, I would stay away if you value your life, for he is hot with anger!"

"My life is in the High King's hands – it is he who protects me. But I fear for your lord. I shall return in the morning and ask if he is ready to see me then."

The pilgrims left the courtyard, leaving a group shaking their heads with a mixture of dismay and respect.

That night when everyone was asleep at the muintir, the sound of thundering horse hooves disturbed the peace. A voice cried out in the night, shortly joined by others. Fillan rose, finding his shoulder particularly sore and his cheek so swollen that he could not open one eye. There was more shouting as Fillan struggled to pass beneath the low entrance to his cell. Several thatch roofs were on fire and more were being torched at the far end of the muintir. Some tried to quench the flames, but lacking a ready supply of water, the roofs burned in no time. The noisy commotion ensured that not one of them was left asleep to perish within his cell.

The riders returned, having torched many more roofs. They rode up to where the community had gathered about the burnt remains of the oratory.

"Pilgrims!" one of the horsemen addressed them. "This is an apt name for you, for tomorrow you are to leave. Anyone remaining by tomorrow night shall be run through by sword or spear."

He spurred his horse, and his fellow riders followed him back to the rock.

The sound of horse hooves diminished, along with the dying crackling of the roof fires. The brothers stared at the burnt-out shells of their cells in dismay. No one spoke.

"Come, brothers, do not be so discouraged," Fillan said eventually. "We still have our lives."

"What are we to do? Where are we to go? Many of us were born and raised here," said one of the younger monks.

"Tomorrow is a new day; and then the High King will direct our ways. I say to you not to be discouraged, for this anger is Domech's frustration with us and with the High King. He lashes out like a dying man, intent to harm, for he feels his own impotence and his reputation is harmed."

"I would say that the unrest is in the hearts of many of Domech's people!" Castantin proclaimed. "Is this not brought about by the Spirit, so that some may find peace?"

"Well spoken. But as for now, find what shelter you can. Rest, and we will meet at daybreak to pray. Be of good cheer, for our Lord is with us and I sense much good will come from this, as we have already seen evidence that many are with us. Remain steadfast."

Near the close of their dawn prayer, two mounted soldiers arrived. Surprisingly, the soldiers waited until their prayers were over, before announcing with a tone of respect, "Abbot Fillan, Lord Domech has called for you."

Fillan had not slept well, which after the fitful sleep at the guardhouse the previous night had frayed his nerves. He wondered what new menace the warlord was preparing. He required a moment to remind himself that the battle was not his, but the High King's. It had showered in the night, and his clothes were wet, clinging uncomfortably to his body. Not only his shoulder and cheek ached worse than before, but all his joints were troubled with rheumatic pain.

"Castantin, come with me, please," Fillan said. "As for the rest of you, gather reeds down at the river and straight branches from the woods, for there are many roofs to rebuild."

One man looked incredulously at him, as if to say, 'Did you not hear that we were to leave this day?'

Arriving at Domech's quarters, they found the warlord sat upon a chair, eating a bowl of porridge. He looked worse than Fillan felt, dishevelled, his face gaunt and haunted.

"Fillan!" he said weakly. He placed his bowl down, and looked their way but did not speak further.

Fillan noticed the warlord's lower lip trembling and that his eyes were more bloodshot than usual. Any residual unease dissipated at that moment, realising some profound change had indeed come over him.

"My lord, how can we be of service to you?" Fillan said simply, sensing the viper had been de-fanged.

"You are always gentle!" the warlord said with a sense of incredulity in his voice. "Does your meekness have no end?" Domech stared at him with a kind of wonder, in no hurry to continue – or perhaps feeling awkward about how to proceed, he had hesitated. "I had always regarded meekness to be a weakness. Who does not? But in you, I see it is a strength. Who, after all, would go to the home of one who has tried to kill you? That is courageous."

"My lord, we are only men, like yourself, hampered by all the natural passions that afflict mankind. The difference is . . ." Here, he paused, licking his dry lips. "We dwell under the shadow of the High Rock that protects us, giving us peace."

"You mean Dindurn?" questioned Domech, confused.

"No. By the High Rock, I mean Christ."

"You – and the druids – like to speak in riddles!" he admonished gently, with a half-smile.

"Forgive me, lord, I will try to speak plainly. Tell me, how may I be of service?"

"I have had that dream again."

"What dream?"

"The one I had all those years back when you came with Kessog to this rock."

"The one about the standing stone being undermined?"

"Exactly. Only this time, the stone was toppled!" He looked fearful and the trembling not only returned to his lip, but this time was evident in his hands as well.

"Do you recall the original dream?" Fillan searched the warlord's face. "Was the stone not inscribed with a new symbol during the night of the enemy's digging?"

"Yes, it had been." The warlord nodded. "It was your cross was it not, freshly made in relief on the reverse side to our customary symbols. In my dream, I only saw the Pictish signs. It must have fallen face down on the cross side. What does it mean?"

"I am no interpreter of dreams. That was Kessog's gift."

"What must I do? I fear death is at my door. As great as my body is afflicted, so is my mind."

"Permit me to speak," interjected Castantin. "I have heard of this dream and it seems the meaning is clear."

"Go on," Fillan encouraged.

"In the first dream, the stone remained upright revealing the cross, because it offered deliverance through faith in Christ. So, if it has fallen, does it not mean that the cross symbol, being considered of no account to you and discarded with contempt, now presents a bleak and hopeless future?"

"Yes, of course," pronounced Fillan, "I do not know why I did not understand that myself!" He wiped his hand forcibly over his face as if urging himself to wake up, but winced with pain from his swollen features. He was not feeling himself, and recent events had impacted more than he had imagined. It felt like a fog engulfed his brain and all his senses were dulled through lack of sleep. How thankful he was to have Castantin with him.

"Not only have I disregarded the cross," Domech said, "but I have persecuted its followers! I am ashamed by what I have done to you who are innocent. But your innocence highlighted my darkness the more, and that angered me. What must I do? I fear for my life and what lies beyond. Can there be any hope for someone who has opposed your God all of his life?"

"The Lord is merciful. Has he not stretched out his hand to you through this nightmare, warning you to turn before it is too late?" He felt more alert now. "But you are to turn wholeheartedly, not just for a day to be relieved from your troubles."

"I see that," declared Domech.

"Then let us kneel!" he said, falling to his knees.

The warlord used the chair to help him kneel. It was a most strange sight to see how one previously so haughty was reduced to this humble posture. Fillan prayed.

Still upon his knees following the prayer, Domech said, "I feel a great weight has been lifted,"

"The symbol stone has been raised," announced Castantin. "Which side are you to show your people?"

"I understand. I shall confess my faith before all this day and revoke my orders to destroy your colony of heaven. Fillan, forgive me, for I have done you much harm."

"I forgive! I rejoice that finally you are with us and not opposing us. You know, Kessog prophesied that you and I would grow old in this place; and it has come true. He did not say, though, that you would repent. That has been my prayer for years, that you would turn from your ways."

Domech smiled weakly. "Today, I will instruct every able hand to repair your cells and to rebuild your meeting place. And, should the Lord preserve me, I shall worship with you."

Chapter Eight

Isles of the Great Western Sea

558 AD to Inis Kayru

Taking up his satchel and coracle the next morning, Taran descended into the forests, heading for the northern shore. It began to rain. He moved fairly quickly over the uneven ground, but it was not so easy to pass through the forest where the trees grew dense, encumbered by carrying a coracle. Despite the rain, he felt resolute, considering the present trial as his ongoing training, which required dogged perseverance if he were to prevail. A readiness to believe in a calling higher than that of the warlord of the Ce somehow urged him on with all the might of his warrior spirit.

The substantial waves, breaking white along the shore, made it difficult to launch the coracle. He flipped himself aboard just before a wave nearly overturned the craft. Instantly, the coracle was waterlogged, making it impossible to paddle beyond the breaking surf; so, when the next wave broke, the boat sank. Fear flickered in his chest for an instant. No sooner than his feet had found the sandy sea floor, he found himself being dragged out to sea by the force of the receding water, clinging to the submerged, but still floating vessel. The next wave did not break, but raised him to the peak of its crest. When its force

111

had passed and he descended into the trough of its wake, his feet found the seabed once more. Bracing his legs, he made a stand and flipped the coracle upside down, righting it so that it floated. When he launched himself upon the side of the boat, it dipped, and taking on so much water, it was useless to board. Tipping the water out, he tried twice more before giving up, accepting this method was futile.

If I could launch myself quickly into the boat, he told himself, then the side would spend less time dipped underwater. Holding the coracle by its line, he went underwater in the rising swell where his feet found the seabed. With the drag of the passing wave, he launched himself with a great upthrust and lunged clumsily into the coracle. Although taking on some water, the craft remained afloat; and now, beyond the breaking surf, he had opportunity to bail out the water.

The spring wind blew wretchedly cold, making him paddle vigorously. Wet clothing clung, impeding his every movement, and before long, started to chafe his skin. Inis y Copa Peer lay to the northwest, out across open sea, but clearly visible with its distinctive hill, rising sheer. After much effort in paddling forward, the island still looked no closer. The flimsy vessel bobbed about like a frail petal on the vastness of an ocean; and, being a round bowl shape, it did not cut smoothly through the water. Although cumbersome to handle; surprisingly it stayed afloat despite its frailty and size. A while later, still labouring towards Inis y Copa Peer's peak that seemed no closer, he looked back to Aird nam Murchan's shore and noted that it had receded, growing fainter, the previous detail of its heights now merging into a single shade of grey.

A good while later, he estimated he was midway. Progress was slow despite his best efforts. The sheer summit on Inis y Copa Peer formed a pinnacle, rising above the whale-back of the rest of the island; and he wondered whether this could be the peak in Fillan's vision, a thought that gave him heart.

Later that afternoon, he came into the sheltered water of a bay beneath the peak soaring up like a single tooth into the sky. The peak had a flat top, and with imagination, it could be said to have been sliced through as with a sword, but not at an angle from this aspect. Reaching land brought huge relief.

He was greeted by one of the several folk curiously watching him, as he passed across the beach and onto the machair. "Who are you, and where have you come from?" Their accent had a lyrical quality, spoken much slower than the more guttural speech of the Ce.

"From Aird nam Murchan. I am a Pict of the Ce tribe."

"Welcome."

"What is this island?"

"Why, you do not know?" another of them responded, surprised. "This is Inis y Copa Peer!"

"I thought so, but wanted to be sure. Tell me," he wiped away the sweat and sea salt that encrusted his face, "Do people pilgrimage to the peak?"

They laughed at the thought, and shook their heads, looking at him a little incredulously.

He sat down on the short grass, exhausted from his efforts, drained by the tension of voyaging in so flimsy a craft. There came a sudden cloudburst, sending everyone indoors.

"Come on in," shouted one man from his threshold, gesticulating earnestly.

He was glad of the invitation, and dried himself by the hearth.

"My name is Gartnait," said his host introducing himself. The man had a good-natured expression with eyes that were set quite wide apart, making him look in a constant state of surprise. He spoke about farming out on this edge of the ocean. Surprisingly, the land looked lush around the bay and part-way up the hillside.

"You should see the land on the north side – it is also good, and more extensive. You will see it for yourself if you are travelling on to Rùm."

"What is Rùm?

"Inis Rùm is the next island!" Gartnait seemed astonished by his ignorance. "We traverse our island when going to Rùm – it shortens the sea-crossing. You are brave to cross open sea on your own!"

The next day brought more rain. Taking up his coracle, he accompanied Gartnait up the rise to the central divide of Inis y Copa Peer. Nearing the low ridge, dark rugged peaks of the neighbouring island came into view: first their rocky summits and then their vast bulk emerging with every step, rising dramatically steep out of the sea. His eyes fixed immediately upon a conical top, its summit rising at an angle as though it had been sliced off.

"It is not good land over there on Inis Rùm!" Gartnait shook his head. "We are much more fortunate to farm here." Removing a strand of grass he had been chewing, he used it to point to a distant section of Rùm's coast. "Make for that dark section just before the end of the coastline that we can see. It is the entrance to a sea loch, at the head of which are some dwellings. Ask for Uvan – he is a relative of mine – and tell him I sent you."

This was his fourth day since setting out from Dunadd. Bidding farewell to his wide-eyed host, he launched off to cross the sound, which was a broad expanse though nothing like as great as what he had traversed the previous day. He realised that Rùm's peaks, looming above the ocean, made it look deceptively closer to Inis y Copa Peer than it actually was.

Without habitation, its weathered slopes rose uncompromisingly steep from the shore, ascending to great crags, where as the weather deteriorated mist now formed and swirled in a mysterious manner before being shredded into tatters. Strong, circular strokes were required to make any headway along the coast, to contend with the considerable rise of the swell. He steered a safe distance from its rocky shore, and around midday rounded the point that had been indicated and turned into a significant inlet. Sighting smoke rising at the head of the sea loch, he made for a distant beach. As he neared the far shore, a cluster of round huts came into view beyond.

"What brings you here?" asked a young man with a pick over his shoulder.

After hearing his explanation, he remarked, "No one comes here on pilgrimage! There is an island to the west where pilgrims go – you will see it as you round the top of our island."

"Does it have a conical shaped hill?"

"No," the man replied, raising his eyebrows at the strange question. "But go over to the big island to the north – Inis Niwl – and you will find many hills there with conical peaks."

"Could I get over there this afternoon, do you think?"

"No!" He exclaimed with surprise. "It is too far. You must leave early in the morning."

"I am looking for Uvan – do you know him?"

The man looked at him slightly taken aback. "That's me!"

"Gartnait told me to ask for you. He put me up last night."

"Gartnait is my cousin, or something like that. He is a good fellow, although a bit wide-eyed!" Uvan smiled briefly, and then started to study the sky. "A storm is brewing," he announced with certitude. "You will need to bide here until it is spent. Come, meet my family and have something to eat. Then, if the storm has not broken, I would be glad of your help in preparing some ground nearby."

When they returned from the field later that day, the rising wind was moist with rain. Clouds covered the high peaks in a dark gloom, full of threatening portents, with mutterings of distant thunder rumbling down from the heights.

That night the storm unleashed its full fury. Loud cracks of thunder accompanied the lightning almost simultaneously. Heavy rain fell in the commotion of a wild wind, making sleep fretful. When the storm subsided, the sea swell could be heard lapping the nearby stony shoreline rhythmically. By the afternoon of the next day the sea had calmed, but it was too late to make Inis Niwl before nightfall.

On the sixth day out from Dunadd, the rising sun ushered in one of those rare mornings when the water in the sea loch looked like polished metal. The April sun had a mellow light that honeyed the faded grasses on the hills. Even the grey of the heather was vividly transformed, giving the hills a lustrous, lead-like quality. Thanking Uvan, he launched out into the bay in good spirits with the prospect of a calm crossing and the hope of seeing the sliced-off conical hill, the finding of which, he considered was becoming something of an odyssey.

Even with the favourable sea state, the journey took much of the day; and he made landfall, but not where he had anticipated on the lower-lying peninsula closest to Rùm. The tide had carried him north towards another of Inis Niwl's peninsulas that stretched out towards Rùm, where the land was austere, rather like Rùm, with stark and rugged mountains rising with vast, black cliffs into the clouds. The beach he had arrived at was boulder-strewn, with spines of black rock protruding out into the sea. Exhausted, he lay down and slept in the shelter of his coracle which he had upended to form a windbreak, weighted down with some large stones. Waking cold and aching, he explored the bay for better shelter for the night and found a cave above the high tide mark. It involved a scramble up to enter its mouth, an adequate place to overnight with the bonus of a strong trickle of drinking water falling to one side from the cliffs above. Weary as he was, he scampered along the rocky bay to gather a quantity of well-seasoned driftwood strewn above the high-water mark. With the pangs of hunger being not as great as his weariness, he brought several bundles up to the cave without searching for a much more elusive food source. With the cheer and warmth of a fire to dry his clothes and soothe his aching limbs, he soon descended into the sleep that comes not only from physical exhaustion, but from the mental stress of a precarious voyage.

Next morning, he prised some cockles off the rocks, which he had seen the people of Inis y Copa Peer do, and boiled these for a meal which only whetted a keen appetite. Hunger drove him on. With the coast to the north leading to the unscalable barrier of a black mountain ridge that arced in a most forbidding manner, he chose to paddle in the opposite direction and, before long, was rounding a point just to the south. With the wind now at his back and, with a rising tide, he was heartened by his rapid progress.

Along the coast, he hailed a man fishing from his coracle, "Have you caught anything?"

"Aye, one or two; but I have had better mornings!"

"Tell me – is there a conical-shaped peak that looks like it has had its top sliced off at an angle, where pilgrims go for healing?"

"Why, of course – it is well-known in these parts!" The fisherman looked at him askance. "You cannot be from around here."

"I come from afar," he answered evasively, keen to extract the information he had been seeking for days. "How do you reach this peak?"

"I can also tell, from your strange accent, that you are not from among the Fidach." Pleased to pass the time of day with another, the fisherman did not appear to detect his eagerness to learn the direction. "Where do you come from, and who are your people?"

"I am Drostan of the Ce."

"The Ce! I have heard about your people, but never have I met anyone from your tribe." The fisherman looked pleased to make his acquaintance, regarding him as an exotic curiosity to break the monotony of his day-to-day existence. He asked more questions about their land, how many days' journey it had taken, surprised that someone would come so far to do a pilgrimage to their sacred peak.

"Just continue up the coast," said the fishermen, finally offering the guidance for which he had been waiting. "Enter into an inlet that leads to the foot of some vast hills, rising black on your left and red to your right. From there, go overland, up an easy strath, gentle, but boggy, that leads to the other coast. Near the end of the strath, you will see the peak that you are looking for. It is an easy paddle to reach Inis Kayru."

Thanking the fisherman, he paddled away with renewed determination. Coming around the point of the inlet, great hills confronted him. On his left, rose sheer crags, many hundreds of feet high, with a broken tooth of a pinnacle upon its much-riven ridge. The higher summit was wreathed in mist, evaporating as it was stretched by wind, yet re-forming at the same time. The sight intimidated him.

From the shingle shore at the loch head, he set off up a V-shaped glen whose steep flanks provided shelter for several pines to grow tall. At a small promontory jutting out into a freshwater loch he dropped a line baited with a worm, and waited patiently. With nothing taking the line, he secured it, and gathering the firewood amply strewn close by, lit a fire. Eventually, a trout took the hook, which he grilled over the fire. If only he had oats or bread, he would have better satisfied an appetite that felt like it was gnawing into his stomach lining. Nevertheless, he was thankful for what was provided.

Further up the low-level strath, he reached the crest of a rise, and caught his first glimpse of the conical peak rising above the water, with its top sliced off at an angle. The sight aroused an intense satisfaction welling up within him. Without delay, he made for a cluster of round houses scattered around a small bay.

"Is that the peak where pilgrims make for?" he asked of a local man.

"Aye, it is! Just earlier, a small family group passed in a boat making for Inis Kayru. They had a crippled daughter with them."

He tried hard not to look pleased to hear news that ought to provoke pity.

"If you make haste, there is time to cross before nightfall."

As the sun sank behind the massive peaks to the west, he paddled out from the bay, wondering whether this really could be the hill of Fillan's vision. It fitted the abbot's description well, for the peak rose from a whale-back of an island.

The next day broke dry – his eighth day since setting out from Dunadd. As he made for the peak, he could see a couple of people in the distance, with perhaps a girl being carried.

Probably they are the ones the fisherman had seen yesterday, he thought. Passing the sparse vegetation of wind-clipped shrubs that covered the lower slopes, the upland way took him along a line of low crags, up to a pass with a loch lying immediately to the north. He had lost sight of the family group. From there, the peak rose steeply in a final ascent, leading to the sloping platform of its summit. From this airy top, he looked up and down the strait, a seaway strewn with islands of various sizes with a mountainous mainland emulating the dramatic wildness of Inis Niwl. He gathered his plaid tightly about him, and nestled down in a niche in the cliff-girt escarpment facing east.

What am I to do here? he wondered. Will something, or someone, appear by way of revelation? What did Fillan say about this place? He wracked his brains and recalled, before long, that it would be the place of his renewal, of recognising the King. From here, I shall enter into my destiny of *bearing fire to the north*! He had been thrilled by the abbot quoting the very phrase that had emerged almost three years ago whilst he was staying with Coblaith.

He waited longer upon this eyrie-like vantage point, scanning the watery straits and scrutinising the far-reaching horizon with its unbroken arc of jumbled hills and vast ridges.

What if this is not the peak that Fillan referred to? He felt frustrated, not knowing for sure, reflecting on how Coblaith's vision of the Stone of Refuge had soon led to the encounter with Ossian. The thought made him despondent, especially after so much effort and many perils at sea. He had been there a good while now, and unable to stay static longer, he impatiently paced the sloping terrace of the summit, flapping his arms frantically to warm himself – like some great flightless bird trying to become airborne. He peered down the sides of the hill in every direction, hoping to see an approaching figure.

No one came. In his mounting frustration, he prayed. "Great High King, have mercy on me and show me what to do. Fulfil your purposes in leading me here."

His stomach complained for lack of food. If only I had a bow, or some traps, I could catch something. Oh, I feel so cold!

Since waiting on this breezy summit seemed profitless, and unsure of what he was supposed to encounter, he descended by a slightly different route, down a steeper brae towards a boulder field and screes that were more sheltered from the cold wind. He came upon a natural basin and walked to a small grove of sizeable alder bushes growing beside a spring. Feeling thirsty, he scooped up the bubbling water and sat on a boulder. It was only then that he noticed a girl suspended from a neighbouring shrub some thirty paces off. They looked at one another in bewilderment.

How did I not notice her? he asked himself, much surprised by his lack of vigilance.

He went over and asked, "Why are you here?"

"This place is known for healing," she spoke in a thin voice that ended with a shiver.

"And what are you hoping to be healed from?"

"I am crippled," she said morosely.

"I think I saw you earlier. Were you not with two others? Of course you were, otherwise how could you come here on your own!"

Chill had driven him from the summit, and he thought how cold she must be without having walked there, even though this hollow was sheltered from the wind.

"It is said," she added, "that some who are crippled have been enabled to walk from this place on their own."

He looked at her pitiful state, feeling slightly repulsed by her unkempt appearance and the baggy clothes that hung from her emaciated limbs. He felt guilty for his revulsion.

Eventually he asked, "And do you feel healed? I mean, maybe you are able to walk."

"I do not know! I have not felt anything."

Her legs hung limp from her torso, powerless, unlike her arms which had strength to hold the branches.

"To whom do you turn, believing you can be healed?" he asked curiously.

"To this mountain – it has powers," she replied as though the answer was obvious.

"Not to the Bulàch?" he quizzed. "She is believed to be the shaper of the earth. Maybe she has willed that healing power comes from here."

"Then you ask her for me!" she replied with some consternation.

"No, I will not pray to the Bulàch; not anymore."

"Then, why ask me to whom I pray and speak about the Bulàch?" the girl retorted with a note of complaint that seemed almost to ask the question, 'Have I not suffered enough already?'

He surprised himself for mentioning the Bulàch. Why should he talk of the goddess when he had consciously decided to try to follow Christ? He chided himself over this unhelpful start, but perhaps it was a natural one in trying to connect with the girl concerning Pictish beliefs. The unexpected encounter had ruffled him and conversation did not flow with one who looked understandably depressed.

"Because that is what I expected you to say," he replied awkwardly. He consciously renewed his intention to trust the King for all things on this *white martyrdom*. He keenly felt their uncomfortable silence and wondered what to say next.

"Let me help you to your feet and see if you are healed," he eventually proposed.

As the girl did not reply, he tried to determine from her expression if she might be willing. Her auburn hair burned with a copper red brightness in the light, contrasting with the pallor of her skin. She blinked her eyes twice with a hint of consternation as she looked at him properly for the first time. As she did not look hostile, he concluded that she would be compliant. After all, he told himself, she is hoping to be healed, so why would she not be willing to try?

She readied herself as he came alongside to disengage her from the shrub. He placed his arm around the back of her shoulders which felt strong, unlike how the lower part of her body looked, so withered and useless! He had mistaken her for a girl until he was close up, when it became obvious that she was a young woman. Taking her weight upon his arm, he gently eased her onto her feet, yet still bearing all her mass. As he eased her body on to the ground, he watched her feet curl over. She looked down, seemingly willing her legs into life.

"It is no good," she cried, "they are still useless!"

He felt her disappointment. What should he do next?

"Let us place you back in the shrub again."

He secured her in her previous posture and paused to assess the situation. What would Fillan do if he were in this predicament? Would he not pray? Had this situation arisen before he had reached the muintir, would he not petition the Bulàch concerning circumstances beyond his control?

"I will pray for you, but not to the Bulàch," he added emphatically. "I shall pray to the one who made you and me."

Her blue eyes seemed distraught as she eyed him, striking him as one who looked trapped, enduring a stranger's unsought attention. He closed his eyes.

"I pray to the Son, full of compassion and mercy,
to the Father, who was here before the earth began,
to the all-powerful Spirit who comes with wind and fire.
Be mindful of your creation hanging from this shrub,
fruit of the earth, blighted by this ailment.
If it be your will, bring fullness,
health and wholeness, beauty and restoration."

He paused, conscious of trying to craft an appropriate prayer that would not have Fillan wince should he have been able to hear.

"Above all, bring glory to your name,
that man may know that you are God, and there are no others.
In the triune name of Father, Son and Spirit – Amen."

He raised his head, opening his eyes, believing the miracle. But the girl hung limp, as helpless as before.

"Come on, let us try again. Attempt to stand and walk!"

His confident tone surprised even him for the words were uttered with such bold assertion. But to have said nothing at that moment would have felt like wilful disobedience to

124

the conviction coursing through him. He believed that he did not entirely have a will of his own in this matter.

The girl shivered. Her lips had turned a dull, almost a purplish hue. She looked scared and turned her eyes away, finding her immobility too great a burden to overcome.

"Try and raise yourself!" he encouraged in a gentle but insistent tone. "Here, let me help you again. I will take your weight as before, so you can be sure that you will not fall. Only try to believe – have some faith!"

"I have had faith so many times before, but what good has it done!" Her eyes filled with tears which coursed briskly down her cheeks, spotting her dirty tunic.

She struggled to disengage herself from the bush and, not trusting his hold, she held on to the branches. Gradually, he could feel her shift some of her weight onto his arm. She bit her wrinkled lower lip and took a sharp intake of breath.

"My feet are tingling, they are really tingling – as though licked by fire!" she said, aroused to a semblance of hopefulness.

"Well, is that good?"

"Of course it is good! I have not been able to feel anything in my legs since my accident!"

When her feet touched the ground, instead of awkwardly hanging limp or folding over to one side, he observed that they slightly turned to position themselves, feeling for the firmness of the ground. As he eased her weight from his arm, her legs braced and stood firm. The girl grinned: not a cautious smile, but one that was animated.

"Keep a good hold of me!" she said, managing a slight step forward. An unintelligible sound came from her mouth, which to him seemed to express delight. She let go of the shrub with one hand whilst still holding on with the other, and took another, faltering step. Letting go of the shrub altogether, and appearing to trust that she had been healed, she stood upright. He gradually released the strain of holding her body.

"I can stand! My legs have regained their ability!" she said ecstatically, wiping away the recent tears from her cheeks. He withdrew his arm from her back, and clasping her elbow, he moved round to face her.

"You are standing," he said in amazement, beaming at her with an equally ecstatic smile. "And you can walk!" he said affirmatively. They looked at one another, sharing this moment of delight. If it were possible, his joy was almost as great as the young woman's.

This miracle seemed to have as large an implication for him as it had for the one-time crippled girl. Had Fillan not prophesied his *renewal* at this peak. Here was the fruit of his *white martyrdom,* gaining a connection with the Presence whereas before, he had only known of the God of the Gaels and learned of his ways. Whilst he may have surrendered to the rigorous disciplines of the muintir, and even at times had been in earnest in his seeking, he realised that he had not known the King.

Had it been my abandonment on this precarious journey that brought awareness of the mercies of the King? Had the faith that tackled turbulent seas in a flimsy craft prepared me for this transformative moment to trust where I have no power to bring change? How amazing that I am the chosen instrument! What affirmation of knowing the King's favour! This awakening has come with my final rejection of the Bulàch, entrusting myself to follow Christ.

No more did this Lord of lords feel distant, nor did the Ethereal One, strangely chanted to in Latin psalms, appear unknowable.

He felt odd to be sharing this momentous experience with a stranger. Letting go of her elbow, he took a step back. She looked at him, questioningly, slightly swaying as though struggling to keep her balance. Appearing as though she would take an exploratory step towards him, she suddenly abandoned the idea and reached out with her hands. Aware that she might collapse, he took hold of her wrists.

"I can feel both my legs, but they are so weak."

Recalling how his own fractured arm had felt when he started using it again, he said, "Of course, your legs will be weak. They are thin and without strength!"

The young woman nodded.

"As you walk, day by day, your legs will become stronger and more able." He smiled confidently at her. "Thanks be to the High King who has given you this ability," he added. "I tell you, it is not this mountain, but Christ who has healed you!"

Chapter Nine

The Boar's Head

556 AD   Rhynie

When Alpia awoke in Fionnoula's hut, her hand instinctively reached for Caltram secured in the sling next to her body, feeling for the reassuring rise and fall of his belly. Ever since Caltram had been born she had slept in the home of the wet-nurse as Caltram demanded regular feeding through the night. Fionnoula had offered to take him, but with two bairns of her own, Alpia reckoned Fionnoula would be unable to give the level of commitment that she as a single woman could provide. She had formed a veritable maternal bond with Eithni's child, for what had started as a matter of honour in fulfilling her dying friend's request had developed into a personal cause to preserve this fragile life against all the odds. She had felt him grow heavier in the sling in which he was always contained, except when being fed or having his soiled cloths changed.

Whilst Caltram was being fed, she had time to wash herself and comb her hair. She felt every bit the mother with her dishevelled appearance, smelling rancid from the milk Caltram posseted over her and with the inevitable reek of urine about her clothes. She had quickly overcome her aversion in her bid to save this precarious life.

Going over to Aunt Conchen's hut, she removed the plaid wrapped around her for Caltram's benefit. She settled down beside the hearth, and with her back turned on Oengus, extracted Caltram, tightly wrapped in swaddling clothes, from under her smock.

"Look Oengus, Caltram is smiling," she said, cradling the still-tiny baby in her arms.

Oengus came over and looked into his son's face. A smile came to his lips. "What a pitiful sight!" he remarked, raising his finger to stroke the baby's cheek and coax another grin. "How amazing that he has survived, despite expectations!"

She partly turned so that Oengus could more easily see his son, all the while unable to contain her own smile as she gazed into Caltram's face.

"You know . . ." Oengus stopped to clear his throat. "This is the first time, I think, that I have smiled since Eithni's death!"

"There is nothing like a baby to move you on from recent sadness." remarked Aunt Conchen, rising to admire her great-great-nephew. "Here, let me hold him." She reached out and took the baby. Caltram gurgled, much to the delight of her aunt, a joy shared by Oengus too. "My, oh my, he is growing!" She looked up at her and added with emphasis, "It is thanks to your devotion that Caltram has pulled through!"

"It has been a group effort," she corrected. "Fionnoula has been the one who has fed him."

"Yes, but your commitment has been extraordinary! You have worn that sling next to your skin to nurture Caltram day and night." Despite her advanced years, Aunt Conchen managed a sedate dancing step about the room, holding the baby firmly against her breast.

"Take care!" cautioned Oengus, coming over when her dance became more animated. "May I hold him now."

"Not yet!" Aunt Conchen turned playfully, stepping aside Oengus. "I have only just taken him." She smiled at her aunt's humorous ways, who had pulled a face to protest against an unreasonable request.

"Look at you all," remarked Fionnoula, who had suddenly appeared, "you are quite the happy family! Alpia, I will be gone a short while whilst I draw water from the stream."

She noticed Oengus' face cloud slightly. Eithni's death was still less than a month ago and, if it still felt raw for her, then surely it would be so with Oengus. After dancing further about the room, Aunt Conchen must have tired, for she voluntarily gave Caltram over to him.

Oengus gently stepped up and down the hut and remarked, "Oh, it is good to move on from the gloom and tension of past days." Going over to the small window, he stooped low to look out on a grey day. Snow lay on the higher ground and remained in frozen heaps between the huts to where it had been cleared.

"We have all been mourning our loss," she remarked, brushing her hair to one side.

Caltram started to cry.

"Oh, look what you have done!" Aunt Conchen chided him good-humouredly. "You lack a woman's touch!"

He offered Caltram back to her.

"No. Better return him to Fionnoula."

"He has just been fed," Alpia remarked. "He probably needs to be winded." Taking Caltram from Oengus, she placed him upright against her shoulder and gently patted his back. After a few small burps from the wee boy, she resumed her seat back beside the hearth. Caltram soon settled.

"Would you take him?" she asked her aunt. "I will draw some water from the stream. I could do with some fresh air." She handed the bundle over and took up the empty water skins that she slung over her shoulder. They softly rattled in a gust of wind as she left the hut.

Aunt Conchen sat down with a satisfied sigh beside the hearth. After clearing some dirt from under a fingernail, Oengus came and sat down beside her and asked, "Did I say something wrong?"

"What do you mean?"

"I thought Alpia replied somewhat prickly to my comment about it being good to move on from the gloom!"

"No, I am sure you caused no offence. I think she needs time to herself without Caltram strapped to her. You know it is tiring for a mother to be always attending to the needs of a bairn, especially one so frail as Caltram!"

He observed Aunt Conchen shift position on the bedding, raising her chin in the manner of someone who had more to say.

"Quite to the contrary," she continued, "I have noticed that she no longer just tolerates your company as she used to do. She is genuinely happy to raise Caltram. He brings healing to us all."

"It just seemed sudden her going, that is all."

"That, I think, is just the need to get out of the home during these gloomy days. Do you not just gasp for space after being cooped up indoors for too long?"

His grief had wrestled with the shocking loss of a woman in her prime, who had been the same age as himself. Clearly the Bulàch had been offended and had brought about this tragedy to punish him. He also had to manage dashed hopes, for Eithni's passing occurred not that long after he had brought her back to Rhynie. Having built their hut in early winter, they had just settled in, imagining how life could be. He felt the familiar wave of anger. They had not even reached spring proper as a married couple! Aware of things being far from ideal, he had tried to start afresh with a woman he had spurned, whom he had married to put right the wrong caused, rather than out of love. Despite the harsh reality, he wanted to prove, even to himself, that he was capable of making good out of wrong. He had struggled to find real feelings until the moment Eithni was abruptly taken from him. His love had been what Aunt Conchen described as a commitment of will to make amends. Her sudden death aroused genuine feelings that previously had seemed beyond reach.

He had observed that Eithni had not been that responsive in expressing love in return, for she seemed under no illusion as to the reality when comparing their relationship with the heady days of their passion. She had appeared quietly grateful for being taken back, to have her own home rather than live under a stranger's roof treated as a servant. Being back in Rhynie meant having her family about her; and she had spoken about the birth of a baby as ushering in a new era. Even if things had not progressed significantly between them after having a child, Aunt Conchen had reasoned with him that Eithni would feel more settled in her role as a mother. In time, he anticipated, their life together would have been redefined, that past hurts would be brushed aside.

Aunt Conchen broke a lengthy silence, "What are your plans now that spring is nigh?"

"Why?" He looked at her curiously.

"Winter days are for planning what lies ahead. Talorgen was always impatient for the winter to pass, so he could get back to the business of carrying out a raid or gathering tribute from his nobles."

"I have not given it much thought. I have been grieving," he confessed, but now with interest in moving forward.

"It is right to mourn and there is a time for that; but perhaps now is the time to put that behind you." He could feel her looking meaningfully at him. "What was on your mind before the days of bringing Eithni back to Rhynie?"

"Ugh, I am not sure," he said, straightening himself. "I had been troubled, I think. You remember? you were the one who made me see reason and make my peace with Eithni."

"And you did that well." She reached out and touched his hand. "It has gained you favour among the people, not least with Eithni's family." She paused before adding in a tone that added significance to what she had to say. "And, I should add, even with Alpia!"

He felt slightly uncomfortable, used to as he now was, in playing the familiar role of the grieving husband. Feelings for Alpia, who he now regarded as a significant carer for Caltram, had receded into the background, deliberately consigned there as inappropriate. Besides, those feelings always appeared unrequited; he did not wish to add further heartache to what he was already experiencing by being rebuffed.

"I should plan to visit Cynbel and see how Derile is faring," he responded.

"Oh, that would be good. I do feel for your sister. It cannot be easy for her to be married to such an old man!"

He felt his cheeks flush.

"I did not mean to chastise you," added Aunt Conchen. "We have spoken about this and what is done is done. But, to visit her would be caring. Are you going to take your mother?"

He did not have the opportunity to reply, for when Alpia reappeared with the full waterskins which she slung over a beam in the cooking area, she asked, "Who are you going to visit?"

"I was thinking of going to Migdele to visit Cynbel and Derile."

She smiled slightly as she glanced at him across the hut before busying herself in preparing their food. He noted that she did not seem annoyed with him. Aunt Conchen, as usual, was right.

He yawned. "Here, let me take Caltram. I am feeling sleepy and shall have him lie with me." He settled on the bedding with his baby son, experiencing a joy that had long eluded him; a delight he had no control of, an unexpected, involuntary gladness that welled up unchecked within. This new life was an extension of himself, a being he was responsible for bringing into the world. The wonder of this miniature person impressed him deeply, as he looked into his face with an adoration and wonder he had never thought possible. Later, he dozed off.

Alpia went over to Caltram and dithered uncertainly.

"Leave them be," Aunt Conchen said, reading her thoughts.

"Do you think Caltram is warm enough?"

"If you are concerned, place a blanket over them both."

"What if Oengus rolls over. He will kill the bairn!"

"Do not fuss. Look, I will sit with them, and ensure Oengus does not move. See, Caltram is fast asleep, quite content."

"Are you sure?" She ran a hand through her hair. "I will finish preparing the lunch."

He woke up later, just when lunch was ready. As soon as Alpia had served his bowl, she took Caltram from Oengus. He ate with a good appetite.

"I think I shall go hunting this afternoon," he announced on finishing his last mouthful. "I should like to get out."

The women agreed it would be good for him and, without delay, he gathered his bow and quiver of arrows, and strapped on a long hunting knife. He put on a bearskin jacket and a hat of rabbit fur; and his dog rose with a tail that so fiercely wagged that his whole rear end swayed. They descended the brae to the stream and climbed up through the woods on the far side. The trees were dripping with a thaw that made the earth smell pungent with humus. His steps were brisk, and the damp air cleared his head. He did not much mind whether he shot any game. In his wanderings, he absent-mindedly came upon the hilltop with the ancient stone circle where he had been tattooed the previous year. Thoughts of Taran came to mind, the Z-rod bearer who was – apparently – still at large, seen by Maevis, sustained by an elderly couple in an obscure place hopeless to find. Was he still a threat? He concluded that Taran no longer presented the same level of risk as in the early days following his escape. Had he not reached agreement with the warlords of their neighbouring tribes, settling on a price for his cousin's head? However, it did not feel watertight, certainly with Cynbel, the traditional enemy, who could still use Taran to the Circinn's advantage.

With the ground being too wet to sit upon, he chose to lean against the Yule stone, which he regarded as his stone, for that was where he had been tattooed with the broch.

"All the better to go to Migdele sooner rather than later," he thought aloud. His dog cocked its head to one side as if trying to understand his spoken words. "That way, I could build up trust, reinforcing the discussion held earlier with Aunt Conchen. But I cannot always be looking over my shoulder, fearing. I need to consolidate my position, attain absolute supremacy to ward off an attack from my cousin."

He thought for a good while, piecing together how leaders established a strong foundation. I could groom some warriors of my age with whom I have trained. I can choose men I know and can trust. He thought of several and how he could inspire them and reward their loyalty. I could host a banquet just for these comrades and provide a new vision for the Ce. He thought of how his people could become eminent, be able to hold their heads high, not only before the Circinn, but before the Fortriu too. How could I build a stronger power base, not for petty skirmishes as was Uncle Talorgen's way, but with a proper army that would establish our reputation?

Feeling stirred, he created the framework for a speech he would make to his young warriors, inspiring purpose and taking pride in becoming a people of standing. He remembered his ideas to improve Rhynie, to make it more befitting a warlord's seat of power. Although it would be beyond his present reach to match the grandeur that Brude and his forebears had created at Y Broch, he could nevertheless extend the palisade to allow for an expansion to Rhynie's population. By adding a second tier to the palisade it would not only look more impressive, but also increase the fire power should they ever face a siege. He would raise the emblem of the boar's head above its gates to rival the fine bulls adorning the gates of Y Broch. This way, he would involve craftsmen, spreading the pride in who they were as the people of the Ce, and creating a vision for their destiny.

He thought for a while, aware that the able warriors were limited in number when just drawn from Rhynie. How would I persuade more people to settle within our defences? How can I attract the noble to come to Rhynie, so we can arise as the new people of the Ce?

The tour is the thing, he thought. Just as I made that tour for gathering tribute from the nobles with Talorgen last year, I can repeat it this spring. As well as collecting tribute, I will have the additional aim of gathering men of fighting ability. I shall take like-minded fellow warriors with me to show my vision for the future and challenge our nobles to yield their sons to be part of the new Rhynie. I will entice them to establish homes here so we can become a true fighting force, trained on expeditions and ready for combat. When these young men come, I will arrange a large celebration. I could have them swear an oath of loyalty and give them vision for what the Ce can be.

Being at the stone circle reminded him of his own druids who should be the first with whom to share his vision. Having their backing would better ensure success. Feeling agitated by his dream for the ascension of his tribe, he moved around the circle of standing stones, recalling Maelchon suggesting that the eight stones represented the year's festivals. He pensively came to the next stone representing Imbolc, recalling Eithni's fear over half of the candles being blown out, which had seemed irrational at the time. He soberly noted that she had died the following day, reminding him that absolute control was not with man and his schemes, but the Bulàch had to be appeased. Next, he came to the Ostara stone. By his reckoning Ostara could not be far off.

Could this not be the occasion to put in motion my plans for our revival? What better occasion than this festival of spring, when the ascendent light became equal with the diminishing realm of darkness. He had established accord with both his tribal neighbours, and there was almost a sense of things being equal with the Circinn. On the other hand, the Fortriu under Brude were a force to be reckoned with.

He briskly returned to Rhynie, turning in at Gest's home down by the stream.

"How many days is it until Ostara?" he asked, on passing over the threshold.

"Well, good day to you!" said his friend, mockingly reprimanding him for his lack of civility. "Let me see." He made a calculation. "In eight days' time. Why?"

"We should celebrate it as we emerge from the depths of winter."

"Why, of course, but why your sudden keenness?" Gest looked at him calculatingly, putting aside an implement in a clay basin he had been busy scrubbing.

"I want it to be quite an occasion. We have been in a season of winter, of death, confined to our homes. But that season is ending." He looked up brightly at his friend. "I now have a son who has survived despite our worst fears. There is a new start to be anticipated and celebrated, not just for my household, but for all of the Ce." He expanded on the thoughts he had had up on the hill.

"You really have been thinking!" Gest remarked, with an agreeable smile that encouraged him.

"I am glad that I can count on your loyalty as a friend as well as a druid." He briefly smiled. "Together, we can make our people great, and bring in a new era. Are you with me in this, Gest? Will you work by my side to plan and bring this vision about? I do need the backing of friends like you, particularly the support of a druid!" He looked at him significantly, eager for his response.

"Yes, of course you have my support. But," he seemed to pause deliberately to gain his attention, "you need

Maelchon's backing more than mine. It is his opinion that counts most and will influence further."

"Aye, I understand. But can I count on you to bring Maelchon around to our way of thinking? He is such a taciturn fellow who seems impossible to influence."

"Maelchon is for the Ce – in that you can be sure."

"But he is a man of so few words!"

"Which does not mean he is closed to what others have to say. You do need his support to better promote your cause."

"I understand that. Was it not made clear to me that a warlord is not above his druid and your kin! Maevis made that abundantly clear last autumn when she called me to account. Much as I wanted to overrule her, I realised that I need the spiritual backing to which you and her kind have access." Recalling that incident, and the strong words spoken to him, caused him to wonder whether that incident had brought about Eithni's death? He shuddered, troubled by the caprices of the mother goddess.

"It is good that you mention the gods! I was beginning to think that you would just push your plans forward through your own strength of character and position."

"Although I am not much of a spiritual person, I do respect the gods. That is why I am dependent upon the likes of you and Maelchon, and . . ." He paused uncertainly before adding begrudgingly, "and even Maevis, the one with the fleet feet of the deer!"

Gest smiled and patted his friend on his shoulder. "I shall speak with Maelchon first about your plans, help him understand that Ostara is to be a festival of some significance. Then, the three of us should speak at length, giving you the opportunity to lay the details of your vision before the chief druid himself. I am sure he will have appropriate insight into this to help prosper your cause."

"Can you find us a good bard?"

"Aye, leave that arrangement to us. We might not find the likes of Ossian and those of his standing at such short notice, but there are other upcoming minstrels, eager to demonstrate their maturing skills."

Oengus smiled, and going over to the threshold, he turned. "Also, I want you to tattoo a boar onto my chest!"

"Oh, the old boar image again. You are quite taken by that!"

"Indeed. Boars are not to be meddled with."

"Have I helped you to cultivate your identification with the boar?"

"How do you mean?" he looked at him quizzically.

"By the tattooed skin I gifted you as a wedding gift!"

"Oh that! Indeed, it is a daily reminder."

"And are you consciously considering the attributes of the boar that you may display its prowess and strength?"

"I suppose I am whenever I look upon the image," he said not sounding as convincing as he would have liked.

"I would encourage you to be more deliberate in your study of the boar, so that you may emulate his qualities."

"Like being stubborn?" he snorted with laughter.

Gest smiled. "I was thinking of the boar's qualities that would serve to be more advantageous, like its wily intelligence. Seriously, I challenge you to study the boar. Go out into the wilds, and rather than hunt them, study their manner, almost in a way of veneration. Consider how his qualities might be of service and how you could display those attributes."

"I see my druid is giving me a lesson and a task!"

They laughed together.

"Regarding this tattoo – could you make the boar's head large; so large that it would spread from one side of my chest to the other?"

"Yes, of course," he nodded agreeably.

"And make him look fierce as though about to charge. I do not want some placid-looking beast upon my chest."

"It seems that you are emerging from a long hibernation and have the renewal of Ostara upon you!"

He paused, still framed in the doorway. "I believe that I am," he replied with a seriousness in his tone. "I am done with regret and mourning," he asserted, as though making a solemn oath to move on. "The dead are buried and new life continues in my son."

"That is good talk, my friend. I am glad to hear it."

"Talorgen's rule, marked by his petty skirmishes, has most decidedly closed. I will lead the Ce into a new era of gathering greatness."

"I do not doubt your bold intentions, which are necessary, for without ambition nothing great can be achieved. However, do not allow ambition to get ahead of you. You might have your dreams, but the Bulàch will have her way. We can intercede with her for you and lay these plans before her. You will need to offer her right sacrifices. But more than that . . ."

"Go on?"

"You need a heart that acknowledges her power, to realise that she can curse as well as bless."

"Do I not know that already!"

"I mean it!" To emphasise the point, he stood with his arms akimbo.

"I accept that I need to pay her homage."

"Good. You need to be patient and humble." Gest cleared his throat. "Last time, when we petitioned the high priestess – well, you did not pay due respect!"

He felt inconvenienced by this reminder, but knew Gest spoke wisely. "I shall be patient and suitably humble."

Chapter Ten

Sorrowful Sunbeam

558 AD   Loch Kilmorkill

The young woman's parents soon returned, shocked and overjoyed to find her walking; surprised too to see a young man with her. Many questions led to explanations and expressions of extreme elation.

"Let us introduce ourselves," said the father, a stocky but robust man with a thick shock of sable-coloured hair. "I am Girom and this is my wife, Alma, and as you are already aware, this is our daughter."

"But I do not know her name?"

"Aleine Brona," replied the young woman.

"And I am . . ." he paused to the mild surprise of everyone. Not feeling the need to use his pseudonym so far from home, he said with certitude, "I am Taran."

"Had you forgotten who you were for a moment?" chuckled Aleine Brona.

"I am not quite myself," he laughed. "No, of course I have not forgotten who I am!"

"Tell me, what brings you here?" asked Alma with an enquiring look.

"It is a long story. But to be brief, I came looking for a conical hill with its peak sliced off at an angle as by a sword." The others were amused by this description. "My abbot had a picture of it . . ."

"What is an abbot?" interrupted Aleine Brona.

"I told you, it is a long story! An abbot is like a druid who presides over a community who worship the Christ, not the Bulàch. The abbot's description has guided me here. I have been travelling over a week looking for this place."

"What a strange reason for making so perilous a journey!" remarked Alma, appearing to sense his ordeals.

"The purpose of my journey seems to be the healing of your daughter."

"And what will you do now?" asked Girom.

"I am not certain." He had not considered this question, so focussed he had been on the quest of finding this peak.

"Then you must come to our home whilst you decide what you will do next," insisted Alma.

"We are only poor," explained Girom, "but you are welcome and can stay for as long as you like. We stay on the mainland, over there," he pointed, "beside Loch Kilmorkill, on the far side of the sound."

"Oh, I do not know." He could hear an echo of his words, sounding vague, even evasive.

"You must come," entreated Alma with apparent sincerity, her plump face aglow with benevolence.

"Oh yes, do come back with us!" insisted Aleine Brona, her features beaming with joy.

"Can you give me a moment to think?"

"You have met our daughter's great need and surely that is the purpose of your being led here," pronounced the father. "Since you have the hair of a druid, surely you are familiar with miracles! Have you not healed others?"

"No, I have not. I have only started on my pilgrimage in following the High King."

"What pilgrimage? Who is the High King, and where does he rule?" asked Girom, perplexed. "Clearly, from your strange dialect, you come from afar."

"The High King is the Creator of the world. His rule is spreading through the kingdoms of earth as warlords recognise his authority." He surprised himself to be talking like this. "Allow me to retire for a moment, to consider what I should do. I understand this will appear strange, but it is necessary."

"Do what you must. We are in no hurry," returned Girom.

He went over to where the spring came bubbling up from the ground and the family withdrew a few paces in the opposite direction, seemingly out of deference.

Surely, this miracle fulfils two purposes, he told himself. The need of this family, and my own necessity to be confirmed in the faith. This encounter led me to earnestly pray. Did I not even feel constrained to pray? The healing came from the Spirit who I felt come upon me with power, just like in the scriptures. Fillan had indicated that this peak would be the place of my 'renewal'? What else had he said? He turned over Fillan's parting comments that he had memorised. *This is your opportunity to turn to know the King and enter on your destiny. And your destiny has something about bearing fire to the north.*

He had truly made a new beginning. What of this mysteriously repeated prediction, though, of *bearing fire to the north?* He recalled that Ossian's inspired words featured various directions, *your transformation is in the isles of the west.* With gladness he recognised another fulfilment. The prophecy spoke next about *the anticipation of the learned ones far to the north.* But where in the north, and how much further? He concluded that he should trust things to become clearer at the appropriate time and meanwhile to bide his time there patiently.

He re-joined Girom's family, "I would be glad to join you."

"Excellent, excellent!" Girom responded enthusiastically by clapping his hands.

"You are a strange one!" remarked Alma, not unkindly.

"Come, our boat is down in the bay and there is plenty of room for you," commented Aleine Brona brightly. Then turning to her parents, she said, "I cannot walk, for my legs have no strength."

"I have a coracle down at the shore," he informed them.

"Then we will put it in our boat," Girom replied, satisfied that he was accompanying them.

Their manner was easy, overflowing with gratitude. Crossing the sound took what felt like half a day, and they rowed up a sea loch. Rounding a small promontory, they pulled into a bay. The sight of Aliene Brona walking brought the whole family together to hear all about the healing.

When all the hubbub subsided, Girom took Taran aside. "This is our home, which is also your home," Girom made a sweeping gesture with his arm towards the round huts clustered on the hillside above the bay. "As you have gathered, all these huts belong to my family. Aleine Brona is our youngest – the only one remaining under our roof. Her brothers and sisters are all married."

Girom's round house was substantial, the largest in the village, with the addition of two smaller huts close by used as a barn and a store. Their village faced east, looking out onto bold hills rising steep from the sea loch to such heights that their summits and ridges disappeared into a blanket of cloud.

"What do you think?" asked Girom.

"It is good," he pronounced. "How is the soil here?"

"The soil is good now that we have worked it. We grow neeps, carrot, cabbage, leeks – that kind of thing."

"And you have oak woodlands beyond. They must be good for game?" he remarked admiringly.

"Yes, there is much game there. But we fish, mostly," Girom paused with an expansive smile brightening his features. "We are fond of fish!"

The light was fading and the sea loch became charged with a vibrant light in contrast to the details of the land being consumed under deepening shadows.

"What sort of place do you come from?" asked Aleine Brona.

"My home is very different," he began a little distantly. "It is way over in the east, beyond many mountain ranges. Our land is fertile, but our village is inland, built on a hillside with a great hill opposite, venerated since ancient times."

This led to more questions about his people and how he came to be there. He simplified his story, stating that his purpose in leaving home was to become a warrior of Christ – which he felt in the big scheme of things was true. He was wary of revealing too much concerning the adventures that preceded his time at Dindurn.

"You know, the timing of our meeting on the hillside was extraordinary," he considered aloud. "I had been eight days out from Dunadd and had stayed on Rùm for longer than expected due to a storm. That added an extra day. If it had not been for that storm, I would have arrived on Inis Kayru a day earlier and, well . . . I would probably have missed you!"

"It was meant to happen," remarked Girom with a thankful smile. "Come, let us go inside – I think Alma has the meal ready, judging by the good smell."

Aleine Brona rose, supported by her father's arm about her, and walked hesitantly with a limp. "It is strange to have feeling back in my legs, but they are really tired even though I have not walked far!"

"Well, you have not walked since your accident," commented her father.

"Why the two names?" he questioned their daughter, as they settled down to eat.

"Aleine is my given name, which means 'sunbeam'."

"It well described her character before her accident," interjected her mother.

"But after my accident the name Brona was added, because I was often sorrowful."

"We then got into the habit of putting the two names together," added her mother.

"Sorrowful Sunbeam," he said aloud, nodding approvingly. "How apt for one whose bright nature had been clouded by misfortune! What happened in your accident?"

"Oh, I was gathering some brambles, just around the point. They were growing on top of a craggy part. I slipped and fell some way, not a long fall; but I landed on a boulder on the base of my back. I never expected to walk again!" Her sorrowful look was short-lived for her features brightened into a broad grin.

How extraordinary, he thought: when she is animated, an inner beauty radiates from her, transforming her rather plain features.

"And how old were you when you had that accident?" he continued, keen to piece together the missing details.

"Oh, I was about six. That is more than ten years ago now, is it not?" she turned to her mother for confirmation, who agreed with her estimation.

The days passed pleasantly for him, providing rest following the tensions leading to his flight and the challenging journey that had ensued. The ordeal of being at sea in so precarious a craft haunted his mind, and took time to subside.

I am in no haste to move on, he told himself, although this period is just a pause. I am sure the next episode will be made clear once the time comes.

Girom taught him techniques of how to fish with a line and with a net, the bait to use, where to cast, and how to interpret the conditions. In return he helped with the breaking up of the land for winter, fertilising the ground with seaweed cut from the plentiful supply growing thick around the bay at low water, in preparation for the spring sowing. He gathered firewood, so plentifully that Girom's sons laughed at the huge pile raised at the side of the hut. Some evenings he crafted arrows, smoothing them with a sharp knife and an accustomed eye, before artfully mounting feather flights to the shaft with pine resin.

With a newly-fashioned bow and a quiver now full of fine arrows he went hunting with Aleine Brona's brothers, showing his prowess in taking game usually with a single shot.

"You have a good eye," observed one of Girom's sons. "You strike things first time, not like us."

"It is not just about having a good eye, but knowing how to fashion an arrow that will fly true." Picking up one of their arrows and looking down the line of the shaft, he remarked, "This shaft is warped. It will not hit its mark."

"Unless you are a bad shot and the bent arrow works in your favour!" said one of the brothers, and they all laughed.

"Where I hail from, we do not have the bounty of the sea to live off like you do. We have had to perfect the skill of arrow-making, since our livelihood is so dependent upon shooting game."

He was liked for the things which set him apart, appreciated for the sense of his foreignness, his accent and the occasional words not used in their dialect. This often led to good-hearted banter. His veneration of Christ was unheard of, something they might have been more suspicious of had it not been for Aleine Brona's healing. They curiously observed his daily discipline of rising early to pray, of giving thanks before taking food and of praying at various stages in the day.

"We observe our own practices, like giving food offerings to the Bulàch, avoiding taboos, heeding superstitions . . . that sort of thing," explained Girom.

"I used to follow those practices too . . . but there is no purpose anymore in worshipping the Bulàch, now that the Creator of everything has been revealed."

"Your god, though, seems so foreign; unheard of until you arrived. However, it has to be said that your ways, although very different, appear more heartfelt than the rituals we follow."

"Before this journey, all that I knew about Christ was knowledge passed on. But now, I have experienced God's Spirit upon me, it has made all the difference and brought about Aleine Brona's healing."

"That seems so," conceded Girom with a nod of the head. "However, our people always talk about repercussions that come from abandoning the Bulàch."

"My people are the same. I suppose, though, if someone abandons the Bulàch without trusting in the power of the High King, then bad things will probably befall that person, for the Bulàch is vengeful. But replace the Bulàch with Christ: then you have the High King's protection."

One afternoon, Aleine Brona found him smoothing a piece of hide after it had been stretched and dried for days upon a frame.

"What are you doing?" she asked with genuine curiosity.

"I am flattening this vellum to write upon," he responded, continuing with his preparations.

"You can write!" she exclaimed, flicking her long auburn hair back with an easy air. She beamed with her characteristic smile, relishing the prospect of watching him. "Show me – show me how you write." She sat down enthusiastically beside him on the bench, as he smoothed the vellum on the table's surface.

"All in good time," he laughed. "I have not got everything ready yet! Do you want to help me?"

She nodded emphatically.

"Fetch a small pot and a pestle and then crush these berries to a paste. I am hoping these might produce a kind of ink."

Aleine Brona briefly left, returning with a shallow wooden bowl and a thick peg. She began pulverising the fruit.

Making a diagonal cut across the stem of a goose feather, then a fine cut at its end, down the line of the spine, he raised it to inspect his workmanship.

"Can you get a little water?"

She skipped off, appearing keen to be involved in a project so new to her. When she returned, he guided her as she pulverised the berries.

Dipping the quill into the basin, he made a stroke on the vellum, which left a thin watery mark on the hide's surface.

"The colour is too faint! Somehow, we need to thicken the mixture."

After some reflection, Aleine Brona announced brightly, "I know – what about using a little clay to thicken it? I know where to get some."

"Let us try."

He watched her walking energetically up the brae behind their hut, recalling almost with disbelief her emaciated form – and the useless legs of just some months earlier. What a transformation! Her clothes no longer looked baggy upon her, now her legs had filled out. Her auburn hair, flicking from side to side as she ran, was accentuated by the mellow sunlight – a hue, he considered, to be like dead bracken when damp.

He looked down again to attend to the hide that was considerably coarser than what was used at Dindurn. Taking some pins he tacked the vellum to the table, and sat back to think what to write. A text that was often quoted at Dindurn came readily to mind, for he had memorised it and Fillan had explained how it expressed the heart of a true pilgrim.

Aleine Brona returned with a ball of clay. He noticed how not only the wet clay messed her hands, but its brown streaks had run their dirty traceries over the milky complexion of her slender forearms.

Mixing some clay into the mixture, he dipped the quill into the ink. As he formed a stroke, he noticed her smile out of the corner of his eye. It strangely warmed him. She moved in a little closer to observe, craning her neck, intently watching what creation was about to happen on the hide. The colour was more satisfactory, although nothing like as fine as the inks used at Dindurn, made from minerals imported from far-away lands.

"What are you going to write?" asked Aleine Brona, rocking gently. She placed her forearms on the edge of the table.

The process of crafting the letters with finesse was painstakingly slow; an act of meditational worship was how the monks had described it. He was aware of wanting to impress this young woman, who was fascinated by the loops, strokes and dots taking form on the vellum. Why should I hurry? he thought to himself, relishing her presence. Daily, I am becoming more aware of her beauty. A vitality seems to burst out of what seems an unremarkable appearance. Her exuberance totally transforms her into something that is especially delightful.

After a good length of time, the text was complete.

"Oh, read it out. Tell me what it says." Aleine Brona spoke impatiently, bouncing more energetically upon the bench.

He straightened himself and cleared his throat: "*Dixit autem Dominus ad Abram egredere de terra tua et de cognatione tua et de domo patris tui in terram quam monstrabo tibi.*"

Reciting this Latin script was met with the anti-climax of a silence. Surely, she had been anticipating something greater, he observed.

"And you speak this language?" she finally asked with hesitant admiration.

"Not fluently," he confessed. "I can read and understand things slowly. I do not speak Latin except when singing the psalms and in saying set prayers. Let me translate for you: *And the Lord said to Abram: Go forth out of thy country, and from thy kindred, and out of thy father's house, and come into the land which I shall show thee.*"

"And who is Abram?" Her blue eyes fixed upon him.

"Well, he was a man who left everything. God said that he would bless him and lead him to another country, by leaving all that was familiar, Abram had to depend upon God to lead and sustain him – and he was blessed by knowing God the more. Abram also became the means for others to be blessed."

"Rather like you, then!" remarked Aleine Brona. The intense blue of her eyes searched his own, as though curious to understand his motivation.

"Some are called to leave the familiar, to forsake all they have known. Such adventures make you dependent upon God."

"I would not like to leave my family," she pronounced in a peremptory manner. "I love them, and they love me, loved me even when I was useless. It is not normal to want to leave your people!"

"No, it is not normal." After a pause, he added, "I am only starting on this journey and have much to learn. Sometimes," he added with feeling, "we are not in control of events and circumstances as much as we would prefer."

She inclined her head to one side, weighing his words.

"It is like swimming across a river. You sight where you want to go, but the strength of the current takes you far downstream. You arrive at a place you had not intended on reaching, in an unfamiliar place, not knowing its ways nor its people. Realising you are alone; you reach out to the One who knows you."

"Are you disappointed to have arrived here?" she looked at him with her melting eyes. He averted his own, aware of the extraordinary beauty and soul in the caress of her eyes.

"No, why would I be disappointed?" He expressed the gratitude felt towards her parents in providing this safe haven.

"And what do you suppose was the meaning of you being brought to Inis Kayru on the very day that I was brought there?"

"Well, it is obvious. It was for your restoration!"

"Nothing more?"

"My journey has been about leaving the familiar and becoming totally dependent upon the King. How was I to overcome the peril of the open seas in a flimsy coracle? Exactly where was I to go and in what direction? To whom could I turn? And then I am directed to the conical peak . . ."

"With its top sliced off at an angle as though by a giant sword," finished Aleine Brona with an endearing smile.

He smiled. "With your healing, I knew the Spirit was upon me."

"And I came to believe in your God."

Their eyes met and neither looked away. They smiled simultaneously.

"Now that you are here," Aleine Brona ventured, "perhaps the King intends you to stay."

Her exquisite eyes flirted for a moment as he looked up.

"My way forward is not clear. I have been pondering that question too."

"Maybe to make a new home among us," she suggested warmly.

"That would be one possibility," he agreed, adding emphatically, "and a most pleasant one!"

"Then stay, do stay, do say yes!" she pleaded, child-like.

"But there are other options . . ." his voice trailed off, reluctant to state what these might be when her suggestion was so agreeable.

"If you want to stay, then you just decide; it is as simple as that!" she declared with the utmost simplicity.

He removed the tacks holding the vellum.

Aleine Brona watched his actions. "What are your other options?"

Freed from the table, a corner of the vellum lifted in the breeze. He noted that the ink had already dried.

"Speak to me, Taran," she said, pumping her foot onto the ground. "What troubles you? Am I not your friend?" she asked gently. Then her tone changed with a hint of impatience. "I am not a child, you know!"

"I know you are not a child," he agreed meaningfully. Struggling to find the words, he finally managed to add, "There are expectations of me."

She cocked her head slightly to one side.

"I have the Z-rod tattooed on my back," he blurted out, believing at that moment this was the one person he could confide in. There, he had said it, and the tension was released.

"What is a Z-rod?"

"What! You do not know? The Z-rod consists of three lines. Two are in parallel and the third joins the opposing ends. Here, let me show you." He produced a Z-rod on the vellum.

She looked at him, none the wiser.

"Do you not have standing stones with images on?"

"We have standing stones, but without images." She chuckled briefly.

Impulsively, he cast aside the plaid wrapped about him and removing his tunic, he presented his back to Aleine Brona. She gasped, before running her forefinger along the line of the Z-rod. Her touch tingled strangely upon his skin. He put his tunic back on and wrapped the plaid about him.

"Where I am from (and it is not just from where I am from, but in all the lands on the other side of the Druim Alban) we use lots of symbols that have special meanings. The Z-rod is a power symbol . . ." he stopped himself from adding, 'reserved for the warlord'. He swallowed and proceeded with his explanation, "The symbol is like lightning, the power from the heavens striking the earth. Well, I have been given this symbol by our druid; and others have prophesied that I have been set apart for a purpose. This Z-rod defines my fate."

"Power from heaven came when you healed me," she said with slow deliberation. "I am sure there would be many opportunities for you to use this power in our area!"

He reflected briefly and spoke with a tinge of regret in his voice. "I suspect that I am only at the beginning rather than at the end of my journey." He rolled up the vellum and rose. Glancing at Aleine Brona, he noted that she looked confused, even a little forlorn.

"I am going to put this away." He raised the rolled-up vellum in his hand and disappeared indoors.

She followed him inside and asked, "What is the meaning of the viper on your back?"

"It is a symbol of resurrection. You know, vipers disappear over the winter and then are re-born in the spring." It struck him how apt this pagan symbol was with his Christian pilgrimage. The thought thrilled him, for a scripture spoke of man needing to be re-born to have spiritual life.

That night he dreamed of Rhynie, especially of Oengus, the favoured of Talorgen, the firer of arrows as he swam for his life. Oengus was triumphant, the new warlord, the wily one who fashions alliances with neighbouring powers. Oengus emerged as the double victor in both power and love, stealing Alpia. He awoke with the old resentment burning afresh in his heart. It surprised him, for he had thought the anger had subsided, but the ire had merely died down like a fire without flames, lying dormant under a mound of ash. Such smouldering embers only required a mere breath to re-ignite.

Chapter Eleven

Hope at Ostara
556AD   Rhynie

"The Ce shall be a great people," Oengus proclaimed in the hall before his warriors, adjusting his posture as he came to the heart of his speech at the Ostara celebrations. "Gone are the days of petty skirmishes with the Circinn. Wait . . . I can see from some looks that they are still regarded as enemies! True, they have been a stench in our nostrils as we have been in theirs. They crossed the border and stole cattle and burnt crops, and we retaliated! Where is the gain, comrades?"

"And what about our brothers and your own father fallen in battle?" interrupted Drust, rising to his feet. Drust was a broad-shouldered man with a strident voice, a warrior that others looked up to and even aspired to be like. Taking a decisive hold of his plaid that had slipped from his shoulder, Drust flicked it back into place.

"It is on account of my father's death – his and the deaths of our fallen comrades – that now we can move on to become a stronger people who choose their fights."

"And who do you propose we fight?"

"I am not proposing we pick a fight with anyone."

This caused surprise among the warriors, particularly the younger ones eager to prove themselves.

"This is the time to build ourselves up, to create an army, trained, disciplined and well-equipped that will make any bold neighbour think twice before stepping over the running Dee or even the flowing Spey. Listen, comrades, our forefathers tell us that the Romans were able to defeat us in battle with much smaller numbers than the men we were able to field . . ."

"We beat the Romans!" interjected another young man, also rising to his feet. Looking around for affirmation, he roused a half-hearted mumbling of agreement. The young man sat down again.

"If you will permit me," Maelchon said, rising to his feet. "The Lord Oengus speaks knowledgeably concerning such things, with truths which are entrusted to our druidic order. Every generation needs to heed that *without knowledge of the past we shall lose the future*. It is an account that is different from how things are represented by our bards."

At this, Drust, who was still standing in the middle of the hall, visibly nodded in agreement. He flattened his long moustaches thoughtfully.

"The Romans inflicted a heavy blow on us at Mons Graupius," continued the druid, "causing our retreat, yet not our demise. Because we were able to harry their legions with surprise attacks, we made them retreat south. In that sense, we did beat the Romans."

"Our warlord and druid speak true," approved Drust. He took a pace forward and scanned his audience with his intelligent eyes. "A smaller number, well-disciplined, can overcome a larger force who are not so well-trained."

Oengus was both surprised and glad to receive Drust's approval. He sent a nod in his direction and did likewise with his druid. Both Drust and Maelchon sat down. He continued to expound his ideas. "This is the opportunity to consolidate our position, not only through training a military force, but also by strengthening our defences. We shall make Rhynie look like a true fort and not like some glorified cattle enclosure! We shall extend the palisade way beyond the existing huts, marking out vacant ground for new comrades to establish their homes and add to our fighting number. We shall also build a second tier on top of the existing palisade doubling its height, erecting a raised platform for our sentries."

"But that is a considerable undertaking," objected Drust, rising again to his feet. He did not strike a hostile posture, but assumed a stance that questioned.

"It is a big task!" Oengus nodded. "But I am instructing work teams from among all the communities of the Ce to fell trees and prepare timber to put up this palisade. Skilled craftsmen shall produce and fix all the furnishings, like brackets and hinges, reinforced struts and all manner of ironwork to strengthen the structure."

His main detractor looked appeased and sat down. With the ear of his people, he was able to elaborate. ". . . and we will bring in four more blacksmiths to make weapons and armour to equip our growing force. In this way, we shall be a people to be reckoned with, strengthening our hand in new alliances, not as the inferior side, but as the equal partner, no longer forced into alliances that impoverish with large tributes."

By the time he had finished speaking, the men looked stirred with their heads raised proud.

"And now, comrades, let us join the rest of the community around the salmon and beast stone to observe the rites that Maelchon and Gest will lead. After that, we shall return to this hall to feast and make merry through this night."

As men were dispersing from the hall, Drust came over. "Lord Oengus, I was outspoken earlier. But your words have shown that you have carefully weighed the matter concerning the standing of the Ce with our neighbours. I had at first thought these were rash words, bold ones without substance! But you have given due consideration. I am with you."

"I thank you, Drust. Plans should be carefully laid before actions test them! Is that not so?" He felt relaxed, enjoying the approval of even the outspoken Drust. He knew this young warrior from former days when they had joined forces with other trainees for joint military exercises and had found him to be a leader of strong character, able to command the respect of his fellows through his ability as a fierce combatant and as a tactician. He was glad of his support, for he could have proved a difficult dissenter who could influence others and frustrate his own plans. He decided to appoint Drust as his man to work alongside him in training their new fighting force, a matter which he would address when this day was over.

Maelchon and Gest, who had changed into clean white robes, were the last to appear outside the gates where the community had congregated awaiting their arrival. The wind was bitterly cold and blew through them, causing them to huddle tightly into a concentrated mass. Those exposed on the group's southwest side stood for as long as they could bear before peeling away around the rear to shelter on the group's leeward side. A flurry of icy rain came which presaged an assault of stinging hail stones that bounced on the ground. He had hoped that this second of the spring festivals would bring warmer weather, but was reminded in no uncertain terms that the reign of winter was not over.

Whilst Maelchon busied himself with a smouldering brazier, Gest opened the proceedings in a confident voice. "We purposefully gather before our familiar standing stone, engraved with a salmon over the beast. It is not only the marker standing in the portal that is part of our identity, a portal that gives access to our community; but this stone makes a statement. The wisdom of the salmon overcomes the fear that the beast incites."

Maelchon indicated Gest to pour a ewer of water upon the grass growing around the base of their standing stone. "This water was gathered at first light from our own spring that wells up on the side of our sacred hill. This is the renewing water from which all things shall emerge. Just as it waters the ground, and helps to bring nourishment to roots and seeds, so shall we, the Ce, be renewed with hope in the ascendancy of Beli Mawr who brings heat to the soil to encourage new life."

Maelchon took up the smouldering brazier suspended from three wires and was about to blow upon the ash when an eddy of wind did it for him. Tiny sparks glowed for a moment, whirling through the air before settling as dull, miniscule cinders. Some of the ash scattered over Gest's robe with remnants stinging the faces of the onlookers. He swung the brazier over the ground wetted by the sacred water, symbolising the warmth of the ascending sun in collaboration with the water of life that would bring about the transformation of the ground.

Stooping with bowed head, Maelchon gave the impression that he had perhaps concluded the required rituals and accompanying instruction.

Oh, has he finished? thought Oengus. If only Maelchon could better communicate when things were at an end.

Raising his head, Maelchon spoke up once more.

Oengus could sense the gathering impatience of the crowd having to endure more of the inclement weather.

"I shall add one more thing which it is not customary to utter at Ostara. However, in view of what we have heard our young warlord say earlier, I feel it would be grossly remiss to be silent upon the matter."

The chief druid had the attention of everyone, no doubt willing him, Oengus considered, to hasten what had to be said. He wondered what this sometimes-difficult druid might add, he had not reckoned on the usually taciturn man to elaborate further. He felt apprehensive.

"It struck me, as we were performing this simple rite, that Lord Oengus' plans of renewing Rhynie and expanding its warrior force and prestige is in alignment with the yearly cycle. Shall we as a people not be renewed and transformed, just as the Bulàch has already arisen as Brigantia?"

Oengus gazed upon his chief druid with surprise, filled with an unexpected gratitude in receiving his support, for Maelchon was exceedingly sparing with good omens as his own experience had born out. Gest has done a good work, he thought, in convincing Maelchon to endorse my rule.

With the druids having completed the simple rites, he caught everyone's attention before they moved indoors with anticipation of the feast. "Just bear with me a few moments more, dear comrades." Standing beside the salmon and beast stone, he could be seen by those near the front of the arced crowd. He raised his voice, just as Maelchon had done, to be better heard even at the back. "This is an occasion of new beginnings, to commemorate our intentions to rise from our humble place. I have had fashioned a special symbol." He nodded in the direction of a young man who started to climb a ladder propped up against the lintel above the portal of the palisade. The man awkwardly carried in one hand something evidently heavy and looking like a very large square shield. It required the guiding hand from another in raising its unwieldy bulk, a task made more difficult by the sudden and powerful eddies of wind that sported around the battlements, gusting with force through the portal. The wind caught the large, cumbersome object in a mocking manner. Upon the battlements waited another person, precariously hanging over the palisade to receive it. Oengus realised that it would have been easier had the shield been taken up to the palisade and then lowered down to the man on the ladder. However, he had figured that the mounting of the shield from below was a piece of drama to captivate everyone's attention and would be well-remembered. He considered that he had succeeded in that. With concern, he watched the uncertain raising of the shield, fearing that should it fall, it might be remembered for the wrong reasons as an ill omen!

Eventually, the shield was aloft and then reversed with much difficulty.

"The boar's head!" he proudly announced, "the symbol of the new Ce, placed in this eminent position as a reminder that we are a people with a future, a people not to be taken lightly, and a tribe to be reckoned with as we fashion a skilled fighting force. Mothers and fathers, brothers and sisters, this is just the beginning, a statement of intent so that we might hold our heads high. It is about raising, not just our chins, but an enlarged and enhanced fortification."

His short speech was met with the approval of raucous cheers and clapping. He caught Gest's eye, who nodded in Maelchon's direction. He was pleasantly surprised to see his chief druid smiling approvingly.

"And now comrades," he continued, feeling particularly bright, "it is time to celebrate. May your platters be full of roast boar and your cups overflowing with mead. Eat, drink and be merry, for this is a night for story-telling, for bards to spout poetry and for all to sing the spring into being."

Chilled to the core, no one waited another second; but all poured towards the portal in such a torrent that there was quite a stampede to regain the warmth of the hall.

Her aunt was already cooking porridge when Alpia came through to her hut. She noticed a man collapsed among a pile of clothing and plaids, not realising at first who it was.

"Oengus came in around daybreak," informed her aunt, responding to her puzzled expression. "He was the worse for wear. They had quite a night of carousing in the hall!"

She shook her head, expressing her disgust, a little surprised by the matter-of-fact tone her aunt had used.

"But why did he come here?"

"Probably could not find his own hut, or maybe just out of custom as he comes here daily." She pushed some hair strands behind an ear and looking up, added, "You know how it is with men when they are drunk."

Oengus lay there all morning, motionless, oblivious to the chores carried out and the cries of baby Caltram. When he did move, near noontime, he groaned and propping himself up on an elbow, he blinked repeatedly before lurching urgently to the door. As soon as he was outside, she heard him vomit.

He came back in shortly after, pale and dishevelled, rubbing his face.

"Is that the way for a warlord to behave!" she chastised him.

Oengus merely grunted and sat down near to where Aunt Conchen was now preparing some lunch.

"You had better drink some water," advised Aunt Conchen in a kind tone, handing Oengus a wooden cup. He sipped it steadily and asked for more.

Cradling Caltram in her arms, Alpia shifted her weight from one leg to the other in a motion that soothed the child. She glanced over at Oengus. "What is the sense of drinking yourself stupid and then throwing everything up?" She turned her back on him as though shielding Caltram from the sight of his father whom she found repulsive.

"Oh, that is the way with men!" sighed Aunt Conchen. "You cannot stop them. They are all the same!"

"Is this the way to build the new Ce?" she raised her voice indignantly.

"Och! Talorgen was the same, especially when he was younger."

How could Aunt Conchen defend men's deplorable actions? She pictured Oengus, just yesterday, standing near his druids at the Ostara rites, looking lordly over his people, commanding respect, his prestige raised by his warriors deferring to him. Now look at him! she thought, staring vacantly at the floor as though dazed after being hit over the head.

"The broth is nearly ready," Aunt Conchen announced as she stirred, sniffing at a steaming pot suspended over the fire. She added soothingly to Oengus, "You can get some of this down you, and then you will feel better."

She speaks to him as though he is a boy, taken ill due to no fault of his own and to be pitied.

"No, I do not want any," Oengus replied in an almost despairing voice.

"I will pour you a wee bowl and give you some bread to dunk. It would do you good – and, if you keep it down, you will feel better." She ladled a small portion into a clay bowl, came over and sat down beside him. Like a mother with a child, she carefully placed it into his hands and put her arm around his back.

Alpia turned away in disgust, thinking how undeserving he was of such kindness.

"Smell a little," her aunt coaxed. "Go on, try."

With Oengus not replying, she could not help looking back. She watched him place his face over the bowl and sniff. Tired from pacing the hut to pacify a fractious Caltram, she sat down opposite and held Caltram against her chest to receive her bodily warmth. Hearing her aunt speak in a congratulatory tone, she looked up and saw Oengus sipping from the bowl. Why does her aunt seemingly reward bad behaviour?

"It is quiet today!" remarked her aunt. "I expect all the menfolk will be feeling like Oengus!"

She wondered whether Taran, had he been here, would have been drunk too? Her aunt maintained that all men were the same! So, yes, he would probably have been no better than Oengus. She surprised herself for thinking of Taran who featured less in her thoughts these days since no news of him brought him much to mind. In the past, how often she used to wonder whether he would have gone over to the Circinn. Surely, if he were the traitor that popular opinion would have you believe, there would have been a commotion by now?

I expect he has perished in the forests and hills, dying from cold and hunger, or killed by some wild beast. Haunted by such thoughts, she had grieved in the early days, mourning the loss of a noble youth, her cousin and friend, a close friend who had almost been more than that. But grief had to stop, especially when not knowing the outcome. It had never been the bitter blow she would have felt had she known he was dead, and yet it was something that gnawed away like an old injury. Still, *he is a loss to the Ce*, she thought, a young man, full of potential with the charisma that others would have gladly followed. But Taran was too kind to survive in this warrior world. She recalled the words she had uttered which had caught in the air like an involuntary portent: *I fear for the lives of the innocent in an evil world*. She recalled repeating Ossian's injunction to be *cunning*, a word that had come to haunt her. She concluded that the warlordship was never intended for Taran.

She nursed this sad reverie, still flattered by his attentions on that heady Beltane evening. There had been a time when she had waited for news of him, dreaming of 'what if' scenarios, daydreams detached from reality. But she had determined to live in the real world; and Taran was consigned to the stuff of fanciful dreams, to a past that was no more and had never really been. He had been untimely taken, like his fellow youth who had never returned from the ill-fated ambush, removed from this world.

Life was so unpredictable, just as it had been for Eithni. But for the moment, she had life; what would she do with it?

Fionnoula reappeared to give Caltram his next feed, and as he was suckling at the breast Fionnoula remarked to Oengus, "That is some tattoo you have!"

Alpia looked at her inquisitively.

"Have you not seen it?"

"And why would I have seen it?" she responded testily.

"Well, he exhibited it to all in the hall last night! A great boar's head bellowing right across his chest. It is most impressive."

Oengus passed her a look that started out as impish before melting into something between regret and repentance. He concluded his silent communication with a shrug of his shoulders.

Looking at Caltram at the breast, she reflected upon the strange workings of fate that had assigned her a mother's role. Who would have dreamt that a year ago, before Oengus and Taran had returned to Rhynie? Such were the capricious designs of the Bulàch. Due to the flirtatious ways of her friend Eithni, she would carry Oengus' child and then on her death bed elect Alpia to raise him alongside Oengus! How had that happened when she herself was so careful, desiring an ordered life?

Well, maybe I am not always so careful, she reflected recalling her impulsive spirit that had taken her by surprise on that Beltane evening. No, not back to Taran again!

She looked at the baby half-smiling at her. She did not resent caring for Caltram; a commitment she had taken to with joy and natural ability. However, it had placed her quite unexpectedly in Oengus' company. She could not easily ignore him as she once had done. And she acknowledged that Oengus had undergone a change of heart, starting from the time he had brought Eithni back to Rhynie. And had he not seemed genuinely grief-stricken by her sudden death? Since then, he had never tried to foist himself on her attention, that had made it easier, as too had the arrangement to raise Caltram in her aunt's home. Thank the Bulàch for Aunt Conchen! Without her, this arrangement could never have worked. Aunt Conchen was kindness itself.

Work commenced in raising the new defences straight after Ostara, with work teams from neighbouring communities joining the vast undertaking. Oengus left Rhynie, along with his entourage for Lord Cynbel's court at Migdele, with the sounds of axes and hammers ringing in their ears. His mother, who was riding with him, was largely silent, a changed character after the demise of her husband, leaving him to speak at length with Drust concerning their plans for the rise of the boar, their euphemism for the ascent of the Ce.

On arriving at Migdele, Derile rushed to meet them. "Mother! I am so pleased to see you," Derile was less than enthusiastic in greeting Oengus who was soon escorted to Cynbel.

"What brings you here?" asked the old man, not with a hostile tone, but with what he detected as a wary manner reflected in his eyes.

"I am coming to visit family and new allies," he replied buoyantly. "How is Derile? Is she a pleasing wife to you?"

Cynbel was slow to reply. "She is often sullen," he said flatly. "She misses home."

After making small talk, he raised one of the matters uppermost on his mind. "Have you heard news of Taran, my fugitive cousin?"

"No. Believe me, I would tell you, for you promised a handsome reward." The old warlord laughed. "But why concern yourself with him – what can one man do against a whole tribe?"

"You are right, I was just curious, that was all." He shifted posture, raising a bag in his hand. "I have a gift for you." He reached into the sack and produced an ornate dagger.

Cynbel smiled. He seemed to genuinely admire the blade. For a few moments he lightly drummed the dagger on his lap thoughtfully, before announcing, "And I have something for you." Cynbel beckoned an aide to lift down a finely-crafted shield hanging from the wall, embellished with a blue swirling pattern. "It was taken from the Lord Domech after he tried to trick us. It is a fine shield which I value. I should like you to have it as a sign of the new favour between us and our peoples."

"It is good to move on from the skirmishes that marked Talorgen's rule."

"Indeed. Talorgen was stubborn." Cynbel looked at him thoughtfully. He seemed to have something on his mind. "Our people are turning to the Christian way." He passed him a searching look. "I am a follower of *the Way*, for it is progress, uniting us with others of the same persuasion. Do you have Christian pilgrims coming to your lands?"

"No." He did not know what to make of this revelation. "Is it not risky turning from our Pictish ways! I mean, why should we be like the people of the south?"

"You surprise me, Oengus! I expected you to say that alliances are better than raids!"

He paused thoughtfully. "Aye, I believe that. But that is me exercising my own will; not conforming to some foreign idea."

"Does it matter?" Cynbel looked at him askance. "If it is of your own persuasion to follow the Christian way, then it is not someone telling you that you should. Why allow pride to get in the way when you agree with putting an end to enmity? You would not want to be left alone in the dark, whilst other people find accord together walking in *the way*, would you?"

"I do not know." He scratched his head vigorously. "I am not saying no, but I do not want to be hasty in saying yes either. And what of the Bulàch? Do our druids not warn us, *Abandon her at your peril?*"

"She seems powerless, they say, to stop the advance of Christian influence."

"Are there other Pictish warlords who have been won over by this new teaching?"

"The Lord Uuid of the Fib is most sympathetic with the Christian way. He and his predecessor have, for a long time now, permitted the soldiers of Christ to form their *colonies of heaven* in their lands, close to his centres of power, even at Abernethy. Then, there is Domech of the Fotla." Cynbel pronounced the warlord's name with evident disdain. "He has permitted monks to settle, even below the rock of Dindurn. I believe he still follows the old ways and remains a most volatile and irritating neighbour. The man is a tyrant and a deceiver. However, I can see the old resistance may pass, once Domech dies, for this teaching has made inroads among his people."

Cynbel paused, inhaling noisily through his nostrils. "But as for ourselves, my predecessor was undoubtedly a Christian. Have you heard his story?"

Shaking his head, Oengus was not disposed to listening any more about such foreign beliefs, but Cynbel was undeterred and there was nothing for it but to listen.

"Uist, my predecessor, apparently had died a natural death, when a pilgrim by the name of Boethius, revived him."

"Who can do such a thing?" he retorted sceptically.

"Well, Uist believed it, for he granted land to Boethius. It was not just any spare piece of land he gifted for the pilgrims to build upon. No! Uist gave them an entire fort to establish one of their muintirs."

He felt irritated. Surely there was some simpler explanation for his apparent returning from the dead! "And is that what you believe?"

"How can you deny it when you have witnessed a dead person coming back to life!"

"Maybe he was not dead, but rather had been ailing from some grievous sickness that had made him appear dead."

"That is what some say," Cynbel conceded. Moving on from the contentious matter, he remarked, "The Britons to the south are already Christian."

"The Britons to the south are soft," he interjected. "They are falling prey to the warrior people from across the North Sea."

"They were unprepared," Cynbel shrugged his shoulders. "Their leaders foolishly invited foreign warriors to keep the peace. But if Christian tribes could unite, we could withstand any incursion from these continental barbarians."

"Barbarians? Is that not the word the Romans used to describe us?"

"That may be so," conceded Cynbel, "but Rome is now Christian."

"That's my point. Since they became Christian, her empire diminished!"

"The empire fell for other reasons. Since she became Christian, Rome has been gathering a far-reaching influence again, uniting others in a common belief."

He was quiet for a moment. "You seem well-informed."

"We get a broad outlook from the soldiers of Christ whose influence spreads across many lands. We are also informed in our discussions with the rulers of the south who confirm these things."

"I will think further upon these things. It feels unnatural, though, to accept teaching and information from foreigners. I would much rather have a trusted source." As he said this, he recalled Ossian broadcasting similar news at Beltane the previous year – and that gave the information more legitimacy.

"You could always have pilgrims come to Rhynie to instruct you in their ways. Then, you can make a judgement."

"We shall see – let me think about it."

On their return journey a few days later, he questioned Drust as they rode alongside one another. "What do you think of the Circinn turning away from the Bulàch to follow this new Christian teaching?"

"It will not last. Besides, there are only a few who call themselves pilgrims, and they seem to live apart from the centre of power."

"Not all," he corrected. "Cynbel seems persuaded, as are others in his court. When the ruler changes allegiance, will not his people follow?"

"Maybe. But Cynbel is full of years. These Christian ideas will disappear with him, mark my words."

He thought more on the matter. If he were to consider Cynbel's suggestion of receiving soldiers of Christ, it would upset Maelchon and Gest. Gest was his closest advisor and ally, so why should he jeopardise that? As for Maelchon, he had unexpectedly gained his favour at Ostara. His chief druid was a man of considerable standing, giving legitimacy to his rule. Had the Bulàch not been good to him? She had marked Taran with the Z-rod before the appointed time, banishing him as a fugitive. With Talorgen out of the way too, there were no further perceived obstacles to restrict the ascendancy of the Ce. Had he not gained the following of the people by mapping out a stronger future? Why muddle that with ideas of becoming followers of a foreign way? Why risk the wrath of the Bulàch and lose the support of his druids? No, the Picts to the south might dabble with new ways to emulate the Britons and the Gaels, but we shall maintain our identity as a warrior people, steadfast in our beliefs that have well served our forefathers.

Chapter Twelve

The Shining One
558AD   Loch Kilmorkill

A whole summer had passed and then a prolonged autumn. Taran's mind reeled with the injustice and frustration from being denied his inheritance. Did Oengus' treachery not call to be challenged? What could he do about it from so obscure a place? Yet he also knew that revenge was inappropriate as a pilgrim, leading to a mounting guilt for entertaining such thoughts.

"What ails you?" asked Girom.

"Oh, just a bad dream!" he replied dismissively.

"It seems to have troubled you. Maybe it is a warning?!"

"Yes, maybe."

"Speak to our druid about it – he is a good interpreter of dreams," suggested Girom, turning to go fishing.

Speaking to a druid was the last thing on his mind. Had he not had enough of druids for a lifetime? Besides, he had a new King; although one who seemed quiet of late.

Several times recently he had awoken from the same dream with great frustration and consternation. Aleine Brona was the one person who knew how to soothe his troubles and so he started to hint, rather than tell, about some of his previous life, keeping it under a veil. He noted how she enjoyed the mystery of his origins; and liking to keep this secret between them, it provided him with the soothing opportunity to be with her. Aleine Brona could empathise, although unable to understand everything. He became careless in his prayer habits, spending more time talking with her, speaking less to his King. When at last he noted this, it bothered him. But his conscience was muted by his growing fascination in this girl in the early flush of womanhood. Every day, he became conscious of some new aspect of her person that intrigued him. He noted too, that she made greater efforts with her appearance, in contrast to the image she had presented when suspended in the shrub, so emaciated and unkempt that the sight of her had repulsed him.

I have not been ruing the loss of Alpia from the thieving hand of my cousin lately, but I do feel cheated of my inheritance, he observed one day when gathering firewood. I cannot recall exactly what Alpia looks like anymore. But with Aleine Brona, I can describe her every detail!

What if he could just be at peace with the situation? Had he not given up on the quest of getting his kingdom back after his flight from Dindurn? That was all in the past, as Fillan had insisted. The transition at Dindurn had prepared him for a new life, specifically led by Fillan's vision to this remote coast where he experienced his spiritual renewal. Void of further guidance, Aleine Brona offered great consolation after all that he had lost; her simple, homely wisdom inviting him to build a new life with her, had strong appeal.

Yet the haunting dream would not leave him, with such an indignation growing within him that it made him question why he was at Girom's household and he began to wonder why his life appeared to come to a halt in this place. Was a prince to settle for the obscurity of these shores?

I am a prince no more, he reminded himself, but a warrior of Christ with expectations upon my shoulders, and a prophecy that one day I will *bear fire to the north*. As before, the lovely charm of Aleine Brona made him forgetful of these concerns. Gazing upon her, all these considerations lost their importance and all that mattered was her favour and the loveliness of her company.

"What ails you?" Girom asked again. "You have become like a son to me, and we are glad that you came into our lives. Aleine Brona is especially thankful – and not just just for the obvious reason that she was made well through you . . ." Girom nodded meaningfully at him.

"She was healed by the King I serve," he corrected, feeling uneasy at where this conversation was going.

"Well, it seems that you are fond of her too. Is that not so?"

"I am."

"Who stands between the two of you to prevent you from becoming man and wife? Alma and I would be pleased to have you as our son . . . So then, you can settle here and grow a family." Girom patted his hand, before taking a step back and saying with significance, "Such things bring peace to a man, a sense of belonging. It is a great thing to be loved and cared for by a good woman. Such a thing will take away your restlessness."

He found himself nodding slowly, but with lurking reservations.

"I see that you are not totally convinced! Do you not like being here? Is our land not good enough for you?" Girom asked, slightly piqued.

"No – all these things are excellent. Believe me, I am grateful!"

"Then what causes you to hold back? Is it the sense of making your new life here, and saying farewell to where you hail from?"

"There is that. But my travels have not finished. I was led here, for the healing that confirmed me in a new-found faith. I know this is only the beginning, but now my way is obscure, shrouded in a fog. Not knowing the way ahead, I have stopped moving."

"Those do not sound like the words of a man consumed by love!" Girom shook his head and his features hardened. "When I met Alma it was like a fire within me that having kindled well then just took hold, burning everything in its tracks: to move away from its light and warmth was unthinkable. I know that sometimes, for us men, losing our independence can seem significant – could it be that which is holding you back?"

He thought for a moment. "There is some truth in that. However, it is the question of where my destiny lies that brings about my uncertainty."

"And if you were to move on, what then of your feelings for Aleine Brona – would they not eat you up?"

"I am sure they will – I have no doubt about that."

"Does that not indicate that you should remain here and take her as your wife?"

Girom's tone struck him as being cool, annoyed by the indecisiveness of one caught between passion and reason. He rested his chin on the paddle and did not answer.

"It is up to you to decide! No one is holding you back from being a couple." He puffed out his cheeks, venting his frustration. After a pause, he spoke with calculation. "My daughter is in love with you, and you with her. We consent to you being together, and there is already a place for you here. Is it not clear man?"

He felt the intensity of Girom's gaze but still made no reply. Girom's face reddened. "You need to decide, otherwise love will compromise the two of you; then, you will have no choice in the matter! Decide whether you will settle down together, or . . ." and he stopped, seemingly struggling to find the exact words. Finally he uttered resolutely, "Or you leave us for good!"

Tact had been dispensed with, making evident that her father's wishes were unequivocal.

"With such an ultimatum, I ought to consider everything you have suggested. Yet it is not only my heart I must examine, but my soul. I need to consult my King."

"It is good that we understand one another," he said with finality. But that did not prevent him from adding, "I will not stand aside to see my daughter dishonoured – I think I make myself clear."

Taran determined to remove himself from the household on the next day to seek his way, and began setting aside the things required for camping in the woods: a bow and quiver, a spear and a knife and a satchel full of provisions. He added a bearskin as a blanket, and recalling the misery of being drenched by rain whilst camping in the Minamoyn Goch, he folded a bulky awning made from leather hides sewn into one piece.

Aleine Brona loitered despondently, watching the preparations but, without assisting him. Finally, she spoke. "My heart does not want to accept that you have to go away to know whether you truly love me or not!"

"It is not like that . . ."

She interrupted him. "I was going to add, though, that my head does understand! I owe my healing to the High King and therefore, sometimes, I do feel that we should not hold back from following his leading."

"Thank you," he simply uttered. He kissed her forehead. She reached out and touched his own forehead with her hand and ran her fingers through his wavy forelocks. The action made him recoil.

"I must shave!" he announced abruptly, and went in search of a razor. How careless I have grown in this place he considered as he removed his forelocks in a conscious effort of re-committing himself to *the way* and continuing with his *white martyrdom*.

Walking about the bay, he crossed low, boggy ground, before ascending the sharp rise of the hill overlooking their settlement. The steepness almost persuaded him to walk the contour around the hill to find a gentler incline, but he checked himself. "I have become soft!" he remonstrated aloud. Determining to endure the difficulty of the slope, he hoped to purge himself of the easy malaise that had crept over him. Despite the frosty chill, the effort made him break into a sweat by the time he reached the hilltop. Through the windswept pines, broken and gnarled by storms that crowned the summit, he caught glimpses of the sea below and the bay where the last months had been spent. To his left was the broader sound where he had crossed from Inis Kayru, visibly turbulent with the ocean's tidal flow. It brought to mind precarious voyages in a flimsy coracle.

Looking up to the head of the sea loch, he detected small scattered communities whose fires raised tell-tale smoke trails onto a cold blue sky. He had been aware of fires at night, winking along the shores. Out in the distance, he could see the sliced pinnacle of Inis Kayru's peak, like the amputated stump of a finger raised to make a statement. He reflected on how his *white martyrdom* had grown a dependence upon the High King, culminating in the miracle at the spring beneath the peak. A sense of shame overshadowed him on recognising the neglect of his prayers, making way for his reliance upon human affection.

The descent from the ridge was gentler, leading to a low pass, dense with trees. Having gone eastward, and keen to avoid returning to the coast he had just left, he veered southwards at the first opportunity, around the flank of a hill. Soon, he glimpsed a loch below in a boggy basin and decided to pitch camp on the higher ground, still in the hill's shelter. His purpose was not to make a long expedition, but to create the opportunity to search his heart before the Presence. This place felt remote with its undisturbed forest, whose stillness could settle his turbulent thoughts.

He draped his leather awning over a branch forming an inverted V-shape and secured its sides with rocks. One end of the awning was fastened about the tree's trunk, leaving the opposite end open to the loch below. He gathered dead bracken until it lay in a heap on the ground before the awning, and collected enough wood to fuel a fire that could burn all through the night. He carefully shaped a sphere of dried lichen, straw and the slenderest of twigs. Striking a flint repeatedly, he watched a flurry of sparks showering the kindling ball, looking as if they would combust the material at any moment. It took a while before a smouldering spiral revealed a tiny bud of fire. Picking up the smouldering sphere with something akin to reverence, he brought it close to his mouth and breathed lightly upon it. The small bundle crackled as it flickered with the smallest petal of a flame. With another three gentle breaths, the flame grew to the size of a rose bud. The flaming orb was quickly placed at the base of the small wood pile just beyond the threshold of his awning, to which he added twigs that soon grew the fire. He arranged the damp bracken in a loose heap about the fire, every so often turning the pile to thoroughly dry it for his bedding.

It felt good to be back on his own in the woods, without the need to converse or to help with someone else's chores. His needs were stripped back to the bare essentials; it felt liberating, producing a deep thankfulness for the necessities gathered about him. As he watched the flames slowly consume the wood, turning a solid mass to ash, he recited some scriptures, but was troubled by his lack of recall. After eating some smoked fish, he prayed, determining to fast the next day and remain in this place above the stillness of the loch.

Icy showers fell intermittently through the night, dampening the campfire and rousing him from his sleep. Logs, dry from underneath the awning, revived the smouldering pyre and warmed him to a renewed state of drowsiness to which he gladly yielded.

Fasting the next day avoided the distraction of finding food, allowing him to commit to prayer and contemplation. Often though, he found his mind wandering, returning again and again to Aleine Brona's loveliness. Such recollections made him smile, until coming to his senses he chastised himself for his lack of focus. That night, having not eaten anything, he felt the cold. The darkness was long. Prayer became more focussed, leading at times to a sense of breakthrough and reconnection, until distraction broke in, leaving him disappointed.

I have not achieved the direction I desire, he declared on the following morning; so I shall continue my fast for a second day. He heated water, hoping that by drinking some, warmth might return to limb and bring cheer amidst the dripping dampness of his surroundings.

Later that morning, he climbed to a hilltop to warm himself and ease the ache in his joints. Catching sight of Girom's settlement in the bay, reminded him that the distance was not far between Aleine Brona and himself. He returned to camp and read the scripture about Abram he had written on the vellum. The words reminded him of the act of leaving all that was familiar, and how he must expose himself to the unknown in an embrace of trust in his God. The mark of the Z-rod he had drawn on the vellum was the stark reminder that he must confront his destiny.

"Lord, show me what is next, what I should do and where I should go. Or – is it here where my journey is to be fulfilled?" He fondly envisaged what it would be like to make a home and to provide for a family. Could he not enjoy her comfort, and care for her and their offspring? The idea usurped all other thoughts, and nagged like a troublesome, spoilt child seeking to have its way. He fought back with prayer through the rest of the day and into the evening, but found no answer. He tried to ponder other options but not knowing where to go, or what to do, he found these too difficult to consider.

"I shall fast for a third day!" he vowed aloud. The thought of going without food was an unpleasant one, for he felt the damp penetrating through to his core until he was quite nauseous with cold.

He woke shivering, his mouth thick and his breath vile. After stoking the fire, he gave himself to prayer, kneeling on the ground to avoid falling into a slumber. He recited the prayers learned at Dindurn, several more than he could recall on the first day of his camp – and spoke the others in his own words. He prayed for peace, which he knew could only come with the guidance of what he should do next. He concluded with one of Saint Patrick's prayers that Fillan had taught him to recite when facing times of turmoil,

"I bind unto myself today
the power of God to hold and lead,
God's eye to look before me,
his might to stay,
his ear to hearken to my need.
God's word to speak for me,
God's hand to guard me,
his shield to ward,
the word of God to give me speech,
his heavenly host to be my guard."

Going out from his camp, he took a spear for protection, but left his bow behind, so as to resist the temptation to hunt for a meal and bring warmth to his body. His teeth began to chatter uncontrollably in the chill of the winter's morning. He wandered down the glen, enjoying the sunbeams that found a way through the forest, and gave thanks. His powers of perception were heightened from fasting and solitude; every manifestation of movement and light awakened in him an acute sense of curiosity and wonder. He came to another small glen, dark with tall pines that formed an unyielding gloom under the heaviness of wintry skies. It seemed a place where the sun rarely penetrated and the damp enfolded with chilling intensity.

A glimpse of bright yellow in the distance caught his eye so alluringly that he went to investigate. He waded through the dead fern towards the enticing warmth of this splash of colour in a faded landscape full of decay. There, a solitary birch grew in a sheltered glade, with most of its leaves surprisingly still intact even after Samhainn; protected by the lie of the land and the shield of the pines. Sunlight broke through and hallowed the ground with a delectable radiance. The sickly yellow leaves of the birch were transformed into a tantalising treasure of gold coins hidden in this secret place. He lingered at length, as sunbeams came and faded, watching the gold turn back to a sickly yellow until another break in the clouds showered the small birch with another benediction of radiance.

He felt like that solitary birch, alone and overshadowed in a wood darkened by tall pines. And however obscure the place he had come to, beyond the knowledge of another as to his whereabouts, he felt reassured by the thought that the High King knew precisely where he was, just as the sunbeams illumined the birch.

Eventually, he turned away as the sun had ceased to break through the closed firmament. As he walked slowly back to camp, he treasured the sighting, over and again, as something rare and special, yet knowing it was only a birch that had held on to its leaves in early winter.

Back at the camp, he resurrected the fire from a few smouldering embers, and soon had the wood catching. He placed a pan of water on the flames, seeking the small solace of drinking something hot to try to rid himself of this oppressive cold.

Sipping the scalding water and cupping his numbed hands around the wooden bowl, he stared mesmerised by the glowing embers of the fire.

"Will you not speak to me, Great High King – and show me the way forward?"

The yellow of the fire amidst the crimson brought to mind the stunning sight of that solitary birch. All other details of his surroundings diminished as he focussed on the birch in the pulsing gold of the fire. His soul sought the Presence wordlessly – rather like a child passing through a crowd in search of his parent does not get distracted by other sights, but wholeheartedly pursues that longing to be reunited. His breathing grew shallow, and his eyes, glazed from looking into the fire, cherished the vision of the birch. It was like looking through a tunnel without awareness of anything on the periphery; just an unbroken, obsessive gaze into the pulsing fire from which the birch had now become inseparable.

The light grew brighter, so intensifying that he narrowed his eyes until they were almost closed. Perceiving the extreme glare to have diminished, his eyes relaxed and looked upon a new image. Someone, like a shining being, stood opposite him, resplendent. Again, the light grew so intense that he screwed up his eyes. When the intensity diminished, he saw the shining one brandishing a sword. His face had a dazzling brilliance, and his clothes were as bright as thin cloud suffused in summer sunshine.

He was filled with both wonder and dreadful fear.

The shining one reached out to him with drawn sword as brilliant as the one who bore it. Despite all his military training, facing the tip of the weapon from so extraordinary an adversary made him feel vulnerable. He instinctively reached for his spear. The sword at the end of a fully extended arm did not pose so deep a threat as it would have done if raised to strike a blow. Then the light seemed to intensify along the shining one's arm, shimmering like a molten mass, until the sword glowed with the same extraordinary brilliance. No longer appearing solid, the weapon looked as if it had been taken straight from the forge, rippling like molten metal. When the figure approached, he raised his spear, unsure of the intent of the shining one. The radiant form passed through the tip of his spear like a shadow.

"Who are you?" he cried out, lowering his spear to the ground, acknowledging its uselessness against so other-worldly an adversary. He also felt compelled to defer.

From the sword's tip, there flowed what appeared like a white-hot beam, striking his sword arm with searing pain. The agony penetrated deep, probing through to the very marrow of the bone that had been fractured when he had fallen into the ravine three years previously.

"Have mercy upon me!" he cried, falling upon his knees. The pain had now become so excruciating that he had to surrender in homage to one he knew to be invincible. The face of the shining one remained expressionless, intent on carrying out some undisclosed purpose. The pain had riven his entire arm, and he felt on the point of vomiting.

"Speak, Lord, for your servant listens," he said wretchedly, feeling unable to endure another moment. His head was spinning, and he feared he would faint.

The flow of light from the sword's tip suddenly ceased, along with the agony it had caused. He looked up, and saw the shining one sheathing his sword, eyeing him with a hint of compassion. "Mere mortal, you are powerless before the High King. It is not for you to seek vengeance, nor to take up arms to kill, nor to take a woman to wed."

He acknowledged the statement with a bow of the head.

"As you have found mercy, therefore be merciful. As you have received, so shall you give." Then he added, rather matter-of-factly, "Come and eat."

To the side of the supreme one appeared a lamb, baked and divided in two. He cautiously reached out with his injured arm that moments earlier had felt shattered. He moved it tentatively and noted that the rheumatic ache within the fracture, experienced keenly since camping out, had gone. The limb tingled with vitality. He took a morsel of lamb – which broke away with ease, for it was tender. The meat was exquisite, like nothing ever tasted before. It was sweet, flavoured with herbs unfamiliar to him.

The heavenly being withdrew a couple of steps, and looking as though he was about to leave, spoke: "Taran, son of Nechtan of the noble Ce, chosen heir through the line of Mongfind: seven quests await you, quests that cannot be gained by human endeavour alone. To succeed requires attaining seven heavenly graces. Obtaining each will prepare you for the next quest. Accomplishing the deeds will be the making of a warrior of the High King, leading you to the final task of *bearing fire to the north.* This will be for the fulfilment of your calling *and for the anticipation of the learned ones far to the north.*"

"Lord ..."

He was interrupted. "Do not call me Lord, for there is only one. I am the servant of the Lord."

"What you disclose is full of received prophecies ..."

"Does that surprise you? Even from pagan lips that speak involuntary, heavenly words can be proclaimed. Ossian was merely the bearer, not the author. When you break camp tomorrow, take your coracle and follow the loch to its head. From there, continue up the glen to where two rivers meet in a V. Take the lesser glen, and where the glens branch, again follow the lesser. You are to reach a pass above a pass, where a sign will be revealed. After seeing the sign, return by the same route. And then continue to the end of the peninsula to the home of one who makes his livelihood from the strait. From him you will learn; and to him will be given your next quest."

With that, the unearthly being faded – like a sunbeam was extinguished by the smothering of cloud.

Was it really an angel? he considered. No, it was just a vision, for he emerged from the flames of the fire. But what about the lamb? I could taste that; and my stomach feels satisfied, yet there are no remains – so was that just a vision? But I picked it up with my hands . . . maybe I can still smell the sweet meat. He sniffed his fingers, and they smelt only of wood and humus from handling fire and vegetation. It does not matter, for I have heard what I must do.

Chapter Thirteen

The Rise of the Aspiring Boar
AD 558   Rhynie

"Dada wing orse!" the young Caltram exclaimed, looking to Alpia and Oengus in turn before making a series of small skips.

"What is he saying?" Oengus asked, turning to her.

"Is it not obvious? He is speaking words now, and not just sounds!" chided Aunt Conchen, with an endearing smile.

Alpia found herself smiling too. "He is saying, 'Dada riding horse.' He said 'chicken' just yesterday, and now it is 'horse'."

"Oh, that was what he was saying! I still cannot hear his words that well, although I hear him say 'Dada' a lot."

"Dada was his first word!" she reminded. "He likes his dada!" She looked up, to determe how Oengus would respond, and noted that he was smiling at his son. Then, he swooped down to gather Caltram in his hands – hands that looked so huge to her, clasped about the boy's chest. Caltram laughed as he sailed through the air and came to rest on his father's shoulders, where he muttered 'orse' several times whilst making a pumping action with his body. Oengus proceeded to prance him around the hut, rising and dipping, making Caltram chuckle uncontrollably. And she laughed with Aunt Conchen.

Drust appeared in the doorway. She managed to catch Oengus' unknowing eye, and indicated the direction of the entrance.

"What is it?" Oengus asked his commander, still smiling.

"My lord, Brude has sent men riding up the valley."

The smile vanished from his face. "Are they many?"

"The guard reported about twenty."

"Then they come in peace," said Oengus, relaxing. "Tell the steward to make the hall ready for their arrival, and give instructions for the cook to prepare a meal befitting the overlord's men."

Taking Caltram from his shoulders, he delivered him onto Alpia's lap. "I am coming with you," he said, turning to Drust. He picked up a sword with its belt attached, fastened it about him and wrapped a russet-brown plaid around his shoulders.

"Here, I think you will need this." She handed him a wooden comb and, after a brief rummage, also gave him a polished metal disc.

Oengus straightened his thick mane of red hair as quickly as he could. And looking approvingly into the disc, he turned to her with the raised brows of an unspoken question.

"Aye, it is better," she said matter-of-factly, conscious not to give the impression of strong approval.

Before disappearing from the threshold he looked back at her, whilst braving a brief smile.

"I wonder what brings King Brude's men here?" said Aunt Conchen, looking enquiringly at her.

"I have no idea!" Alpia replied.

"I thought that perhaps you knew," she suggested, meaningfully.

"I think it was as much of a surprise to Oengus as it was to us!"

What was her aunt implying? She finally asked, "And you do not know why Brude would send a delegation here?"

"I do not know! Brude has never been here. His predecessor had, but that was only once. Oh! what was his name?" She knitted her brows.

"Was it not Galam?"

"Aye, that is it, Galam! The Fortriu warlords expect us to be the ones who make the journey between our courts."

They were quiet for a while, feeling a certain tension about the impending arrival. She could hear the commotion and saw figures passing with purpose outside.

"What did you mean by suggesting that I might know something about this visit?" she finally challenged her aunt.

She half-expected an innocent, 'nothing', like most would say in those circumstances, not wanting to be drawn. Instead, Aunt Conchen came over and settled beside her, reaching out to stroke Caltram's hair. It was red like his father's.

"Oengus seems much more at peace with you these days. And, I might add, you with him." Her aunt looked at her meaningfully.

She felt a brief blush come to her cheeks. "Well, I cannot deny that it is easier between us. But there is nothing more to it than that!"

"Oh!" Aunt Conchen let her exclamation hang in the air suggestively.

"And what do you mean by that?" she challenged good-naturedly, feeling a smile play around the corner of her mouth.

"Look, it is only natural. You share a common house, and only go home to yours to sleep. And you also share a boy who is like a son to you, as much as he is to Oengus. You are already like a family!"

She felt another blush, this time coming more forcibly to her cheeks. She flicked her long hair back over her shoulders.

"And Oengus is fond of you," continued her aunt. "He always has been, even in the days when Eithni was alive!"

"That is Oengus for you!" she replied with a touch of disdain. "He has a roving eye, and is an opportunist with women."

"That is maybe so," Aunt Conchen replied without pause. "But I know he has a high regard for you. It is plain to see!"

"Aye, it has always been plain, from the time when he and Taran returned to Rhynie at their coming of age."

"Ah, Taran!" her aunt sighed melancholically. "I was very fond of him. It was tragic what became of him."

"It was evil!" she corrected. "And Oengus had a major part in driving Taran into exile. That is hard to forget!"

"It was your uncle who should take the blame. Talorgen was impressed by unscrupulous ambition. Oengus was always his choice, and there was nothing I could say that would make him change his mind. After that failed ambush claimed such loss of life, Talorgen was anxious to settle the warlordship and confer it upon Oengus. Maelchon was saying that the Z-rod was a deliberate act of the Bulàch to claim Taran for herself. She is a wanton goddess, and Taran was quite the catch." She looked up at her. "You had quite a thing for him!"

"Oengus was not innocent in the whole affair," she said, sidestepping her aunt's remark. "Do you not mind him firing arrows at Taran from the crannog?"

"He is impulsive and a warrior," said Aunt Conchen unexpectedly defending him. "Besides, Talorgen and the druids had already decided that Taran was the one to be sacrificed. That was not Oengus' decision. Taran was already marked for execution, and you could say that Oengus was only playing his part!"

"Aunt, I cannot believe you are saying this! Oengus and Taran were cousins and one-time close friends. Is there not honour in such bonds? No, Oengus was definitely wrong in what he did."

"And are you still waiting for Taran?" her aunt asked after a silence.

"Why does everyone assume that Taran and I were a couple?" She felt annoyed, and was aware that it showed in her tone, more than she had intended.

"Well, you were, were you not!" her aunt said, not so much as a question but as a statement.

"We were just good friends and relatives. Yes, I admit to liking Taran. He was a noble youth, no-one could not help but admire." She looked out beyond the threshold and uttered wistfully, "He loved me, though. It was Taran's unconcealed love for me that made people assume that we were a couple. But I checked his passion, questioning its longevity when it began so swiftly."

"Let me ask you again. Are you still waiting for Taran?"

"No." She could say that without pretence or hurt; something that would have been inconceivable in the year when Taran had disappeared. "Three years have passed now since Taran became a fugitive and, with there being no word from anybody, we have to assume he is dead. That is what I have come to believe."

Aunt Conchen looked down in her lap and unhurriedly agreed with her assumption. "So, my dear, if Taran is no more and you are not waiting for him, what are your hopes now?"

"It is not straightforward, is it? It is a question I have been asking myself. Moreover, it is a question muddled by me being like a mother to Oengus's child." The usual feelings of being entrapped returned. "I love Caltram. He is like my own. It is not difficult for a woman to love a child."

"No, especially after the way you cared for him as a wee bairn. That was extraordinary what you did, strapping himself to you like you did. That saved his life for sure. No one really expected him to survive; and it is all thanks to you! But anyway, would you not like bairns of your own?"

"Caltram is like my own child. I suppose it would be good to have bairns of my own one day, if the gods permit."

She could sense her aunt studying her and still having yet more to say upon so sensitive a matter. Who else could she have this talk with other than Aunt Conchen? And although it was difficult to pursue, she was finding it helpful in putting things in better order in her head.

"Let us talk about Oengus again . . ."

"Must we, Aunt?"

"Yes!" Aunt Conchen said, emphatically. "You have chosen to dwell on all the negative traits and suppositions! Not all which you consider negative, is wrong."

"How do you mean?"

"Take his ambitious nature for example. A leader needs ambition to move his people forward. That is not a bad quality, but a necessary one – something that can be approved, even admired, when right choices are made. Look at what Rhynie has become under Oengus' rule. He has expanded it, built up its defences to be a proper seat for a warlord. He has created a large band of horsemen properly equipped, with armour even for the horses."

"The armour was Drust's suggestion!"

"It might have been Drust's suggestion, but Oengus chose him as his commander. Oengus should take credit for making a wise appointment. A warlord is not just his own person, but becomes the sum of those he chooses to advise him. Oengus has shown discernment, and should be applauded!"

Seeing her aunt's point of view, she did not protest.

"You also accused Oengus of being a womaniser. It is a fair judgement, but he is a young man after all. And, as the warlord, there are women who will lure him on."

"And what is your point, Aunt?"

"Has Oengus ever been inappropriate with you?"

"No! I would not allow him to be," she replied, with her upper lip turned in contempt on one side.

"Knowing how he has strong affections for you, does that not show self-control and indicate his respect for you?"

"Well, I suppose it does," she conceded somewhat reluctantly.

"These things should be acknowledged." Her aunt sat back with a self-contented air.

She felt slightly annoyed by her aunt's clever arbitrations, not that she considered her to be meddling in her personal affairs, but because her words challenged her own long-held assumptions. Oengus had always been regarded as the bad cousin, something of an untamed beast, uncouth, unscrupulous, self-serving; the list could go on. But she could not deny Aunt Conchen's assessment, making her own judgement seem uncharitable, perhaps even unfair. Were his achievements not to be applauded? Had he not always acted with honour towards her? Did he not hold her in high regard, respecting her opinion? She could not deny that she already played a significant role in his life.

She admired Oengus unhesitatingly as a father, when the true substance of a man could be seen without being contrived before the gaze of others. He was down-to-earth and fun, loyal and committed. He was not the brute when playing with Caltram, and could even show tender love. That tenderness was surprising in one who could be ruthless. She recalled Oengus' grief as he cradled her dead friend in his arms. That was a surprising reaction from a man who a few months earlier had spurned Eithni. When he had brought Eithni back to Rhynie, Oengus had been raised in the eyes of the community, but not in her own. She had doubted his intentions, not believing kindness and contriteness could have driven it. She had not expected much from her cousin because she perceived him through Taran's eyes. Now that Taran was dead, should she not reassess her views?

Oengus reappeared briefly in the hut looking for something.

"What do Brude's men want?" she asked.

"Uh! It is the matter of tribute payment."

"I thought you had paid him," said Aunt Conchen.

"Aye, I did!" His rummaging started to become more frantic.

"What are you looking for?" she asked impatiently, rising to her feet to come to his aid.

"The ornate silver cloak-clasp. I thought it was in this box."

"I think it is on the shelf over there." She went over and, reaching up to a shelf that was above eye-level, she felt along the top of the board. "Is this the one?"

Oengus came over and on closer inspection, declared that it was. She handed him the heavy clasp.

"If you have paid him the tribute already, then why are they demanding more?" she asked.

"Oh! Probably Brude considers what I gave him previously was not enough."

He looked slightly uncomfortable, and made to leave.

"And did you pay him the usual amount?" she pursued.

"Well . . ." He stopped short of the doorway, turned and looked her in the face. He looked worried, "I might have withheld a portion."

"Why would you do that with the overlord?" asked Aunt Conchen, slightly shaking her head in disbelief over his indiscretion.

He had no ready reply.

"Because you thought that the Ce are more on an equal footing now with the Fortriu?" Alpia tendered as a possible explanation. She observed him, searchingly, and noticed how his hand tightened around the silver clasp. He evaded her eyes. Although he paused, and looked on the point of replying, he said nothing. Turning abruptly, he left with a determined manner.

"Did you observe that?" she looked at her aunt.

"Yes!" she uttered a sigh. "A case of overreaching himself!"

Being close to the kitchen and to the hall, they could hear all the commotion as the various parts of the meal were prepared and served. Going over to the door, she could see the rear entrance to the hall where two unfamiliar guards stood. One of them bore a shield with the bull emblem of Y Broch on it. "So, Brude's men are standing guard!" she exclaimed.

As it was already evening, the men remained in the hall. She could hear the occasional song from the bard but there was no applause, no spirited revelry.

Fionnoula came later to feed Caltram. He has really out-grown breast-feeding, Alpia thought, but it does seem to soothe him for his night-time sleep. It would not be long before he would be weaned. She watched as Caltram grew sleepy at the breast, and then he was laid down to rest beside her aunt who was already sitting on her bed winding a ball of wool. She decided to retire to her own home.

The next morning, when she reappeared at Aunt Conchen's home, she asked, "Is it not dangerous when a man overreaches himself?"

Her aunt did not reply.

"I mean, when a man overreaches, does he not tumble forward?"

"It is true – Oengus will need to take care. I will talk with him later."

"Did you not see him again last night?"

"No. They were up late in the hall, drinking. Oengus must have gone directly home afterward."

"And did you not see him this morning?"

"No."

"He must be breakfasting with them in the hall." She moved over to the door.

"Where are you going?"

"To observe how things are going." She wrapped the plaid about her torso and added, casting a backward glance over her shoulder, ". . . from a distance, that is."

Brude's official and his men were at the table in the hall with Oengus, Drust, Gest and Maelchon. The Fortriu looked like it was they who were the hosts. Their manner appeared particularly exaggerated, whilst her own people looked subdued and awkward. She sat down with a few others, loitering in the dimness at the rear of the hall, unable to make out the words of their conversation. Matters were clear enough without hearing words. Brude's official was served food first, as she would expect. He immediately set into his meal before the others were served, and did not pay a single compliment, devouring his portion as a man with a big appetite, insisting more be brought. He even demanded wine. How could they drink at so early an hour!

After the meal, the official nodded to one of his companions who produced a large sack into which another man cleared all the plates and goblets with a heavy clatter. She looked at Oengus who appeared inwardly furious, but in fact was powerless. What humiliation, she thought. And what a fool Oengus is for thinking he was bigger than he really is. Will everything the Fortriu delegation has gathered be considered sufficient payment by an indignant overlord? Will the previous failure of paying the full tribute be now considered a debt cancelled? She doubted it. Oh, it would take a long time before Oengus could redeem himself, if that were even possible. What a stupid man, she thought, risking not only his own reputation, but the welfare of the Ce. To think that I had been persuaded to think well of him!

After the valuables had been cleared into the sack, the delegation rose and filed past her with a superior air. They stopped just outside the entrance, and she could plainly hear the official address Oengus: "Show us around Rhynie." He sniffed and pulled a disparaging face. "It is quite the humble place! Lead us along the top of the palisade where we can look over this small community, and assess everything."

She did not like the way the official elongated the word, 'assess'.

When the Fortriu mounted their horses, she joined other curious onlookers at the gate to witness the overlord's men's departing.

"Be sure to send your warriors – and without delay – when we ask. Dal Riata is making trouble to the south; we shall call you, and you shall be there." With that, the official turned his horse and spurred him to lurch forward in a highly spirited manner.

Oengus and Drust lingered at Rhynie's gates, and spoke in subdued tones, feeling piqued by the overbearing treatment from these unbidden guests.

"Things do not bode well!" observed Oengus, aware of stating the obvious. "Brude is out to make an example of us – it is plain to see."

"As it stands now, we do not have a chance of withstanding an attack from the Fortriu. They are superior in number, and can also call upon the Cait to provide men."

"But I do not think he will try to make an example of us, not yet; not before fighting his bigger adversary, Dal Riata."

Drust did not look as if he would respond to this calculation, for he seemed to be pondering something weighty. Finally, he announced, "We shall have to rebuild the fort on top of the sacred hill!"

"Do you think we need to take that measure?" Oengus replied, biting his thumbnail, overwhelmed by the prospect of such a building task.

"Our palisade, although much improved, is vulnerable in the parts to the rear where there is no downward slope. It would be easy for missiles and arrows to be fired upon us from the flat ground behind."

"I see. But the hillfort has not been used in living memory."

"We should ride up there. Much stone has fallen, but the walls are still partially standing. With a big work-team and carpenters, we could get it back in shape. It probably would not require quarrying much new stone; although will require new timber to realign the walls."

"And the building of homes within!" he added, not making so light of the task.

Drust nodded. "Each can build their own. That way, the work will be quick. The fort is a proper defence and large enough to contain all of Rhynie. From up there, on clear days you can see most of the flatter ground to the north, and beyond to the lands of the Fortriu across the waters.

You can even make out the lands of the distant Cait in the far-north!"

"Let us go now and *assess* everything." He consciously aped Brude's official in elongating the word. The visit had intimidated him; but the sense of impotency was being replaced by a bold resolve. He felt pleased to have so quickly found a response to the threat, so that action could replace crippling fear and inertia. More would be needed for sure, he told himself, but this was a bold start. His mind raced on to other ways to counter his neighbour's belligerence.

Chapter Fourteen

Broken Arrow

558 AD   Glen Kilmorkill

"Why must you go? You have only just arrived!" demanded Aleine Brona, confused by Taran's sudden appearance only to announce his imminent departure.

"You were not supposed to see me. I have come for my coracle." He spoke without properly looking up, intent on gathering some belongings. "I am pursuing the same quest as I set out on five days ago."

"You would just come and go ... without greeting me?" she asked quietly, her eyes fixed on him without blinking.

"I know – I should have greeted you. But, I was afraid ..." He stood up straight, giving her his full attention.

"Afraid of what?"

"That your beauty would compel me to remain."

She faintly smiled.

"But I have to leave."

"Stay tonight at least," she pleaded. "I have missed you!"

He paused, warmed by her effusive nature.

"I am sorry, I cannot!" Feeling a choking sensation, he cleared his throat. "I must complete my purpose."

Aleine Brona looked downcast. "Then, you do not love me." She bit her lip petulantly, and a heavy tear ran down her cheek.

"That is not true. I love you, and that makes this quest far more challenging."

"If you love me," she stated with childlike simplicity, "you will stay." There was a note of finality in her tone.

"I cannot!" he protested, struggling with his own inclination to remain with the one whose charms, made all the keener for his absence in the forest, were intoxicating.

"Cannot, or will not?" she challenged.

"I have said that I cannot." He felt like one drowning in circumstances that conspired against him, annoyed at not better mastering the situation. If only he could be more articulate in explaining the conflict between real affection and his spiritual search. "I have two tasks to fulfil, and then another, and so, God willing, after that I shall return to you."

"You say two tasks, but then add 'another'– that makes three tasks, not two!" she protested over what she probably perceived as deception.

Whatever he wanted to say came out wrong and caused more hurt. Aleine Brona stared vacantly down at the bay. He could understand how she thought she was losing him. All her usual vigour had vanished as she hung her head, refusing to meet his eyes. He crouched to peer up into her face, thinking frantically how he might assure her, distraught to have upset the one person he cared for most. He took her in his arms and gave her a comforting hug. She did not push him away but yielded to his embrace.

Still holding her by her shoulders, he stepped back and stooped so that their eyes were at the same level. She looked vulnerable. Feeling most perturbed, still the right words would not come.

He kissed her lips for the first time. They were so soft and yielding that he kissed her again, longer than intended. A powerful intoxication coursed through him.

After their embrace, he felt an extraordinary tenderness towards her, and that they had been inextricably joined together. His chest grew damp with her tears, tears that dissolved his will to continue on his quest. All that mattered was their togetherness. The smell of her hair, the caress of it upon his cheek, the pressure of her body against his – was all so inebriating. For the remainder of that day there was harmony without further talk of leaving.

He had planned to leave the next morning, but on seeing her face, glowing with the warmth of a young woman in love, his resolve just evaporated. She busied herself preparing him breakfast, and he knew such completeness in being cared for, as though they were already man and wife. Like a thorn in his foot, guilt troubled him though, a guilt as strong as his love. Had he not tried to leave? The sorrow of failing vied with the pleasure of remaining. He conceded defeat for today. Tomorrow, he would leave before dawn, before the household was awake.

All morning they were inseparable, sharing common tasks, talking endlessly, taking every opportunity to touch hands or rub shoulders. Come noon, they still had not achieved a single chore.

Girom returned late afternoon with a catch for their evening meal, and asked for his help to fix a fence. The older man halted halfway up the brae, asking "Have you decided?" Girom looked at him sternly from beneath his taut brows. "Will you wed Aleine Brona?"

"I do not know!" He was taken aback by the directness of the question. "I do love her!"

"I can see that! And she loves you. I need your word before your love threatens to destroy the thing it loves. I will not stand by and watch my daughter being mistreated." His voice was menacing.

"Mistreated! Do not be absurd. But, I cannot give you my word."

"What do you mean, man? You cannot give your word about marrying her, or mistreating her?"

"About marrying her, of course!" He now felt heated. "I cannot believe you had to ask me that!"

The father breathed heavily, and seemed to have nothing ready to say.

"I have three quests to complete first," he explained, trying to reason with him. "If I were to say I will marry her now, then I abandon the King's business."

"This is foolish talk," remonstrated Girom, his face flushed afresh. He raised his voice, "Stop this talk about your King! Your King does not rule here; we do not recognise his overlordship and we will not bend the knee to him." He wiped some saliva from his lips with the back of his hand. "I have been reasonable, treated you as a son, taking in a ragged wanderer, clothing and feeding you. You eye the one who is precious to me, my only daughter and the last of our offspring. I cared for her following her accident and held nothing back. I will speak straight, so that my meaning is clear. Either you marry Aleine Brona, or you leave!"

The summons was hard – its timing deplorable. To follow the King meant losing Aleine Brona, although maybe only for a time. Could he not trust his King to work things for the good, eventually? But he remembered the angel had said that he would not wed Aleine Brona. Who was he to obey: man, or angel? Put like that, his choice was clear and he made it known.

"Then you are no longer welcome here. By the Bulàch, you will not rest another night under my roof, nor sup another glass of mead, nor take another crust of bread or pinch of salt. Take your coracle and be gone," adding in a most disparaging tone, "you warrior of Christ. You have dishonoured my hospitality in taking liberties with my daughter."

"I have done no such thing!" he replied hotly, "although I could have done, had it not been for my Lord." He looked at him in dismay. "You can discredit my Lord, but know this, if it were not for the King, Aleine Brona would still be crippled! Heed your words less your insults turn out bad for you." He took a deep breath and continued, riled by the unfairness of accusations. "I have received your hospitality; you have received the sweat of my labour. You have taught me to fish; I have shown you and your sons how to craft arrows that will reach their target. This is a fair exchange, and I do not think there are debts I owe. There is nothing for me to feel guilty about, for nothing shameful has been committed." Taran turned to walk away.

"No one talks to me like that!"

Girom forcibly grabbed him by the arm, and turning him, threw a wild punch. He ducked, narrowly missing what would have been a punch that would indeed have floored him. Taking hold of Girom's arm, he wrenched it around his back with difficulty, locking it into place, and managed to seize Girom's other arm. He held him in a posture of surrender. The older man was powerless.

"I leave of my own accord, for no man sends me away," he breathed heavily. "I heed my King's summons, not your false accusations." Feeling Girom's resistance slacken, he released him; then made for the house to take his belongings placed to one side for the departure he had been putting off.

"What has happened?" entreated Aleine Brona.

"I am sorry. I have to follow my King – though it breaks my heart!"

211

"But it is nearly nightfall," reasoned Alma.

Just then her husband appeared in the doorway, confronting him.

"Move aside."

Girom breathed heavily, filling the threshold threateningly.

"In the name of Christ, move aside – I choose to show no violence."

"Papa, what are you doing? Why are you behaving like this?" demanded Aleine Brona.

"What is happening?" Alma appealed, fraught by what looked like a skirmish about to erupt. A torrent of questions and exclamations from the two women followed without let-up, which allowed no opportunity for response.

"For the last time, in Christ's name, step aside!" Taran demanded, raising his voice over the womenfolk. "You have been warned three times and that is my final warning."

Girom bowed his head, as though tired of resisting, and stepped aside.

He moved past, with his arms full of the things he needed for his journey, and walked swiftly down to the bay to where his coracle lay upturned.

"What sort of power did you place upon me?" Girom shouted after him. "I had no intention of standing aside!"

Without turning, he remained alert to every sound and prayed that violence could be avoided. He heard Girom shouting as Alma cried out for an explanation, mixed with Aleine Brona's shrieks. He pushed out in his coracle into the bay. Looking over his shoulder, he detected figures running through the twilight from the neighbouring huts.

The water lay languid in the bay as his paddle with its figure-of-eight strokes formed spinning pools of turbulence. The discord faded as he withdrew and, by the time he reached the wooded islands standing sentinel at the extremity of the bay, the brief twilight was almost spent. His refuge of the past months was only discernible by two flickering tongues of flame from handheld torches, small in the great darkness of the winter's night. He plied his paddle purposefully in the direction of the head of the loch, as the shining one had instructed him, looking along the dark reach of the sea wending its way deep inland.

Benefitting from the flow of the rising tide, he slackened his strokes, plying his paddle more for steerage than speed, resting from his exertions for a while. The waters became turbulent mid-channel, but aided his course towards the hidden head of the loch. The shoreline, with its lofty hills reaching up into the night, was etched in a jet-black silhouette between the dull lustre of the water and the night sky faintly illumined by the first stars. He passed islands and skerries; and upon reaching the narrows of the straits his craft, caught in the tidal race was propelled swiftly through onto the upper reaches of the water.

Having found his second wind, he settled into a rhythm, paddling with purpose while the tide was still rising, propelling him far inland along this sleeve of the sea.

When the water slackened, he observed that it must be near high water. Tired from his exertions, he placed the paddle inside the coracle and looked ahead. The rising hills of the glen at the loch-head arched with grandeur, dark against the night sky.

"Just a little way further, and then I can rest on the shore."

Soon, he felt the pull of the ebbing tide as the waters began to drain back through the narrows. Later, when he had reached the shore, he walked beyond the high water mark, and finding a tree with a branch protruding over level ground, he secured his awning. He spread out his possessions. Due to his abrupt departure he had brought no food, but reflected that he had eaten three wholesome meals since returning from the forest. Moving about his camp, he found a dead shrub and some dry grass, and soon had a fire burning on the threshold of his camp. He lopped some limbs off a spreading juniper, and lay on these for his bedding, wrapped in his plaid. The sudden turn of events caused him to groan, recognising that he was deprived of what most men enjoyed and took for granted. He prayed for Aleine Brona's well-being.

Tired from waking many times through the night, he broke camp in the bone-aching damp of early morning. He could hold his head high before Girom's insinuations. Although he might never be justified in the eyes of others, he took satisfaction in knowing his innocence was known to the King. He need not fear for Aleine Brona's well-being either; for her father was a good man, and life would become normal once his temper had abated.

As he plied his way up to the loch's head waters, he relived his fraught departure, the stand-off with Girom and the hysteria of the women. The sense of personal loss was immense. Such an ultimatum had abruptly put an end to his wish to manage things well. Images and sounds of conflict, replayed over and over again, drove home the huge loss of what he held most dear.

He prayed for calm, for the High King to take charge of his thinking; but the images continued to haunt and mock. He was an exile once more, alone in a coracle in the vast emptiness of the loch, beneath imposing hills and the illimitable sky. Here, there was no sign of human life. His spirit reached out to the Presence striving for that connection which would enable him to view things as seen from the throne room of heaven.

Reaching the end of the loch, he secured his coracle onto his back with a strap around his forehead, and picked up his possessions. He shouted out his anger as he stumbled over the shaly sands and mud of a river's delta. His voice sounded small in the vastness, lost in this desert expanse between the water and firm land. Reaching a stagnant creek, he boarded his coracle and paddled into the marsh maze of languid watercourses – and before long arrived at a dead end. He attempted to wade across the marsh but had to give up, impeded by deep, stinking mud. Frustrated by this futility, he returned to the loch head and took a different stream of this ribboned delta – a course that was somewhat broader, penetrating into the marshlands. Unlike the former, this waterway turned a bend and joined a river whose shallows, although impeding progress, opened a way inland.

The river ribboned like a snake along the flat basin at the start of the glen. With marsh all about he remained in the riverbed, paddling his coracle where he could, but otherwise wading and using the line to tow his craft containing his possessions. He arrived at a confluence, where a swift mountain stream had deposited grit and pebbles, an ash tree grew with drooping boughs, reaching elegantly towards the ground. Hanging his leather awning to dry from a branch, he strung his bow and crouched concealed amidst a nearby reed bed. Watching a dipper sport under the water a few feet off where the mainstream flowed with purpose, he felt encouraged by the example of its spirited display. He scanned the riverside for something worthy of shooting for food. The mournful, soul-wrenching cries of a skein of geese, rhythmically passing overhead, deepened his sense of wretchedness. He considered trying his luck at spearing one of the fish that he could see occasionally darting among the shallows before him.

No! I'm tired of eating fish; he craved meat. At the back of his mind, though, was his poor hit-rate at taking fish from a stream. He had a lengthy wait, contending with his gnawing hunger, before hitting a duck. The gathering of firewood, lighting a fire, plucking, and preparing the bird were tasks that took up the remainder of the morning. After eating, he snoozed beside the fire.

He awoke cold, smelling of woodsmoke. He prayed, asking for strength and a cessation of the previous day's events being replayed as an endless cycle. He pressed on with renewed determination, reaching a loch where he could paddle in a straight line without hindrance. Beyond, progress was slow again with the coracle bottoming out on shallow sandbanks and boulder fields.

Coming to a steep brae where a stream tumbled down between hill flanks, he wondered if this was the glen he was to follow, indicated by the shining one? It rose precipitously, soon losing the character of a glen: for vast crags barred the way. Surely it could not be that one, for no subsidiary glen branched off from it, and he also noted that the confluence did not form the V-shape that he was instructed to look for. He pushed on upstream and came to the confluence that fitted the description. To his right rose a steep-sided glen cutting deep into the mountains before disappearing out of sight. The November light was dwindling; and knowing nightfall to be nigh he made camp. He felt disappointed not to have travelled far that day, but acquiesced as he realised it was warmer to camp down in the valley than to make for the cold of the heights.

After praying, he managed to reflect on the previous day's events more philosophically, thankful to see the endless cycle of his thoughts had finally been broken. He recognised that a decision he had found difficult to make had been made for him. A bad experience had worked for the good. A semblance of growing acceptance, emerging from his rationalising, created an island of peace amidst the turbulence of his emotions. Once again love had been thwarted – and he wondered how much longer he was to wait before a settled life could be his.

The next day broke with the brooding gloom of low cloud dark upon the hills, making him feel apprehensive as he recalled past ordeals under the duns of the gods. He prayed for vigilance to walk in the way indicated and to see the sign upon the high pass. Going about breakfast preparations, he continued to pray, "I will kindle my fire this morning, knowing the favour of a loving Lord upon me, the friendship of the Son to walk with me, and the helping hand of the mighty Spirit to guide."

He resented having to endure further tests in the mountains: reluctant to leave the warmth of his campfire. Then, he reminded himself that *white martyrdom* involved hardships, that to overcome these would require his spirit to focus on wanting to know his King the more.

I need the mindset of my military training, he told himself. Hardships can be faced and overcome with the right attitude. But if I cannot do this, then failure will follow for sure. I need the right desires that Fillan has urged me to adopt, to order my thoughts, and have the right objectives. I need to rein in my emotions if I am to counter self-pity.

Looking up to the foreboding cloud lying upon the high ridges, darkening the fawn-coloured land below, he prayed aloud, "Although the sun does not shine upon my glen, your light still shines supreme beyond the clouds of doubt that smother my way. I shall not fear the gloom, the setbacks, for I determine to persevere."

He broke camp, leaving his few cooking utensils placed under his upturned coracle, hidden in a thicket of shrubs not far from the spent ash of the fire. The way was hindered by dense bracken and trees clawing at his body and catching at times on the leather awning and bear-skin draped over his shoulder. Further on, where the trees thinned, the ground became difficult with tough, tussocky lumps of grass catching his feet among bog-filled hollows. A lynx trotted briskly across the open landscape, several times its head turning in his direction. He used his spear as a steadying-staff and reached a vantage point from where he looked back. The river valley was already a good distance below.

"O great King, strengthen my spirit to push on, whatever the effort to rise to the heights to which you call me. May I tread the crags like a mountain goat, and move swiftly like a deer across open ground."

As the upper glen came into view, he clearly saw the subsidiary one to the right, *the lesser glen* of the angel's instruction. The incline was steep, but walking over the short grass growing close to the mountain torrent, made for an easier way. Even the boulder field further on presented no real obstacle, as he skipped from one to the next. It was not long before he had reached the pass, clear now of the earlier cloud and revealing a steady descent into the forest on the other side.

I am to climb to the *pass above a pass* where the sign will be revealed. The instruction is clear, but I remember nearly missing the description that led to the Stone of Refuge – I was not being so vigilant back then. I wonder though on which side this higher pass may lie?

Hills rose on both sides. A lower ridge-like section became visible beneath the lifting cloud, and thinking this might possibly be the *pass above a pass,* he ascended towards it. He climbed briskly, and after a while, he arrived at a level area where sections looked as though they had been laid out into a stone pavement. Although roughly set, they had a flat, slab-like appearance, criss-crossed by scars; striking him as being unusual. He slowly paced the pavement, curiously trying to determine if the scar-formed patterns could indicate the sign.

Cloud smothered the peaks on either side; and having ceased to climb he began to feel cold. Wrapping the bearskin tighter about his neck, he secured it in place about his waist with a cord. Not a single tree grew from which to suspend his leather awning, nor was firewood to be had to light a fire. A cloud of mist, sweeping up from the steep gully to the south, enveloped the pass in a murky, twilit world.

"How can I see the sign if the pass is shrouded in cloud!" he complained aloud.

Shivering, he took to pacing the ground, still attempting to 'read' the slabs for a possible sign, as mist continued to pour steadily over the pass. He reached the far side where fallen boulders upreared spectral heads in the gloom, and there spied a cleft, large enough for him to enter between two large sections of rock. Within this niche, out of the wind, he unfurled the leather awning. Draping it as a hood over his head and wrapping the folded bulk about him, he kept warm for a good while until his inactivity and the freezing weather started to take their toll. Crouching, he brought his knees up to his chin, and adjusted the awning to shut out every perceived draught. He prayed to concentrate his mind on something other than the cold.

"Majesty and mystery are in this place of swirling cloud where mortals never tread. Make me alert to view what you will reveal, not to be blind to what might be obvious or easily passed over."

Still he saw nothing. Sleet blew on the wind and settled on the short grass, but thawed upon the rock. Aware that his feet were growing numb he grew anxious, wondering how much longer he could endure these inhospitable heights.

A little while later, driven by the numbing cold, he cast off the leather awning and ran back and forth across the flat ground many times until he started to warm. He flailed his arms and could feel his cheeks thawing from their frozen ache. The flurry of sleet that had settled on his pelt started to melt from his hair.

When the shower had passed, the mist thinned and began to disperse. The straight pavement of stone, traversing the pass and dipping into the gully, was highlighted by the sleet that had only settled on the grass about it. Again, the stone pavement seemed curiously significant, although he could not detect any sign. The daylight was dimming and the cold began to assail his limbs once more, bringing thoughts of descending to camp for another night in the shelter of the forests far below. He could hunt and cook, and warm himself by a fire – and then return tomorrow.

It is probably about timing, and today is just not the day! He recalled how his delay on Rùm had meant meeting Aleine Brona on Inis Kayru. Then a less pleasant thought came . . . what if the delay at Girom's household had caused him to miss the sign? Had he jeopardised his *white martyrdom*? Angry, and recognising that he could not remain at that high pass, he went to retrieve his awning from the cleft. With difficulty, he folded the leather now made stiff with the cold, and draped it over his shoulder: before he turned resolutely to the pass. Again, he was struck by the sight of the stone pavement, clear of sleet, that formed a clear V-shape.

"The V-rod!" he exclaimed out loud. "Does it not represent a broken arrow or a bent sword?" He considered how warriors would heat a prized sword in burning charcoals and then beat and bend it until it was rendered useless into a V-shape to present as a costly votive offering, then thrown into the depths of a loch or thrust into a bog. He had seen that sign before on his adventures in the Minamoyn Goch when approaching the Stone of Refuge, struck by the two courses of water that had formed a V-shape, running down the great sloping wall of rock below the corrie. Had that not been a great turning point, raising his hopes? It was there he had met Ossian, who strengthened his arm when most in need.

He recalled the shining one's words: *As you have found mercy, therefore be merciful. As you have received, so shall you give.* He considered what further significance it taught, keen not to miss its intended meaning.

It is not my votive offering of a ruined sword, or a broken arrow, but one made by another. Therefore it cannot be my pleading for victory over my foes, for I am to be merciful as is befitting of a warrior of Christ.

The image of the spoiled weaponry made him recall Fillan reading a scripture about swords beaten into plough shares. Living by the sword had to be renounced, for those who did not do so would die by the sword. Scripture, which had often been hard to recall down at Girom's home, now came with greater ease and clarity, charged with significance.

What if the V-rod is offered by the High King, as his pledge of victory for me?

For a time, he could gain no further clarity. He walked on purposefully, frozen to the bone.

Did the prophetic words of Fillan's prayer not indicate something about my surrender and obedience? My will is to be surrendered so that the intentions of the King shall prevail. If I follow him implicitly in all things, his Spirit shall be my guide and victor. If I exercise self-control and resist vengeance, then this heavenly sign indicates that I will be given victory over my adversaries.

Words of a scripture that had impressed from the earliest days at Dindurn, came to mind. *Not by might, nor by power, but by my Spirit, says the Lord Almighty.* He smiled with the dawning revelation and exclaimed aloud, "By heaven's might, not by my own endeavour, will I succeed in this quest of *bearing fire to the north.*"

Domech's ways came to mind, illustrating the lesson well. For all of the Fotla's impressive strength, the vigilance of their intelligence network and the wiliness of its ruler – the sum of all these strengths was nothing when confronted by the power of heaven. Fillan always remained one step ahead, enabled to know the secret thoughts and the whispered words of scheming men. He considered too how he had been enabled to outstrip Domech's men in his own flight to Dal Riata.

The High King is strengthening my arm at such a time when I am homeless, dispossessed, torn from the girl I love; when I am a pitiful adventurer, barely holding body and soul together in these raw elements! How alike my situation when I had fled from the crannog, stripped of position, family, tribe, and of Alpia!

For a moment, he felt he was starting all over again, sensing its apparent futility – until he remembered that the battle is not always won by the strong, but by the favoured, by those who are meek, aware and reliant upon the Presence.

His ambition to seize the rule over the Ce finally expired on that pass. "Who are the Domechs and Oenguses of this world? What is their power? But what is the significance of my bearing the Z-rod if I am not to rule?"

Taran 'the de-prized prince' was laid down to rest; and Taran, the wandering pilgrim with a warrior's spirit, emerged resurrected from those ethereal mists. He knew the favour of an invincible Lord and protector King.

Chapter Fifteen

Strengthening of Hand

558AD   Rhynie – Migdele

"You can see almost a day's journey from this height," Oengus remarked to his commander, raising his voice to be heard over the din of the hammers and chisels of the masons. The resurrection of the old hillfort upon the Pap of the Bulàch, with additional fortifications, was well underway.

"It is a fine vantage point when the weather is fair. Here we can better withstand any assault," expanded Drust.

"Look-out sentries will still be required along the Spey to relay any significant movement of men from the Fortriu, for we cannot depend on clear visibility at such a height!" He rubbed his cold hands energetically together.

Drust nodded. "It is cold up here, even though it is summer! We shall have to hope that we do not need to take refuge here in the winter. Traditionally though, warlords go to war in the spring!"

"Aye," he assented thoughtfully, "but we cannot depend upon that; not with the likes of Brude."

"Then we should ensure a plentiful supply of firewood and provisions to withstand a winter siege. Mind you – it would be tough for an attacker as well, to withstand the winter blasts up here!"

"We must be prepared for any eventuality so that we are not taken by surprise." Seeing the overseer of the building works behind his commander, he caught his attention, "Uuid! Do you think this fort will be ready by Lughnasa?"

"That will be, what, seven weeks away? Yes, lord, it shall be ready before then. As you can see, work has already started on the buildings upon this summit."

"Many of these, though, are outwith the fort!"

"We are too many to all build within the fort. For this reason, we have put up an additional wall."

"The rebuilding of the walls is looking particularly solid," remarked Drust, nodding his head approvingly.

"We have interlaced the stone with timber to give it form and make it more robust."

"I can see that," he said approvingly, placing his hand along one of the horizontal timbers. "Good. We shall celebrate Lughnasa here. Ensure that things are complete enough for us to stay overnight upon this hill."

"They shall be. The work has progressed fast since you brought in the work-parties from afar."

"That is the way to ensure a job is done quickly," Oengus felt the pride swell within him. "We learned that from how quickly the palisade extension about Rhynie was completed."

"And various homes are already taking shape," observed Drust. "There is a good supply of timber here! Ensure that a huge store of firewood is gathered, at least enough for three full moons."

"Yes, lord – it shall be done."

He clapped the overseer of the building works on the shoulder, glad to leave it in capable hands whilst he turned his attention to other pressing matters.

The following day he rode with Drust to Cynbel's court, together with Gest and an entourage of bodyguards. It was summer, and warm breezes winnowed through the long, wavering stems of the barley, promising a good harvest. It felt like heaven's fortunes were shining upon him, for additional grain would be required for winter provisions should there be a siege.

The Lord Cynbel received them civilly and with all the due courtesy towards an ally and a brother-in-law. After the preliminaries, Oengus cleared his throat to state his business. "Brother! Are you aware that there was a raid last week? Some of your people crossed the Dee to waste crops and lift our cattle!"

"No!" He looked visibly surprised. "That should not be. Where exactly?"

He indicated the region, upriver from the ferry-point that he was well familiar with.

"It shall be investigated and the cattle returned. I will see to it that extra are given by way of compensation for the spoiled crops."

"Good! We want to avoid the return of the old days!" he added meaningfully.

"Indeed. We value our alliance – peace is prized between our peoples."

Oengus paused ponderously, weighing the matter that had really brought them to Migdele. "Our alliance is being tested by this incursion, and I have had to restrain my people. In Talorgen's day, he would have sent a party across the Dee to spoil your land. Now, though, we seek cooperation."

"Quite!" Cynbel exclaimed emphatically.

"It is good that we are of the same mind, which brings me to another matter, brother."

He noticed that Cynbel looked at him with slight unease. So, the old mistrust was still there. But that was natural, for the animosity between their peoples had been long-standing and trust takes time to build.

"The Fortriu are behaving belligerently towards us, so much so that we have had to add extra fortifications in case we need to defend ourselves."

"I see. I thought you had an alliance, you and Brude?"

"We do, but he seems to be wanting to make a name for himself!"

"He is not a peaceful man," Cynbel uttered with contempt.

"I am glad that you can see that." Feeling his mouth go dry, he took a mouthful of ale given upon arrival. "We would request your assistance should things come to a head."

"How do you mean?"

He detected the old suspicion again. "Let me speak plainly. Should the need arise, would you send us two hundred men to Rhynie!"

"Two hundred!" The old warlord looked aghast.

An uneasy silence between them ensued. Deciding to say nothing, he forced Cynbel to answer.

"We are a peaceful people," Cynbel stroked his white beard, regaining his equanimity. "As you know, we follow Christ and do not seek conflict."

"And nor do we!" he interjected with visible indignation. "You will recall that you made that observation about me previously, congratulating the new era of peace between our peoples, which I will remind you I brokered."

"Lord, if you permit me to speak." Drust addressed his words to Cynbel. "It takes two to keep the peace and only one side to make war. Brude is a menace and an opponent to peace."

Cynbel nodded in acknowledgement. "I am aware that there are skirmishes on Brude's border with Dal Riata. That, though, is so far away that it is hard to understand the true situation. Brude will say that the Dal Riatans are expansionists, seizing new coasts. However, Dal Riata is a Christian realm, and if truly Christian, will not be looking for a fight!"

"Do you think so?" he questioned dubiously.

"Well, maybe not. Old ways die hard!"

"As you can see, things are uncertain, hanging in the balance," added Drust.

Oengus's impatience was rising. "What do you say about two hundred men to help defend our land and our people."

"Two hundred is absurd. That would leave me with insufficient men. What if Domech, hearing about it, should push forward his advantage?"

"And if Brude goes unchecked and the Ce fall, that leaves the Circinn next on his borders . . ." Drust lent forward to drive home his point.

Cynbel thought for a while and finally uttered, "I do not like it!"

"We do not like it, either, but this is the unpleasant truth. Your brother is being threatened, and I would at least expect a better understanding!" He could feel his face flush as he curbed his indignation.

"Do not speak like that!" Cynbel's tone was conciliatory. He lent forward, stretching out a hand.

"How do you expect me to react if you refuse us help? It is as though there is no alliance between us!"

"We have shown restraint," reminded Drust, "by not retaliating after your border incursion."

"There is no need to speak like that!" retorted Cynbel.

"Then show your hand of friendship, brother." He fixed his brother-in-law with a stare and perceived that Cynbel was reconsidering. A tense silence ensued, awaiting the Circinnian's response.

"I could send you fifty men," offered Cynbel, leaning back in his seat.

"What are fifty men," he retorted with a contemptuous snort, "when Brude will field hundreds!"

"As I said, I cannot leave myself exposed to the Fotla."

"Listen, brother," he continued, eager to share a new thought. "If the Fotla were to attack you, do you think we would even hesitate to come to your aid if asked?"

"And it would not be a mere fifty men!" added Drust in a tone that ridiculed so small a figure.

"Well, maybe we could spare seventy-five."

"That is better, but it is not the two hundred that we request!" Drust rubbed the back of his sunburnt neck with a huge hand.

"Let me speak with my commander, and see what we can muster." Cynbel rose and left them.

Drust lent forward and spoke in an undertone lest anyone could hear. "Maybe we can fashion an alliance, agreeing a fixed number of warriors that each would send to the other when under threat. So, if the Circinn are to lend two hundred men, we would likewise provide two hundred should Domech threaten the Circinn."

"That sounds good," he agreed, glad to see how the threat from Brude could be contained. "Do you know what else I am thinking?"

"What?"

"That we should extend this tour and speak with the king of Dal Riata himself."

"That is a long way!"

He could tell from Drust's tone that he was indicating the distance more, rather than state an objection.

"It is good thinking, though," continued Drust with a wily grin. "Make a friend of your enemy's enemy!"

"Precisely."

The two men talked about the journey, estimating its length, approximating when they would return to Rhynie.

Cynbel returned to the hall with his commander.

"We could spare a hundred men," announced the aged warlord.

"Although that is better it is still only half of what we requested!" He straightened himself in the high-backed chair, keen to bring the matter to a proper conclusion. "We have a proposal. Drust, set out the plan."

Drust outlined the terms of an alliance of matching like for like in manpower should the need arise on either side. Cynbel consulted with his commander.

"Put like that, then let us agree to a hundred and fifty, but that is our final offer. I will not spare more."

Drust conveyed, with a look, that it was an acceptable offer, confirming his own take. "Then we are agreed."

"I have another condition," added Cynbel.

"What is it?" It was Oengus's turn now to show the old mistrust.

"That you agree to have the instruction of a soldier of Christ at your court."

"Ah!" Oengus exclaimed involuntarily. He glanced behind to where Gest was seated.

"The Ce have our own spiritual guidance," remarked Gest, addressing Cynbel. "We follow the age-old ways in the tradition of our forebears."

"I know." Cynbel nodded with understanding. "And so did we until recently."

"But why turn your back on the Bulàch? She provides fertility for our cattle and ensures our crops prosper."

"That was our opinion too, at one time. But look at us now! Did you not notice how the fields are ripening with grain? The harvest looks particularly promising this year! Does that not show the favour of Christ?"

"Our own crops are looking equally good, thanks to the Bulàch," interjected Oengus.

"I am only indicating that although we have turned from the Bulàch, we have suffered no retribution from the goddess attributed with fertility." He looked at them with an air of confidence.

"Would you excuse us a moment?" he said to Cynbel.

Taking Gest to one side, he said, "Although it is not an agreeable thought to have to suffer the instruction of a soldier of Christ, it is a small condition for a significant gain."

"Oengus, I must protest! We should not trifle with the Bulàch — it will lead to retribution."

"I understand, and I know that you have to say that as my druid!" He winked at him, and placed a conciliatory hand upon Gest's shoulder. "But we are only paying lip-service to this request. We shall not change our ways, I assure you."

"But even giving ear to another teaching will arouse the Bulàch's jealousy."

"Oh, I do not think so. I will renew my vows to her before the soldier of Christ comes, and afterwards when we send him away. It would merely be a ruse. If our neighbour is only asking that of us in return for an agreement of one hundred and fifty fighting men, then why should we not agree? We only have to listen to what the soldier of Christ believes — but we will not change. It is a small ask."

"It seems you have made up your mind. But let it be known that I have warned you, and I have no part in this agreement!" Gest slightly shook his head, stepping back disconsolately, and lurked in the gloom near a corner of the hall.

He stood quietly for a few moments with his back turned to Cynbel. Going over to his druid friend, he placed a hand upon his shoulder. "I am sorry, Gest. You are my friend and ally from the beginning and I do not like to cross you. Brude's threat though is so great that I cannot do nothing about it."

"Aye, do something, but not this!" His eyes looked distracted, not settling on anything although they momentarily looked into his own. "It would be better to re-build your alliance with the Fortriu, for like us, they are not turning to new gods."

"I know the argument, and that was Talorgen's choice; but it puts us in a subservient role. That is not what we have been working towards these past two years." He realised that Gest was quite opposed to his wishes. But as much as he would have liked to have agreed with his friend, he also realised that to forge a stronger alliance with the Fortriu meant undoing what the rising boar had been working to achieve. He walked over to Cynbel, aware that Gest had not followed.

"Well, do you agree to the terms?" Cynbel asked, curiously.

He nodded, feeling the disquiet in his spirit with Gest not agreeing. Somehow I will show him that my allegiance has not changed, he pledged.

"Then let us seal this agreement with a drink," Cynbel announced cheerfully, and came forward to embrace him.

Later, he quizzed the old warlord. "Do you personally know the king of Dal Riata?"

"Aye, we are acquainted."

"Would you give me a letter of introduction to him?"

"Well, yes. But what is your purpose with him?"

"If we are to consider being a Christian realm, then it would be useful to make his acquaintance!"

"Then you should also go to the courts of the Fib and Din Brython. Both are following *the way,* like ourselves, but for much longer, particularly in the case of the Britons."

"Are these realms not a little far off?" questioned Drust.

"You would naturally pass that way when going to Dal Riata! Unless you want to chance journeying through Domech's lands." He grimaced. "I would not advise that."

The route they would take was indicated and Cynbel was glad to provide letters to the warlord of the Fib, as well as to the kings of Strath Clud and Dal Riata. "They will receive you well and provide for your needs."

Oengus felt much had been gained, more than had been originally envisaged when setting out to Migdele. He might not have achieved quite the number of warriors he had hoped for, but he was extending his knowledge beyond his immediate borders and intent on courting the favour of new warlords who might be of help. If he had to pay lip-service to the Christian way, then why not? – if it meant new allies to shore him up against Brude. The once disagreeable idea of having a pilgrim instruct him back at Rhynie, suddenly appeared useful, so that, in time, he could be familiar with their beliefs, and able to converse credibly with these Christian warlords.

Indeed, much has been achieved, he thought to himself, considering how he was bringing the Ce out from their insignificant backwater and into the main current of world affairs. Suddenly, the future seemed brighter, less overshadowed by Brude, although also still acknowledging the threat that remained.

However, the following day, Gest declared that he would not continue on the journey to the courts of the Christians, insistent that since his counsel was held of no account he was returning to Rhynie.

Chapter Sixteen

The Waterfall

558-9 AD   Loch Aloninn

Returning from the mountains, Taran approached the islands out in the bay where Girom and his kindred lived. He thought of turning aside – for he longed to see Aleine Brona. But what of Girom's wrath? Surely, he will have cooled down, he hoped. As for himself, he could hold his head high before false accusation, knowing that he had brought no dishonour on their household. He dithered, indecisive, beyond the islands out in the bay.

This desire, though, did not sit easily with following the quests the shining one had assigned. Fear of having possibly missed the sign upon the pass, due to his delay with Aleine Brona, persuaded him to continue along the coast, reluctantly conceding that love was a distraction to his immediate purpose. The shining one's instructions had been to continue to Loch Aloninn at the end of the peninsula, to the home of one who made his livelihood from the strait between the mainland and Inis Niwl.

He journeyed into ever broadening expanses of water, under the watch of the conical peak with its top sliced off – that now had become a visual reminder of the High King's faithfulness. With the completion of the first quest, could he not trust him more? All the uncertainties ahead were only 'unknowns' from his limited perspective; but for his High King with his illimitable panorama, there were no constraints.

Arriving at the narrows of Loch Aloninn, he found no evidence of the ferryman.

"There is no ferry nowadays!" he learned from an elderly woman.

"Is there still a ferryman alive?"

"You know Carvorst?" she asked, with mild interest.

"Not exactly, but I have heard of him."

"You will find him in the hut over there." She pointed to a dwelling whose thatch looked the worse for wear. "Come, I will introduce you. No doubt he will be glad of company. He took ill many weeks ago, unable to get out. He is in a fair wretched state, without livelihood and dependent upon the goodwill of his family."

Coming under the low opening into the dim interior of the hut, she called out, "I have brought you a visitor!"

A man was sitting close to the hearth in the centre of the hovel, his knees tucked up under his chin. "Bring him closer," came a rather thin voice. "I cannot make him out."

"In you come," she gestured to him impatiently. Turning to Carvorst, she said, "I will bring you that cabbage I promised you the other day." With that, the woman left.

He stepped forward into the light of the fire. An emaciated man confronted him, with a shock of wild grey hair matted with ash. Carvost must have been sleeping close to the fire to have ash in his hair, he thought.

"I am Taran," he introduced himself, wondering how best to proceed. "Do not trouble your mind trying to recall who I am, for you do not know me!" This did not sound an encouraging start, even to his own mind. "I have come to see if I can be of help."

There was a lengthy pause before the dejected man asked, "Why would you help me if you do not know me?"

"Someone who knows of you told me to come."

"And what is his name?" It appeared to him that the old man was having trouble focussing, and frowned.

"I never learned his name. He told me that you run the ferry across Loch Aloninn to Inis Niwl," he stated a little uneasily. He suddenly changed the subject: "You do not look too well! How long have you been sick?"

"Och, these past few weeks! Something within my belly hurts. Even the slightest movement upsets and causes weakness!"

"Do you stay on your own?"

"I do. But I have neighbours – most are my kinsfolk. They keep an occasional eye on me."

"Is no one prepared to keep up the ferry crossing?"

"No. Word is about now that there is no ferry, and so folk are making other arrangements."

He thought for a moment. "What would you say if I were to run the boat again and bring you the proceeds to help you be better fed. You are not looking strong – and although I do not know what you looked like before, you are thin, very thin."

"And why would you do that?" asked the old man suspiciously.

"To earn my keep so that I might stay under your roof these winter days. Food and warmth are all I seek."

Carvorst studied him, then turned his face dismissively away with a sullen expression. They sat in an awkward silence.

"I see that you distrust me!" he observed aloud. "Who would not, given that I had no introduction. I will be frank with you . . ."

"Aye, do that, young man!" Carvorst spoke with a sense of finality.

"Some days ago, I was in the hills, not far from here, seeking my purpose in life. I had been fasting for three days, when in a vision I saw a shining one, bright as the sun . . ."

"A shining one, you say?" queried the old man, with renewed curiosity.

"Aye. He sent me on a quest, instructing that when completed, I was to come *to the home of one who makes his livelihood from the strait.* So that is how I was led to your door. I am a man of peace, and bear only good intentions."

The old ferryman looked him over with an incredulous air.

"Give me an opportunity to show I mean well," he implored mildly.

"A shining one, you say?" – the old man's eyes looked lustrous in the fire glow. "That is strange – I dreamt of a shining one the other night! The dream made such an impression, and although I wanted to pass it off I have not been able to, for it offered a token of hope, that help was at hand. If you had not mentioned the shining one, I would not want you staying under my roof. But it must be the gods who gave this sign and sent you here."

"Can I stay, then?"

"Aye, you can, for who are we to resist the gods and expect things to go well!"

Taran became the ferryman. Although there were hardly any passengers at first, the two who next day did use his services provided the food they ate that night. As the boat was leaking, he made it more sea-worthy by caulking the seams with a mixture of sheep's wool and pine resin. Over the following days, word spread that the ferry had resumed.

Carvorst found it difficult to fend for himself; so much so that after a day of running the ferry, Taran also cooked for and tidied after the old man. He wondered how this could be when most of Carvost's neighbours were his kinsfolk? He felt indignant having to care for so unwell a man. Carvorst's neglect seemed strange – since he had stepped in to help, the scant help from his family had come to an end. He felt taken advantage of. There seemed no limit to Carvorst's needs, requiring assistance even in going to the toilet.

"I am sorry," Carvorst muttered. "Believe you me, I would rather you did not have to do this!" Carvorst's embarrassment was so great that it seemed to make him reluctant to speak much, or to even thank him.

Taran struggled to be gracious, helping another in so intimate a detail. He had been trained to be a warrior, and although that was not to be, he questioned whether there were limits to being a saint. Despite his aversion, he pitied the neglected man and performed this service. He reflected, philosophically, that his only other option would be to fend for himself in the wilds during a long winter that was fraught with a damp cold that seeped into his bones.

"I am more or less useless to anyone now!" remarked Carvorst, despondently – "My kinsfolk must be thinking, why go on feeding the old blighter when he will probably not pull through this winter? Why waste precious food, during the lean season, on one who will not be fit to return the favour? That is how their minds work, and I suppose, who can blame them? I am a lost cause!"

"No, no one is a lost cause!" he returned emphatically. "Although I am young, I have been through much. I have been brought so low that I have wondered how I could survive." He spoke about breaking his arm and how he had found refuge with Coblaith and Elphin – giving credit to the High King in bringing him through such ordeals.

"Who is this High King of whom you speak?"

"The true God!" He went on to relate his sea exploits and how they had led to his arriving on Inis Kayru; and then he told him all about Aleine Brona's healing.

"I have heard about that. So, you are the miracle worker!"

"No! The power was from Christ. That incident made me a true pilgrim."

"If this Christ has power, then maybe he could heal me?"

"We should pray and hope."

Despite his faith that had seen Aleine Brona walk, his prayer was not answered. Daily, he prayed for Carvorst, sure that the King was testing his persistence before finally granting them their hope. The disappointment was keen.

Feeling that he had failed in his prayers, he questioned what sort of pilgrim he was? Why did healing power come for Aleine Brona but not for Carvorst? Although coming to terms with the practicalities of remaining in Carvorst's home, he did feel uneasy about being drawn into a situation without knowing how long he would be needed. Being unable to see the end of things brought consternation – for how would he become free and move on?

When considering things from the old man's point of view, he saw things differently. He understood Carvorst's humiliation at being dependent upon a stranger and felt the sting of rejection from his own kin. This human empathy caused him to want to know Carvorst, to draw out his life story, to hear about better days and to see beyond this malfunctioning body. This process helped restore Carvorst's human dignity; and he responded to this kind treatment, becoming talkative and showing a will to recover, even challenging himself to do chores about the house, most of which he accomplished.

He thought much about Aleine Brona, with her just being a short distance along the coast. Every time the urge came to set out, a contrary thought would resist. He felt caught hopelessly between desire and self-restraint. Girom's ultimatum to marry his daughter, or to leave, had presented a stark choice. He wrestled in prayer, and by degrees, gained a certain acceptance, and along with that, peace. He acknowledged that his life had been set on a new trajectory since the Z-rod was tattooed upon him, ultimately making him a fugitive, dependent upon strangers like Coblaith, Fillan, Girom . . . and now Carvorst. This *white martyrdom,* without a permanent home in this world, formalised his status as a pilgrim.

At times it felt a high calling – like being set aside to become a warrior as a boy of six. Still, it was a costly one, requiring denial of a normal life. When sent away from the family home as a child, he had cried, finding little comfort in his foster-father's reasoning. Now, as a grown man, he had to apply reason, rebuking himself for thinking that he was destitute. Had not Fillan reminded him, that at the low points that he was not alone? With the knowledge of the Presence with him, he hoped to strengthen himself. Upon the pass, he had been shown the broken arrow pledge of victory, conditional on his maintaining that surrendered, dependent state, of walking in *the way*, a lesson begun from the time of his flight from Dindurn.

As Carvorst improved with his care, he showed interest in the young man's life. Taran was open with him. Maybe it was the vulnerability of the older man that broke his reserve, but for the first time since leaving Coblaith, he became totally transparent with another, relating all his circumstances and his struggles. "Surrendering ambition has been hard," he confessed one evening, "but renouncing love for Aleine Brona is as difficult!" His brow furrowed, "Sometimes it keeps me awake at night!"

"That is the way when you are young!" Carvorst nodded, which Taran thought implied recollection of his own distant struggles.

"I wonder where my life is going? What is to pass next, do you suppose?" he mused aloud, watching the tongues of flame lick the logs on the fire.

"I would not worry too much about what is to come," replied Carvorst in a matter-of-fact tone. "Destiny works its own way out, irrespective of our wishes and efforts. Better to focus on today. Work hard to provide for today; and tomorrow will come soon enough, with fresh challenges that we are better off not knowing in advance!"

"That is true enough," he nodded, "except that I do believe effort can change things."

"That is only partly true. For years I had strength to row the ferry, provide for my family, and all is well. Then sickness strikes. Within days, my strength is gone and my kinsfolk do not want to know me. I thought I had reached the end of my days when a shining one appears in a dream, followed by a stranger appearing at my door! That is what I mean about destiny playing a part that we do not control."

"I am grateful to have a place for the winter," he replied with genuine feeling. He had rowed the last ferry-crossing of the day in driving sleet. "Fire and shelter are my rewards. There is always enough food, unlike some days last summer when I slept under a coracle on an empty belly!" When he maintained this perspective, his spirit quietened within him.

He recognised a growing fondness for the old man, that caring for his needs was no longer done so much out of duty, for Carvorst's well-being now mattered to him.

As he presented these matters to the King, he found consolation and an ability, strange and unexpected, to deal with the sense of bitter loss. But not long after grappling with the issue, the loveliness of Aleine Brona and her understanding nature, haunted him with renewed vigour. Her soulful look, the eyes of a young woman in the flush of first love, were images difficult to eradicate. He knew a sense of completeness when with her, and he longed for those times.

One day when he was down at the jetty, a voice hailed him in a friendly manner. He knew the voice and looked up with a degree of trepidation. As Girom drew near, he noticed the man's expression became serious.

"I was unjust with you. I have come to ask your pardon." Taking hold of his hand, Girom wetted it with his tears. "You were sent and healed my daughter. You removed the curse that had descended as a blight upon her young life. You restored my broken daughter, and she blossomed into a beautiful young woman." He paused to control his emotions. "Whereas, look at my response! I falsely accused you and drove you away. Will you no come back again?"

"Come, my father, do not be anxious. These things have passed!" He was about to add that no harm had been done, but checked himself. Although no one had suffered bodily harm, he had known much anguish. The same would have been true of Aleine Brona.

"Can you pardon me for my foolishness?" Girom fell to his knees.

He found himself involuntarily saying, "As the Father has forgiven me, so do I forgive you." The words felt liberating.

All-pervasive was the need to forgive, suffused with a love hard to have perceived before this encounter.

"I am sorry I have maligned you and your God." Girom rose to his feet and brushed the dust from his knees. "Will you no return to our home?" Without waiting for a reply, he continued rapidly, "We recently heard that some young stranger was ferrying passengers across the straits to Inis Niwl. I reckoned that it was probably you." Girom was excited and agitated, continuing without pause despite his attempts to interject, ". . . Aleine Brona is still awaiting you." Then lowering his voice, he lent forward and uttered, "although, truth be said, she has perhaps lost hope – I have caused that. Once I knew you had not taken advantage of her, I wanted to make amends. Will you no come back?"

He felt confused. Why this sudden turn of events? – and just when he had recognised the need to renounce this girl.

"I am not saying you are to marry her immediately," continued Girom, playing with a cap in his hands. "Come under our roof again, and let it be as it was. Alma very much wishes it so. And as for Aleine Brona . . . What do you say?"

He looked at him with incredulity. "You are presenting everything on my terms. A few months back, this was everything I desired." He looked wistfully beyond Girom's shoulder to the ruffled waters of the strait. "As I declared back then, I cannot marry Aleine Brona – and that has not changed. My destiny lies elsewhere."

"All because of your King?" Girom spoke without his former disdain for the Lord.

He nodded, noting the gentleness in Girom's tone.

"You are very devoted."

"The King is committed to me, and has not failed me. By his grace I am alive, and no longer am I full of hatred and vengeance. I have received mercy and now am enabled to show mercy. I have been preserved through all kinds of trials, more than most could bear, exceedingly more than I could have borne on my own. Yet I am here, wiser, at peace and serving my King."

Girom grunted. He looked at him with a side glance, "It seems that you have made up your mind."

He nodded, suppressing his natural instincts.

"Would it make a difference if I were to say that Aleine Brona now worships Christ rather than the Bulàch?"

"Then I am thankful that she continues to trust and that my being with your family has brought life to more than her limbs." It had been simple to say, but deep down he felt the age-old ache for a companion. Sensing his imagination about to run wild in presenting all kinds of possibilities, he checked their riotous course.

The older man stepped forward, embraced him, and departed with tears in his eyes.

That evening, he told Carvorst about Girom's visit.

"You are a good man!" remarked Carvorst.

"I am not good. Left to my own devices, I would probably hurt many people."

"That is what I mean! You are a good man because you exercise self-control. To control anger and lust is to become master over yourself."

"It is not enough to master oneself. I only succeed because I have a Master over me. I am accountable to him, and he gives me strength."

Carvorst smiled approvingly. "I was not like that as a young man, I got myself into many a difficulty by not reining in my passions. Fights were fought, and liberties taken with girls. But you are different. You have followed your king, who as you say, has become your master, and I can see that he sustains you. Will you teach me to pray?"

Taran smiled, and said that he would.

The weeks went by, days and nights of great storms were followed by days of grey calm and a rippling of silver around the straits. The mornings grew lighter, and days lengthened with the sunshine gleaming on the wetness of sand and rock. And the hills were swept clean with the keen wind, blessed by warming rays of light. The season brought a sense of renewal to man in these northern climes.

Taran noted that Carvorst was able to do many chores, eradicating the image of a bent old man, he now held himself erect and spoke with renewed determination. He thought he looked ten years younger.

After finishing evening prayers together, the old ferryman cleared his throat and pulled awkwardly at the loose skin on his neck.

"There is a strange thing I feel I have to tell you."

"Oh? Go on then," he encouraged, sensing the hesitation.

"Tomorrow, you are not to take the currach across the straits. I do not really understand this, for you are to sail down Loch Aloninn to the isles at the entrance to a lesser loch. It is a narrow but quite lengthy loch, leading into the hills. From the loch head, you are to walk to the highest waterfall."

"Thank you! The shining one said that I would be directed to my next quest by the ferryman."

Carvorst looked with a sense of wonder.

He left in the currach, straight after breakfast, following the instructions. By late morning, he reached the isles on either side of the narrow loch and turned the boat into the opening.

"How's the fishing?" he greeted some men who had a net stretched from shore to a boat.

"Not bad. It is better now the tide's rising. Where are you off to?"

"I am looking for a waterfall!"

The man laughed. "There are many waterfalls in these parts!"

"I am looking for a great one beyond this loch. Do you know it?"

"Why would you go looking for a distant waterfall? They are everywhere – which is not surprising given all the rain."

They parted. The rising tide made it easier for him to pass through the narrows into broader waters. He rowed, and by the time he came to more narrows the tide had started to slacken, requiring more strength to reach the loch's upper reaches. As the tide began to ebb, the sand banks and mud flats at the loch head began to be laid bare.

He pulled the boat beyond the seaweed-strewn high-water mark, and walked to the confluence of two rivers beyond the loch. Not knowing which to follow, he crossed the mouth of one and suspended the leather awning from a tree, spreading over an inviting patch of ground. He carefully examined the pools and shallows upriver, and saw a good-sized trout and bided his time to spear it.

With firewood in abundance, he had a fire in his camp and a fish to grill. He took a nap under the awning, and awoke as the sun sank behind the snowy hills, which cast a freezing shadow over the land. Building up the fire, he wondered whether the bears were still in hibernation and in case they were not, he took some small comfort in the protection of the fire and spear, recalling Aniel's way with animals. The night was cold and so damp that he regretted pitching camp between two rivers. Intermittent sleep meant that he could feed the fire through the night. During his morning prayers, a young, fair-haired stranger hailed him from across the river. "Where are you coming from?" he enquired.

"From my land upriver. What brings you here?"

"I am looking for a waterfall, the highest one in these parts. Do you know of it?"

"There are many waterfalls here," the man began reflectively, and Taran anticipated being teased again. "There are a series of waterfalls along the north side of the river, but they are not as high as the ones opposite. There are at least three significant waterfalls on the south side. The last of these is the greatest."

"How will I know the way to the third and last of these waterfalls?"

"That is easy. The streams that flow from the waterfalls travel straight to join the main river, whilst the stream from the great waterfall makes a dog-leg shape around the jutting foot of a mountain spur. Follow that. It is steep, and it will take you up high. You will hear its roar before you see it."

"Can I get there and back in a day?"

"Oh, hell yes! . . . unless you are sickening from something!" The young man looked at him a little incredulously before going on his way.

He took with him a spear and some day-old bread. And he set off along a well-trodden path through the woods which soon brought him to a cultivated field, probably belonging to the fair-haired man. The land was good, enhanced by soil washed down from the heights. Beyond the fields, a waterfall came tumbling down halfway up the hillside. From there, the hills closed in, and the forest became dense. A wintry wind whispered mournfully in its stirring crest. He felt he was an intruder, and the chill penetrated through to the marrow of his bones. He crossed several streams, wondering which had flowed from unseen waterfalls. It seemed a lengthy walk before he reached the dog-leg indicator to the big falls. His way climbed up a steep and narrow gully to the snow line. Fresh traces of wolf prints and hare criss-crossed the way. Further up, he disturbed a small herd of deer who made a noisy escape through the forest. The fast torrent of the swollen stream twisted to the right, and as he rounded the bend the distant roar of a waterfall raised his spirits.

At the foot of a high crag, he caught sight of a vast plume of falling water that at times seemed momentarily suspended mid-air before striking the rocks below with a thunderous tumult. He stood amazed at the height from which it fell. Upon the fringes of this water plume, he watched with fascination separate cascades that descended with slender meteor-like trails only to disperse, seemingly into the nothingness of a mist, without reaching the base. The extreme narrows of the gully reverberated with noise, which seemed to him to contain the echo of the roars which had tumbled in that secret place throughout the centuries. Hidden from the haunts of man, and powerful in the extreme, the waterfall held him with a force that was beguiling.

"Who could resist?" he shouted above the cacophony of sound. "Who could withstand your onslaught?"

The forest could not stand its ground in a place dominated by water that uncovered the bare groin of the hills.

"*Deep calls to deep in the roar of your waterfalls; all your waters and breakers have swept over me.*" He chanted part of a psalm and, although unable to recite more, he recalled that it echoed parts of his *white martyrdom*.

A dense mist rolled up from where the waters came crashing upon the rocks, feeding the mosses and keeping the ground clear of snow. Icicles had formed: whole clusters, thick and some gigantic in length, hanging above the steep valley sides, poised like an array of weaponry. As the mist billowed up and enveloped him in its pure and freezing embrace, he felt imbued with its irresistible power – not a force that would slay him, but an energy that imparted its vitality. Kneeling in homage to the Presence, he felt suffused by a warm sensation, in contrast to the cold of the gorge that tingled through every fibre of his being. This sense had a personality which struck him as the might of God's love. It descended and flowed over him, washing and renewing him as in a baptism. The fantastic roar, obliterating all sound but its own, was utterly compelling and became all-consuming.

All beaded by the mist from the falls, he beamed with wonder as he made his way slowly from the gorge.

Chapter Seventeen

The Dress of Purple

558 AD   Rhynie

"Where have you been?" Alpia greeted Oengus on his return to Rhynie.

"Our travels took us further than envisaged." He threw back his head with an easy-going laugh. "We went to Dunadd!"

He looked tired but pleased with himself, which further roused her curiosity. Caltram had rushed to greet his father, fastening his arms around his legs and pressing his cheek into the side of his lower thigh. Oengus quickly cast off his plaid from his shoulders and scooping his son up, raised him towards the apex of the roof. Caltram laughed, and as he was lowered, reached for his father's neck to give him a hearty hug. She was aware that Caltram had missed him, uttering 'dada' every day of the absence. Oengus looked absorbed receiving his son's attention, and although she was bursting for news about these far-off destinations, she too could not help but admire a father's delight. This overdue homecoming was a relief, for the responsibilities of raising Caltram could be shared again. His presence brought a sense of completeness to the family unit.

"Why would you go so far?" she asked, unable to contain herself longer.

"Alpia! It has been a most worthwhile visit." He looked at her with a broad smile. "First an agreement with the Circinn for military support; and then we met with King Gabran MacDomangart of Dal Riata."

He did look very pleased with himself, she thought. "What is the Dal Riatan king like?"

"A man of strength, for sure, in an expanding kingdom. He has quite a fleet of boats, able to move his fighting men quickly. He is like an overlord within his own realm; for the land is far-reaching, scattered over many islands, and there are other strong lords, each controlling their own clan lands, but subservient to him as their king. He has strong ties with Erin too. His arm continues to stretch north along the coastlands, beyond the Great Glen, including many an island. No wonder they cause Brude concern! And he is not afraid of Brude either! It is like King Gabran is spoiling for a fight, confident to emerge the victor. Living in peaceful co-existence with Strath Clud leaves Brude as his only adversary."

He took a piece of cheese from a cloth, cut himself a large slice and ate it with hunger, but continued to speak with animation. "We also stayed at Din Brython twice on our travels. What things we have seen! Foreign vessels loaded with fine clothes and wine, glassware and gems! These ships call almost daily into their ports – and you should see how these kings are apparelled! Even their court officials wear foreign finery! I felt quite the peasant from the hill country!" Throwing his head back, he laughed generously.

"Blind should be the eyes in the abode of another," she quoted, mindful of how Oengus' head had been impressed. "Did they look down on you?"

"No, not at all. They were curious to learn about the Ce, knowing so little about us. No, they accorded me much honour and served me strange meats at their table; and oh, wine like I have never tasted before!" He went on to describe at length various table delicacies.

"I take it that it was not just a tour of curiosity?" She felt impatient to learn more.

"Listen, I will tell you all. But first, I have brought you a present."

"For me?" She was genuinely surprised, and watched Oengus go through his belongings to finally pull out a package of purple fabric, neatly tied with twine. He handed it to her with a flourish.

"Go on – undo it!" he said impatiently.

Her hands felt the fine material, the likes of which she had never touched before, and undid the simple knot holding the package together. Holding it up, the fabric unfurled before her in a cascade of purple finery. It was a long dress, embroidered lavishly with gold brocade around the neckline. An additional section of brocade tapered down the front of the dress. Such exquisiteness was unimaginable.

"Oengus, I cannot accept it!" She lowered her arms.

"But why? It is only a gift. I bought it with only you in mind. Who else am I going to give it to – Aunt Conchen?" He laughed nervously. "It would be too small for her." Oengus looked slightly taken aback, clearly not anticipating her reaction. He did not convey annoyance, or disappointment; but his look insisted that she should keep the dress. As she said nothing, he shifted somewhat uneasily, seemingly questioning whether he had done right.

"Oengus, just tell me about your visit – not about the finery you have been dazzled by! You know what we were taught as youths, *character is better than wealth*. Tell me about the agreements you have reached. That is what most interests me."

"Truly?"

"Yes! I am not a dizzy young girl whose head is turned by a fine article of clothing." Becoming aware of her fingers caressing the quality of the fabric of the dress upon her lap, she placed it to one side.

"You do not like the dress?" He sounded genuinely disappointed.

"It is very fine. But tell me, what did you learn from King Gabran?" She heard the note of impatience in her own voice.

"So, you might accept it?"

Ignoring the comment, she compressed her lips and turned towards him with growing expectation. Caltram was sitting peacefully on his father's lap, and she wondered how long he would be content to bide there.

"There are no agreements as such, except with the Lord Cynbel . . ." He proceeded to outline their understanding.

"And you would have a soldier of Christ come to Rhynie?" she queried with surprise.

"Oh that! Cynbel was keen to include that as part of the agreement, and it seeming a small matter in return for one hundred and fifty fighting men, I agreed."

"That explains why Gest came home from Migdele!"

"He was not pleased." She noticed that his eyes slightly clouded. "Of course, he has to take that line – he is a druid, after all! But we are friends; and he will understand. Besides, I have vowed to remain steadfast to the Bulàch."

"And Maelchon?"

"I will talk it through with him, and will do whatever is required to maintain our position with the Bulàch."

"You seem confident that you can appease Maelchon."

"Times are changing, Alpia; and we have to move with them. All those who can help us are Christian realms."

It seemed to her that Oengus had carefully weighed the matter and was not responding impulsively.

"Something else that I have observed," continued Oengus, "is how well connected the Christian rulers are with the world beyond the lands of the north. They also have scribes who draw up agreements and write clear laws for their subjects to adhere to – it seems a great idea. There are things we can learn from them without having to turn from the Bulàch, things to prosper us and make us stand proud – even before the eyes of our enemies."

She deliberately changed the subject. "You will be glad to know that the work is completed on the hillfort, including the extended ramparts that enclose the new settlement. I took Caltram up there the other day. It is quite a steep climb but looks impressive."

"It is well-situated. Our ancestors appreciated what a defensive position it is."

"The hall is complete and thatched. Things have been made ready to celebrate Lughnasa."

"Good." Oengus beamed with the air of someone establishing himself, not just as ruler over the rising boar, but appeared to Alpia as one who was confident in taking his place among the rulers of the north. "Well, Caltram," he said, rising, and placing his son down on the ground. "I must leave you for the moment. I should speak with Maelchon." With that, he took up his plaid and left.

Alpia admired what he was achieving without resorting to force, and it surprised her. Oengus was maturing from the brash, hot-headed boar he had started out to be. Recognising he did not match the strength of the bull, he compensated by being astute. Were boars not known for their intelligence? She checked this unexpected enthusiasm, recalling his miscalculation in reducing the tribute payment to the Fortriu. Had that not been a lesson for him? He may have emerged from the situation, reeling; but had it not spurred him on to act more wisely? His actions added to his acclaim for reversing the petty skirmishes with the Circinn. Had he not proved himself as a visionary with his newly trained fighting force and elaborately constructed defences? Was the balance of power about to shift in favour of the Christian rulers? With their prestige growing, Brude's threat would perhaps wither; especially if Dal Riata were able to put Brude in his place. Their own position, though, still felt precarious. However, Oengus seemed to be keeping his head, acting intelligently to secure their position.

Aunt Conchen appeared from visiting a neighbour.

"I hear Oengus has returned?" her aunt remarked keenly.

"Oh yes. You just missed him."

"How did he look?"

"A little weary from his travels, which is not surprising since he went all the way to Dal Riata!" She updated her aunt on all that she had learned.

"What is that on your lap?" Aunt Conchen asked curiously.

She looked down, surprised to discover the dress was on her lap again. "Oh! something that Oengus acquired at Din Brython!"

"Let me have a look." Aunt Conchen came over to inspect the garment. "My! what a beautiful colour . . . Purple is costly! Oh, and it is so fine to touch!"

"I am not accepting it!" Alpia added quickly.

Her aunt took the garment from her, holding it up to admire its whole form. She lingered in appreciation of such rare finery, before carefully folding it and handing it back. Alpia received it, putting it aside dismissively.

"It is quite the gift!" said Aunt Conchen, breaking a silence.

"Yes, and for that reason I cannot accept it."

"I see," she remarked with a judicious air, sitting down next to her.

"Caltram! Do not touch that!" She rose, and took a sharp kitchen knife from the small boy. He cried, so she found a small basin which she placed on the ground and filled it with some water for him to play with instead . . . "Look! You can float your boat on the loch," she said, placing a bowl in the basin.

"He obviously thinks a lot of you!" continued Aunt Conchen, fondling the purple dress.

"Well, you know Oengus!" she remarked dismissively.

"He has always had a tender spot for you, my dear!"

She grimaced.

"I know that it was not welcome in the beginning," her aunt rapidly continued. "And quite rightly so."

"Aunt!"

"Yes, I know. I did not think well of Oengus either back at that time. But he changed his ways and that should be acknowledged. You know, I remember a discussion with him back in those early days when he realised that the course he had taken was damaging his reputation. He put off emulating your uncle and chose a new style of governing, leading to where we are today. He has learned to use his head more than his arm – which has not been natural for someone as impulsive as Oengus."

"I have to agree there. Oengus has changed. But I cannot accept his gift. I mean, it would be declaring that I am now his woman if I were to wear it!"

"And is that such a bad thing?" Her aunt studied her with a lingering stare. "Are you still waiting for Taran?"

"Taran!" she returned impatiently. "No. I accept that he has perished. Besides, we were never a couple!" She rose from her crouching position beside the basin and flicked the water from her hands a couple of times. She saw Aunt Conchen pass her a knowing look. "It is true! We were never a couple – how many times do I have to declare that!" Her protest felt in vain.

Aunt Conchen did not contradict, but observing her look, it appeared she thought otherwise. It was wearying to have people being presumptuous, thinking they knew better than she knew her own feelings. Well, maybe she did have a high regard for her vanished cousin, but hope had died – and she was relieved that he no longer came to mind, or that when he did, thoughts of him did not cause her unrest. Taran was just a faded memory, a pleasant although melancholic one . . . consigned irrevocably to the past.

"What are you going to do with your life?" Aunt Conchen pursued afresh, as one who was not going to let go of this unwelcome discussion. "A young woman has a limited time to turn heads!"

"Aunt!" she said in protest.

"Who else will you have this conversation with, disagreeable though it be to you?"

She was right about that, she thought. Had she not become like a water-skin that because of a jammed stopper no one bothered to pick up? Her aunt knew her well and loved her like a daughter. As she trusted her, should she not receive her insight on the matter? Had her homely wisdom not turned a head-strong ruler into a discerning one?

"Go on, then," she replied with a degree of resignation, but not wholly closed.

"I take it that you do not have your mind set on becoming a spinster – few women do – it is one of those things that unhappily befalls a woman."

"It is true, I should like to have my own bairns one day; although, Caltram is like my own son."

"And do you have your eye on anyone?"

She felt herself flinch inwardly at having to endure this probing. "No. There is no one who remotely comes to mind."

Her aunt studied her for a moment, in no hurry to pursue her line of argument. When she did speak, it was gentler with the voice of tried reason. "You know, we can become too choosy for our own good, looking for perfection in a man. I mean, has there ever been a man who is perfect – or even one who has come remotely close?" She threw back her head slightly and laughed. "As for us women, there are one or two who come close to sheer perfection!" She laughed again, and Alpia found herself smiling.

"Oengus," Aunt Conchen continued, "has changed for the better. He is teachable, at times demonstrating that he is open to instruction and correction. A man needs a woman to steer him, otherwise he is like a boat without a rudder, thrashing and splashing away in every direction with a lot of commotion and little direction."

Again, the two women laughed.

"Alpia, you have been in this household for some time and have witnessed the rule of your Uncle Talorgen and the uneasy handover between him and Oengus. You have observed the rise of the boar. You have looked on, watching men blunder and at other times managing to do a half decent job. You are clever, my dear, and can be a force for good for the Ce."

Aunt Conchen raised her hand to the objection that she was about to make, insistent that she had her say. "I speak from experience – a wife has a leading role to fulfil, in influencing events by tempering the choleric feelings of her man. You have seen that with your uncle, and surely have noted that there were times when he did adhere to my reasoning!"

Alpia nodded, recalling several instances.

"Some women marry for love!" Her statement came emphatically, stating a new direction. "But not all. Love can be so blind, unseeing what a man is truly like, wanting to believe the best, believing that what they see is truly what a man is. But men are flatterers, skilled at saying what we want to hear, practised in the art of deceit. How many of your friends can you count who have gone into marriage all dreamy-eyed, to wake up the next day appalled by the uncouth beast they have married! But you, my dear, are not so controlled. You see what a man like Oengus is truly like, and have not had your head turned by flattery. You can refuse even so costly a present as this purple dress!"

"Yes, I have refused it!"

"Marrying for love can be a big mistake. I speak from experience. And having made my bed, I had to lie in it and make the best of things."

"Knowing what you know now, are you saying you would not have married Uncle Talorgen?"

"Probably I would have declined him. But, as I said before, a wife has a pivotal role – a sacred role, appealing to the Bulàch in mediation, seeking wisdom. Unwelcome as the marriage was at first, I came to discern my purpose and, because I was sometimes able to influence events for the better, I no longer despised my marriage."

She folded her hands upon her lap and shifted her posture round to face her more directly. "Anyway, enough about me, it is you we are talking about. I do wonder whether the Bulàch has chosen you for a mediatorial role in the household of the warlord! You are practically that person already, eminent, a mother to Oengus' son . . ."

"I know," she interrupted, "and I do not like that assumption!"

"And, I am going to add," Aunt Conchen went on undeterred, taking hold of her hand in both of hers, "Oengus cares about your opinion. He is malleable, respecting your cool, intelligent head, seeking your approval. In a way he is the perfect husband, one who is open to your influence; and you are the perfect wife, not dominated by your heart, not eager to please your man, knowing your destiny is to steer the passage of the warlord through troubled waters."

She clearly understood her aunt's rationale. It had been eye-opening to learn about her aunt's true thoughts about marriage to her difficult uncle. How often had she looked up to her, admired her gracious ways and gentle but persuasive manner. What she spoke about love echoed her own observations when considering how Eithni had been allured by the wily Oengus, and then had been compromised, trapped and rejected. That kind of love was something to be avoided. Anyway, it was unlikely to happen to her, even with the charmer that Taran had been, enthusiastic to win her. No, she was not like Eithni, or many of the other young women in Rhynie, eager for a man. She was cool-hearted as well as cool-headed, she surmised, and a likely candidate for remaining a spinster. That was an unpleasant prospect . . . not that becoming Oengus' wife appealed. She was in quite a dilemma.

"I will leave you with these thoughts," her aunt concluded, moving to the edge of the seat. "I see these words are still unwelcome, but they are worth weighing up. You could have quite a destiny before you."

"Is everything ready?" Oengus asked at the threshold, turning back to Alpia.

"Caltram, you hold this." She handed him a small bouquet of wildflowers picked earlier. "Hold on to them. Do not drop them until we reach the top of the hill. Dada will carry you on his shoulders."

Taking hold of the flowers, Caltram did a little dance on the spot.

"I have the barley sheath, the first fruits of the harvest cut earlier today, and a blaeberry cake baked in a skillet. Yes, all is ready." She looked about her, seeming to question whether she had overlooked something, whilst fastening a basket over her shoulder.

They left Rhynie, joining a line of people climbing the Pap of the Bulàch. A group broke into song ahead, chanting rather raucously along the way until coming to the steep ascent. They veered off along an offshoot to the sacred spring, following a well-trodden way by others who paced sunwise around the source. Offerings of flowers strewed the grass beside where the water came bubbling up from the breast of the hill.

On reaching the newly-raised walls of the fort upon the summit, they joined the crowd gathered about an open trench.

"Caltram," Alpia spoke to attract his attention. "Throw your flowers in there as an offering to Lugh."

Oengus led him over to the trench, where the young lad happily released the small bouquet he had been holding firmly all the way, adding to the many offerings of grain and flowers in the shallow trench. He watched Alpia offer her small sheath of barley and noticed a copious amount of blood staining one corner of the trench. That, he thought, will be where they sacrificed the bull earlier. A waft of cooked meat confirmed that preparations were near complete for the feasting.

Now that the warlord was present, along with most of the community, Maelchon addressed them from the far side of the trench. "We celebrate this day, commemorating Lugh's victory over the hideous race that opposed him and his people. Today, Lugh symbolises our strong champion who rescues the harvest from the clutches of the lord of the underworld. Let us invoke his name as we pray."

Raising his arms, Maelchon lifted his voice. "O Lugh, the bright one of skilful hand, prevail against the threat of blight, or storm, that these first fruits offered may be the promise of a full harvest. Protect our crops! May the grain become fully formed and be abundant to sustain us through the long winter."

The chief druid sang something, but the words were not clear. He tried to be joyful, but his rhythm was sometimes lethargic. Was that significant, he thought, or is it just Maelchon's morose nature, incapable of singing with joyful abandon? He noticed Gest gesturing to someone in the crowd, who emerged fully clad for combat, with a sword still belted about his waist and brandishing a spear. The warrior bounded with lightness of foot into the human arena, raising a war cry. Running up to a human effigy at the far end of the trench, he proceeded to make various acrobatic leaps about it, turning in the air as his spear came close to piercing its victim. His warrior's dance was skilful and elaborate, entertaining to watch, making people smile and some to even laugh. He made the most of his part before finally dispatching his victim, raising a cheer.

All eyes were fixed upon the two druids busy discussing something, concluded by Gest picking up a large, round garland. The sun had sunk behind the hills in the west and lighted the horizon with what looked like a vast forest fire burning along its ridges.

"Spread out and form one large circle," ordered Gest, making a sweeping gesture with one hand. "As you know, the garland represents the wheel of the year. Whilst waiting your turn to receive it, bring to mind the things that have been accomplished this year and what you would like to take forward. Give thanks to Lugh, and invoke his craftsman's skills to help you in the things yet to be done. *Beware what you wish for, for the gods may grant it to you.* Pray too for the gathering of a bountiful harvest."

The garland was circulated. On receiving it, he inspected it briefly in the fading light, it was heavier than it looked. Outwardly, it was woven from braided rushes and straw; but within, short, thin sections of wood had given the frame rigidity and weight. He considered this year had been like no other — with many accomplishments, not least the completion of the hillfort, a strengthening of an alliance and the good favour of far-off warlords and kings. Even Alpia was friendly.

What would I take forward? he considered. Consolidating our fighting force to withstand an attack. Brude presents my only threat to what otherwise is a peaceful rule.

His hand combed through Caltram's hair, and he looked down upon him with pleasure. He is of age to join me on forays into the woods. I will make him a small bow and show him how to fire arrows. His thoughts wandered, anticipating what knowledge and skills he would pass on and how he would instil in him the pride of being one of the Ce. Caltram, in time, would take his eminent place.

Having completed a whole revolution about the gathering, the garland came back to Gest. Twilight was fast encroaching, smudging out the details of everyone's faces. "The wheel has passed beyond its zenith. Lughnasa represents the downward turn as the growth slows, whilst fruit matures and grain reaches its full ripeness."

Maelchon came over with the brazier.

He noted how it always seemed to be the function of the chief druid to tend to the fire. He watched them kindle a flame and then set light to the wheel. Gest raised the burning disc on the end of a pole which the breeze combusted. He walked it over to the edge of the summit, with the crowd drawing in swiftly behind. Gest gestured them to stand back as he slowly drew the flaming garland behind him towards the crowd. With an energetic sweep, he sent it hurtling down the steep slope in a spinning, fiery mass, much to the delight of the onlookers who whooped and cheered. They watched the progress of the incandescent wheel as it bumped over the screes, propelled ever-faster by the steepness of the brae. The blazing garland bounced high into the air, and scattered tongues of flame that momentarily stabbed at the gathering darkness.

"Will you take Caltram for a short while?" Alpia asked. "I have something to do."

Oengus led his boy to the new hall that smelt of pine, and finding Aunt Conchen already seated at the high table, took his place beside her.

"Where is Alpia?" she enquired.

"She said she had something to do but would be with us shortly."

"Oh, I am ready to eat! That climb has given me quite an appetite." Turning to Caltram, she continued, "Is it not exciting to be sleeping on a mountain top this night!"

Caltram looked at her with an earnest expression. "I ride dada!"

"Oh, he is telling me about you carrying him up here on your shoulders." Aunt Conchen elucidated.

"I understood that."

"Flo'ers, flo'ers!"

"What is he saying?" he was forced to ask.

"I think he is saying 'flowers'."

"Aye, that will be it. He carried a bunch and never let go until we reached the top, just as Alpia had instructed him!"

"Oh, clever boy!" Aunt Conchen pinched the wee laddie's cheek. But she stopped as she looked beyond his father's shoulder. "Oengus, look behind you!" Alpia was approaching.

"She is wearing the purple dress!" remarked Aunt Conchen, significantly. "You know, Lughnasa is a time for joining hands. Take note and do not be reserved."

He knew what she meant by 'reserve'. That was not his usual manner, not holding back with women. But with Alpia, she was territory where he felt he could not trespass. As much as he admired her beauty, she had a sanctity about her: mother to his child, but not his wife. If it were not for Alpia, Caltram would not have life. He remembered, with extreme gratitude, how she had cared for the premature baby, faithfully executing her vow to Eithni. They had learnt, in time, to play their respective roles without the awkward embarrassment that had characterised their early days of parenthood. Now . . . it felt normal, that was until he had brought the dress from Din Brython. He had intended the gift to show respect and thankfulness for raising Caltram as her own and had been surprised by its rejection, regarding the gesture as an act to make her his woman. If misunderstanding were to arise, then it most often occurred with Alpia.

She looked exquisite, he thought, as she gracefully walked over to take her place at the table beside him. Her long, auburn hair appeared unusually voluminous that evening as it cascaded over her shoulders and accentuated the purple finery of the dress. And she was perceptibly smiling at him, with that signature of an enigmatic look. Even though many heads were turned in her direction, arrested by this exotic, foreign attire worn so splendidly by a woman in her prime and eminent among the Ce nobility, she continued to hold him in her gaze.

What did it mean? he asked himself. She told me she could never accept the gift – and now she is wearing it before the eyes of all! Can a man ever fully understand a woman? Was it not significant, though, her wearing his gift? She has accepted it! And wearing it on Lughnasa, of all occasions, which as Aunt Conchen has reminded me, is the time for the binding of hands. He felt unusually nervous, at a loss of what to say, his palms clammy, and he swallowed with difficulty. His aunt had warned him not to be 'reserved'. How he wished that he could just be himself.

"Alpia! You look wonderful tonight." The words spilled out, stating truly what he beheld.

She smiled vaguely in return. A brief, economic smile, but it felt lavish for she was certainly sparing in showing, especially to him, any favour, maintaining her haughty exterior. She always came across as inaccessible. He had guessed her dress size well, which he took pride in. Well I have observed her form, he thought to himself with pleasure. Throughout the evening she was attentive to what he had to say as now they spoke about inconsequential things that characterised the domestic life lived under Aunt Conchen's roof.

Oengus felt a growing unrest with how mundane a course their conversation had taken. What could he say to bring it round to something significant, to break the terrible reserve that crippled his tongue?

"So, you decided to wear the dress after all?" he remarked, his eye giving her a lingering approving look from head to waist.

"I thought it wrong after all, to reject a gift well-meant."

"I am glad." His mouth was dry and he reached for his goblet. "And you do not mind people perhaps thinking that you are my woman?"

He noted that the remark was not well-received. He was annoyed with himself for being indelicate – and it seemed he was destined to say the wrong thing to her. He was a straightforward man who liked to say things as they were. "Alpia, I am not a smooth-tongued man – you know that! I never seem able to say the words I ought to with you."

She looked at him steadily, but made no effort to say anything to assist his fumbling efforts. The fact that she did not cut his words short, he took as an encouragement, for she was not slow at nipping things in the bud when they displeased her.

"I have always admired you!" There, it had not been so difficult to say and he felt immense relief to have transitioned from mundane, domestic talk, to state his true feelings. "Even when I was with Eithni, I thought of you . . ."

Alpia held up her hand. "Please, do not say more." She frowned and turned her attention to what was on her plate. She cut a strip of beef and put it in her mouth with a delicate movement of her slender fingers.

He was not going to allow this opportunity to pass. It had taken two and half years to say what he had always wanted to utter, and she should hear him out. Even if the outcome were disastrous, he would have the satisfaction of having said what was always on his heart and not live with the constant regret of his silence that gnawed away within.

"You have always been the one." He cleared his throat, and she did not protest. "When I am with you, I aspire to become a better man. Your opinion matters and I want to do right in your eyes, but it appears that I always fall short!"

Spirits were high in the hall, making for lively chatter and laughter. She lent closer to catch what he was saying, which encouraged him.

"Can there ever be hope for me? When we are together during the day, the world is all that it should be, with everything in its rightful place; but parting at night reminds me that I am quite alone!" He felt pleased to articulate feelings he thought himself incapable of expressing.

Just then, a familiar face appeared before them leaning across the table. He could not place who it was immediately, but the intensity of her eyes, that stared boldly into his own were familiar, reminding him of someone he had already met. Once she began speaking, her identity was unmistakeable.

"You are chosen by the Bulàch on this auspicious evening!" she announced with confidence. "The man of strength, who like the boar, pushes carelessly through the thicket, little minding what gets in his way. And with him the goose with the noble neck, haughty in her defence and loyal to her flock. She has ability in her wings to soar high."

She withdrew suddenly from the table and disappeared among the melee in the hall. They looked at one another in dismay.

"Who was that?" asked Alpia.

"That was Maevis, the high priestess of the Bulàch."

"Uh! I have heard about her and her reputation for seeing hidden things!"

Maevis' negative illumination of the boar came as no surprise given their previous exchanges, revealing her contempt for him. Alpia, though, had received a commendable comparison that he could not argue with. Was Maevis saying that the goose would make the boar noble?

He half expected Alpia to rise and abandon the table, but she remained. She appeared thoughtful, perhaps confused, or was she appalled? *You are chosen by the Bulàch!* he repeated to himself. The 'you' had been addressed to them both as she deliberately fastened each in turn with her meaningful stare.

"First it is Aunt Conchen, then you, and now this all-seeing woman all saying the same thing!" Alpia began unexpectedly. "And I suppose even myself, with my decision to wear your gift. All indicate that we should be together!"

She looked somewhat crestfallen, to Oengus' eye, a victim of fate. It was not the consent he had in mind. He would have preferred her glad acceptance, not her surrender, and it troubled him for a moment. Then he acquiesced. If he obtained what he so eagerly desired, did it really matter whether it was with glad consent or obedient submission? What mattered was that she would be his. Perhaps his own love for her might awaken love within her for him? Damn it, he said to himself, I so desire her that it does not matter how I should acquire her. For once, he thought well of Maevis.

"The boar needs the wings of the goose!" His utterance seemed to make an impression.

"You know, our great-grandmother Mongfind gave me an amulet when I was a girl and became a woman." She felt about her neck, and catching hold of a leather thong, she reeled it about her finger until quite a large stone, equally speckled with red and white, emerged. "Look! What do you see?"

She leaned forward. The neckline of her dress gaped and he saw, beyond the amulet, her bosom voluptuously heaving with some agitation. They were more ample than he had imagined. With an effort, he re-focussed upon the stone. It had an engraving of a goose, with its head looking back in a posture of alertness and defence.

"A goose! Did Maevis know you wear this amulet?"

"No! I have never met her before! That is what makes it strange and noteworthy!"

After the feasting was done, he took a stroll outside the hall. It took a moment for his eyes to re-adjust to the darkness. Going over to the wall, he mounted the steps to the top of the recently completed fortification. There he met with Maelchon conversing with Gest, gazing up into the night skies.

"Oengus!" Gest greeted him engagingly. "Listen – we saw a star fall a short time ago, burning a silver trail."

"Oh! What does it mean?"

"Certainly, it is a sign," replied Maelchon with some levity. "It is quite cloudy, but this star happened to fall in the very quarter where the heavens were laid bare. It has clouded over since, making it the more significant that we noticed it!"

Another sign, he thought. Could it emphasise Alpia's surrender to becoming his wife?

"A falling star usually points to a grave event, for troubles in the heavens precede commotion upon the earth," pronounced Maelchon.

"Who, do you suppose, the star represents?" enquired Oengus, feeling a tad impatient with the indirect ways of his chief druid.

"A battle and a defeat I would think!"

"Oh! Involving who?" he asked, a little detached, knowing Maelchon was usually pessimistic but also still savouring the dawning prospects with Alpia.

"Something that is going to be significant for us, I would say."

"Are you always set to be a harbinger of doom?" he challenged boldly.

"I do not decree such things; I only search for their possible meaning that we may be forewarned and take heed."

"Could it be the falling of the Fortriu at the hands of Dal Riata?" he suggested himself. "They are the ones preparing for war."

"Or it could be our falling at the hands of Brude," Maelchon glumly predicted. "His officials have revealed what a menacing threat he is to us."

He shook his head at his druid's interpretation.

"You want a favourable outcome, but you are careless in your manner of venerating the Bulàch!" challenged Maelchon.

"What have I done now?" he felt the heat rising from his bowels.

"You have agreed to have a soldier of Christ come to Rhynie! The Bulàch is jealous and such notions should not even be entertained!"

"I did warn you," reminded Gest, looking sullen.

"Yes, I know. And I have said that this arrangement is purely diplomatic to gain the support of the Circinn. I will do whatever it takes to show that I am for the Bulàch!"

"And what if the Bulàch has sent this sign to show your fall?" Maelchon reminded him unpleasantly.

"Bah! You are insufferable! As you have said, there are several interpretations as to what this star's fall may mean. Why fixate on the worst outcome?"

"Huh!" Maelchon grunted, in no hurry to reply. Finally, he looked him in the eye. "To have more clarity on this matter, it would be well that you sacrifice a bull to the Bulàch and I will look for signs among its entrails. That way, you renew your commitment to the goddess, and we might have further insight as to what we should anticipate."

"Agreed. When shall the sacrifice be made?"

"Tomorrow, over on the hill with the stone circle where you first received the broch."

Chapter Eighteen

A Surprise

559 AD   Loch Aloninn

"There is a fellow on the far shore who has been waiting a long time!" Carvorst greeted him on returning from the great waterfall.

"Oh, my strength is spent!" Taran brought the boat alongside the wooden jetty.

"I will take the oars," Carvorst said, climbing into the currach with an agility that surprised Taran. "I am ready to cross the straits again."

He was pleased to see Carvorst ably manoeuvring the currach. Further out into the strait, the currach's bow caught the cross current, and he watched with interest how Carvorst would fare. The old man kept the vessel under control, either by pulling harder on the right oar or by taking a double stroke. Reaching the slacker water on the far side, Carvorst corrected their course, aiming for the jetty. He observed that their passenger was an older man, still robust, with a great beard.

"Well, I have proved to myself that I have the strength," Carvorst winked at him. "But maybe we can row back together for the tidal race is strong."

Something about the posture of the waiting passenger reminded him of someone. The old man had been looking down into the water, and when he looked up, he called out, "Well, well, if it is not young Drostan!" A broad grin radiated across his face. "I heard rumour of a young man, foreign to these parts, ferrying people across these straits."

"Ossian!" He took hold of a wooden upright of the jetty. He leapt ashore, holding fast to the line, and the two hugged enthusiastically with much back-slapping. Holding him at arm's length, he noticed that Ossian looked greyer than three years previously when they had parted after their meeting at the Stone of Refuge.

"It seems that you two know one another well," remarked Carvorst.

"This is my very good friend, Ossian, a bard who travels the courts of the warlords. What a singing voice he has! – and no one can tell stories better than him."

"Well, I have had years of practice," said the bard modestly, with palms upturned.

After completing the introductions, Carvorst enquired, "What brings you to these parts, when no warlord holds court here?"

"I have been looking for this young man these past few days." Again, Ossian slapped him on the back, looking relieved to have ended his search.

"Come, let us get back before nightfall," suggested Carvorst. "This strenuous row has given me an appetite."

That evening, Carvorst managed to beg meat and mead from his kinsfolk. "It has been nearly five moons," he explained, scratching his chest vigorously, "that this young man has cared for me. He has been like a son looking after his father." He paused, and laughed ironically. "No, better than a son; more like a daughter; a son and a daughter combined! I had been useless, a bag of bones on the verge of giving up the ghost; but now look at me – I have rowed the straits again."

He felt his cheeks blush.

Ossian plied Taran with questions until he had pieced together the outline story of the past three years. Knowing all these details, Carvorst remarked, "The hand of the High King works in mysterious ways!"

"So, you are a follower of *the way* too?" asked Ossian.

"I am persuaded by what this young man has taught me, especially by his deep concern for others. And as for his self-control – it is so untypical of young men."

Although he did not comment, Ossian appeared pleased with the reply. His mind appeared to be elsewhere, though. After further talk, he came to the matter of what brought him to Loch Aloninn. "Fillan sent me, saying that should I find you, to bring you to Dunadd by Easter. He would like to celebrate the occasion there with you. It is not like Fillan to be leaving his muintir, especially at so ripe an age; but there are rumours of war, as Dal Riata is intent on flexing its muscle, and the abbot is much concerned for what lies ahead."

Making a calculation, they realised that further delay should be avoided if they hoped to reach Dunadd by Easter.

"I had hoped to have arrived sooner, but the only description I had to go by was of a conical hill with its peak sliced off!"

". . . at an angle! You will understand something of my travels then."

"There were a few peaks that came to mind, but finally I felt drawn to Inis Niwl. When I heard news over there of a young man from foreign parts plying these straits for a living, I had to investigate."

They dined well that evening. And those who provided for the meal partook of it, making merry as seemed appropriate for the recovery of their relative as much as the sense of occasion of having a bard in their midst. After regaling them with songs, Ossian settled to tell a story.

After a rambling introduction, which Taran attributed only to Ossian being tired, the bard finally became animated. "Arthur and his men, after his subjugation of the foul warriors from across the seas, led a raid on the far distant underworld of Annwn. In the course of so many battles with the Saxons and Angles, Arthur had lost many of his own warriors, and therefore determined to seize from Annwn the famed cauldron which restores men to their prime. Into this cauldron he could immerse his dear slain – and thereafter lose no more heroes to the underworld."

"Oh, what a prize!" exclaimed Carvorst.

"It was not a straightforward journey, somewhat like my own these past days, and that of young Taran here before, seeking the peak sliced off at an angle as though by a giant blade." He paused, smiling upon his own adventure. "Arthur had to cross a vast sea where no land is sighted, only the expanse of ocean in every direction, where storm assailed and monsters of the deep appeared to discourage mariners from sailing further. Their ship, named Prydwen, was like no other, fashioned, they say, not by mortal hands. How this band of heroes acquired so magical a craft that could withstand the worst of tempests, remains a mystery. But surely, the favour of the gods was upon their venture. Arthur penetrated through to the realms of the dead, the only living person to have ventured there, and seized this prized cauldron that gives immortality. However, as to its whereabouts now, no one knows."

"Immortality! the longing of man," he remarked. "The cauldron, though, did not prevent Arthur from dying."

"It is said that he is not dead, but that he sleeps beneath the Eildon Hills with his warband awaiting the hour of calamity when he shall rise to the dire need of his people."

"It sounds rather like the retelling of the Christ story, our true hero who has fought the fight, who lives – although he did die for a short time – lives to impart life to all who look to him, and who will rise again at the end of the age." He was aware of how Ossian looked strangely at him.

"Well, my friends, with all this talk of strife and plunder, as the Fidach what are your thoughts, on the looming war?"

"What war?" asked a wizened man, almost toothless.

"Between Dal Riata and the Picts!" Ossian exclaimed, visibly surprised by such ignorance.

"Why? What is the quarrel?"

"Territory. Dal Riata is ambitious. Theirs is a kingdom considered too small, populating thin coastlands. The mountains are a barrier to any expansion east; and around their southern flank is Strath Clud, too formidable an opponent to attack. They have already occupied every island west of Dunadd, so northwards is the natural direction. They are lured by taking control of the trade-route up the Great Glen. The revenue that could be demanded would be considerable. It could even prepare expansion to the rich agricultural lands of the north-east."

"What do you suppose the outcome will be?" asked Carvorst.

"King Gabran assumes that as ruler of a Christian nation heaven will favour him against the heathen Picts. I believe he underestimates Brude's ability. The Fortriu have several alliances with their neighbours, including the Ce, Taran's own people. They are likely to be drawn in, along with the Cait, and possibly yourselves too. Does Brude's influence extend this far?"

"We have heard of Brude," answered Carvorst, "but we are such small and scattered communities that no one really bothers with us. We get on with our own business – too humble to feature in the affairs of the wider world."

"But you might be drawn in whether you like it or not," remarked Ossian, evidently keen to open their minds. "If Brude does not stop the advance of the Gaels, you will face them sooner than you might expect. Either your lands will be seized, or you will be forced to pay tribute to Dal Riata."

The wizened man shook his head. "What is the world coming to!"

That evening, Carvorst managed to arrange passage for them on a larger vessel, owned by his cousin, bound for Aird nam Murchan. Provisions for the trip were supplied by Carvorst's kinsfolk as expressions of thanks for Taran's care of their relative.

A small group of people congregated on the wharf early the next day.

"I am much indebted," began Carvorst. "My home will always be your home. I give thanks for the shining one whom you saw in the woods and who appeared to me in my dream . . ." He paused to clear his throat. "Now, the High King summons – and we must part." His eyes grew lustrous as tears welled up, which somehow, he managed to restrain himself from shedding. "Goodbye, my son."

"And I have much to thank you for, because man needs shelter through our long winters. But a greater gift was given: your friendship. I am so thankful that the King has restored strength to your limbs once more, and that in him you have a new companion."

He fixed his eyes on the old ferryman as the boat sailed away from the wharf, wondering whether he would ever come here again. Would he see Aleine Brona again? he considered with keen regret.

Another adventure commenced upon the restless seas of March, marked by especially high tides and freezing nights. It took the best part of three days to reach Dunadd, giving the two men time to talk at length.

"You have fared well, Taran!" observed Ossian. "You are changed."

"Because I chose to become a warrior of Christ!"

"The world is changing fast."

"You played a part – for you spoke well of Fillan and his God. But it was far from straightforward, for I stubbornly resisted."

"You know," Ossian began ponderously, "we walk by the light we have. Can a man be faulted for stumbling around in the twilight, when the dawn has not yet risen? But when the sun appears, the shadows, with all their fears . . . shall flee away! Then he can truly see and gladly walk in that light."

"Has that dawn light broken upon you?"

Ossian considered the question as his mouth chewed on something. Eventually, he exclaimed, "It is like the first rays are striking up from the horizon and they light the heights above!" Ossian looked out to sea peering into the distance as their craft rose and fell in a heavy swell. "These are unsettled days," he continued after a lengthy pause. "Fillan will be glad that I have found you before armies move north and Brude marches south to clash with them."

"Is the battle that inevitable?"

"It has to be. King Gabran has been stretching out his hand too far for Brude to tolerate. The Fortriu have also been preparing for a showdown now that Brude has consolidated his position in Fortriu and amongst his neighbours."

"What do you think will be the outcome?"

"They are well matched and it is too difficult to call." Ossian cleaned a fingernail with a small knife. "Should Brude triumph, it will exalt his position beyond his neighbours. Such a victory will send shockwaves through our world. And the same is true should Gabran defeat the strongest Pictish warlord. Dal Riata shall be exalted, bringing tribute payments from more than just the Fortriu. Domech will be forced to bow if he wants to avoid an invasion of the Gaels, and Strath Clud will feel uneasy about a growing power to their west!"

They reached Dunadd two days before Easter. With the acclaim the bard commanded in Dal Riata, together with the anticipation of Fillan's imminent arrival, expectations were much raised for an Easter celebration like no other.

After an evening entertaining the king and his court up on the rock, Ossian met up with him once more the following morning, close by a wooden oratory beyond the marshes. Below them extended a large complex of stones in alignment and set in circles with burial cairns all about.

"It appears no one performs rituals down there anymore," he observed.

Ossian nodded. "This place was once pre-eminent in the land. People would travel for days to fashion cup and ring marks in the rock all around these hills, marking their pilgrimage and making known their supplications." He took a deep breath. "Dal Riata follows *the way*, like yourself, and other Picts are being persuaded. The old ways are being abandoned."

"What news is there from court? Dunadd seems astir."

Ossian's face was grave. "Oh, as I have said all along, they are flexing their muscle for an imminent battle."

Fillan arrived at midday, wearied from his journey and from fasting. He soon learned that Ossian had arrived with a young pilgrim. He made directly for the muintir, beyond the marsh, reckoning on finding Taran there. He arrived at the conclusion of the noonday prayers. Leaning on his staff, he watched the brethren file out of the oratory, and was greeted by the older monks.

May they take my distraction for weariness, he thought to himself as he conversed sparsely with each. I wish no one any discourtesy; but I long to see Drostan.

"Ah, Drostan!" he called out. The young man rushed over and embraced him. "It is good to see you!"

"I am delighted to see you and sooner than I might have expected!" returned Taran effusively.

"Come, let us take some water, and then we can talk down by the River Add."

Taran gave a lengthy account of all the developments since they had parted. He listened intently, sometimes adding, 'praise be to God.' The spring wind blew chill, rippling the water and rustling the faded reeds along the water's edge. Coming to a more sheltered spot where willows and alders grew abundantly around the river's bend, they sat upon a fallen trunk. Although he relished the light of the spring sun, it cheered him more, with its hopeful light, rather than warmed with its rays.

"It is clear," he spoke after a reflective pause, "that not only have you found Christ to be your closest companion, but that the challenges you faced have created a certain grace. How you are changed! That was my experience in my youth, although it took years of enduring difficulties, often despairing over the lack of progress." He smiled sympathetically, briefly placing his arm around Taran's shoulders, drawing him affectionately to his side. "I have prayed ceaselessly for your renewal. This grace, the visible evidence of change, brings to mind our Lord's words, *you will know them by their fruit*." He paused thoughtfully, mindful of what Taran had endured. "You have had to persevere since the days you fled your home, have you not? And there is purpose to it; suffering is the proving of a soldier of Christ!"

"I wish there were some other way," responded Taran with feeling. "I have suffered much: riding in a flimsy coracle upon the unruly ocean, going without food, and sleeping rough."

"I also found the sea a sobering experience when I left Erin. Mind you, I was in a larger currach with a sail and navigated by seasoned mariners. Nevertheless, it felt precarious, as I was not in control and resulted in me vomiting. I still remember feeling an acute sense of loss, leaving home for the wilds of the north. 'North' conjured up tales of hostility, pagan dangers, and an unkind climate." Aware of talking about himself more than he felt he ought, he looked up at the bare branches of the trees with a chill shudder.

"Sailing on the open ocean is one thing, but you have had to deny yourself a woman's love, the lure of settling down, and also to renounce your birthright as warlord of the Ce."

"You understand well." Taran returned a sad smile. "But the warlordship does not concern me now."

"Does it surprise you to admit that?" Fillian lent back, clasping his hands around a knee studying the young man intently.

"Should you have said that last year at Dindurn, it would have surprised me." Taran smoothed his moustache away from his lips. "It has been a hard lesson. Several times I thought I had relinquished ambition and revenge, only for it to resurface."

"Such is the way of the disciple. The warrior spirit, along with our natural worldliness, has to be bridled if we are to turn in a new direction." He paused, adjusting his cloak to eliminate a draught. Had he been on his own, he would have walked on to warm himself; but noticing how Taran sat deep in thought, he avoided an interruption. "You will know from your military preparation that suffering makes a warrior out of a soft boy. Your *white martyrdom* has produced character with the mark of godliness about it."

Taran nodded thoughtfully.

"Once, you despised what you perceived to be the way of losing; but now you recognise it as the path towards a higher calling." He observed the young man leaning forward, as if intent on receiving every word to bring clarity to his soul. "The struggle will continue – we are never done with it," he continued solemnly. "As soon as you overcome one wrong attitude, or misconception, you become conscious of another. Our weaknesses will always be felt, especially at the low ebbs, in the conflict between wanting an ordinary life and our dying to the allurements of this passing world."

Inhaling noisily, he continued with renewed conviction. "You know, I perceive the things that you have learned on your quests. Be of good cheer, for you are progressing swiftly in *the way*. He raised an index finger to enumerate his points. "Mercy is something that you have known for some time now. You found mercy when escaping the clutches of your people conspiring to make you a sacrifice, and again at Coblaith's home. When going through the wilds of the Minamoyn Goch, to your coming to our muintir, mercy was upon you; as indeed when escaping Domech's clutches and surviving the Great Western Sea. But you have also shown mercy: to a wretch hanging from a shrub, and to Carvorst." He paused, surprised by so many examples.

"That is a lot of mercy! And I could add other examples too, particularly the mercy I received from the shining one," declared Taran, animated.

"Yes, indeed! Just as you have received mercy, so are you to show mercy *to confound the foe and to bind up the injured,* as the prophecy says. By these means, your way shall prosper."

He smiled when raising a second finger. "Showing *mercy* requires *humility* and," he paused to raise a third finger, "*perseverance* too. As the prophecy indicates, both are *characteristics* that you are *to be known by and be outstanding in.*"

"Humility was foisted upon me at Coblaith's home!"

He noticed the narrowing of Taran's pupils as the young man stared vacantly into the distance. "And humility is a discipline at the muintir," he continued. "As for perseverance, I think you have excelled!" He extended a fourth finger. *Surrender* is perhaps an alien concept for a warrior, but it is a requisite for Christ's soldier. It is the giving up of reliance on our own understanding, self-effort, and the use of the sword. Surrender is something that has characterised your journey from the time you left your life as a prince, stripped of position, power, and influence. Surrender is, in a way, reliance upon the Presence – as experienced upon the high seas and up in the snowy mountains."

"Then finally," he raised his thumb, raising his whole hand to indicate five graces, "you received a precious token of his love, spilling incessantly over the great waterfall. Knowing the Father's love in a deep way is the yearning of all true pilgrims and the reason for undertaking the *white martyrdom.*"

"Five of the nine graces acquired already!" Taran exclaimed brightly. "It should not be long before all nine are acquired, which will accomplish the ultimate mission of *bearing fire to the north.*

"It does not follow that the acquisition of the other four will be so swift!" He felt a certain heaviness come over him. Did he detect a momentary scowl come across Taran's face? He did not want to discourage him, but nor did he want to give the impression that acquiring the final four graces was something of a foregone conclusion. In his experience of *the way,* it had the tendency to get tougher the further one progressed. *The way* was a journey often shrouded in mystery, especially with, at times, the apparent aloofness of the Presence. He recalled with shame his own wish to return to Erin in the early years before the breakthrough occurred at Dindurn, and how he had to be contained by Kessog's fatherly concern and counsel, preventing his flight.

Perhaps grappling to understand mysterious ways, he noted that Taran's mouth was slightly open, on the verge of wanting to say something.

"Permit me to ask a question," the young man's brow knitted. "Why did God not answer my prayer – and even though I did not doubt – when I prayed for Carvorst's healing?"

"That is often our question, is it not?" he sighed, with empathy. "Why are people healed sometimes and not at other times?" He considered his words carefully. "It is always our wish to find the short cut, but there is purpose in the longer journey. However mysterious things may seem from our very limited, earthbound view, the panorama from heaven's throne is different. The King acts in the most appropriate way." He raised his chin, keen to impart comfort as well as wisdom. "It would seem that our Lord had a bigger purpose in not healing Carvorst immediately."

"What do you mean?"

"Ponder this. With you remaining all winter in his house, Carvorst was provided with a companion through the valley from which he had despaired of ever being able to find a way out. You pointed to the light beyond the valley, and not only that . . ." He shifted on the tree trunk to more directly face Taran. "What effect did this have upon you? Humility and compassion for your fellow man, would you not say? A similar feeling to when you discovered Aleine Brona hanging from the bush."

"It was easy to love Aleine Brona – it just welled up instinctively," Taran nodded. After a brief pause, he emphasised his next words, "But loving Carvorst had to be worked at!"

"Caring for an infirm, old man was not so easy, was it?"

"It was not at first, but later I found empathy and compassion."

"It had to be intentional, and, at times sacrificial. It contained something of Christ's love, would you not say: a love springing up for an unlikely individual?"

He could see Taran deep in thought as the spring wind lifted some strands of hair across his face. "Resenting some of the things you had to do," he continued, "you learned a lesson in loving your neighbour as yourself. This prepared you for what you received at the foot of the great waterfall – the immersion in the love of the Father." He lifted his hands heavenward, in a gesture of thankfulness.

Taran had a look of more fully comprehending something. As the wind made his eyes moist, the April light gave them a lustre. "Such love does not come from within," he began falteringly, "but emerges as a choice. Such love is allowing God's Spirit to have unhindered sway."

"Well said," he congratulated, surprised by the depth of Taran's understanding.

They sat quietly, enjoying the spring sunshine, despite the regular reminders that winter was not over. The wind sounded mournfully through the bare branches of the willows.

That evening, Fillan went up to the citadel in search of Ossian. Most were not observing the Easter fast, but he was surprised to see the bard drinking only water.

"Why are you not eating like most of the others?"

"I am concerned for my soul!" Ossian replied, with startling sincerity.

"How is that?"

"Have I not seen great things in the young Taran! Who would have believed it? What a transformation from a prince, distracted from the big affairs of the world by the beauty of a woman, and then to find his peace as a pilgrim! He has wrestled with much: exile, status, identity, bitter vengeance – renouncing all, wholeheartedly, to become a warrior of Christ. In so brief a time, how he has risen in stature."

"Those are my own observations. But enough of Drostan, what about you?"

The bard eyed him sheepishly. "You will recall I once cursed you for turning people from the Bulàch."

"Yes, I do recollect. But I detect that the Lord has softened your heart since then?"

"Your kindness, the love that emanated from you on that day, deeply convicted me. And I have not been the same since. I asked myself why did the Bulàch not frustrate your purposes? Why did the Lord Domech not turn against you much sooner? When he did, he was thwarted – as the High King so clearly intervened at the moment of your execution!"

Seeing the bard becoming misty-eyed, he asked. "What is your persuasion now?"

"I am persuaded that the kingdom of the High King is evident. A kingdom of love and peace. And yet, those who purport to being followers of the High King still persist in the old ways by force of sword!" Ossian furtively gestured with his eyes towards the king's table.

"I understand. But do not speak of another. What about yourself?"

"I fast this day and shall celebrate Easter tomorrow, believing in the one who died for all, who rose from the dead and has power to raise me also."

"If you are of this persuasion," he fixed him steadily with his eye, "then why not join those being baptised tomorrow?"

Ossian did not look taken aback, but smiled. "Have I not been an instrument in the High King's hand? It was at my behest that Taran came to Dindurn. I recognise that the Lord has been gaining control of me for quite some time. Tomorrow, I should publicly declare whom I now follow."

"I am delighted to hear this." Fillan thought of the years that had passed when Ossian remained steadfastly rooted in the old ways. And he was so surprised by Ossian's declaration that he rebuked himself for being taken aback. I should have believed all along, he told himself. And had I not prayed for this man's renewal?

"I do believe that the kingdom of the High King shall unite us Picts," Ossian continued. "I am not the only bard, or druid, to embrace the new: for several recognise in Christ the fulfilment of the prophecy concerning the sun god coming to heal the wrongs on earth."

All the faithful at Dunadd, including King Gabran MacDomangart and his entire court, greeted the breaking of

Easter morn with the joyful singing of psalms down by the River Add beneath the citadel. Fillan presided over a large gathering; and some who were not of the same persuasion looked on with varied interest. He stepped aside, to allow two elders instead, to baptise over sixty men and women that Easter Sunday. The large number he considered was partly due to mortal concerns over the imminent conflict with the northern Picts.

"Is that Ossian over there?" asked Taran, looking along the line of those to be baptised.

"Yes, and you have had no small part in opening his eyes."

"I did not recognise him at first. His whole person radiates a pure joy that quite transforms his features."

When Ossian joined them from the river, Taran greeted him. "This is a well-kept secret!"

"A secret no more," he winked.

Ossian had a far-off look in his eyes, peering beyond Taran's shoulder to the knobbly hills fringing the great mossy plain. "But do you remember the prophetic words, Taran?" Ossian lent forward, tapping the side of his forehead. "*Take heart my son, through one you will overcome the world.* That part of the prophecy that had me puzzled has been fulfilled, not just for you, but for me as well."

Taran smiled, and gave the bard a hearty embrace. "Concerning the prophetic . . ." Taran seemed stirred by what Ossian had introduced, and asked urgently "how will I be guided in my next adventure?"

Ossian raised his chin and also looked towards him. "Aye, where is Taran to go from here?"

"It is time for him to study and be better equipped as a soldier of Christ," said Fillan, decisively.

"I have been thinking the same myself. But how can I return to Dindurn with Domech eager to gain by turning me in?"

"Have you not heard? Domech is changed." Fillan briefly related the incidents of their persecution, leading to the warlord's repentance. "When the oratory had been rebuilt, it was too small to contain the numbers who had now joined us from Domech's entourage and also others from the citadel. We had to meet in the open field between the muintir and the citadel. Even in the rain, the Lord Domech sang psalms with us."

Taran looked incredulous.

"Although it would be safe for you to return to Dindurn, you will learn more by studying at one of the great seats of learning in Erin. Clonard is pre-eminent among these, founded by Finnian, which became his place of resurrection . . ."

"How do you mean?" asked Ossian.

"That having died there, he will rise from that place when the King returns. Finnian gave up his mortal body over ten years ago, but by that time he had established a style of exposition which has become something of a distinctive at Clonard."

Taran looked uncomfortable, struggling with something. "I know that I need to prepare for what lies ahead, for this *bearing fire to the north*, so study seems right. But I will struggle to go to Erin, for that lies to the south."

"Aye, it is to the south," he simply replied.

"The prophecy, spoken through Ossian, does not mention going south again, but to the north!"

"It is true," Ossian interjected. "After *your transformation in the isles of the west; your fulfilment coincides with the anticipation of the learned ones far to the north.*"

Both Picts looked to him for an explanation.

"Prophecies, by nature, are not necessarily so detailed as not to permit other developments taking place in between the events being highlighted" he explained. Judging by their looks, they remained unconvinced.

Taran, seeming to have difficulty in giving voice to his thoughts, began uncertainly. "If I am to study, what will that take – two, three, four years, right?"

He nodded.

"Then surely, something that is to take years to accomplish would be in the prophecy?"

"Think about the first part of the prophecy in which you were to head south to Dindurn – did that come to pass immediately after your flight from the crannog?"

"No – I had a year in the home of Coblaith and Elphin."

"That is what I mean, prophecies do not state absolutely everything, even events that take a year to unfold." He noticed that Taran still looked perturbed. "Well, consider also that the prophecy speaks of *much strife, like a blight threatening to consume. Heartache and anguish lie before you. Many a journey awaits* . . . Those words warn of extra events and things that will seem to frustrate you to the utmost. With war about to break out in the north, it is not the place to be, and . . ." he paused, reaching out to pat the young man's hand, "there is an obvious, practical detail . . ."

"What is that?" Taran looked up enquiringly.

"There are no muintirs to the north! At least not yet, but I suspect that is about to change!"

"Muintirs to be established as a result of a Dal Riatan victory?" asked Ossian with evident displeasure.

He shrugged his shoulders. Noticing Taran's foot beating away restlessly, reminded him of the impatience of youth. Taran had been raised to be a warrior, a man of action. Wishing to conclude the matter, he said to Taran, "I shall write you a letter of introduction to take to Clonard."

"I am not happy about going to Erin for possibly four years. It deflects from the purpose of what is outlined in the prophecy."

The objection took him aback. "Perhaps the issue should be regarded as a matter of surrender, then?"

"Well, I am of the mind to come back with you to Dindurn, if that is possible, to study," announced Ossian, perhaps feeling somewhat uncomfortable at Taran's objection.

"And you will be made most welcome."

"But not for four years!" continued the bard. "I might not be granted so many earthly years. Maybe a year, though, to better understand the faith I have embraced, to give food for contemplation at the end of my days."

"I am not afraid of the war about to erupt!" Taran stated tensely.

He noticed how tightly Taran was grasping the end of his plaid, the tassels of which, he had been fingering with agitation.

"Maybe as a result of this outbreak of hostilities," Taran continued boldly, "men will be more inclined to take note of this heavenly fire I am to bear!"

"Spoken like a true warrior!" congratulated Ossian. His smile was brief, for he quickly acquiesced. "Taran – you are young, and therefore tasks will appear to need to be done if not now then no later than tomorrow!"

"I disagree!" Taran replied forcibly. "I feel strongly that so little of consequence gets done in the world because man will procrastinate! Whilst I accept that further study would be very useful – something which I am disposed to undertake, as I stated at the beginning of this conversation – four years is too long; and I cannot help but believe the recommendation is taking me in the wrong direction!"

He observed Taran's brow was flushed. Had Kessog not forewarned that this prodigy would be hard to disciple? His own dream that had disturbed him just before Taran had come to Dindurn, indicated a troublesome disciple. But he was comforted by Kessog's foreknowledge in seeing these forty years before, and how it was all coming to pass. There was also the prediction of the young man's ascent. He marvelled over the High King's long view, which so often in man's own impatience, seemed slow to transpire.

"Your objection is noted, and I do understand. However, you need to be better equipped to face the challenges ahead. I see harsh ordeals and events that are far greater than what you have encountered until now, involving whole groups of people, and huge shifts in the state of the world as we know it. As your abbot, I am saying that you are to go to Erin!"

Taran was red-faced, and did not immediately respond, but when he did; he bowed his head. "Because I trust you, I will do it."

With that disagreement sorted, he observed Ossian's countenance was tinged with a certain melancholy. He could not sense the reason for it at first, not believing that the bard had a change of mind and supported Taran's objections. Ossian had been obstinate too, refusing previous opportunities to change. Perhaps it was in the nature of the Picts to be stubborn? After further reflection, he deduced that Ossian was subdued because he was in the latter stage of his life, like himself, with goodness knows how little time remaining, unlike Taran who was young, brimful of possibilities.

Ossian confirmed these reflections by saying, "It is well that you respect Fillan – a man who never disappoints. We might not now clearly see what is to pass. But I move ahead with joy and peace, trusting in the one who ultimately oversees our times."

"I find comfort in that outlook too," agreed Taran. "But I would like to return to my original question earlier: how will I know guidance for the next part of the adventure beyond the hiatus of my studies?"

"The High King, my son, will let you know." He reached inside the inner pocket of his cloak and extracted a small parchment which he handed him. "On here I have written the words of the prophetic prayer spoken some time back in my cell at Dindurn. As I surmise, the prophecies in that prayer – not being as specific as what you received from Ossian with points of direction – are perhaps not so familiar to you, but nevertheless are guidance for your way ahead. They concern spiritual quests, which when completed will equip you with graces, the sum of which will be required for *your fulfilment* to coincide *with the anticipation of the learned ones far to the north.*

Chapter Nineteen

The Call

Rhynie   558-559 AD

Oengus and Alpia were wed straight after Lughnasa.

Why did I have to choose the boar image to describe my own aspirations? he considered to himself. Why did I not consider something nobler, like a horse? I had admired the boar for its ferocious strength and wily intelligence, but had not considered its baser instincts of grunting and wallowing in the dirt! The contempt of Maevis' words came repeatedly to mind.

He saw himself featuring increasingly, as Maevis would portray him, as the brute having his way. Their wedding had left the impression of the boar's menace causing the goose to yield; her fine, slender neck bent ungainly beneath his brutish advances. It was a conquest he had wildly imagined; its fulfilment, though, tasted bitter-sweet. Had this been the significance of the falling star? Alpia seemed resigned to her fate, not truly making an effort, to his mind, to welcome their union. She continued as their lives had been before, with her chief role still being mother to Caltram. Was she unable, or more unwilling, to explore the role of being his wife except through apparent surrender? Why did she lack capacity to embrace her new status? It brought sore regret that his desire to wed her had not brought him happiness.

Six weeks after their marriage, they celebrated an abundant harvest at Mabon, a garnering like no other in living memory. This confirmed an interpretation Gest had revealed to him in private, of the falling star being the defeat of the lord of the underworld in his attempt to seize the harvest. However, Maelchon's own take on events lurked in the background, unsettling him. Maelchon's reading of a sacrificed animal's entrails had been inconclusive, and even then the druid could not help suggesting gloomy outcomes. Maelchon seemed a man who forever veered toward portraying the future as ominous, just in case things did evolve for the worse – and then no one could blame him for not warning the community. But when there were good outcomes, Maelchon would merely shrug his shoulders, give one of his rare, almost apologetic smiles, and all would be well.

Two soldiers of Christ arrived at Rhynie, men Oengus found particularly dull, full of speech, quoting from their book, laboriously translating word by word, slowly from the Latin. They caused him indigestion. He tried to extract from among so much that was alien whatever what might be of use when conversing with Christian lords and kings, fresh concepts that ran counter to his own view of the world. It felt a futile task. It was hard to concentrate on so many foreign names and places, along with strange teachings. Alpia attended all these sessions, for which he was grateful, for she grasped things quicker; and she helpfully paraphrased the gist of the pilgrims' lengthy monologues. He was relieved to release the men after a fortnight, and realised they also had grown tired of being in Rhynie.

"You have nothing to fear," Oengus remarked to Gest. "The Christian teaching is not for us! It does not serve the purpose of our warrior society. It has strange talk, like *the last shall be first* – and if someone strikes you on one cheek then you should present your other cheek to be struck!"

"What did I say?" And to emphasise his point, Gest proffered his hands forward in a gesture to convey, 'I told you so!' – "You ought never to have entertained these soldiers of strange peace!" Gest continued to whittle down a wooden peg he was fashioning to make a repair, and did not look up from his task.

"It had to be done, and now it is over!" Oengus said brightly.

Gest did not acknowledge his conclusion.

He is still sulking, he thought. Wanting to close the matter once and for all, he asked, "What would it take for you to know that I maintain the traditions of our forefathers?"

Putting the peg to one side, Gest looked up. "It is not just for me, but for the people of the Ce to know, and above all, for the Bulàch to be convinced. Make a public demonstration at Samhainn before the mound of the ancestors. Then, folk will know that you have not sold yourself to these people of another *way*."

"Fine!" The word came forcibly from his lips, irritated by being held on trial. They briefly discussed what was required to be done.

The nights were closing in rapidly with an irrepressible veil of darkness, thickened by the overcast weather and much rain. A cold, damp wind made it abundantly clear that winter was advancing inexorably upon them. The earth endured the reeling spell of crisp frosts, stripping what leaves remained upon the trees. He felt the grim change of season, knowing the lengthy inertia of winter would lay upon him heavily.

He ensured that he was seen to be organising the Samhainn celebrations, overseeing the construction of two bonfires before the mound of the ancestors, and directing where large canopies were to be erected a good distance from the fire, in the likely event that it would be raining on the eve. Cattle were brought down off the hill to their winter pastures and byres; and he selected a fine bull from his own herd to be sacrificed. Taking the fine dagger that had been gifted by Uncle Talorgen at his initiation, he polished it until it gleamed, showing off the exquisite swirls engraved along its blade. The last time the dagger had shed blood it was his own on the day of his initiation, alongside his cousin's, when they spilled blood onto their ancient soil to express their union with their ancestral lands. He wondered about the whereabouts of the twin blade gifted to Taran; for surely it existed, even if his cousin did not? He underwent the purification rites, overseen by Gest, implicitly following every instruction with meticulous observance, so that he might be absolved of wrongdoing in his friend's eyes.

At the close of day, when all had gathered before the mound of the ancestors, Maelchon got the proceedings underway. "At this year's end, we give thanks to the Bulàch for the yield of an exceptional harvest, and to Lugh for safekeeping it from the grasp of the lord of the underworld. Beli Mawr brought warmth to ripen the grain at the appropriate time so that we cannot fail to observe his munificence – for we know from past experience how blight can spoil and how rain can bring mildew."

Maelchon took a step towards him, for they had agreed that as warlord, he would have a ceremonial part in the required proceedings.

"And now, our Lord Oengus will light the fires that are to cleanse the cattle from all impurities brought from the hill as they pass through the sacred smoke. The fires bear testimony to our need of warmth in the coming time and commemorate Beli Mawr's heat in providing sufficient winter provisions. Although the light appears to diminish, still it shall burn on our hearths through the darkest times at this onset of decay."

The two bonfires combusted well. Having strategically placed pine resin, ample tinder, and kindling in the bonfires himself, he knew exactly where to apply the flaming brand. A rousing crackle thrilled his heart as he stepped back from the rising flames.

The druid paused as he slowly scanned the crowd with a rather withering look. "Regard the flames as an opportunity for you to cast into their consuming fire all harmful influences." Maelchon nodded at him.

He took from inside his red centurion's cloak, a written scroll. "Fathers and mothers, brother and sisters," he declared, raising his voice over the sound of the crackling flames. "Upon this parchment are written the teachings of the foreign god that the people of the south call the Christ; the god brought by the Gaels from Erin, challenging us to abandon our time-honoured traditions and turn our backs upon the Bulàch and forsake all other gods. We will have nothing of this teaching among us, and I commit this parchment to the flames as a harmful influence."

At this, he tossed the open scroll onto where the fire was burning fiercest. For a moment, the flames appeared to illuminate the words upon the scroll; and he felt alarmed, doubting his action. Then the flames darkened the parchment, rendering the words illegible before suddenly combusting, becoming one with the pyre. He smiled, glad to have publicly demonstrated, and most importantly before his druids, his rejection of this foreign religion. He touched the torc about his neck with its terminals of two boars' heads facing one another, and smiled. The warlord's ornament, inherited from Talorgen, felt reassuring to his touch, prophetically stating the significance of the boar for their tribal identity. The boar had been an inspired choice, despite his recent misgivings.

After the cattle had been driven between the two fires and secured within an enclosure, he took the one remaining bull, leading it through the purifying smoke, bringing it to Maelchon by a cord strung through its nose. Four others came forward, each tying a rope around the legs of the bull, who was beginning to snort and grow restless. But it was the nostril cord that he forcibly held that kept the bull in check. The bull submitted, giving him opportunity to reach for his ceremonial dagger to present to Maelchon. The druid said something unintelligible before running the blade with considerable force and skill through the bull's throat. The beast flinched, taking all the strength of the those restraining him. Briefly the bull emitted a gurgling noise, before keeling over on one side, causing Oengus, and two others to deftly step aside of its fall. The blood spilled so liberally that his sleeve was soaked in its life, a flow which felt warm and sticky. He saw that the bull had expired.

Whilst a team butchered the bull, Maelchon and Gest stood at the entrance to the mound of their ancestors. Its stone portal had been removed to reveal immense stone slabs lining a very narrow passage into the chamber. What might their ancestors communicate? Would this falling star omen now be consigned to the past, confirmed as the interpretation he and Gest had favoured? Or was Maelchon about to hear a dissenting voice from the dead, predicting dire events yet to transpire? What if Talorgen should speak from the grave? His difficult uncle would surely have something unsavoury to utter that would cause Maelchon to nod in an all-knowing manner!

The druids were then joined by Maevis. Where had she appeared from? he thought, not expecting her to be part of the proceedings. His heart felt heavy. How was it that she, who had never been present in Rhynie during Talorgen's rule, was now making appearances at their feast days? If there were to be some rebuke, then Maevis could be counted on making it. What an odious pair Maevis and Maelchon presented – and he waited gloomily for them to utter words of chastisement. He had been briefly thankful for her intervention at Lughnasa, for bringing about his marriage union. Alpia had been kinder, easier to live with, before she became his wife. But marriage brought none of the anticipated advantages, only the bitterness of acquiring his heart's desire that yielded no fulfillment.

Part of the meat to be offered to the ancestors was placed in a newly-woven basket, and presented to Maelchon. The druids briefly conversed. Gest took the basket, and bending double entered the exceedingly constricted confines of the chambered tomb, with considerable difficulty.

He reflected that the passage was too narrow for the ageing Maelchon to negotiate.

Gest had been gone some time, making him feel restless. What had detained him? he thought. I cannot lose my sole ally from the druid fraternity. Surely, I have done enough for the Bulàch to accept my contrition. Had she not favoured me over Taran, given me prosperity and helped establish the Ce as a force to be reckoned with? Surely, this exhibited her favour, so why should I unduly worry?

He felt relieved to see Gest emerge from the tomb, and the rituals were confirmed to have been completed. Gest was smiling, and made a point of nodding at him as if to convey that all was well.

"Friends! Let us sup and eat well this evening," Oengus addressed his people. "To the hall for song and cheer!"

Just then, Maelchon stepped forward, calling for everyone's attention. What did he have to say now? Is he going to dampen our spirits with something unpleasant?

"Remember, before you go home this night, to take a flaming brand from the fire. I trust that you have all extinguished your hearth fires before Samhainn so that proper observance shall be kept and new fires shall burn from this consecrated flame, symbol of Beli Mawr to preserve the light through the coming decline."

Maelchon had nothing further to say.

He felt relieved.

The descent into darkness passed with Yule. Daylight began its noticeable resurgence with Imbolc, which by Ostara, shared equally with darkness. The ascendancy of the sun bore his hopes forward, leaving him confident. Less cattle had been slaughtered, for there had been ample fodder; and their grain stores were plentiful enough to avoid the necessity of slaughtering the usual number of cattle for meat. No one went hungry. Neither he, nor anyone among the Ce, experienced the vengeance of the Bulàch.

Brigantia was now in ascendancy as the wheel of the year turned, bringing in a season of hopeful expectation and renewed energies. He reflected that exactly four years had passed since his return to his birthplace. Tattooed with the broch, he had triumphed over his cousin, despite Taran ominously receiving the Z-rod.

He observed a staging of geese, arriving in extended family groups, gathering on the pasture to the south of Rhynie. They stalked about the meadow, alert and seemingly in conference about the long migratory flight ahead of them. This attracted other family groups passing overhead to spiral down cautiously, before committing themselves to swell the ranks upon the ground. He reckoned a thousand or more geese had assembled, with their elders maintaining a purposeful conversation with one another, as they strutted about with self-importance. Impressive in number, they struck him as a highly organised unit. He had never noticed them congregate to the south of Rhynie before in this manner; possibly they had escaped his attention. But the fact they had caught his eye this year was a favourable sign, for the geese were Alpia's emblem. Over three days, the geese mustered a huge flock – and the comparison with the three years it had taken to assemble the fighting force of the Ce did not escape his attention. He made a purpose of going to the edge of their pasture, morning and late afternoon, observing their manner closely, intrigued by their unity and the authority of their elders.

When he appeared on the fourth day, they had flown. He felt sad to have missed their departure, for surely the sight of over a thousand birds rising into the air would have been impressive. In their place, he heard a solitary male curlew practising his courtship call as a rather incomplete and melancholic song, bringing to mind his own brief courtship of Alpia.

We are all caught up by this drive of nature to procreate, he mused gloomily. How it can dominate, distract from all other considerations. He then heard a blackbird chattering blithely with exuberant abandon, and felt strangely warmed. The hawthorn was just coming into leaf, and the willows down by the stream were covered in a pale green haze, laden with furry blossom. All was well in the world, he thought; and he and his people had prospered knowing the favour of the gods, despite Maelchon's gloomy half-predictions.

Shortly before Beltane, a messenger came.

"Lord, I come in haste from King Brude. Dal Riata has mustered a great army, and the overlord requires the Ce to send warriors to join battle with the Gaels."

"Where have the Gaels reached?" he asked, roused by this unwelcome news.

"To the south of the Great Glen. They are vast in number, swelled by the alliance of three significant clans."

"And where is your own fighting force?"

"They are already on the move, south of Craig Padrig."

"So, your men are going to engage the Gaels in battle?"

"No. We are moving into position to contain Dal Riata from advancing up the Great Glen into the lands of the Fortriu. Lord Brude will wait until your own men arrive before he attacks." The messenger paused, looking, to Oengus's eye, somewhat uncomfortable. "My lord reminds you not to delay, nor to send a shortfall as you did with the tribute payment. But he graciously adds that past debts can be cancelled by your acting swiftly."

"What past debts! They have been paid in full – your officials made sure of that by taking more than was required."

"I was informed that you might have a different understanding of events!" The messenger had lost his previous reserve, and Oengus became aware of a slightly insolent air.

"And how many men does your lord expect me to send?"

"Three hundred."

He repeated the number incredulously. "What makes him think we have so many? We are a smaller tribe than the Fortriu."

Ignoring the question, the messenger took on an air of authority. "You are to make your way down the Great Glen, and meet with my lord there."

Once the messenger had left, he went down to the stream to see Gest. He needed to ruminate with another, whose opinion he respected, to quell the great unease this message had brought. Not finding Gest at home, he proceeded, somewhat hesitantly, to Maelchon, hoping that his friend might be with the chief druid – a hope that seemed confirmed on hearing Maelchon talking within his hut. Summoned to enter, he was surprised to find Maelchon alone. Perhaps he had been reciting some ancient lore aloud to himself, he thought.

"What brings you here?" Maelchon greeted him, matter-of-factly.

He shared the unwelcome news, which Maelchon listened to with equanimity. As soon as he had finished explaining, the druid replied with an engagement that slightly surprised him. "We have heard about Dal Riata's expansionism for some while now, and Brude's own expectation of a clash sooner or later: so the inevitable is finally happening."

"With this being expected, do you understand how events might unfold?"

"There will be a falling – that much is clear from the star we saw plummeting back at Lughnasa."

"Not the star again! That was a while ago now." He still held firmly to other interpretations of the celestial event.

Maelchon ignored his protestation. "What are you going to do?"

"I have to be seen to do something!"

"Indeed." Maelchon returned, in a voice that sounded repressed, as though enduring a bout of indigestion.

"Can you divine what the outcome will be, more than that there will be a falling?" he asked, knowing that the druid had been stating the obvious before an impending battle.

"Yes, yes, I shall come to that." Maelchon tried not to appear flustered. "But what are you intending to do?"

"I met with King Gabran last year, and was impressed by his ambition and well-ordered rule. But then, the Fortriu are bold and many, and it is hard to determine who might come out on top. But I would say the odds are against Brude."

"Is that what you truly believe – or what you want to believe?"

Oengus paused thoughtfully. "I suppose it is both."

"So, what is the 'something' that you say you have to be seen to be doing?" pursued Maelchon.

"To send our men! Brude has asked for three hundred!"

Maelchon did not look surprised. Not proffering anything to say, he felt that the druid's gaze had an air of impatience. Oengus proceeded, "My hope is that we might arrive after the battle. If King Gabran is victor, then our enemy will either be wiped out, or will have been put in place, and we will not have to bow to Fortriu's hegemony. But if Brude emerges victorious, then we will have been compliant with his command to send men – so he cannot protest."

"Ah, but he will protest. He will assume that you did not act fast enough upon his orders!"

"Even though we have three hundred fighting men to send, I am loath to lose them and leave ourselves exposed."

"What are you proposing?"

"To send maybe a hundred trained men to lead and make up the rest with peasants who are yet seemingly equipped."

"I see!" Maelchon placed his elbows on the tabletop and rested his chin in his upturned palms. Not speaking, he gazed fixedly into vacant space.

This is typical Maelchon behaviour, he thought, exasperated. "Well, will you not consult the gods and our ancestors?"

Maelchon stirred as though coming to his senses. He rose from the table and unexpectedly placed a hand briefly on his shoulder and said, "Of course."

He left, walking briskly up the hill to the palisade. Pausing at their symbol stone, he remembered Maelchon's instruction at his initiation that the salmon was purposefully placed above the beast to indicate that wisdom overcomes fear.

"Where have you been?" Alpia asked, when he reached home. "We have heard about the call to battle."

"We need to ready our men." Oengus informed her about the messenger's demands, and summarised his discussion with Maelchon.

"I think a hundred warriors among peasants would be too obvious. And suppose you are enjoined in battle – how would they protect you? Or if Brude turns on you – you would be wiped out!"

He stared at the ground, knowing that his wife spoke wisely. "I do not like leaving Rhynie exposed, though, by taking all our men from here. I could ask Cynbel to send us some men here, but . . ."

"They might take advantage of our being defenceless?" she finished his sentence.

"Precisely. Better that the Circinn do not know about this! Have you seen Drust?" He rose.

"No, but is he not normally drilling the young warriors up at the hillfort in the afternoons?"

"Yes, you are right!" He was not thinking clearly. He went to the door, picked up the red centurion's cloak; and then, changing his mind, placed it back on the peg. The ride up to the Pap of the Bulàch would make him warm.

When he had returned late afternoon, he shared his plans with Alpia. "We will take three hundred men, fifty of these recent recruits. This way, we will leave just over a hundred here in Rhynie. We shall set out at dawn."

"And Drust will ride with you?"

"Yes, he is our most capable commander who knows his men."

"And who will you leave in charge of the men here?"

"I am still undecided. Have Maelchon or Gest come here?"

She shook her head. "Nechtan would be the obvious choice, would he not?"

"Possibly, but I do not trust him. I would prefer to have him with me where I can see him!"

"What can he do with a fraction of the fighting force?"

"What if we lose men in battle, and are outnumbered when we return with Uncle Nechtan holding the hillfort?"

"Do you think he would do that? If he did, you could get a force from the Circinn or perhaps even from Brude!"

"Maybe you are right. Uncle Nechtan is competent," he admitted reluctantly. "And I would not have to abide having him under my nose."

He went off in search of his druids, but no sooner had he reached the citadel's portals, people were gathering before the mound of the ancestors where a fire had been lit. No doubt, he told himself, they are appealing to our illustrious battle heroes of the past.

He watched one warrior stop before the tomb, his body taut and upright. Holding out both hands, palms upwards, he offered an arrow, bowed his head several times, before looking up at the Pap of the Bulàch beyond the shoulder of the cairn. His long hair moved in a gust of wind. Gripping the shaft of the arrow, he tensed his hands, causing the wood to suddenly snap yet still remaining a single piece. He placed the spoiled shaft on the ground and stepped back with slow steps, bowing a final time before the heroes of the past.

As Gest was busy with the intercessions, he decided to return home to fetch a sword, a hammer and a reed fan. Returning with these, he readjusted one side of the bonfire and raked among the burning debris to expose a bed of glowing embers. He placed his sword into the fire and waited. More of his warriors gathered, ritualistically spoiling more arrows and even one or two spears, adding to the offerings on the ground before the tomb. Several times he took hold of his sword wrapped in part of his plaid about the hilt and tested it upon a flat boulder with his hammer before placing it back in the embers. He used his reed fan to feed air into the glowing mass of embers and from time to time, raked the charred remnants of burnt wood to form a small mound over where the blade lay buried.

He thought of the campaign ahead, wondering how many days they would be in their saddles before meeting with Brude's men, envisaging the part of the country he knew where they would ride through before venturing down the Great Glen where he had never travelled before. Reports of a far-reaching glen, running as a vast corridor from coast to coast and filled with long lochs, flanked by rising hills, presented him with an unknown challenge. It made it difficult to calculate how long an army would take to pass through, unaware of the conditions under foot. Would Brude await their arrival? What if King Gabran struck first? Brude would then have to engage him and he considered the outcome – which proved futile, not knowing the numbers involved, or the terrain held, or the tactics employed. Maybe the Gaels had a different approach to battle from theirs and would spring the element of surprise to their favour.

As for his own men, that was a known quantity. With Drust, he had built up a highly trained force: men who were fit, able with sword, spear and bow, highly disciplined to follow commands. From Maelchon's store of historical knowledge, he and Drust replicated, as best as they could surmise, the Roman war machine, their ability to fight as a single unit and not randomly as individual warriors. He had their blacksmiths prepare long shields after the fashion of the Romans, which he and Drust had trained their men to interlock, giving a troop protection to withstand enemy fire power. He was proud of them. They had undergone so many drills that were now to be tested – as, too, was he as their warlord, backed by the intelligence of his right-hand man.

Reaching for his sword again, he tested it upon the stone with the hammer and felt a slight give in the metal. He struck it four times, and with the shaft slightly bent he returned it into the embers which he fanned into a lurid hot commotion. He did this repeatedly until his sword had been truly spoiled into a V-shape.

"O Fionn," he whispered, audible only to his own ears. "I thank you for the favours you have shown me, the making of a fighting force and the construction of great defences. Thank you, Lugh, for the blessing of an abundant harvest. And Brigantia in your spring transformation, show us your favour." He looked up to the heights of the Pap of the Bulàch and offered the spoiled sword in outstretched arms. "And Gruagach, the long-haired, valiant warrior and sorcerer, go before us and confound our foes, along with Fionn, famed destroyer of giant and monster. Grant us victory, that we would not be wasted on foreign soil in a fight that is not of our choosing. Keep us vigilant, wise to the schemes of others, that we may return without disgrace to our homes. Keep us in the ascendancy, and I vow to follow you all with greater devotion."

He surprised himself by the way he could pray. He recognised that the mounting tension had brought on the impulse, knowing that whatever care had been taken and strength of hand shown, the outcome was still with the gods.

Gest joined him soon after he had laid the sword on the ground among the other spoiled items of warfare. "I have decided that I will ride with you," he stated simply.

He felt pleased. This announcement, coming just at the close of his prayer, surely was a token of Brigantia's favour. He felt better equipped and ready, having a druid among his military retinue, especially with Gest's friendly disposition and more positive take on the world of the gods.

"Have you received any sign or word from our ancestors?" he asked with genuine interest.

"No. But Maelchon and I have observed all the due rites, and made the required offerings. We can ride with confidence that all has been done as it should."

Drust arrived shortly after, with the last of the warriors, who likewise made votive offerings before the tomb. In the gathering dusk, he stood with his back to the cairn of the ancestors, and addressed a great body of warriors. Many wives, parents and younger siblings assembled on the slopes that fell away from the mound.

"... We shall ride at dawn," he said, concluding a speech marked largely by practical talk, "with the rising sun at our backs casting long shadows over the lands of the Fortriu, moving forwards with the gathering strength of Beli Mawr. We shall not be ashamed, brothers; we shall not be despised. These are not empty words of bluster, but are uttered in the knowledge that we have trained for years and are ready for the testing. We shall hold our heads high before Brude and the Gaels, and cause them to take note that we are not an ill-prepared backward people from the hills. We shall surprise them, and cause them to wonder and question, 'How is it that we have not noticed before these men who advance with ease, compact in their military precision, bristling with spears, bearing huge shields with the mark of the boar?' They will say with some trepidation: 'The boar slumbers no more. And now we must heed him with extreme caution, careful not to excite his wrath.'"

The concluding book to the Z-ROD trilogy will follow soon.

Glossary

With many of the original Brittonic/Pictish place names forgotten, educated guesses have been made using the Brittonic (Welsh) equivalent of current Gaelic names and Norse names in areas beyond the influence of Dal Riata in the mid-6th century. Although little is currently known about Pictish language, it did have its linguistic variations from the rest of ancient Britain. The pronunciation has been phonetically transliterated (at the expense of correct spellings that are complicated to pronounce for non-Welsh speakers) to help with the flow and enjoyment of the drama. Besides, as the Picts were largely an illiterate people, their language would have been more of an oral tradition.

Aird nam Murchan – Ardnamurchan, the lengthy peninsula jutting westwards, forming the natural divide and marking the boundary in the era of this story between Pict and Gael.

Alt Clud – Brittonic for 'rock on the Clyde' which is how the inhabitants of the rock referred to Din Brython, modern day Dumbarton.

Y Broch – major seat of power of the Fortriu warlords; modern-day Burghead.

Cartray – 'the town of the fort', named in recognition of the Roman garrison at modern day Callander that lay in ruins at the time of our story. Callander is an anglicisation derived from Gaelic, Calasraid, with different possible meanings.

Craig Padrig – Craig Phadrig in Gaelic, stronghold of the Fortriu at the top of the Great Glen, standing above modern-day Inverness.

Dal Riata – Scots Kingdom in modern day Argyll, west Scotland.

Din Brython – Literally 'Fort of the Britons', capital of Strath Clud (Strathclyde), also known as Alt Clud; modern day Dumbarton.

Dindurn – hillfort of the Fotla Picts, near St Fillans, Perthshire.

Druim Alban – mountainous country separating Dal Riata from the Picts.

Dunadd – hillfort capital of Dal Riata, near modern day Kilmartin.

Eilean Bhòid – isle of Bute.

Eilean Creagach – Scarba (Norse word). As the Gaelic name is unknown, I have chosen this Gaelic name, meaning 'Rocky Island', which describes its appearance.

Erin – (Ireland) divided into sub kingdoms, e.g. Munster – Connacht – Leinster etc.

Hinba – probably the Isle of Jura (Norse origin). Although contested by some, Jura seems identifiable by Hinba's early description as having a 'sea sack', referring to a large sea-loch indenting its coast.

Inis y Copa Peer – Isle of Eigg, one of the Small Isles, the Brittonic name meaning the isle of the sheer summit.

Inis Kayru – modern day Raasay (derived from the Norse) meaning roe deer island. Kayru is a generic Welsh word for deer.

Inis y Mynachon – 'isle of the monks', 'Inchtavannach' in Gaelic, on Loch Lomond.

Inis Niwl – Brittonic rendering of 'isle of mist', referring to the Isle of Skye. It is unknown what Skye was called pre-dating the Gaelicisation of the Northern Hebrides. At the time our drama is set, the influence of the Gaels did not extend north of Ardnamurchan.

Loch Aloninn – meaning 'restless loch', Loch Alsh in Gaelic.

Loch Gunalon – Loch Earn (derived from the Gaelic: Eireann, simplified as 'Erin' – Ireland). This watery route, east to west, was used as a place of passage by Irish monks.

Loch Kilmorkill – 'loch of the narrow strait', modern day, Loch Carron.

Loch Lengwartha – Loch Katrine, literally meaning loch of the cattle hustlers.

Loch Lumon – Loch Lomond.

Luinn – modern day, Isle of Luing.

Manau or **Maetae** – a one-time eminent people group in Roman times, confined in 6th century AD to the environs of modern-day Stirling, with their fort at Dumyat.

Migdele – modern day Meigle in Angus.

Minamoyn Goch – a Brittonic rendering of 'the red hills' by which the Cairngorm Mountains are known, rather than by their lesser-known Gaelic name of Am Monadh Ruadh, 'the red hills'.

Muile – Gaelic for modern-day Isle of Mull.

Pap of the Bulàch – the hill above Rhynie now known as 'Tap O' Noth'.

Pictish Tribes (7): Fortriu – Fotla– Fib – Fidach – Cait – Ce – Circinn [see map].

Rhynie – seat of the Ce warlords.

Rùm – Isle of Rum, one of the Small Isles, keeping with the name it is identified by today as there is a case for the name being pre-Gaelic.

Saoil – Gaelic for modern day, Isle of Seil.

Strath Clud – Strathclyde.

Definition of other words

Anam cara – soul mate, denoting a mentor.

Angle – Saxon – Jute – Germanic tribes who established themselves in current day England.

Annwn – the otherworld, paradise, home of the righteous dead.

Bairns – children.

Bannock – a round, flat bread baked on a sandstone slab in the Early Historic period.

Beli Mawr – Celtic sun god.

Beltane – early summer pagan festival.

Brae – a slope.

Brigantia – the transformation of the Bulàch (mother earth goddess) from the old hag into the young maiden at springtime.

Briton – the indigenous Celtic peoples of Britain before the arrivals of Angles, Saxons and Jutes.

Broch – an Iron-age tower with double walls, two to three storeys in height, occupied by high status people for domestic and defensive purposes.

Bulàch – probably Brittonic/Pictish for 'old hag' or 'witch', the mother earth goddess known by the Gaels as the Cailleach, and in 20th century Scotland, as 'Beira'. The Bulàch transforms herself into the youthful goddess 'Brigantia' come spring, when the Bulàch drinks from the well of eternal youth.

Coracle – a light craft for one person made of stitched and pitched animal hides stretched over a wooden frame.

Currach – a leather craft, larger than the coracle, powered by rowers and a sail.

Din – dun, an Iron-age hillfort.

Gael – refers to a speaker of Gaelic, the language of the Irish and of Dal Riata.

Imbolc – the first of three spring festivals, commencing at the start of February.

Lughnasa – the early harvest festival celebrated on 2nd August, following the reaping of the hay and in anticipation of the growing grain that would be gathered in the following month.

Muintir – Gaelic for 'family', the term the monks used to express their Christian community, or 'colony of heaven'. The term 'monastery' is avoided as it gives an unhelpful impression of a medieval equivalent far removed from the basic building structure used in this early time.

Oratory – the simple chapel in the centre of the monastic community.

Ostara – the spring equinox festival.

Pict – the indigenous peoples north of the Forth-Clyde divide.

Saint – an early biblical term for a Christian pilgrim, not referring to the special holy status conferred on an individual by papal decree.

Samhainn – Halloween festival, honouring the dead.

Strath – a long, wide valley.

Torc – a neck ring adornment worn by high-status warriors.

Vallum – an earth mound about a settlement.

Vellum – parchment.

Yule – end of year, winter solstice festival.

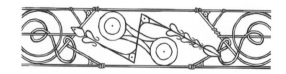

with Nature

STICKY WICKET

Gardening in Tune with Nature

PAM LEWIS

SPECIAL PHOTOGRAPHY BY
Andrew Lawson

FRANCES LINCOLN

To Peter

Frances Lincoln Limited
4 Torriano Mews
Torriano Avenue
London NW5 2RZ

Sticky Wicket: Gardening in Tune with Nature
Copyright © Frances Lincoln Limited 2005
Text copyright © Pam Lewis 2005
Photographs copyright © 2005 Pam Lewis
except jacket and pp 2-3, 5, 6, 13, 16-17, 32, 35,
37, 40, 44, 48-9, 63, 65, 86-7, 98, 109, 116,
121, 132-3, 156, 158, 163, 170-1, 198
copyright © Andrew Lawson
Illustrations copyright © Anne Wilson 2005
except plan illustration pp 14-15
copyright © Ed Brooks 2003

First Frances Lincoln edition 2005

British Library Cataloguing-in-Publication data
A catalogue record for this book is available from
the British Library

ISBN 0 7112 2480 3

Conceived, edited and designed for
Frances Lincoln Ltd by
Berry & Co (Publishing) Ltd
47 Crewys Road
Child's Hill
London NW2 2AU

Edited by Susan Berry
Design and illustrations by Anne Wilson
Plan illustration by Ed Brooks
Index by Marie Lorimer

Printed in Singapore

9 8 7 6 5 4 3 2 1

Contents

PREFACE

Sticky Wicket is primarily a wildlife garden but also a romantic and peaceful place of great character and charm. In the following chapters, I describe my inspiration and incentive, my design and planting and the link with the immediate environment and how our garden is holistically managed to be in tune with nature. By "nature" I refer to the interrelationship between the soil (which underpins all life), the garden plants and associated creatures, the aspect of the land, weather patterns, light and shade, the scent, aroma and other virtues of plants, their tactile quality and the sounds we hear. By "gardening in tune with nature" I mean understanding, respecting and working in step with all these elements so that organic garden husbandry is more logical to undertake and much more rewarding to carry out.

Human nature also has to be considered; notably our emotional responses, our inherent need for order, our desire to enhance and embellish our surroundings and our penchant for acquiring and cosseting a collection of plants. I, too, want to satisfy these human needs. I try to use my wildlife-friendly plants to paint beautiful living pictures in the garden and in the way I grow crops but without inflicting chemicals on my soil, my plants, my wildlife or myself – in fact exactly the reverse.

By adopting this holistic approach, encouraging a natural equilibrium between plants and beneficial wildlife, I can successfully manage my garden using organic methods. A finely balanced interrelationship has developed between living things, including plants and creatures, and the less evident, but crucially important fungus and bacteria. "Good guys" will prey on those that are pests to gardeners and our flowers will be pollinated to provide seed and berries for ourselves and our wildlife.

I observe, enjoy and allow myself to be guided by nature as I "nudge things along" rather than "enforce an extreme regime". The trick is to be patient, pragmatic at times, and to temper reasonable measures of control with a sympathetic and lenient attitude. The pay-back I get for my work and forbearance is enjoying the response as I watch my garden flourish artistically and simply buzz with wildlife, and being able to help and encourage others who may wish to achieve similar goals.

The principles and practices of making and managing a natural and wildlife-friendly garden can be scaled to size and applied to even the tiniest backyard which, multiplied by a potential 270,000 hectares of amassed garden wildlife oasis, signifies great hope for an enlightened future for our environment.

Pam Lewis, Sticky Wicket, January 2005

INTRODUCTION

W E CAME TO STICKY WICKET with all our possessions and animals, including a horse and several hens and ducks, stacked in a cattle truck. It was October 1986; we had moved from Hampshire to Dorset with no job, no money and no idea what we would do.

On the plus side we now had our own home with five acres of land. We also had open minds and were used to hard work and "making do". Peter and I had enjoyed a life-long, hands-on connection with the land, both as farmers and gardeners. We had loved our farming life but times were changing both in agriculture and in the countryside. Over the years, we had witnessed the destruction of so much of our natural and semi-natural wildlife habitat, for which farmers hold a large share of the blame. Giving something back to the environment seemed the right thing to do, and making a wildlife-friendly garden was our first intention. I wanted to throw all my experience, energy and artistic inclinations into making a joy and a success of this project and Peter, with his extraordinary physical strength and tenacity, would help to shape it. The five acres of grass pasture that surrounded the house were in a neglected and dejected state. There was limited appeal for wildlife and only the faintest indication that someone had, at one time, vaguely intended to make a garden. With some previous experience in designing and making gardens, Peter and I immediately focused on the ways we could change and manage our few acres efficiently. We wanted our land to become a safe haven for wildlife and, at the same time, be beautiful, creative and productive for us. All these elements were to guide our garden-making and our future in Dorset.

One writer, Chris Baines, had a very positive influence. In his excellent and inspiring book *How to Make a Wildlife Garden*, Professor Baines explains how gardeners can help to make sanctuaries for much of our displaced farmland wildlife. As the face of the countryside continues to be dramatically changed, wildlife is increasingly harassed and displaced by modern farming practice, political manipulation and building developments, and many species of flora and fauna have become victims, some even driven to extinction. Fortunately, our gardens can become a constructive part of the vital network of alternative habitat that exists in our road verges, canals and riversides, coastal regions, parks and open spaces.

There needs to be a "green corridor" system, through which the creatures and plants can move and spread from one small safe haven to another, and find shelter and sustenance along the way.

There are, of course, certain plants and creatures that cannot adapt to the sort of habitat most of us have on offer in our gardens; for instance, the green-winged orchid, the chalkhill blue butterfly and the otter all have very specific habitat requirements in order to be able to survive and breed. We have to rely on a very few dedicated individuals and conservation organizations, such as the Wildlife Trusts, to protect such rare species. However, with our garden wildlife projects we can boost the chances of survival for thousands of less exotic species which also desperately need safeguarding.

I realized that this is where our individual patches of land are so important – we can all do our bit to help and the more gardeners who do so, the less fragmented and more connected our web of wildlife corridors can become. In Britain around two and a half million acres of land are said to be cultivated as part of the fifteen millions of gardens estimated to exist. To some extent, these gardens can be made to mimic some vital natural habitats such as woodland glades, wetlands and grasslands. These mini-habitats can be made viable in just a few square yards of garden – or even on a balcony – but of course with a larger area the opportunities and chances of success are multiplied. The design of the garden, the plants we select and the way we manage our gardens are the keys to success.

A pond, of whatever size, with native water plants is a very good start and is guaranteed to generate instantly gratifying results. Trees and hedges can be planted to mimic semi-woodland type of wildlife-friendly habitat, especially if British native plants can be included. Well-sited bird-feeders, bird-baths and nesting-boxes will further boost the chances of supporting and increasing the local bird population. There is a vast selection of glamorous, ornamental garden plants and wildflowers that will appeal to bees and butterflies and other important insects, such as hoverflies and beetles, which will feed on the pollen and nectar. In return, they help pollinate our plants and some will prey on insects we regard as pests. Most of these plants need to be grown in an open but sheltered place – the natural equivalent of a sunlit woodland glade. Fruits and berries, and seeds and nuts, will feed many of our birds and some of the small mammals that most of us can most easily accommodate in our gardens. There is a wealth of both wild plants and garden plants to help in this respect. Thousands of acres of lawn consume thousands of gallons of fossil fuel and chemicals to keep them maintained with only a limited value to wildlife. A little patch of fertilizer- and herbicide-free meadow, on the other hand, can support thousands of creatures and, although some are so small as to be invisible to the naked eye, they are all vital links in the food chain for wildlife.

With all this in mind, I drafted the "grand plan" for our land and, in 1987, we began making our Frog and Bird Gardens. By then we had had time to assess the site and our immediate environment and we fully understood the nature of our fertile loam-over-clay soil, which needed to be very carefully handled. The following year we began preparations for the Round Garden, where we intended to lavish our attention on growing nectar plants to attract beneficial insects. At the same time we planted the small birch copse, the little orchard area and the great hawthorn hedge which were to eventually shelter and enfold our "sunny glade". We already had one enormous asset for wildlife: the 350m (400yd) of hedgerow that formed the boundary of our land and, amongst the wide range of native species, the five mature oaks spaced along it. In 1990 we forged on with the making of our White Garden, which was intended to be much wilder than the other gardens and would help to merge our garden discreetly into the beautiful surrounding countryside.

We spent part of the next six years consolidating our work, learning how best to apply organic methods to manage the garden sensitively, and trying to persuade our pasture and part of the White Garden to be conducive to growing wildflowers. This was altogether a different ball game! Peter and I had many years of previous experience managing grassland but the nature of our soil, with its high fertility, showed a remarkable resistance to change. This set us a challenge that was to grasp our interest, change our lives and eventually commit us to a future specializing in and dedicating ourselves to the conservation of the flora and fauna of grassland. Only after thorough research, much physical effort and hours of soul-searching did we take the plunge and scrape the topsoil from half an acre of land to make the species-rich wildflower meadow (the New Hay Meadow) adjoining the White Garden (the subject of my first book, *Making Wildflower Meadows*).

My finely prepared life-size canvas was blank before I began the systematic planting of each individual garden. We had been very thorough in the planning, design and construction of our garden before carefully preparing the soil. We were at opposite poles to the quick-fix make-over teams we so often see on television! Eventually it was time to put the paint on the canvas and begin planting. During the design stages I had begun to loosely sketch out my thoughts on planting. The major structural planting such as woodland copses, hedges and shelter belts were settled in my mind. Design and planting must run hand in hand to some extent but I find it best not to get too caught up in detailing specific plants in the early stages unless very special planting conditions are likely to be required.

I had clear ideas about which colours I wanted to use in each garden. The colours were to relate to the seasonal and ecological focus I was placing on each garden area. For instance, several of our native pond and bog plants and early spring-flowering plants are yellow so I followed their lead and used yellow as the main colour for my Frog Garden. In the Bird Garden I chose pink because I wanted an extended range of plants giving me a long season of flowering; there are pink forms and varieties of most garden plants and many of our wildflowers are pink. Insects, such as bees and butterflies, are very often attracted to plants in the blue/violet/magenta spectrum so my Round (nectar) Garden needed to include these colours. Many plants with fruit, berries and autumn colour have white flowers and there were plenty of white wildflowers that would contribute handsomely to my White Garden with its "fruit forest".

I started off in a very disciplined way before unleashing my creative inclinations. I researched my subject in great detail and made a long list of all the plants I could possibly need for a thriving wildlife garden on a neutral, loamy but heavily clay-based soil. Garden wildlife requires plants to provide a variety of both food and habitat. Food plants include those that supply nectar, pollen, fruit, nut, berry or seed and very often some leaves for the infant (larval) stage in the cycle of insect development. Useful habitat plants provide shelter from the elements and protection from predators as the creatures hunt or forage for food, court, mate and rear their young and perch, roost, hide-out, hibernate or build nests.

I also listed the plants I wanted to grow to nourish my own body and soul. I intended to continue my tradition of growing as much of my own food as can be easily produced in our home conditions. I wanted my plants to be grown "cottage-garden style" in that they would be arranged in a seemingly random mixture of edible and decorative plants seasoned with useable herbs. I most certainly yearned for a sequence of scented and aromatic plants – particularly surrounding the house.

Fragrance often triggers nostalgic memories and there were some favourite plants I needed for emotional stimulation. I am passionate about meadows so wildflowers and grasses would be a thread running through all the gardens. Although I love to pick and browse my way around the garden, I am not a bit interested in gathering quantities of plants for interior flower arranging. However, I do love to have a little "nosegay" of fresh flowers and herbs on my kitchen table and beside my bed. The lists grew longer and longer but I knew they would be rationalized because I am a composer of plants rather than a compulsive collector.

While I was mulling over the proposed composition, I found this inspiring quote by George Eliot in *Scenes from Clerical Life*, first published in 1857:

> "A charming paradisiacal mingling of all that was pleasant to the eye and good for food. You gathered a moss rose one moment and a bunch of currants the next. You were in a delicious fluctuation between the scent of jasmine and the juice of gooseberries."

She had perfectly expressed my own romantic notions.

I had brought a "Noah's Ark" of plants from my previous garden, many of which were herbs. Most of our British native plants enjoy a reputation of having herbal virtues, capable of curing any complaint from the bubonic plague and wounds inflicted by mad dogs to modern-day allergies and even some cancers. I am fascinated by herbs and astonished at the power and the potency of plants. I find it terrifying to think of a future where genetically manipulated plants will inevitably escape into the countryside and into gardens. Some may hybridize with our wild plants and potentially pollute the genetic stock of plants which, as yet unbeknownst to us, may hold health-giving or even life-saving attributes. By happy coincidence, many of the top-of-the-range insect nectar plants are herbs and they are all beautiful – lavender, rosemary, fennel, marjoram and thyme are old favourites. I was delighted by how well the interests of wildlife, wildflower gardener and herbalist neatly overlap.

Having developed my planting brief I began to dreamily compose the picture I would paint. I wanted my borders to vary in terms of rhythm and pace. The style

Undulating grasses glisten at the feet of the upstanding valerian (*Valeriana officinalis*); foxtail barley grass (*Hordeum jubatum*) and *Stipa tenuissima* are signature plants in our garden.

of some would seem to be measured and controlled – almost static and becalmed. In other places I wanted the assembled plants to wave, flow, flutter and blow or weave, tumble and thread together. I tried to foresee and capitalize on the way sunlight and shadow, wind and rain, frost and dew would contribute, casting their magical spells over the images, making them sparkle, shimmer, glisten and glow. I think these less definable qualities of planting need to evolve from a hands-on relationship with the garden and by giving the plants sufficient space and scope to express their character and charisma. Some of the most magical planting events have resulted from a smouldering idea that has "spontaneously combusted", perhaps because of the way the plants have spilled over each other or from some self-set seedlings volunteering their services. The combined design and planting is like arranging a stage set, then directing the dance choreography to the music of the sounds of the countryside: a somewhat clichéd but nevertheless descriptive comparison.

PLAN OF STICKY WICKET GARDENS

Our two-and-a-half-acre gardens are surrounded by a further two and a half acres of varied grassland, mature, species-rich hedgerows and small wooded areas that provide vital natural habitat for the wildlife that visits the garden.

1 THE FROG GARDEN
Creating ponds and wetland habitat was an
urgent priority when we first set out to
transform our land from neglected pasture
into a flourishing wildlife haven.

2 THE BIRD GARDEN
A special focus on attracting birds close to the
house and a very personal garden where we
joyfully watch and welcome the ever-increasing
numbers and range of visiting and resident birds.

3 THE ROUND GARDEN
A paradise for bees and butterflies and
beneficial insects and an equal attraction for
all who visit this sheltered, sunny glade.

4 THE WHITE GARDEN
Our white-flowered wilderness garden with
its "fruit forest", grassland, woodland edge and
hedgerow habitat provides for all creatures large
and small.

5 THE GARDEN MEADOW
A mixture of wildflowers and naturalized
garden plants grows in the fertile, loamy
grassland within the garden.

6 THE NEW HAY MEADOW
An important conservation project where
topsoil was removed to enable us to grow
a diversity of wildflowers harvested from very
few remaining local, traditional hay meadows.

7 BIRCH COPSE
Just a few birches and a couple of Scots pines
were all that was needed to satisfy many species
of woodland flora and fauna.

THE FROG GARDEN

The Frog Garden has predominantly spring and early-summer planting with yellow and blue colouring. The special features are the recently enlarged ponds and bogs where amphibians breed and birds drink, bathe and gather mud for nesting.

Just six months after construction, the new ponds look long-established and local wildlife is already settling in.

T HERE ARE CONSIDERABLY fewer ponds left on farmland in the countryside nowadays. Some ecologists suggest, as a result, that if it were not for our garden ponds, the frog would be in danger of becoming extinct. What an alarming thought both for the frog and for the gardener, for whom he is a slug-consuming friend. The garden pond can provide a constant, local source of water for pond-life battling to exist in a particular area. Amphibians lack the mobility of birds, mammals and insects, which can easily travel many miles seeking pastures new, so if just one pond is destroyed, an entire ecosystem could be wiped out.

The reduction in farmland ponds began to occur as water became easy to pump and pipe around the countryside, and the ponds were filled in to increase further the acreage of surplus crops. There are still some woodlands (which are the best for pure water), nature reserves, disused quarries, depressions, dew ponds and village ponds, but farmland, anyway, is a hostile place for a frog. Harmful chemicals that run off agricultural land often contaminate the surviving, undrained wetlands. Frogs and other amphibians are very susceptible to harm from such chemicals, especially the toxic ones associated with the growing of maize – whether conventional or genetically modified. These chemicals run off the soil surface of fields, enter the watercourses and all too easily end up in the places frogs use as a breeding ground. Since frogs and toads cannot survive without still water in which to breed, many now seek asylum in gardens where, although not all ornamental ponds are wildlife-friendly, they often get lucky and find the right sort of unpolluted, predator-free, alternative habitat in which to spawn their young. However, they do run the gauntlet of strimmers and mowers when they settle for the comparative safety of our gardens. What a predicament!

BALANCE OF AQUATIC SPECIES   There are many other fascinating creatures that also live in water or require water during part of their life-cycle. Besides frogs, we love to see toads, newts, dragonfly nymphs, caddis larvae and water beetles. There are also native water-loving plants and marginal plants, such as yellow loosestrife and flag iris, which need a safe home. Their natural riverside habitat is being eroded by invasive alien species erroneously put on sale in garden centres. Once these escape from gardens and enter watercourses, they can block waterways and cause irresolvable problems in the countryside. Some of these greedy species, such as parrot feather (*Myriophyllum aquaticum*), floating pennywort (*Hydrocotyle ranunculoides*), water fern (*Azolla filiculoides* and *A. caroliniana*) and Australian swamp stonecrop (*Crassula helmsii*) are aquatic. Himalayan balsam (*Impatiens glandulifera*), Japanese knotweed (*Petasites japonicus*) and giant hogweed (*Heracleum mantegazzianum*) can proliferate excessively at the water's edge. The all-enveloping plants are further boosted by the chemical nutrients entering our waterways, giving them an unfair advantage over our native wildflowers, which are swallowed up by the rampant vegetation. Once there is an imbalance to plant-life, there is an automatic distortion to animal life.

How can we gardeners help? Garden pond-making is one of the most instantly gratifying wildlife projects, with a guaranteed result if the basic construction and planting guidelines are in place. Almost as soon as the project is complete, the pond dwellers miraculously gravitate to the habitat they crave. In fact, our local frogs were found loitering all around us, as if queuing up for a place, when we filled our first pond with water. The whole of this lower garden soon picked up the nickname the "Frog Garden" and the title stuck.

DESIGN

The design for this garden began with, and centred around, the desire to make a wildlife pond. We mentally positioned it where we could see it from some of the house windows and, most conveniently, at the lowest point on our property where we noticed water had a tendency to gather but not, fortunately, in depths that could make excavations complicated.

We were actually making the best of what could have been a tricky situation for most ordinary gardening. The water-logging we had experienced was as much to do with land abuse as it was land levels; previous builders' disregard for the soil strata and structure had been absolute. The worst imaginable topsoil/subsoil mix had occurred where a cesspit had once been installed and then later filled in. We had inherited a sticky, swampy, nightmare corner, but this lent itself ideally to our wetland project.

In this sheltered south-westerly corner there were good light levels so we could easily reach our aim of having one third of our pond as open, sunny water surface and two thirds of it shaded, at least for part of the day. Fortunately there were no nearby conifers (which produce an acidic run-off that pollutes water) but the nearby oak would be a mixed blessing come autumn when it shed its leaves and acorns. However, for bats and many insects the positioning would be highly appropriate and the tree would provide a little of the pond's necessary shade for part of the day.

BORDERS AND LAWNS I decided I would arrange the borders and lawn in the space left after we fixed this main feature and after siting some screening trees in strategic positions. As the ideas began to gel, I set out the design using sketch plan, thick pencil, assorted sticks and yards of yellow hose and bale-string – all very high tech! The exact position and shape of the pond, and its attendant planting area, were paramount; the rest of the design would follow logically from that starting point.

SURROUNDING HEDGES, ROADS AND WATERCOURSES I wanted my planting to integrate softly with the views of our highly valued boundary hedgerows, preserving my vista of the bustling wildlife already in residence. Because the road was so close, the sides would have to be trimmed annually but that would stimulate dense, twiggy growth as well as keeping access and vision clear along the narrow lanes.

We (and our wildlife) would be well contained and sheltered, and the thorny plants, such as blackthorn and dog rose, would help keep both the creatures and our property secure from intruders. Apart from the intermittent sound of traffic we need hardly know the road was so close. However, roads are a dreadful hazard to wildlife, especially frogs and toads that move slowly and are not the least bit streetwise. I like

With plans set for three of our four gardens, work began in 1987 as we laid out and constructed paths, pergolas and borders at the entrance to the Frog Garden.

to think they would prefer to stay at Sticky Wicket rather than be tempted to migrate away. Even though I sometimes find one or two squashed on the tarmac, I can never be sure if they were our residents leaving home or newcomers looking for a place to breed as the neighbouring gardens do not always have wildlife-friendly ponds. The River Lyden trickles by within 300 yards of the garden but frogs, toads and newts require water which is quite still and with reasonably constant depths; the river is too variable in all respects to be ideal for pond-life.

NEIGHBOURING WILDFLOWER OASIS   Although a fairly busy country lane borders this garden on its north and west sides, to the east lies the village cemetery – nice quiet neighbours for us and very special extra habitat for wildlife. The graveyard is a tiny oasis of the kind of wildflowers that grew in the ancient meadowland before it was set aside as a burial place about 50 years ago. They have fortunately survived because no chemicals have ever been applied, it is mown several times a year and the cut grass always removed (which helps to prevent nutrient build-up).

OUR SMALL GRASSLAND PROJECT   Inspired by what we had observed over our hedge, Peter and I wanted to make a "weedy-by-design" lawn which would become a colourful, nectar-filled and seed-rich mini-meadow. We noted that, next door, where the yellow meadow ants had worked away over the years, some of the grave mounds had slowly grown into well-drained heaps of crumbly clay and formed curious shapes (I refer to them as the "spooky humps"). The queen ant has her nest below the soil surface but the workers beaver away to make the anthills, which maintain an ambient temperature to create premium breeding conditions for her. The most delicate of wildflowers grew at the highest point of these mounds. We would use this intelligence to help us mimic suitable planting conditions with our own interpretation of these "spooky humps".

We divided our lawn into two parts: one would remain damp and fertile but, if we wanted to try to imitate the favourable conditions of the grave mounds in our garden, we would have to actively create a dry, nutrient-starved lawn feature using rubble and clay.

Like the rest of the five acres of land, the existing turf in the frog garden site was comprised of a mixture of grasses with white clover and creeping buttercup. We needed a grassy arena in the centre but certainly not one of those over-manicured, over-green, stripy jobs. I saw the potential for making my lawn interesting and useful to wildlife while also providing a play area for my three dogs in their ebullient youth, and us with the perfect place to enjoy a well-spread picnic with our friends, as I had an area of about 7 by 10m (22 by 32 yd) left after the borders and ponds had been carved out.

We intended to design all the gardens with fairly limited lawn space to minimize mowing, which is not an eco-friendly activity. Paradoxically though, even mown lawns can be very attractive for wildlife, provided they are never treated with chemicals, which we would never do. The best way forward in this situation was to make a virtue of what existed, adding more wildflowers to make a flowering lawn that would be mown for most of the year but with periods of flowering in spring and early summer. I placed a wildlife-friendly, shapely specimen tree in the corner of the lawn to provide a shade for the seat I would, in my dreams, one day set beneath the leafy canopy. The bird cherry, *Prunus padus*, turned out to be a first-class choice in all respects.

CONNECTING ONE GARDEN TO ANOTHER Although the adjoining Bird Garden was to be a separate "room", the rhythm of the design flowed from one to another, so the two were mapped out at the same time. The gentle, sensuous curves of the ponds and the borders and grassy areas of both gardens have been designed to give an illusion of depth at the points where the boundary hedge is closest to the house. I insisted on a wide path to surround the entire house, which would allow me to wander, sandal-shod, around the immediate vicinity, at any time of the year. Apart from bird-feeding, pond-watching and pot-watering, I had to allow for meeting my sudden impulses: to capture a moment on camera or rushing out for some impromptu weeding or dead-heading as the spirit moved me! The existing patio, a tacky-looking affair, was easily dismantled and reassembled to help with the necessary hard landscaping for a path-cum-terrace-cum-flight of shallow steps on the north side of the house.

PLANTING

The pond and bog planting would comprise almost entirely native plants to suit the needs of the amphibians and insects associated with water. The tangle of vegetation would provide cover for the creatures who would be competing for their place in the pond. I would need oxygenating plants and some aquatics with large surface leaves to shade the water below. Blanketweed and other algae are almost certain to be a problem in any artificially made pond so I needed to follow the best advice for minimizing such unwanted vegetation.

With our border planting, I took into account the other non-aquatic wildlife that would be attracted to the pond to bathe or drink, or would be drawn to the garden for other reasons. To coordinate the borders visually with the pond, bog planting and flowering lawn, I used yellow flowers (and some foliage) as the common denominator. Many pond plants are yellow and flower in the early part of the year: it is a wonderfully cheering colour, very much associated with springtime so I wanted to make this an essentially spring-orientated garden with a concentration of bulbs, and with some blue flowers to complement the yellows.

Grasses and grass-like plants in the borders and bog would unify with the fine grasses in the flowering lawns so the whole garden would have relaxed, coherent and natural style. I was pleased to find there are one or two beautiful ornamental yellow grasses and sedges that are closely related to our British native species.

For wildlife cover, *Cornus* would be ideal beside the pond, the leafy foliage offering a cool, shady retreat for frogs, toads and newts during the summer while the vibrant stem colour would be gloriously reflected in the inky pools in winter. Bearing in mind my office window faces the pond corner, there would be plenty of all-year-round action to distract and delight me as I struggled with the computer.

CONSTRUCTION – FIRST PHASE

We made this first, and lower-lying, pond using a flexible waterproof butyl liner. I wish I had had the confidence to puddle our own clay because we certainly had plenty of it but in this corner it was mixed with topsoil and not pure enough for puddling. There is a product that can be used as a substitute or addition to line clay ponds but we were advised this was not suitable for novice or faint-hearted pond-makes, and hadn't the nerve to gamble with the prospect of a dismal, fissure-edged hole if we failed in our endeavours. In hindsight this may have looked rather less depressing than the conspicuous butyl edges that can appear in periods of drought. However, butyl has distinct advantages over other man-made materials and, for first-time pond builders, it was probably the best choice.

POND EXCAVATION Once the pond site was approved and marked out, it took a body of four strong men (two of us were girls!) to hand-dig the (roughly) 4 sq m (4½ sq yd) hole during a weekend. The excavated clay soil was then used to reinforce the rubble bank on two sides to provide us with a level water surface.

Working with soil that seems to be three parts plasticene to one part goo has its advantages; it was easy to mould to the dips and shelves we wanted to create just below the water's edge. These anomalies would create gentle level changes, including warm shallows and ledges, for both plants and creatures. We removed any offending sharp stones or bits of root from the fashioned sides of the excavated hole to make certain the surface was entirely smooth (vital if the butyl liner was not to be punctured and the pond to then leak). We lined the base and sides with bits of old carpet, overlapping sheets of thick polythene and a layer of sand to protect the butyl sheet that we then dragged carefully into position.

To help the wildlife and pond plants feel at home, we put a thin layer of sand and finely sieved subsoil in the bottom of the pond. It is important to avoid over-fertile soil and especially any which may have traces of fertilizer or indeed any chemical. We slowly three-quarter filled the pond with a gentle trickle of water that barely disturbed the sand and soil base. The pond was fully filled only after the finishing touches were complete.

I can only describe the shape of this original pond as "irregularly square with rounded corners". It was over 60cm (2ft) deep in the centre and had sloping sides so that any visiting wildlife could easily come and go without getting trapped. The pond centre must be deep enough for aquatic wildlife to survive when the top portion of the pond freezes in winter. Ideally it should have been deeper, but we found with a small, saucer-shaped pond further excavation would have been difficult.

POND HABITAT The pond needed some "furniture" for the wildlife to find privacy, safety and asylum from each other; where subterfuge rather than speed is the criteria for survival such "hidey-holes" for escaping the enemy are essential. Several large boulders were placed both at the pond side and in the water and we laid some smooth stones of assorted sizes, like a pebble beach, near the edge. We then planted flag iris and kingcups to form small islands on the shallow shelves near the rounded corners, to help hide the liner in case our landscaping and water-technology skills failed to do the job. We could afford only a limited amount of materials for landscaping but were given a few large stone slabs, which we used to edge our approach to the pond. We laid them to overhang slightly and disguise the liner, and to create little areas of shade and protection for extra habitat. Setting them with small spaces in between helps to prevent wildlife getting trapped. As clay soil begins to settle it is difficult to prevent the stones from gradually sliding towards the water, especially if they are not quite large enough; as we had mixed-sized stone slabs, we had correspondingly mixed results as time went by.

THE SECOND POND   We built our second pond some years later when we began to regret not having made a larger one in the first place. We made fewer mistakes with the second pond, the worst of which was using concrete to construct it. The passage of time revealed the truth about concrete ponds; they are prone to cracking in freezing weather and seem to provide perfect conditions for blanketweed to become a menace in warm weather. Also, concrete contains harmful chemicals that leach out into the water. In theory, this can be removed after several rinses with fresh water but this is not easy without a pump and a suitable place to dispose of the contaminated water.

However, we were full of enthusiasm when we – the same heroic team that dug the first pond – set out to excavate another with similar wildlife specifications. Design-wise, the pond was teardrop-shaped, any surplus water spilling gently into the first, lower pond. Hardly a gushing waterfall, this nevertheless made a pleasing trickle, and we installed a circulating pump so that it could be prompted at the flick of a switch.

THE BASE FOR THE SECOND POND   We needed to dig a hole at least 15cm (6in) deeper and wider than the ultimate pond size to allow for the necessary thickness of the concrete. This time we set aside the clay spoil to make the grassland feature described below. Once the hired concrete mixer was in operation, it was all hands on deck – shovelling, barrowing, tamping, slapping, smoothing and moulding the

mixture onto the base of pegged-down heavy-gauge chicken wire that reinforced the structure. It is recommended that a 10cm (4in) layer of concrete is needed to minimize cracking but it is difficult to avoid being a little inconsistent in places, as the whole process is a race against time as the concrete begins to set mid-operation.

Finally, we mixed up a barrow-load of concrete with a few buckets of coir to make a reasonably attractive tufa-style rim to the pond and peppered it here and there with round stones that Peter had spent many hours picking out of the path gravel. We set groups of substantial-sized rocks at strategic points to make varied habitats in the pond. I can't remember how many days we left it draped in polythene to allow the concrete to set but it seemed ages to me – the most childlike member of the construction team, who couldn't wait to see the job prettied up with plants. Even when we eventually filled the pond, and could see that it looked good, we still had to wait a couple of weeks while emptying and refilling the pond twice more to remove the toxic chemicals that leach into the water from the cement. Six weeks later it was deemed habitable and the covers removed to allow creatures to begin to colonize.

ALL ABOUT WATER As tap water can exacerbate the growth of problem weed, such as blanketweed, and it may contain chemicals that are not good news for wildlife,

Shaping and excavating the site for the concrete pond was a messy and inevitably disruptive exercise but nature is very forgiving and, in the blink of an eye, the pond soon looked glorious and brimmed with pond life.

we channelled rainwater off the house to top up the pond (also helping to conserve water). A wooden barrel acts as a water butt, storing several gallons before the surplus cascades down the sides to a soakaway, from which it is piped to the pond. Admittedly, in long spells of dry weather we have to run tap water into the butt to supplement the supply but at least our input is diluted with the stored rainwater and used only in emergencies. On high days and holidays we switch on the pump which circulates and aerates water whilst yielding a pleasant sound.

We are currently researching the use of solar power, as an environmentally advantageous form of resourcing energy. I feel sufficiently confident to scribble a conspicuous note on our Christmas list alongside the request for the solar lights I have been wanting for some time. I have not yet been able to discover whether the advertised floating globes would be efficient in keeping an ice-free breathing hole for aquatic wildlife during a freeze. It would save me having to fiddle about with bowls of hot water to melt the ice (cracking it can be traumatic for underwater creatures).

POND GARDEN FEATURES

There was only one "garden feature" at Sticky Wicket when we came. The former owner had built what could be loosely described as a patio – a conspicuous square platform of slabs protruding from a doorway with four rounded, coniferous blobs at the edges. You needed to be either seven foot tall or an athlete to get on and off the "patio" without straining some part of your anatomy. We re-homed the conifers (far away in another county!) but recycled the paving as part of the construction of the wide path-cum-terrace along this north side of the house. We also reused the paving to make a flight of shallow steps to abolish the need for the death-defying leap onto the lawn. The paving slabs were at first rather grim, but reset in gravel with creeping plants threaded in and out of the patchwork, they have gradually begun to mellow. Cobbled sets would have been a preferred option but were way beyond our budget.

Recycling was an essential part of the brief for our low-cost garden-making, but I promised myself I would one day revamp some of the economy landscaping once the priority wildlife initiatives were up and running. In the meantime we saved a pile of stones from the builders' rubble dug out of the proposed planting areas. We managed to beg, steal or borrow a few more to build some dry-stone retaining walls, which formed part of the restructured terrace. As dry-stone walls are built without mortar they have lots of useful crevices for all kinds of wildlife to occupy. The skill in building such a wall is to have a good eye for exactly the right size and shape of stone to fit securely beside its neighbour. As an amateur dry-stone wall builder I am only average, but Peter revealed a superior skill and practised eye that way outshone mine.

THE SPOOKY HUMP We were diligent in making our planting preparations suitable for extremes of both wet and dry conditions. More stone was needed on the upper edge of the Frog Garden lawn where we constructed our triangular patch, known as the "spooky hump" (see page 21). It is really just a gentle mound

We constantly explore different ways to persuade a diversity of wildflowers to grow in the varied conditions required for them to cohabit alongside selected native grasses. The "spooky hump" is designed and constructed to mimic the very special grassland habitat in our neighbouring graveyard.

but produces a sufficient micro-environment to create the well-drained and impoverished conditions that many wildflowers favour. Most fortuitously, one of our neighbours offered us some assorted rubble from his building demolition. Rubble is always a useful component of many a wildlife feature and we happily accepted. We first laid a tough horticultural fabric over the fertile soil at the base of our proposed artificial, over-sized "anthill" to form a barrier and prevent nutrients being taken up by deeper-rooted plants. Then we piled rubble on top – larger pieces first, then those of a finer grade mixed with some of the clay saved from pond excavations. To level it off, we capped it with about an inch of limestone chippings and sand. We laid a patchwork of irregularly shaped pieces of ryegrass-free turf with gaps between each – like a chequerboard. From our store of mixed wildflower seed harvested from our local churchyard we propagated about fifty plants, setting most of these into the gaps and some actually into the patchwork pieces of turf. Then we scattered the rest of the seed very finely over the whole area, crossed our fingers, and hoped for the best!

Within months our own "spooky hump" became a great joy to behold. It now helps conserve the local flora while attracting legions of insects and invertebrates, which, in turn, help to feed birds and sometimes a visiting fox or hedgehog. How wonderful it would be if the green woodpeckers that visit these humps in the neighbouring churchyard in search of ants also visit our own.

Sadly, these extremely special grave mounds and anthills were perceived as "untidy" by the parish council, and have recently been removed or tampered with, thus desecrating the locally distinct landmark and impacting on the ecosystem. Our personal quest to conserve the wildflowers became more urgent. We realized the ecological importance of these grave mounds and knew that we cannot possibly recreate such a phenomenon that has taken decades to evolve. We could, however, address the lack of awareness in our local countryside and resolved to do our best to compensate for any indifferent stewardship that contributes to the demise of Britain's wild plants and interdependent wildlife.

CONSTRUCTION – PHASE TWO

By October 2003, our original butyl pond – then 17 years old – was leaking and so overgrown it was hardly visible. It was still very much the domain of our frog population so we thought long and hard when contemplating a third, much larger, pond for our wildlife that seemed to be outgrowing the two we had. The disruption would inevitably be a bit traumatic for all the creatures in the vicinity but before we started, we carefully rescued all the pond life we could find. Many creatures were given temporary lodgings in large plastic tubs, along with some of the pond sludge and vegetation. The very few frogs in residence at the time were persuaded to visit other parts of the garden. It was some way off their breeding time and we were determined to have the pond ready before they needed to hibernate (around October) or spawn (beginning in February).

PETER'S PONDS   Peter took command of this project. There were to be no half measures this time. In spite of all the careful overall planning of the gardens, I must be honest and admit that, in our enthusiasm, we rushed into our first pond project without sufficient forethought and made mistakes. In the first place, we should have allocated a larger space for the pond, preferably further away from the nearby oak. It is not close enough to harm the tree or for the tree to cast too much shade on the pond, but the leaf-fall causes a build-up and overload of silt. Secondly, we should have considered more thoroughly the feats of water engineering needed to supply the pond with rainwater channelled from our herringbone land-drainage system. However, we were daunted by the logistics of seasonal "feast or famine" rainwater supplies. It was too technically challenging to deal with the surplus water pouring off our land during the increasingly wet winters, nor could we begin to evaluate the quantities of water that might flood in or how to deflect the surplus back into the particular watercourse we could officially access. We would just have to top up the pond with tap water in dry weather although we recognized this resolution was not ideal.

This time around Peter designed, excavated and constructed not one but two large ponds to replace the single original small one. Why two? Well, in terms of biodiversity, a series of ponds with varied habitats is more valuable than one large body of water. In our case it was also to do with land levels, the reinforcement of the sides and aspects of water engineering that left me perplexed and unable to visualize. I was grateful to be a passenger in this, and to marvel at Peter's ingenuity.

Peter applied the same successful construction principles to the new ponds as he had to the original but, with the size of this one at least tenfold the original, there was far more scope for a greater depth of water and more varied shelves and bog

areas. The increased size and depth would eventually help regulate fluctuations in temperature but brought with it technical hitches when it came to making the water levels precise and when finishing the edges and disguising the liner. At each stage of the construction he used a plank and spirit level to check the levels in both directions.

He used a tufa mix for the edging about half-way around each pond. This tufa mix was made using the same combination of ingredients as before (see page 26) but with one difference. We wanted to avoid using peat and even imported coir is not really ecologically friendly. Peter used organic peat-free compost instead. It seemed a good substitute and the

Peter's ambition was to enlarge our wetland habitat from the original small ponds. He pauses momentarily while installing the pond liner during one of the construction stages in this major project.

dark colour resulted in a mix that looked like baked mud. With its reasonably organic and unobtrusive appearance, it held the edge of the liner secure and helped to protect the potentially exposed parts of the butyl from the ultra-violet rays of the sun as and when the tide-line fluctuated in dry weather. Random groups of stones, logs and both pond and marginal plants distracted from the rim-like appearance. Of the remaining edges, some were turfed and some paved as with the previous ponds. Peter also made a small bog by sinking part of the butyl lining and back-filling with soil, retained by a dam of sandbags.

Peter entrusted me with the habitat creation part of the project once his construction work was nearing completion. The large pile of leftover assorted stones waiting in the wings were randomly shaped, so to avoid the risk of leaks or damage to the liner we used mats of additional butyl, saved from the trimmings, underneath them. They were held down with small hessian bags of sand and soil into which we anchored some oxygenating plants.

More dragonflies than ever before visited the garden while our pond's progress was hurried along to beat the advancing wet winter weather. How frustrating it must have been for them to find preparations still incomplete for what promised to be a superbly safe breeding ground! For the robins, chaffinches and grey wagtails, however, the amenities were immediately usable and they were bathing in it even while work went on. Within days the frogs were back, too, and Peter was never short of wildlife company as he worked on resolving the edges. Even though we were now in October, I was unable to resist a dip before it became sacrosanct for wildlife. Peter could not believe his eyes when, on a sudden impulse, I dived into the pond fully clothed: "More like wild wife than wildlife", was his only comment. Tongue slightly in cheek, we buried a time capsule at the pond edge to remind or inform future archaeologists of our good intentions and our antics!

THE PLANTING

My first priority was to introduce some oxygenators to the muddy bottom of the pond. Water starwort (*Callitriche* sp.), spiked water milfoil (*Myriophyllum spicatum*), hornwort (*Ceratophyllum demersum*), and curly pondweed (*Tamogeton cripsus*) are recommended natives that root into the mud and improve the health of the water. I used hessian bags of sand and soil to start some of the plants going and anchor them at the appropriate depth. They multiply at a great rate and provide food and hiding places for tiny creatures.

Next I put in some plants with leaves that would float on the water surface and help reduce the light levels: The fringed water lily (*Nymphoides peltata*) is free-floating and therefore not fussy about water depths, making it ideal for any dimension of pond. With an ability to spread very rapidly, it is efficient in making a dark covering to exclude sunlight and so hamper the spread of blanketweed. In our situation, it also has the advantage of having delicate yellow flowers and small leaves that are perfectly in scale with the size of the little pond. However, for the large new ponds I have cautiously introduced the large yellow native water lily (*Nymphaea lutea*) that has much bolder flowers and leaves. I have also included broad-leaved pondweed (*Potamogeton natans*) with its olive-green oval leaves, which also lie on the surface.

The sun sets over Peter's pond, creating a serene view from our house as a community of native plants and wildlife rapidly become established during the first year.

Greater spearwort (*Ranunculus lingua*) has long, horizontal, underwater shoots with large spear-shaped leaves and huge buttercup-like flowers. It is one of the most invasive of my selection but I love it and the excess plants are easily weeded out to make good compost fodder. The bog bean (*Menyanthes trifoliata*) has leaves like a broad bean and delightful white flowers while burr reed (*Sparganium erectum*) has contrastingly sword-like leaves and globe-shaped fruits with seeds that some birds enjoy. Whether I wanted it or not, duckweed (*Lemna minor*) spread from pond to pond. The tiny, bright green leaves multiply like crazy and are a bit of a menace, but they redeem themselves by using up nutrients and helping to shade the water. To relieve the pond of a surplus, I net the excess and compost it or feed it to my very appreciative ducks.

POND MARGINS Most of my marginal plants are British natives and it is interesting how many of them are yellow. There are just a few blue ones to help unite my selected colour arrangement. At the edges of the butyl-lined ponds, at various depths of mud and water, I grow flag iris, kingcups, water-mint, water forget-me-not, and brooklime and creeping Jenny, which will both grow in the water as well as in fairly dry conditions. The damp, clay soil is ideal for yellow loosestrife, meadow buttercups, lesser spearwort, silverweed, yellow archangel and bugle. I have allowed just a few non-native plants to join the throng. Among them are: *Mimulus guttatus*, *Primula florindae*, *Iris sibirica* and a very special geranium I have named Geranium 'Blue Shimmer'. This is a beautiful and dynamic Sticky Wicket seedling that I selected for propagation. It is the progeny of our native meadow crane's-bill (*Geranium pratense*). Just for fun I added *Juncus effusus* f. *spiralis*, a crazy-looking relative of our native soft rush.

Rosebay willowherb and purple loosestrife set seed nearby and although they are somewhat at odds with the colour scheme, they are excellent for wildlife. I find them so beautiful that I eventually weakened and gave up any serious attempt to remove them. I do, however, attempt to confine them and at least regulate their spread by cutting off their seeding heads.

I had a useful idea for disguising the butyl edges. I stacked up a pile of turf removed during the excavations, covered them in black plastic and left them in the heap for about a month until the grass had been killed off but before the fibrous root

Shafts of sunlight strike the foliage of the variegated flag iris, accentuating the form of the swordlike leaves mirrored in the inky darkness of the clear water.

system had totally decomposed, so they could be easily handled. I laid them out and planted their undersides with the roots of ground-cover plants, such as periwinkle, creeping Jenny, brooklime and lamium, before draping them gently along the pond edges with an inch or so dangling into the water (making sure the turf sloped gently downwards towards the pond, to avoid drawing too much water out). This made a good job of hiding the liner and gave us a pleasing green edge that needed no mowing or strimming – operations best avoided near frogs and toads.

SHADE AND GROUND COVER Our young frogs and baby toads now benefit from the shady protection of the several varieties of cornus which grow well in the heavy clay soil turned up by the excavations. In winter we enjoy their vibrantly coloured stems. The cornuses are carpeted with Russian comfrey, which forms an immensely effective weed-suppressing ground cover that is abuzz with nectar-hungry bumble-bees in spring. The comfrey grows willingly on the sticky clay and actually helps to break chunks of it down into an almost crumbly tilth. The price I pay for growing such a useful plant is the struggle to control its advance into neighbouring plants. As I could not win in all ways, I accepted that my choice of additional planting would be limited. The silver variegated *Lamium galeobdolon*, whose yellow flowers provide a good early source of nectar, competes fairly gallantly beside the comfrey.

Years ago I made the unfortunate mistake of planting lyme grass (*Leymus arenarius*) too close to the edge of the liner. I doubt if there is, in fact, a safe distance for it. During its first summer it forged its way several feet towards the pond; its powerful underground stems managed to creep under the butyl liner and lurk there, unnoticed, until the following spring. At the first sniff of warm weather, it emerged triumphantly, the virulent strength of its new shoots piercing the liner and creating a leak, which has remained a 17-year-long thorn in the side of the plantswoman who underestimated its power! I have now learned my lesson and avoid growing such furtively creeping plants – or at least within a good stone's throw of a pond.

GARDEN BORDERS

I wanted the planting on the northern boundary to be "fuzzy" – in other words, devoid of any plants with a distinctive form to achieve my intention of softly blending the garden into its surroundings. A densely wooded patch in our

neighbour's mature garden made the perfect background for our conspicuously new one. I wanted to echo the quiet look of our immediate borrowed landscape and a non-confrontational planting style would give the appearance that our land extended further into the distance. In the same respect I also wanted a stretch of mown grass between the house and this boundary to maximize the existing space and enhance this impression of distance.

"FUZZY" PLANTS Bearing in mind my yellow and blue colour scheme, I wanted an early-flowering shrub in the background of the "fuzzy border". My choice of forthysia may seem odd as most are glaringly conspicuous. However, I planted a very pale-coloured, sparsely-flowered, dark-stemmed variety called Forsythia suspensa f. atrocaulis with Clematis alpina as a nearby companion and a mist of forget-me-nots as

The strong form of the mature yellow borders and the tapering gravel and grass paths make the entrance to the Frog Garden inviting. As you pass through, Peter's ponds (see page 30) are revealed among the more naturalistic planting background.

ground cover. The combination was very easy on the human eye and an attraction for the early bees. The summer flowers include the soft-yellow, scabious-like *Cephalaria gigantea*, fennel and *Nepeta govaniana* with *Deschampsia cespitosa* 'Golden Veil' to make the border seem even more hazy.

This was all very satisfactory until an uninvited *Clematis montana* hijacked the hedgerow and tried to spread its curtain of growth over the border. You may wonder why I allowed this to happen to a precious native hedge. Well, beguiled by the waft of the vanilla-scented flowers, I began to weaken. In what seemed like the blink of an eyelid, the opportunist invader infiltrated the hedgerow and set its sights on scaling the oak tree, which was just when the first pair of thrushes chose to nest in the mounting tangle. No nature-loving gardener could dream of interfering with thrush habitat, certainly not me! Pruning time was at odds with nesting time, the thrushes won and the clematis rampaged out of bounds.

YELLOW AND BLUE BORDERS With a preponderance of yellow flowers adorning the ponds and borders, the relaxing blues of herbaceous plants such as *Campanula latiloba* and *C. lactiflora* and our home-bred *Geranium* 'Blue Shimmer' make a welcome contrast. This combination of colours always looks both fresh and calming. At the same time, yellow has a notably "uplifting" effect, which is particularly cheering at springtime when the countryside first comes alive with primroses, cowslips, dandelions, wild daffodils and celandines in the hedgerows. When it comes to working with colour, as in all things, I like to take my lead from nature.

SCENTED AND AROMATIC SHRUBS The gardens are all sweetened and spiced with fragrant and aromatic plants, especially in the borders closest to the house. The honey-scented *Euphorbia mellifera* appears to be dripping with nectar, but I am surprised to find little obvious reaction from wildlife, though perhaps I could watch more attentively. Some of the early-flowering shrubs, such as *Mahonia japonica* and the flower-smothered broom (*Cytisus x praecox*), are blessed with an ample supply of nectar which the queen bumblebees need for vital sustenance to start a new brood. Both shrubs fill the late-winter/early-spring air with scent and the mahonias provide summer berries (edible, but best left for the birds). I can also tap into the stimulating aroma of rosemary, santolina, sage, or bay anytime I care to brush past or pick a sprig or two from these aromatics, which flank my well-trodden routes around the garden.

Wildflowers, herbs and ornamental garden plants mingle in a relaxed way that characterizes our planting style. Cowslips, tulips and fennel cohabit charmingly while satisfying the needs of many beneficial insects.

BULBS Spring bulbs are a feature of the Frog Garden borders. I have taken some old-fashioned narcissus under my wing, caring for the shy-looking and rather unimposing varieties which I find in some of the very old gardens I manage. These natural and modest-looking narcissus seem to have been superseded by some oversized, over-coloured and downright peculiar newcomers, many of which appear to have been bred to shine on the show bench. They look embarrassed in the garden and confound the nectar-seeking bees. Of course, there are some very lovely modern varieties as well. Far and away my favourite of these is *Narcissus* 'Jenny'. She has a grace and elegance of shape that reminds me of my whippets.

There are also other bulbs, such as aconites, 'West Point' tulips, grape hyacinths and some yellow and blue crocuses which grow among my fresh, limy-green grasses and sedges (*Milium effusum* 'Aureum' and *Carex elata* 'Aurea', for example), and other delectable foliage plants, such as *Physocarpus* 'Dart's Gold'. The golden hop twines through the yellow-berried *Cotoneaster salicifolius* 'Rothschildianus' and *Viburnum opulus* 'Aureum' then rambles on into the hedgerow, scaling field maple, hazel, hawthorn and blackthorn.

Hops are the most favoured food plant of the beautiful Comma butterfly. They are said to accept the golden form so I hope they find breeding conditions suitable here.

FREE-RANGING HERBS Self-seeding herbs, such as evening primrose and fennel, are welcome to squat where they will, since they attract and feed moths and other

pollinating insects. Herbs are not confined to a regulation "herb garden" here at Sticky Wicket. They are set free among the borders and encouraged to self-seed in a fairly random way. However, allowing the entry of ginger mint was a serious mistake. Although its colouring is absolutely perfect, it has become much too headstrong and is terrorizing other species with its rampaging root system. I ferociously drag out as much as I can once a year, accept that it has the better of me and we muddle along as best we can. At least it is efficient ground cover and the bees and hoverflies like it.

WILDFLOWER VERSUS WEED   It is interesting how we call our native plants "wildflowers" when we like them and "weeds" when we don't. I grow and try to love both (almost) equally. The harebell must be one of the most beautiful, delicate and well-loved of our wildflowers. Some have seeded in my pots to make a perfect marriage of colour and form with the bell-shaped flowers of the more muscular agapanthus — a South African guest. Gardeners usually regard wildflowers such as nipplewort and greater celandine as weeds, but they are reasonably non-aggressive,

Ornamental and wild grasses, such as *Molinia variegata* and *Deschampsia cespitosa*, soften the pond edges, modestly supporting the yellow colour theme and integrating with native rushes and sedges.

quite pretty and good for wildlife, so I let some of them join the throng of other yellow flowers, provided they do not trespass too heavily on my hospitality. Greater celandine is quite different from its pesky relative, lesser celandine, which can become a weed in the fullest sense of the word when it invades a border, although I happily let it grow in my lawn. Cowslips and primroses, being far more restrained and domesticated self-seed in the borders and in the flowering lawns.

YELLOWS AND YELLOWS All the yellows I have so far mentioned are what you might call "full on", not necessarily harsh or too much on the side of chrome but, well, yellow. I have a collection of more subtly coloured plants that share their yellowness with the amber or brown overtones that I like to combine for a more painterly composition. The part of the border that greets me at my entrance gate needs to be a gentle transition from the countryside beyond, so the yellows are more subdued and the foliage colour understated.

THE BROWNISH BIAS Corokia cotoneaster, sometimes called the wire-netting plant, has tiny brown-bronze leaves on wiry, zigzag stems with minuscule yellow flowers, rather like mimosa. *Muehlenbeckia complexa* is similar in foliage but rather too adventurous in habit for those who need sanity in the border. As a sharp contrast in foliage size, *Actinidia deliciosa* has huge, leathery leaves that hide its creamy beige-yellow flowers. It makes yards of growth and anchors its thick, knobbly tan stems with conspicuous winding tendrils. The fine, tall, grassy leaves of *Chionochloa rubra* make an extreme contrast of form, but the colours include those of the aforementioned shrubs and, on close examination, extend the range to subdued orange, olive-green and buff. This quietly understated grass draws my attention and admiration all year round and, as a bonus, has a fountain of sprays of oaten flowers in summer. The grass is a match made in heaven for the unique colouring of *Diervilla sessilifolia* with its young foliage which, if you mixed its colours in a paint-box, would contain pale olive-green and an apricot blend. It has pale yellow flowers which in no way vie for attention.

SOFT, TINTED YELLOWS   Spires of yellow foxgloves punctuate the foliage composition. *Digitalis grandiflora* has a soft colouring, gentled by a hint of dull apricot, which makes it a perfect companion for the group I have described. The colours have a similar gentle hint-of-a-tint to those of *Buddleia x weyeriana* and also to the divinely perfumed *Lonicera periclymenum* 'Graham Thomas'. The strangely scented *Rosa* 'Maigold' and the more discreet *Polemonium pauciflorum* also fit well amongst these assembled plants, which all have amber tones in their various flower parts.

SPECIFIC HABITAT BOOSTERS

It is incredible how, given the right conditions, wildlife soon finds its way to a new garden habitat. Adult amphibians have a strong homing instinct so it is cruel to import them as adults, but it is permissible (although frowned upon by some ecologists) to transfer spawn, especially where it is rescued from a pond with tadpole-fancying goldfish. (There is, however, a danger of spreading a very unfortunate and little understood wasting disease called 'red leg' that is affecting frogs in many parts of the country.) Fortunately, for us, our frogs arrived of their own accord.

We certainly did not want to add fish, which compete for food and gobble up the aquatic life we sought to conserve. The only imported pond wildlife were pond snails from a friend's pond. They make a marvellous job of helping to keep the pond clean and free of excessive weed.

AQUATIC WILDLIFE   Pond skaters and water boatmen were the first pond-dwellers to move in; the former skimming the surface and the latter scudding around just below it. Heaven knows where they came from but our ponds were barely filled before they started to arrive. Whether by mutual agreement or as a result of ferocious contest, the butyl ponds are used by scores of frogs and sometimes toads, while the concrete one is occupied predominantly by newts and/or dragonfly larvae. Frogs and toads lay a massive amount of spawn to compensate for the vast

Lonicera 'Graham Thomas' provides a sweet fragrance for the rustic arbour, which is set among the softly tinted yellow flowers and foliage of the border. The seat and arbour are made from locally coppiced hazel.

quantity eaten by other creatures. Toads contribute to the health of the pond by eating decaying plants and algal growth. They hatch two weeks after the frogs and it is five years before they become sexually active adults; hence the importance of a safe, damp, shaded, muddy habitat where they can grow and survive to maturity. Dragonfly larvae, diving beetles and water scorpions gobble up a huge proportion of the pond community. I tend to champion the less tyrannical newts, which consume the larvae of mosquitoes and other undesirables when in the water and insect pests when in the garden. Of course, I have no control in the matter; I get what I am given. Some years we have a good newt season and see both common and palmate types; it seems to be swings and roundabouts when it comes to claiming and defending domains.

LOG AND STONE HEAPS While Peter slaved away at the finer details of the landscaping, I began the fun part of the construction. At the water's edge, I piled

small stacks of logs from a range of native trees. Yearling newts particularly appreciate damp logs so the wood was deliberately gathered in varied states of decomposition. A hollow elm log had for years served as a seat by the back door but in its ancient crumbling state became an ideal woody cavern for toads or frogs. Some lengths of wood were then partly submerged for extra wildlife appeal. I make it all sound as casual as it was intended to look, but in fact each piece of wood was selected as carefully as if my composition were a possible entry for the Turner prize.

I heaped groups of large stones beside the pond and tried to avoid them looking like a third-rate rockery. Being swamped with billowing meadow crane's-bills and sedges soon took care of that. We hoped both frogs and toads would appreciate our specially constructed stone "frogarium" and "Toad Hall" – mini-caves made out of flat slabs of stone – and other built-in nooks and crannies that simulate the small, cool, damp cavities and hollows where they might naturally shelter or hibernate. I also submerged some rocky hideouts and hibernation places in the new ponds. First I gently lowered in a couple of hollow breeze-blocks and then randomly surrounded them with air-bricks and rocks, creating crevices and hollows of varied dimensions. I settled these piles with some subsoil and disguised the rather ordinary materials with some attractive stones. One such pile formed an island and the other formed a promontory from the water's edge. The frogs came to their new home in droves.

ATTRACTING OTHER WILDLIFE Hedgehogs are delightful creatures that very helpfully consume slugs as part of their varied diet. I have often seen these prickly characters in the garden but neither of us have ever actually witnessed one visit the pond to drink, although we like to think they do. Judging by the numbers that come to grief in our modern world, hedgehogs are either very unlucky or they have suicidal tendencies. They are very good at falling into ponds with steep sides, which make escape impossible for them – another good reason to make sure at least some of the pond edges are gently graded so they can drink easily or crawl to safety.

Placed at the water's edge, my carefully selected and composed "eco-heap" of mixed logs is perfect habitat for insects and young newts. The pebble-edged concrete pond is filled with fringed water-lily foliage to help suppress the growth of blanketweed, while the outer fringe of *Molinia caerulea* 'Variegata' is peppered with self-seeding mimulus.

INSECTS AND INSECT PREDATORS   Bats are another creature of the night that I rarely encounter. I know we are visited by them but I see no evidence of a roost on our property, although I believe they inhabit our oak trees. Or maybe they live in my neighbours' buildings and fly in, just as our swallows do, for a gourmet feast on the insects that fly around the pond.

HOSTAS AND SLUGS   I find hostas rather too solid and "static" for my liking but there are one or two places where these qualities are appropriate. I quite like to grow *Hosta* 'Honeybells' by the pond, where my population of frogs and toads help me to deal with the slug problems associated with these plants. Hostas are martyrs even more to snails, and the thrushes help here, using the stone pond surround as an anvil. We hear the tap-tapping, and see the crushed shells, evidence of their welcome feast and our much-valued organic pest control. I'd much rather see a thrush in the garden than a perfect hosta! The hostas lure the snails away from other plants and I know just where to find them. There is no question of using chemical slug control in our garden, since any poisoned creature can become food for another and the toxins get passed into the intestines of the innocent bystander; often the natural predator that would have dealt with the problem. . . had it lived.

VISITING BIRDS   Apart from the underwater-dwellers and nocturnal individuals, there are other more easily discernible creatures. Our birds are predictable pondside visitors and it is a great joy to watch them bathing in the shallows and splashing water over the nearby marginal plants. Thrushes, blackbirds and starlings take their turn to bathe and drink. Pigeons drink in a very distinctive manner; both collared

Several species of visiting and resident birds like to drink and bathe in the stony shallows of the small concrete pond and thrushes use the larger stones as an anvil for cracking snail shells.

doves and wood pigeons suck up water as if they were drinking through a straw and give the impression they are getting immense relief from a burning thirst. When they treat their "bar" as a washing facility, they extract yet more water using their amazingly strong wings to splash a cascade over the edges.

It is quite hard to leave bare, wet earth for swallows, martins and other birds to use for nest building. Every patch of earth soon becomes colonized with vegetation, but I suspect the birds are astute at spotting nesting materials without my thinking I must leave glaringly obvious mud-flats to help. After all, when your property has previously been christened Sticky Wicket, there is plenty of sludgy ground around, especially where horses and chickens have scraped and scratched bare patches.

IN CONCLUSION

We learned a great deal as we met the challenges of pond making and can honestly say that this project has been a huge success story in terms of the pleasure we have received, the beauty we see and in constructing a truly important wildlife and wild plant conservation resource. The more gardeners who make wildlife-friendly ponds, the greater the chances of survival for our poor wetland refugees. Whether the pond is the size of a lake or just a washing-up bowl, results are guaranteed to be rapid and encouraging, providing hours of lively entertainment watching the constant buzz of wildlife activity in and around the water and surrounding planting.

So far we have had a pond unfailingly crammed with frogs at mating and spawning time in February, when the resonance of croaky frog-song is quite astonishing. I was determined not to be put off by Peter's comment that this strange cacophany sounded like "the reverberation of a submerged moped" – a typically unromantic, male interpretation of a unique sound – but an accurate description, nonetheless!

THE BIRD GARDEN

*In our Bird Garden the focus is on providing
features, many of them hand crafted, to
attract birds so that they can best be viewed
from the house. The pink and plum-coloured
plants in this part of the garden provide a
long season of attractive flowers and foliage.*

A home-made bird-bath, set into a carpet of nectar-rich
plants and grasses, provides the centrepiece for this area.

A S WITH ALL OUR BRITISH WILDLIFE, birds are having a tough time living in 21st-century Britain. Numbers of some species are in steep decline; the population of thrushes and skylarks, for example, has halved in the last twenty-five to thirty years. Much of this misery is attributable to the extensive and excessive use of agricultural and horticultural chemicals, particularly pesticides and herbicides. They eradicate all but the most persistent insects and weeds, and in doing so remove the birds' natural food supply. Added to this, the ever-diminishing areas of natural habitat left for wildlife and pockets of unspoilt woodland, grassland and wetland are becoming increasingly isolated as more – and larger – roads scar our landscape and building developments gobble up the remaining green space.

Mile upon mile of hedgerows is ripped out every year and many that survive are ill-managed. Now that 40 per cent has been removed, every single stretch of hedgerow becomes incredibly precious – particularly those that are older and more species-rich. There is some welcome and positive work being done by conservation organizations, but I believe much tighter legislation is required to prevent this increasingly widespread harm. It is apparently illegal to destroy a bird's nest and there is a fine of up to £5,000 for doing so: yet there is no law to prevent farmers from trimming or cutting and laying hedges at bird-nesting time and thereby causing disruption or devastation. An exposed nest is a nest that is wide open to predators and therefore just as doomed as one that has actually been flailed to bits.

Gardens provide a useful habitat for at least 20 per cent of the country's populations of house sparrows, starlings, greenfinches, blackbirds and song thrushes, all of which are declining across the UK. The Royal Society for the Protection of Birds (RSPB) reckons that over 50 million birds a year become prey to cats, with house sparrows, blue tits, blackbirds and starlings being the most frequently caught. This is a disturbing figure but cats apparently thin out the weaker or sickly garden birds before they die of natural causes and the RSPB does not regard cats as the greater threat to the bird population UK-wide. They attribute the declines to habitat change and loss.

There are many wonderful breeds and groups of birds which need very specific surroundings – wading birds are an obvious example. Our garden habitat is clearly no substitute for the estuaries, mud-flats and reed beds that such birds need, nor is it likely to be suitable for some of the birds which belong in forests. It is fortunate that there remain many species with less exacting requirements, and these have adapted well to our garden environment. For instance, robins and blackbirds were originally shy, woodland birds but they now seem perfectly at home among our lawns and borders. Even rarer and more habitat-specific species (such as reed bunting) are reported to be venturing into some gardens and parks. There are many ways of encouraging birds to the garden, a wealth of plants to feed and support them, and several measures we can take to protect their welfare. Isn't it heartening to think that we gardeners are so well placed to help conserve many of our songbirds?

We are fortunate here in Dorset that there are many mature oaks in our vicinity; that a river rises just a mile up the valley and there is both dry chalk and wet clay grassland as well as wooded hills within a mile radius. Some of the visiting birds, or those which pass overhead, are there because of the features of the landscape which immediately surrounds us, and it is possible to echo some of them in microcosm using elements of design in the garden.

Several of the gardens in our village remain pretty, unspoilt cottage gardens with good hedgerows and mature trees. Sadly, others are becoming increasingly suburbanized and are no longer even faintly sympathetic to their natural surroundings. New "low maintenance" gardens, with a minimalist approach to planting may be fine for the busy householders, but they make distinctly barren places for birds and other wildlife. However, by far the most distressing consequences are wrought by the "slash and burn merchants", who move into old properties and proceed to destroy hedges and valuable cover – even during nesting periods. It is so sad when this happens because it has an inevitable knock-on effect on the wildlife in all the surrounding gardens. We need at least to fight back and explore all the ways in which we can help to compensate.

Our allocated "Bird Garden" site was approximately 5 by 9 m (15 by 18 yd) square and our design, special features and choice of plants were planned to draw in a wide range of birds and maximize our pleasure in watching them prosper. I try not to drive a wedge between the "art" and the "science" of wildlife gardening, or "gardening in tune with nature", as I call my style of design and gardening methods. In this instance, the welfare of the birds is paramount but my Bird Garden is also a very satisfying and beautiful place, both to be in and to look out upon.

DESIGN

I wanted the focus of bird activity to be centred on the part of our garden that we can see from the kitchen window, so that Peter and I, and our visiting family and friends, could enjoy a grandstand view. Throughout the year we are able to watch many more birds from within the house than we could outside in the garden, where we often inadvertently disturb them with our activities. We purposefully designed the garden to incorporate many features that would bring an abundance of birds close to the house and into the frame provided by the kitchen window. With the backdrop of an existing native hedge, the stage was already well set when we arrived in 1987. We just needed the right "props" in the foreground, some essential "furniture" and some exciting bird-friendly planting. Naturally, the results would also depend enormously on the wildlife-friendly habitat we could create in the other four areas of the garden; the pond, meadows, woodland, hedgerows, compost heap and artificial habitat-boosters contributing to the overall health of our garden ecosystem.

Some birds visit our Bird Garden regularly and reliably throughout the year and breed close by. Others call in from time to time, varying their habits with the seasons and the availability of food elsewhere. Of this group, some are resident on our land but are timid or rely exclusively on wild food. We also receive summer or winter visitors who may stay for a season or just call in briefly on their travels. There are a few birds, such as owls and swallows that are seen on other areas of our five acres of land but not actually in the Bird Garden.

PATHS, PERGOLAS, FEATURES AND PRACTICAL ACCESS   My vision for this garden began at the point where I needed to blend house with garden. The wide gravel and paving path was to turn at right angles from the Frog to the Bird Garden, to skirt the east side of the house. There were to be generously plant-clad pergolas extending from the house, crossing the gravel surround and casting intermittent shade and interesting shadows. For spring and summer treats, pots with bulbs and tender perennials would be set among the tangle of entwining plants. In winter the same pots could display coloured winter stems and could contain cut stems with seed-heads for the birds. Right through the seasons I would be able to admire the plants and savour the scented and aromatic ones while on my daily feeding-round – one of the highlights of my day.

There would be a concentration of attractive features for the birds, most of them positioned where they could be seen from the house windows. Similar feeding and nesting apparatus would be scattered around other parts of the garden; inviting them exclusively to one spot would make the birds over-conspicuous to predators and overcrowding can result in hygiene problems where feeders are concerned.

Some birds enjoy the challenge of visiting manmade feeders whereas some are less adventurous or simply not designed to feed in that way. Many birds are adapting to our garden environment and learning new tricks (such as hovering), but a few remain unimpressed or not physically equipped for the antics involved in hanging onto the edge of, or upside down from, a natty, manmade feeding device.

My 7m- (8yd-) diameter "floral carpet", as I call it, is designed as a safe and decorative arena to accommodate and show off both ground-feeding birds and those visiting the bird-bath and sand-bath. I wanted this gravelled planting space to be in the middle of the garden but to look part of the whole gently curving pattern rather than like a bed plonked in the centre of the lawn. I sketched the lines of the design of this garden without lifting pencil from paper and this left me with a fluid-looking horseshoe shape, defined by narrow ribbons of surrounding grass. In the high-profile centre, flagstones could be set into a slightly mounded gravel bed, spiralling inward to the large central bird-bath, and diminishing in size as they reach the epicentre. I called the whole feature "the swirl".

PLANTING BRIEF

As with the Frog Garden, I was lucky to have a particularly bountiful stretch of hedgerow bordering the Bird Garden. This natural hedgerow "larder", with the ground below, has most of the provisions needed to sustain many adult birds and their nestlings. With our two mature oaks nearby, it would be difficult to better the planting formula. Some entomologists estimate that between one and two thousand different insects live in such mature, mixed hedges.

Many wildflowers arrive in borders, either by intention or default. As usual, I would be quite prepared to negotiate with the "volunteer arrivals" (the weeds) provided they were the right colour, but common sense would have to prevail if I needed to prevent things getting completely out of hand. A range of native plants would attract the right sort of insects for the birds to feed on and the hedgerow plants would supply fruits, nuts, berries and seeds for the vegetarian residents. There is a drainage ditch and bank which forms an integral part of the hedge. This is a bonus zone of habitat for wildlife as it offers dry, rooty crevices and crannies as well as moist and muddy places for many months of the year.

BORDERS   Admittedly, not every single one of the plants I selected for this garden had special bird appeal, but 90 per cent of plants, as well as being beautiful, would also provide food and habitat for birds and/or for interrelated wildlife. I chose plants that would not only help provide a natural diet for birds but would give added protection for them when they were roosting or nesting. My selection included thorny or spiny shrubs and those that form dense thickets, some of which would be evergreen. I picked one or two selected trees to screen the intrusive view of nearby houses and others to help shelter the garden from the prevailing south-westerly winds. I would plant cornus and willow to continue the winter effect of coloured stems which was a feature of the adjoining Frog Garden. I love to watch plants whose vision is enhanced by gentle summer breeze or even wild winter wind. Swaying grasses and fluttery, silver-backed leaves would meet the criteria for making a windswept site a dramatic one.

PINK FLOWERS AND PLUM-COLOURED FOLIAGE   For orchestrating a prolonged season of flowering with a wide range of bird-friendly and people-pleasing plants, pink is an good colour to work with because there is a wealth of choice, so I chose pink as the principal colour for the flowering plants, supported by foliage in plum, bronze, burgundy and ruby shades, according to the variations in the pink tints and tones of the flowers. Among my pink selection I wanted to include scented plants such as viburnums, lilies and roses and position them where, in my year-round sequence of daily feeding-rounds, my meetings with them would be intimate. If I wanted to grow a few tender perennials in pots, then this much visited and viewed part of the garden would be the place where they would give me the most pleasure and be guaranteed to receive my full attention.

HOUSE-WALL HABITAT   Birds appreciate the warmth and protection which buildings can offer. If lavishly plant-covered, as ours were intended to be, the walls would offer warm roosting sites and space for safe nesting places. The support wires for the climbers were to be held in place about six inches from the wall so there was a spacious gap where birds could benefit from the microclimate that is eventually created. The leaf litter at the base of the wall plants would be an important asset in providing insect cover and winter warmth for birds.

CONSTRUCTION

PATH, PERGOLA AND STEPS We continued the path around the house using the same low-cost materials for the pergola as for the Frog Garden (see page xx). Peter and I wished we could have afforded chunky green oak but had to make do with regulation, treated softwood. The construction was simple and also low-budget, using bog-standard 8 by 8cm (3 by 3 in) uprights and 12 by 4cm (5 by 1.5 in)

cross-members. They looked very ordinary until I dressed them to have a more "organic" appearance. One post is now trimmed around with hemp rope, which the birds like to use for beak wiping after a greasy dinner of home-made bird-pudding (see page 78). Another post is now a pillar of ivy. By annual hard pruning of the new growth of the latter, and training the leading stem in a spiral, I have created a gnarled, woody, evergreen column. It is arguable whether the post supports the ivy or vice versa! Other posts are decorated with spirals of willow or hazel stems.

We adorned our pergola with hand-crafted willow features for birds to feed, perch, roost and nest, and used fragrant plants, such as honeysuckle, lilies and Rosa 'Debutante', to cover the walls and the woodwork.

Close to the house, where there was a change of level to deal with, Peter used old railway sleepers to make a set of shallow steps and we gravelled the surface in between. We used these same economy materials to make a path to intersect one of the borders and allow access to the adjacent gardens.

FEATURES AND PLANTING SPACES The "floral carpet" or "swirl" needed to be well drained, so we employed topsoil from the path excavations to raise the ground level with some gravel mixed in to help. The flat stone slabs that form the spiral design would also provide additional conditions to help certain plants to thrive and they would doubtless be useful for snail-bashing thrushes. At the centre I used a tufa mix (see Frog Garden, page 26) to make a shallow bird-bath that is slightly more generously sized than any I have seen in garden centres. Some birds, such as sparrows, enjoy communal bathing and sometimes small birds will actually stand at the edge and take a shower in the tidal wave caused by larger birds splashing about

in the centre. The swirl and the borders were prepared with our usual diligence; we first ensured that the area was entirely free of grass and perennial weeds before thoroughly conditioning the soil with well-rotted manure. Only then did we begin to plant the first trees and shrubs.

THE BIRD-FRIENDLY LAWN   Although I intended to minimize grass mowing, I make no apologies for mowing the small proportion of the grassland which is central to the design of this garden. The lawn also defines and strengthens the design and is cool and comfortable to walk on. Some birds really do appreciate fairly close-mown grass when foraging for invertebrates, so my green "ribbons" of turf form part of the varied habitat in the Bird Garden. The fact that the turf is, by chance, composed of approximately 50 per cent white clover is a bonus; we have a self-feeding lawn that enriches itself with its own nitrogen, which is naturally manufactured by this leguminous plant's own roots. Our lawn is always verdant and lush, full of worms for the birds and with the bonus of the little white flowers to keep our bees happy.

A pattern of close-mown grass paths surrounds this swirl, bringing the insect- or worm-seeking visitors, such as pied wagtails, robins, blackbirds and thrushes to the fore. Thrushes are a fine spectacle and, though increasingly scarce, a joy to behold. Unfortunately they are easily scared away by the more competitive birds – blackbirds being the main antagonists. Starlings are the masters of organic leather-jacket control, penetrating and aerating the turf with their mighty strong beaks as they search for the grubs. Jackdaws, with their even more powerful beaks, drop in from time to time, cantering sideways endearingly across the lawn as they forage. I am not sure of the criteria that move them to desert their usual feeding territory around our stables, but I think perhaps the older birds become more domesticated.

Although swallows nest in our stables and outbuildings, from the Bird Garden we only hear and see them flying above us and swooping to catch insects on the wing. Buzzards, too, can be heard and seen overhead, but much higher up, soaring over the open hills and woodland that surround us.

Vibrant Japanese blood grass (*Imperata cylindrica* 'Rubra') punctuates the floral carpet of insect nectar plants, including oreganos, thymes and *Geranium striatum*.

We rarely see more than a pair of pied wagtails in this garden at one time. They usually forage on the lawn but just now and again, presumably when insects are short, these most delightful, uncompetitive birds will make their selection from the least complicated and open of our seed-holders. The related grey wagtails are just a hop away in the Frog Garden, where they are drawn to the recently enlarged ponds.

PLANTING

When we began this garden, the first thing we did was to allow the existing eastern boundary hedge to grow tall. Peter cut and laid (and regularly trimmed) a stretch of it to invigorate and thicken the base and to make dense, rich habitat which is ideal for nesting. The remaining hedge is allowed to continue to grow tall and produce hips and berries on the mature wood. There is always a hub of activity as hundreds of birds chatter, perch, forage and make their homes among the branches. The mixed native hedgerow plants provide first-class living accommodation for the birds and are a vital source of food. The oak offers acorns for jays, wood pigeons, great spotted woodpeckers and nuthatches. Hawthorn, blackthorn, bryony, nightshade, elder,

guelder rose and privet provide a sequence of luscious berries. In particular, brambles supply seed and flesh for blackbirds, warblers and finches. Greenfinches are partial to rosehips, while the robins seek out spindle berries. Ivy berries are the last in the season to form and cater for wood pigeons, robins and blackcaps. In spring, willow – especially goat willow – attracts early insects to supply the birds with body-building protein. Among the herbaceous hedgerow species, numerous "weed" seeds also supply part of their nutritious diet. Chickweed, colt's-foot dandelion, groundsel and sow thistle are by no means the gardener's first choice of wildflower, but they are fine in the hedgerow and if they inevitably turn up in borders then at least it is a comfort to realize they do have value. I know that finches like the seed of nettles, but I try to confine my nettles to wilder parts of the garden.

The shape of birds' beaks gives a strong clue as to their required or preferred diet. Some, such as finches, have short, robust beaks that are brilliantly engineered for seed dehusking. Others, such as blackbirds and starlings, have longer, more slender beaks for ferreting out worms, grubs and insects.

GARDEN TREES My first choice of tree is appropriately named for this garden. The bird cherry has black berries on the beautiful bronze/purple leaves of the pink-flowered form (Prunus padus 'Colorata'). These berries are devoured early in the season but I must admit I am not convinced the coloured form is as remarkably well-flavoured as the slightly less ornamental, white-flowered parent (Prunus padus) which is host to a seemingly bottomless supply of insects while appearing to be quite cosmetically unchallenged by them. This tree is constantly full of birds, particularly tits – blue tits, great tits, coaltits, long-tailed tits and marsh-tits – all of which also visit the bird-feeders. There are also tree-creepers, flycatchers and occasionally nuthatches in the bird cherries. Each day I watch the birds busily working the stems but I can never determine exactly which bugs or insects they find so thrilling.

Crab apples produce masses of fruit which the birds eat once they begin to rot. The purple-foliaged, red-flowered Malus 'Red Glow' is always heavily laden with delightful pink fruit. The ornamental cherry, Prunus cerasifera 'Nigra', has brownish-

When we cut and laid our boundary hedge we recycled some ash branches to make an "eco seat" to offer a good habitat for wildlife and a place for us to pause to enjoy our plants and the birds they encourage and support.

purple leaves with pale pink flowers, the buds of which are beloved by bullfinches. It doesn't worry me if they pinch them because, when it comes to non-fruiting ornamentals, potential fruit and berry pickers (bird or human) are not deprived as a result of their sabotage. It was not long before the trees became of significant size to be used as song posts and this cherry tree, with its upright form, was one of the first.

BIRD SONG AND ACTIVITIES   Fortunately for us, when birds broadcast their territorial rights to each other it manifests to us as the most delightful song. Blackbirds and robins are the tamest birds and yet among the most aggressive when it comes to fighting for territory. Dunnocks are also charming songbirds but far more timid. Wrens and thrushes bring indescribable joy with their sweet song and are always around the garden, though not in large numbers. These two are very independent as far as supplementary feeding is concerned. Blackcaps, those very fine songsters, whose music is often likened to a nightingale, usually only come to our feeders in winter. Of the other birds in the same (warbler) family, chiffchaffs and garden warblers are summer visitors, the former bringing its distinctive sound to our hedgerows. Peter developed a finely tuned ear for distinguishing individual birdsong and an astute eye for the rare or unusual visitors, such as bramblings and reed buntings, which have pitched up on odd occasions.

Tree-creepers are most furtive in pursuit of their insect prey and stay close to the bark of trees, always ascending them from the bottom to the top of the trunk. I only see these tiny birds in winter but I expect they are around all year. Nuthatches are larger, more striking and conspicuously coloured, and work the tree trunks from top to bottom. We seldom notice spotted flycatchers in the Bird Garden; although they are around, they conduct themselves in a secretive way. We obtain a better view of them in our poly-tunnels where they find easy pickings as unfortunate insects get trapped against the polythene. Goldcrests also flit about among the tree branches and stems. These are the tiniest and one of the most engaging of our British birds. They can be distinguished by their neat little mohican-style gold caps and bold eye stripes.

There are herbaceous plants among the pink and plum-coloured shrubs, including *Berberis* 'Harlequin'. The chocolate-scented *Cosmos atrosanguineus* glows brightly beside dusky pink *Sedum telephium* 'Matrona', which has long lasting and attractive seed-heads, often harbouring tiny insects that attract garden warblers.

SHRUBS I like the continuity provided by using garden forms of native hedgerow plants to integrate garden and boundary. The purple form of our wild elder (*Sambucus nigra* 'Purpurea') has scented and very beautiful pink flowers, bronzy-purple foliage and black berries that are as well received as those of its native cousin. Purple hazel (*Corylus maxima* 'Purpurea') has large purple leaves with nuts to match. Jays are the only birds with strong enough beaks (and the inclination) to extract the kernels. I have never seen them at work but I have found nuts showing evidence of their industry. They leave the shell more fragmented and less neatly accessed than dormice, which also feed on hazel nuts. There is an interesting coloured form of our native blackthorn, *Prunus spinosa*. The soft plum-coloured foliage, which turns red in autumn, looks striking when combined with the blue-black sloe berries. Plants such as this may be a new way forward for the gardener with an interest in wildlife. They offer the glamour of a garden plant with, hopefully, all the specific, associated benefits that the native parentage offers in terms of food and habitat.

Lonicera rupicola var. *syringantha* is a rather rambling shrub that is early-flowering and sweetly scented, and has just a few red berries for birds. This is a tough cookie and uncomplainingly puts up with the occasional violent assault necessary to keep it vaguely in bounds. If allowed to grow reasonably unimpeded, it forms a densely-branched thicket with narrow grey-green leaves. Thickets provide a remarkable level of protection against the cold wind. I'd hate to be without this rather wayward hunk of a plant and so would the gang of sparrows who, for some reason, love to socialize in the maze of stems in winter, reminding me of giggling gangs of little children.

Lonicera pileata and L. *yunnanensis* form dense evergreen cover for winter shelter and well-secreted nesting sites. They make quite a secret of their purple berries too. I have never witnessed the birds eating them but maybe they enjoy them as much as the pink berries of the deciduous *Symphoricarpos chenaultii* 'Hancock', which holds its pink berries at the end of long wands of tightly massed cascading stems. There is one other impenetrable shrub which makes outstanding bird habitat: *Cotoneaster conspicuus* is a strapping, arching, evergreen shrub with powerful visual impact and is also an outstanding provider for wildlife. Honey-bees are drawn in their hundreds to the masses of pink-tinged flowers in spring and, occasionally, there is even an early butterfly or two. Oddly, the berries have no appeal for the birds but it is the tangled network of tough branches that draws several species to compete for shelter and to roost and breed within its confines. Sparrows, dunnocks and blackbirds are almost always scuttling about in its stiff skirts and, if I throw some food nearby, I can be quite certain of one or another popping out from within.

The "pheasant berry", or *Leycestera formosa*, is a sadly underrated shrub in my opinion. I love both its pink and red dangling flowers and the red berries which form while flower buds are still coming out. Where feasible, I allow it to self-seed – which it does with great generosity – because it has both bird and bee appeal, as well as great personality and shiny green stems that add a verdant element to the winter scene. The apple-blossom-pink-flowered *Chaenomeles speciosa* 'Moerloosei' has quince-like fruits which, when they finally begin to rot, offer emergency rations in harsh, late-winter weather.

By autumn, the pink flowers in this garden give way to red hips of dog roses and the berries of *Cotoneaster horizontalis* and C. 'Coral Beauty', which spread along the ground and hug the house walls. In the border there is a very dark maroon-stemmed dogwood (*Cornus alba* 'Kesselringii') which has bronze foliage. The berries are white and soon eaten in September and then, after the yellow autumn leaves are shed, the gleaming bare stems steal the show when set against the varied red, yellow and orange stems of willows and other cornuses. Imagine how stunning our birds look in such a dramatic setting!

Fieldfares and occasional redwings call in and raid the fruit and berries in late autumn and winter. I love to see them but they cause dissent amongst the blackbird population, which seems to resent this daylight robbery of their winter provisions.

SCENTED PLANTS AND OTHER TREATS FOR US Closer at hand, *Lonicera x purpusii* frames the window and is a favourite place for small birds to shelter. During mid to late winter, we relish the astonishing fragrance of this shrub when the bare branches are covered in flowers. The power of the perfume defies belief when you consider the diminutive size of the flowers. It has a few succulent red berries which the blackbirds take gratefully in early spring when most other berries are gone. Other scented plants include *Viburnum farreri* and *V. x burkwoodii* which flower in sequence from about November to May and they have a few berries to follow. When selecting a healthy, scented, pink-flowered climbing rose, I chose 'Debutante'. She is smothered in clusters of flowers for several weeks, produces a few small hips, and then pops up a few surprise and welcome sprays of flowers right up until Christmas. She spreads sinuous arms right across the east side of the house and I train a few of her long stems along the cross-bars of the pergola. *Lilium* 'Pink Perfection', grown in pots at the base of the pergola, has splendid steely-pink trumpets and a rich and penetrating scent in June; later there are the reflexed, spotted petals of *L. speciosum* var. *rubrum*. They

There are moments of pure human indulgence as I pause from bird-feeding duties to imbibe the extravagant fragrance of the aptly named Lilium 'Pink Perfection', partnered by the perfectly colour-matched *Diascia rigescens*.

both attract hoverflies but I admit I have seen no noticeable direct benefit to birds, unless they eat the seeds.

The chocolate-scented *Cosmos atrosanguineus* is a real indulgence for Peter and me, and any chocoholic garden visitors. Although it has no obvious bird-appeal, it draws plenty of bees to its amazingly rich claret-coloured flowers. All these fragrant plants give me great joy as I wander round on my daily bird-feeding schedule. This part of the garden is not exclusively for birds – there are other creatures to consider and this includes the owners! Gardening "in tune with nature" also requires that our human nature is considered and all our senses satisfied.

As an extra treat for myself I grow a few tender and not-so-tender perennials in pots; *Diascia rigescens* and *Verbena* 'Silver Anne' associate most pleasingly with each other and with the nearby *Penstemon* 'Apple Blossom' and an airy pink gypsophila. With regular dead-heading and an occasional dose of seaweed liquid, the verbena and diascia flower continually for about five months of the year. They sprawl through, and are loosely supported by, some of the woven structures which also function as bird perches. In winter these same woven supports hold arrangements of harvested seed-heads.

THE FLORAL CARPET CENTREPIECE   From the framework of my kitchen window, I painted a living picture – a set staged for the extra dynamics of colour, sound and movement provided by the birds. The spiral of stones in the floral carpet have now become obscured by the tapestry of plants, such as thrift, thyme, marjoram and ajuga, that thrive in this open, sunny, well-drained site. This pretty carpet of flowering plants is punctuated by waving grasses and the vertical accents of dieramas, whose graceful, swaying stems yielding to the slightest breeze are often momentarily bent to the ground by finches raiding insects for their young (or eventually taking their seeds). Bullfinches do a bit of spasmodic blossom- and berry-raiding and visit "the swirl" from time to time. They look particularly striking and add to the effect of the combined colours I have used.

To echo the motion provided by the birds, I use delicate grasses such as the wispy *Stipa tenuissima*, and waving foxtail barley grass, *Hordeum jubatum*, which sparkle with

Poetry in motion! Barley grass (*Hordeum jubatum*) is one of the most admired plants in the garden. Steely-pink flower heads gracefully bow and dance in the breeze.

dew and seem to dance demurely amongst the more static plants. The barley grass is one of my most cherished plants. I often stand transfixed by its beauty and the sheer splendour of the natural "choreography" of the dancing movements of its pink-sheened flowers as they softly twist and sway from side to side. The ornamental grasses seem to interest the birds so I think they must attract insects to their flowers and seed-heads, and to the foliage which forms good insect habitat as the clumps mature. Old stems and leaves are certainly a bonus when it comes to selecting durable nesting materials.

I try to use such plants in a way that concedes to the extraordinary effects of light and shade. For instance, the glowing red blades of the Japanese blood grass (*Imperata cylindrica* 'Rubra') are best placed here in open ground where the sunlight can penetrate all around. In fact, they look to me as if they are illuminated by a force of light drawn through their roots and fuelled by the dynamic force of earth's energy. The emerald green, combined with the dual blood and ruby reds, make the plant versatile in complementing different ends of the pink/plum/red colour spectrum of flowers and other foliage. It is noteworthy how there is a mellow reflection of these colours in the plumage of some of the birds – male chaffinches and bullfinches in particular. Perhaps this takes "set design" to an extreme level, but my kitchen window frames a fabulous living picture and I never tire of watching the scenes unfold.

THE BIRDS Seldom has there been a prettier event than this year when Peter and I stood transfixed as we watched a small group of garden warblers at work picking the aphids off a self-set *Angelica sylvestris* 'Purpurea'. Their antics seemed to give them a need for refreshment and they made sorties to the nearby bird-bath to drink and bathe together. In and around this same bed, dunnocks, sparrows, chaffinches, greenfinches and occasionally yellowhammers forage for the seed I scatter. Collared doves are one of my favourite birds and I love to hear their soft cooing calls and to watch them feeding here. I have a soft spot for their heftier and often quarrelsome relations, the wood pigeons, which regularly drink from the bird-bath and satisfy their hearty appetites. It is a bit unnerving when they haul out long stems of thyme

Sometimes a stunning and useful nectar plant, such as *Angelica gigas*, will have unexpected extra wildlife attributes and discreetly harbour insects that attract birds to feed among its flower- and seed-heads, adding extra dynamics to an already dramatic image.

for nesting material but the plants somehow survive this rather random and brutal pruning. Choosing aromatic foliage is a good way to disguise the presence of chicks and help deflect predators but I wonder if the chicks benefit in other ways from being hatched into a fragrant world?

Sometimes seed from the bird mix germinates and adds an impromptu touch. Not all of these volunteer plants are appropriate here so some are removed but millet looks most handsome and is left to provide an extra food source. We are frequently visited by pheasants which seem to blend with the autumn and winter shapes and colouring as if camouflage had been an intrinsic part of the design.

CLOTHING THE HOUSE WALLS A tangle of roses, clematis and honeysuckle with one or two berry-laden cotoneasters is a good formula for starting to clothe the walls and provide the habitat birds need. I have mentioned my first choice, the great climbing *Rosa* 'Debutante', which occupies a huge space and is regularly used as a roosting and nesting place. Pruning 'Deb' is a task and a half, but also a labour of love as the end result is a wall-covering extending at least 11m (12 yd) across the house, and with long arms reaching along each of the four cross-members of the pergola.

The even more delicate-looking, tiny-leafed, tiny single-flowered *Rosa* 'Nozomi' makes a perfect companion to thread through, and add extra "armour" to, the ubiquitous *Cotoneaster horizontalis* which I grow all around the house at the foot of the walls. The unassuming beauty and fragrance of the shell-pink 'New Dawn' puts this beautiful rose in the "desert island selection" league, as far as I am concerned. The scent has the perfectly balanced blend of sweetness and aroma that I would choose to imbibe when taking my last breath on earth. Ivy arrived uninvited but it has been allowed to grow within a defined space because, among its many virtues, it creates a valuable evergreen roosting and nesting place for wrens, which also feed on the spiders it harbours. The house walls have no loose mortar so the ivy can do little harm and it helps to insulate the building. In late autumn the flowers are rich in nectar for the late butterflies and in mid-winter its black berries are an extra welcome food source when other natural food supplies dwindle.

PINK WILDFLOWERS AND VOLUNTEERS   Wildflower or weed? It depends on whether we judge the volunteers to be guest or gate-crasher. With a little thinning now and again, ragged Robin, lady's smock and fumitory are most welcome pink-flowered natives that have turned up and work happily with my pink colour-scheme. Herb Robert and campion have their place but need to be confined to it and, in this garden, I prefer them not to stray too far from the hedgerows. I stand accused, justifiably, of being too lenient with some of these plants in the recent past. When we began our garden-making, I was a much stricter disciplinarian but I dropped my guard when, increasingly, I began to value the impact and respect the need for allowing in as many native plants as possible. A heather turned up uninvited and unwanted, but its seeds are useful to birds so I put up with it. They also like the seeds of the marjoram which germinates in all sorts of places so, naturally, I weakly give in and leave the plants untrimmed. If I cared less for birds and more for plants, I would take matters in hand and prevent the mass colonization of dynasties of inferior seedlings. Never mind, they are quite easily thinned out where necessary and weeding aromatic plants is first-class therapy – aromatherapy au naturel, so to speak.

Cotoneasters, such as C. x *horizontalis* and C. x *watereri* 'John Waterer' (seen here), provide a sequence of berries as well as joining the throng of plants on the house walls that help to provide habitat for the summer nesting period.

OTHER SEED-HEADS   Although we dead-head some plants to prolong their flowering period, we leave almost all our last crop of seed-heads for wildlife. Birds visit seed-heads not only for the actual seed content but also for the numbers of insects that visit or set up camp in certain plants – such as the dark, dusky-pink Joe pyeweed (*Eupatorium purpureum*), the fluffy pink meadowsweet (*Filipendula rubra* 'Venusta') and the rather sultry *Sedum telephium* 'Matrona'. All these plants, along with the stately varieties of miscanthus, have a forceful visual impact and make a splendid contribution to the performance of the garden. Birds particularly like the seeds of *Geranium pratense* 'Striatum', the scabious-like *Knautia macedonica* and the purple plantains, which are just a hop away from being truly native.

Three of my most admired late-summer plants also leave a legacy of fine seed-heads. *Angelica sylvestris* 'Purpurea' is a tall, stately plant with purple foliage and stems that perfectly partner its beautiful, umbelliferous, pale pink flowers. With *Actaea simplex* 'Brunette' there is a similar, and possibly even more striking, association of colour and form, the deeper purple foliage colour being concentrated in its weightier palmate leaves. With a fine, upstanding, vanilla-scented flower spike, loved by Red Admiral butterflies, along with unusual seed-heads as a finale, how much more could any plant offer? *Sanguisorba officinalis* (greater burnet) is also an outstanding and very garden-worthy native plant. It stands about 1.5m (4-5ft) tall with branched flower-heads and bears oval, small but vibrant maroon flowers and seed-heads that eventually turn earthy brown.

WINTER WAYS WITH SEED-HEADS   After a long period of flowering, my tender perennials are eventually taken in for the winter, but the empty pots

Teasels are somewhat free-spirited in the places they choose to grow, but I harvest some mature seed-heads to place in pots to attract goldfinches close to the house, where we can watch their feeding activities in winter.

are not left idle. I fill them with coloured willow and cornus stems which look splendid and also help to support the bunches of seed-heads I import from other parts of the garden. I then have an interesting and ornamental winter arrangement to look out on and one that provides hours of entertaining bird-watching. I include eryngiums, sedums, crocosmia and teasels. The teasels are the best "draws" because they can be relied on, eventually, to bring our brightly coloured goldfinches close to the house. It is fun to try out different plants; one year I may try an edible amaryllis, another I might bring in orache (*Atriplex hortensis*) or sunflower heads from the vegetable garden. I can then determine which birds favour which seeds. Lately, my winter-pot scenario has been in some confusion owing to the seasons being so strange. Teasel seeds usually last well into winter but there have been recent problems with extreme warm, wet weather, which causes the seeds to germinate in the seed heads in autumn. This means some of the food supply will not be available when the birds come to rely on it. I have begun to harvest some teasel heads in September and keep them in a dry place until later in the winter. Then, provided they don't go mouldy, I can deal them out as and when it is timely.

HABITAT BOOSTERS

In our Bird Garden there are many artificial habitat boosters to provide extra roosting, perching, feeding and nesting places. Beginning at the house, our east-facing aspect with its high gable-end is ideal for tit nest-boxes – a choice of three being the maximum there is room for. Birds need their own space and seclusion just as we do, so there is no point in overdoing the numbers of nest-boxes in one space. We can generally accommodate two lots of tits in this garden, at least one blackbird on the house wall, a wren in the ivy just around the corner against the north wall and goodness knows what goes on in the well-occupied hedgerow opposite! Birds bravely make their homes here in spite of the fact that I inadvertently disturb them as I patrol the area at least once a day to fill feeders and water-baths, or as I work in the garden. Remarkably tolerant of quiet, non-confrontational human presence, the home-seekers' criteria seem to be protection from predators, prevailing wind and over-heating. (An exposed south wall can be just too hot for baby chicks.)

For some reason, the tiled house roof is attractive to pied wagtails, which is very gratifying, but I can never discover exactly what it is that appeals to them. The chimney is used as a song-perch and some years we are treated to the melodic music of a resident song thrush so, all in all, our building serves the birds well in many ways.

NEST-BOXES There are many designs and varied constructions for nest-boxes. The RSPB, the British Trust for Ornithology (BTO) and various manufacturers are producing an ever-widening, scientifically designed range to meet the growing need for artificial bird habitat. Different birds have different requirements and some are very specific. As far as possible, I prefer to try to create protected habitat where the birds can nest naturally, but a sprinkling of nest-boxes certainly helps to boost the natural sites and can often act as an extra safeguard against predators. The main things to take into account are camouflage and protection; aspect and access; weather-proofing; hygiene; and whether the bird naturally chooses a ledge or a hole.

With tit-boxes, the exact size of the entrance hole is crucial as to which species will take up residence. A 28mm (1in) hole is correct for tits and nuthatches and 32mm (1¼in) for sparrows. Woodpeckers will sometimes widen the entrance of wooden boxes with sinister intentions towards the resident's eggs or chicks. A protective punched-out metal plate helps prevent their intrusion. A custom-made box, constructed of cement and sawdust, is the answer to some of the problems with safety and hygiene, but I have to say that some of them lack style and others are distinctly aesthetically challenged. Nevertheless, "handsome is as handsome does", so we invested in, and tried out a few of these and the birds seem well satisfied. We also make tit nest-boxes by hollowing out chunky logs, which are then attached to walls or trees. This is closer to the conditions the birds would naturally choose but these homemade ones are difficult to clean out and if I fail to be diligent in the necessary "spring- (or rather autumn-) cleaning", I worry about the hygiene factor when the same sites are used year after year.

ROOSTING POCKETS This is one feature that I particularly delight in designing and crafting. I use a combination of willow and grasses to weave roosting pockets in which some birds may also choose to nest. It is apparently common for several small birds to share cosy overnight accommodation, their combined body warmth helping to centrally heat these roosters. There are all sorts of products on offer commercially but I like to be a bit adventurous with the design and sizes. When I heard that up to 50 wrens have been found roosting in one place, I couldn't resist weaving a "three-door terraced property" which I hid in the ivy. In fact, it was some time before it was hidden away in its final position because it looked so fascinating and attractive that I gave it a season as a "nesting-material dispenser". I incorporated it into the pergola decoration and stuffed it with hair, moss and dried grass so the birds could make their selection and I could have the fun of seeing which bird chose which material. I now have several generations of roosters tucked away all over the garden in safe, sheltered sites. I very much doubt if there are two the same among them because when I begin with a few twigs I never know quite how they will turn out. If one roosting pocket saves even one little life on a freezing night, then a few hours' twiddling will have been well worth the sore fingers!

PERCHING PLACES   Queuing and competing for a place at the feeders and bird-bath is an extremely important social issue for birds. For every two or three we see feeding, there are probably dozens enviously waiting their turn. They can use up and waste a lot of precious energy struggling with the logistics of, and contention involved in, acquiring food. The pergolas and the well-selected and carefully positioned nearby garden trees, shrubs and hedgerow, allow them all a chance to gather, "socialize" and sort out an order.

On the ivy-clad pillar I echo the spiral stem pattern by weaving a willow or hazel "helter skelter" from top to bottom, doubling the circumference of the pillar. This is one of several places for dozens of birds to perch or queue for the feeders. Blackbirds and chaffinches, lacking the athleticism of the tits, use some of these perching places as a launching platform to attack the fat-filled coconut halves which hang like bells from the pergolas. Other posts are variously decorated by wrapping them with willow and attaching curious willow objects to them. For instance, willow "cobwebs" decorate the pergolas and are often threaded into the designs of other woven features. One pergola post is perforated with holes into which I cram a mixture of fat and nuts for the woodpeckers, nuthatches and any bird with the ingenuity to extract the food. I am hoping a tree-creeper may visit but it is a healthy sign that they seem content with the natural fare in the garden.

We planted a weeping silver pear (*Pyrus salicifolia* 'Pendula') at a comfortable 10m (11yd) from the kitchen window. Dozens of small birds gather among the dense branchwork, chattering away as they watch for the right moment to approach. Our home-crafted willow and hazel woven features are a great additional asset in this respect, providing many extra perching and tarrying places while the hierarchy is debated. These bare, twiggy perches are a bonus in summer too, because many of the bird activities are otherwise hidden from us by the great covering of dense foliage and flower. I watch every detail of the various birds' behaviour and then weave different items to try and cater for their needs.

Each year I discover new ways of trying to help. For instance, dunnocks are notorious ground-feeding birds but I have made a feeder which they find totally acceptable and regularly use, thanks to the exact position of the willow perch at the entrance. The particular, spherical, open, willow-woven feature is placed about 1.2m (4ft) high in the top stems of a mahonia. A hollowed-out coconut food-holder hangs centrally and one of the horizontal woven stems is just a couple of inches from the opening in the coconut. Now I am trying to discover which their favourite seed ingredient is. (I don't think I am quite a "bird anorak" – yet – but I happen to be very fond of dunnocks!) Different species vary significantly in their behaviour, choice of food and agility in acquiring it. I am not sure which of us is most entertained; our entrancing birds or we who bird-watch, enthralled by their antics, as we breakfast and then (very happily) wash-up in front of our kitchen window.

BIRD-BATHS These double as drinking places and ours is used daily by a great variety of birds, although many of them also use the shallow edges of our wildlife pond in the Frog Garden. It is important that fresh water is unfailingly supplied, especially in very dry or icy weather. Our bird-bath is situated in full central view of the kitchen window, so there is no way we could overlook topping it up. As far as possible I try to use rainwater for this. The fluctuating level of water seems to affect which birds use the bath from day to day and I still haven't fathomed out the criteria, but I don't think it is as simple as "deeper water = bigger bird".

Preoccupation with ablutions can result in golden opportunities for predators to take advantage and attack. Cats are a major hazard to the survival of birds and although for this reason we did not replace our elderly cats when they died, it is difficult to deter the neighbourhood cats from visiting. It would not be appropriate for me to capture these intruders and equip them with collars with warning bells but I am often sorely tempted when I spot them on a furtive mission or, worse, carrying away a victim. Our low surrounding planting allows good vision and decreases the risk that these intruders will creep up and catch the birds unaware as they drink or "scrub up". Keeping their feathers clean, free of parasites and well preened is of paramount importance to birds so they can survive cold, wet weather and fly with maximum efficiency. Good insulation, together with speed and dexterity, can make the difference between life and death when push comes to shove in a hostile world where predators often lurk nearby.

DUST-BATH   Bearing the birds' flight performance in mind, I have recently introduced a large stone saucer of mixed fine soil and coarse sand into the same area (and try to remember to put a lid on it in wet weather – easier said than done!) Dust-bathing is another efficient way of removing parasites and "dry-cleaning" feathers. The tray also contains grit because some of the finches swallow grit to help their process of digestion. I expect they will snub my offering because they share dust-holes and grit with my hens in their run but it will be gratifying if we see a positive result. It is interesting how sparrows relish communal dust-bathing. One year I tipped a barrow- load of fine gravel near the swirl with a view to topping up the surface mulch. The little birds made at least a dozen indentations and so joyfully did they engage in their grooming activities that I was compelled to leave the heap unspread.

HANGING BIRD FEEDERS My woven-willow feeding "cages" help protect ageing birds from predators, such as the sparrowhawk and the neighbours' cats. They are either suspended from the pergolas or from a bracket on the house wall (the feeders, not the cats!). I weave round or ovoid globes or spheres which are about 45cm (18 in) in diameter and inside them I hang either a hollowed-out coconut shell seed-holder or a metal peanut-holder.

The open weave is amply large enough for birds to move in and out of but the gauge is small enough to confound the attempts of cat or sparrowhawk to catch their prey off-guard. They are, unfortunately, not squirrel-proof, but I sometimes weave a decorative extra willow "skin" to encircle the custom-made metal feeding cages, especially where peanuts are involved. Part of the fun is to find a practical way to make the Bird Garden amusing and glamorous for us, as well as extra safe and appealing for birds. I have actually seen sparrowhawks trap birds in the manufactured metal feeders but never in my willow ones. I find it strangely surreal to have birds fly freely in and out of what appears to be a cage. An amusing deception!

CUSTOM-MADE FEEDERS   The RSPB and the BTO offer excellent, specially designed custom-made feeders and there are all sorts of products on sale at garden centres and pet shops. Some of them function better than others and only one or two of them have much visual appeal. Peanut feeders are usually efficient and some are quite stylish. Seed dispensers never have a very "organic" appearance because of the plastic components. They are designed to keep seed dry and therefore free-flowing, but if water gets in – and it sometimes does – the thing blocks up and wet seed starts to germinate or rot. One or two of the fancier devices are the very devil to take to bits, clean out, dry and reassemble. The viability of the "free-flow" facility may lie in choosing exactly the right seed mix which may just happen to be the most expensive. However, when they do work efficiently they are fine and they save having to do a daily top up – as I do. It depends on whether you are in a position to commit to a regular agenda and whether you regard the exercise as a tedious chore or one of life's pleasures. The most important thing is to somehow provide a regular supply, especially when the weather is harsh or when there are nestlings to rear. Some birds come to depend on us completely to ensure a constant food source and the worst thing would be to let them down and affect their survival. In very wet weather, peanuts can go mouldy before they are eaten and these must be removed to avoid poisoning the birds.

HOMEMADE COCONUT FEEDERS   Coconut shells make good holders for both fat and seed. They can be halved, drilled with holes near the edge, and low down for drainage, threaded with cord or wire and suspended as open-cup or bell-shaped containers. Two or three birds can feed from these at one time, although competition may result in lively confrontation. The open-cup containers are fine in dry weather but when it is wet the seed gets soggy and the birds reject it. As a drier alternative, we carve out an opening into a whole shell and the birds can take it in turns to help

Reading across, from top left: Bluetits approve the concrete nesting box; a young robin perches on a garden seat; a bluetit pauses before entering the coconut feeder; willow-woven features for feeding, perching and roosting; a robin claims his turn on the feeding log; a lonesome yellowhammer joins ground-feeding birds on the lawn; the bird-bath is a good size for the greater spotted woodpecker; woodpeckers explore one of our range of woven feeding devices.

themselves to the dry seed. Some of the birds squat inside, guarding their pitch and feeding voraciously until they are so full I wonder they can fly! They often chuck out the unfavoured seeds, which become a bonus for the ground-feeding birds such as dunnocks and collared doves, and also our garden-orientated pheasants. At night the field mice sometimes move in to the coconut holders and finish off the leftovers. It is quite strange to go to fill the coconut and, on occasions, find it still full of indignant mouse! I have also known geriatric birds use them for night-time shelter.

It is amusing – but time-consuming and certainly inessential – to draw quirky faces onto the face of the coconut and carve these out. I combine the uses of an electric drill and a hack-saw to get the detail required to give them impish expressions. I get quite attached to my little "coco characters" as they become weather-beaten over the years of service. They start off bearded or top-knotted and end up slap-headed and walnut-like. Damaged or "retired" coconuts, having served our resident wildlife well, are eventually secreted securely into the hedgerows as potential roosting or nest sites.

Some of the halved coconuts are suspended as bell-type fat-holders. During cold weather I melt lard, dripping or any left-over fat, stir in some flour, cereals and small seeds and pour the mixture into the shell as it begins to re-set. An hour or so in the fridge and the "bird pudding" is firmly set and ready to hang up. Birds such as blackbirds, robins, chaffinches and starlings manage to alternate hovering and "missile" attacks to snatch the odd bite from the lower edges. I must admit I worry a little about this. Do they use up as much (or more) energy in acquiring the food as they gain from consuming it? Hovering is said to use up massive energy reserves and propelling oneself off the ground to make an upward spear-attack must similarly clock up a fair few kilowatts. I suppose it is wrong to doubt the birds' judgement in energy expenditure. Most creatures are more astute at measuring resources than mankind seems to be!

Some birds are well designed to hang upside down and can cling to such receptacles without any effort or needing to weigh up the logistics. The tits, for example, have the advantage over the others in that they can thereby feed very easily and reach any fat in the deepest recesses of the bell. Bearing this in mind, I can shape the bells and/or adjust the food levels accordingly. When natural food supplies are more abundant, or if I want to single out the smaller tits for special treatment, I cut the rations and just smear a daily portion of the fat mixture right inside the bell. It helps if the inner surface of the coconut is roughened up so that the fat sticks more firmly. The only downside to preparing coconut-shell features is sorting out the actual coconut flesh. My birds will eat a limited amount but mould attacks the white kernel before they can consume it all. Mouldy food is as bad for birds as it is for us so I gouge out the flesh to make a clean, long-lasting receptacle. I then feed them the chunks of coconut, which I wedge into some of my willow woven items. At nesting time it is better to grate the coconut to avoid any chance of chicks choking on oversized offerings. The long-tailed tits are particularly attracted to this food so I freeze some of the coconut flesh to have in reserve to supply regular rations over the winter. I have several of these feeders so that I have spare ones to interchange while soiled ones are cleaned out. Hygiene is an important part of any animal husbandry – birds included. I use boiling water and sometimes bicarbonate of soda as a safe cleaner but there are also special disinfectants (and brushes) now on the market to help with bird-feeder hygiene.

LOG FEEDERS A very simple fat-feeding device can be made by drilling holes in a log, sticking a hook in the top and suspending it. The holes are then stuffed with food, such as a fat, cereal and seed mix. It is possible to buy these ready-made but we prefer to choose a large, chunky, interesting-shaped branch, "plant" it in the ground and go to town with the drill, making holes of varied diameters. We may use a branch of hazel if pruning or coppicing has been necessary but sometimes we chat up the electricity board tree surgeons and get cast-offs when they clear the local power-lines. The wider the drilled hole, the easier it is to push the fat in; the deeper the hole, the more chance of leaving a deep reserve for the spotted woodpeckers, which can probe further with their long beaks. Sometimes they deepen or expand the holes to their own design! Smaller holes are left unfilled for insects to shelter or breed in, and all the holes are horizontal to prevent water gathering inside.

When the branch eventually begins to look tatty, we retire it into the hedgerows or hedge bottom to become exclusively insect habitat. As it biodegrades it continues to feed and house a changing range of insects and also fungi. We can start again with a new branch each year. This exercise keeps us entertained and the product is a great habitat provider – a winner all round.

APPLE BASKET We store several trays of apples for the winter, sharing the harvest with the birds as, one by one, the fruits inevitably begin to rot. I became rather tired of treading squelchy, rotting fruit into the gravel where the blackbirds had chased them offside. I tried skewering them onto a hazel stick, like an apple kebab, but they soon ended up underfoot again. Eventually I came up with a solution; yet another sphere but this one made with twisted willow (*Salix babylonica* var. *pekinensis* 'Tortuosa') which makes a fascinating object of curiosity. First I weave a globe with a dense skin of intertwined, shiny, wiggly stems. I then pull it apart and, using extra willow stems, reinforce two or three entrance holes for the birds' access and for me to drop in a daily ration of apples. This neatly contains both the fruit and the birds, which can feast away in safety, seclusion and a degree or so of shelter.

The apple basket is held on a tripod of stout hazel stems and placed near the house where blackbirds often lurk, especially in cold weather. Of course, some other apples are chucked further away onto the lawn to provide for birds which do not care to visit the feeders or make a public exhibition of themselves. There may be good sense in birds choosing the natural approach because rotting apples attract the worms and other invertebrates that inhabit the lawn. Thrushes, for instance, prefer a carnivorous diet and eat fruit only as a last resort. A wormy apple would be a bonus for them.

BIRD-TABLE   Peter made our bird-table, roughly following the design of an original, custom-built RSPB one, but giving ours a distinctly rustic character of its own. The roof is "thatched" with strips of split hazel stems and it is set onto the branched top of a mature piece of hazel wood, gleaned from our winter coppicing programme. The table is set within the protective skirts of the prickly *Berberis thunbergii* f. *atropurpurea* 'Harlequin', making it pretty well cat-proof or at least slowing the rate of feline harassment and giving birds time to forestall an attack. The original construction incorporated a nest-box but this is said to be confusing and disruptive for brooding birds, which need seclusion and are very territorial. However, our original apparatus had always had particular appeal for great tits, which took up residence and successfully reared large broods for several years in succession. For their sakes we repeated the design in spite of the somewhat contentious planning regulations – but decided to compromise. We use the bird-table as a feeding-station only occasionally during the worst mid-winter weather, leaving it free as a regularly used maternity unit in the breeding season. I should point out that if this bird-table happened to be the only feeding-station in the garden, I would not allow the dual-purpose facilities and I would make a firm choice between feeding or nesting.

FEEDING "PLATTERS"   One of the great joys of sharing a garden with multitudes of birds is to watch them at close quarters. My pergolas bring them within a few yards of the window, and the wall-planting which frames the windows brings them within inches. Arguably, the close proximity to windows may invite disaster with birds crashing against the glass but I believe there may be a case for inviting them close enough to familiarize themselves with the vagaries of glass and thereby teach them to avoid catastrophe. Who knows? Anyway, to bring them into close perspective, I weave an intriguing object resembling a primitive tennis racket or a carpet beater, the "handle" of which I persuade into the branch-work of the wall shrubs surrounding the windows and secure it with string. I then have a platform (or platter, as we call it) in which to incorporate a coconut feeder-cup for seed, and for crumbs which I can conveniently add through the open window. This amounts to a rustic extension to the window sill – which has just set me thinking ...

DISTRIBUTION OF FEEDERS   Perhaps this is the moment to point out that it is possible to overdo the feeding-stations in one area. I use some of my feeders in rotation, catering for the slightly varying appetites during the year. To overfeed is wasteful and a surplus can attract unwanted visitors, such as rats. The other problem is that a heavy concentration of birds in one place will inevitably attract predators such as sparrow hawks. Overcrowding may also create hygiene problems and increase the risk of infectious diseases spreading among the birds. To avoid these potential problems, I distribute some of the daily food quota in other parts of the garden and on the other sides of the house, and rotate the use of some of the feeding- stations, resting one or two at a time and scrubbing any soiled apparatus. I crank up the amount of food in adverse weather conditions, or when the adults are struggling to meet the appetites of a hungry brood. My birds leave me in no doubt whatsoever when they are in need. In fact some of the ailing and geriatric birds seem to throw themselves on our mercy and, in their "twilight days", come right up to me each day for special titbits.

VISITING BIRDS   Finches are a regular part of our bird community as are house sparrows, which live and work in little flocks that, I am happy to say, are increasing in numbers each year. They have become increasingly ingenious in adapting to using feeders. Chaffinches (like robins) have also learned new skills in hovering in order to extract fat from our coconut "bells". They prefer to feed on the ground but I think they are increasingly adjusting their habits. Certainly our feeding "platters" are very much to their liking. Greenfinches are almost always in this garden, often arguing with each other and taking advantage of the food we provide but becoming conspicuous by their absence when they go off on feeding forays for a short while in autumn. Bullfinches have quite recently begun to use the feeders in mid-winter but more often we see them taking seed from plants such as oregano, which self-seeds in abundance. The spectacular goldfinches much prefer to frequent our meadows and more open surrounding hedgerows. However, they cannot resist my winter display of teasels and will take peanuts and wild bird-seed mix when their natural food sources are scant. The canary-like siskins usually appear at the feeders for a while in cold weather although, since our alders have matured to provide their most favoured seeds, we see them less often in the Bird Garden. Similar-looking but ground-feeding by nature, yellowhammers also venture in from the hedgerows when the going gets tough in winter. Blackcaps (Peter's favourite songbird) seem to find an abundance of food in our trees and hedgerows but come to the feeders from time to time, especially in winter, giving us a rare chance to see them at close quarters.

The tit family are well represented and particularly welcome our supplementary feeding in winter and when rearing broods. Great tits, blue tits and coal tits are always around, chattering and chirping to make sure I never miss a beat with handing out their provisions on time. Long-tailed tits arrive in little family gangs from time to time. We usually hear their conversational twittering just before we spot these pretty little "flying mice" which often arrive just before dusk. The very smart marsh tits feed routinely with us in winter and also have a distinctive, high-pitched call. They can easily be confused with coal tits but on close inspection are sleeker and have less white on their heads.

Our one or two visiting nuthatches have no routine that I can fathom but when one does arrive it dominates the peanuts until well re-fuelled. What a stunningly smart bird it is! Greater spotted woodpeckers are also spectacular and exotic-looking. They, too, seem a bit erratic with their feeding patterns but they check in far more often than the nuthatches. When they do feed, provided they are not disturbed, it is as if they are eating for England. We hear the green woodpecker's yaffle more often than we see them. They live close by but only occasionally do they call in to raid an ants' nest or drink from the pond.

SUPPLEMENTARY BIRD FOODS

All the above offerings are to boost the food which occurs naturally in the garden. Contrary to the way it may appear, I do not need to feed vast amounts of these extras because the birds forage on the fruit, berries and seeds plus insects and other invertebrates. It is noticeable how concentrations of birds flock to even tiny plots of organically managed land but, as there is a diminishing amount of chemical-free land to satisfy their needs, popular haunts, such as Sticky Wicket, soon become heavily stocked. This is most gratifying for us but a little supplementary food seems to be required if the needs of the increased population are to be served. Birds can be fed scraps or more conveniently – and consistently – fed with bird seed and nuts, which are readily available in shops or by mail order.

READYMADE FOODS   There are one or two points to be aware of when buying or preparing bird food. There are lethal moulds which can affect the peanuts we eat ourselves or feed to birds. Peanuts are a nutritious addition to their diet but they may be affected by aflatoxin, a toxic fungus that can poison birds (and humans). It is vital to purchase seed that has been tested and certified free of disease and sold as "safe peanuts". I order premium nuts from the RSPB or the BTO or from very reliable suppliers, such as Ernest Charles. I am assured by both bird conservation organizations that it is safe – and indeed advantageous – to feed certified peanuts all year, providing the birds cannot take the kernels away whole and risk the possibility of choking their chicks with oversize pieces.

I wonder, therefore, why some less reliable suppliers sell mixed seed with whole peanuts in? The responsible bird-seed companies do not include these nuts in their all-season mixes unless they are finely chopped. There are plenty of mixtures to choose from and those with a high percentage of black sunflower seeds will be most valued. With the black, as opposed to white or striped, seed, it is said to be easier for the birds to extract kernel from husk. Cheap seed mixes often have disproportionate quantities of fillers such as wheat and linseed. I find linseed is fairly universally disregarded by the birds but perhaps that is because I don't have linnets in the garden. Linnets are said to like linseed so perhaps there is an arguable "chicken and egg" case for having a tiny proportion in the mix – just in case they arrive and decide the Sticky Wicket habitat has become favourable. Rape seed seems to find its way into many mixtures. The birds eat it but inevitably seeds are rejected or dropped and often germinate, grow to maturity and flower. Now, can anyone convince me that bird seed merchants can put hand on heart and declare the rape to be GM-free? Cross-fertilization between GM and non-GM rape is inevitable and will be guaranteed to result in some genetic pollution of non-GM rape and certain brassicas. I do wish more gardeners and bird-lovers would press for "reassurance", if only to generate some response from suppliers and from government, and so force the issues of extensive and responsible research, together with much tighter controls.

LIVE FOOD It is possible to buy mealworms and other grubs to satisfy birds with an appetite for meat. Most seed-feeding birds forsake their vegetarian diet when rearing chicks. Baby birds need lots of protein and demands on their parents are immense. I have given my birds these treats on occasions but I prefer to concentrate on creating suitable habitat and managing the garden to encourage a natural and varied food source. This is just one good reason why the wildlife gardener needs to have a generous tolerance of insects and never ever use pesticides. The natural predators, including birds, will gradually sort out a healthy balance.

BIRD PUDDING AND SCRAPS About once a week I melt a block of fat, stir in a mixture of cereals which might include some oatmeal, ground semolina, flour, flaked millet and other seeds. Just lard and brown flour will do and is cheapest. Each day I put the required ration into the coconut fat holders so that it never hangs about getting stale. Of course it would be much easier to buy blocks of prepared "bird cake" but I prefer to do it the hard way so I know what I'm feeding.

Birds' appetites vary but most left-over offerings are gladly accepted. However, I have found feeding of mixed kitchen scraps often attracts crows and starlings whose presence in large numbers can be a bit overwhelming for the small birds normally frequenting the feeders. There are also the questions of keeping the bird-table clean and hygienic, and avoiding cooked foods which might attract rats. I generally stick to seed, nuts, fruit and a little coconut. In very cold spells I make exceptions but I make sure any uneaten cooked scraps are removed at night. Wrens, so minute they can freeze to death in cold spells, are said to accept grated cheese so I sometimes put a little emergency ration in their favourite haunts although there is no certainty they find it before other birds, mice or even our dogs do!

IN CONCLUSION

Our Bird Garden is, of course, only a small part of our five acres of land and naturally the way we plant and manage the rest of our land has a direct bearing on the results. Our other gardens with their special habitat features all help to support birds and – most essentially – the creatures on which they depend. At night we hear the plaintive calls of owls close-by. A few pheasants stray away from local shooting estates and feed with us during the winter – they are all welcome. Our hospitality wavers when starlings bring a rabble of noisy, greedy mates to the feeders and chase off our small birds. It is a shame because, in small doses, they are handsome, amusing characters and their plumage is most striking (as are their evening pre-roosting displays). I admit to a distinct feeling of hostility towards the sparrowhawks, crows and magpies when they attack our smaller birds. However, predators are part of nature's system so the best we can do is to try to create super-safe nesting sites to give our garden birds a fighting chance of survival.

As I close my chapter on the Bird Garden and look out of my kitchen window where all my thoughts began, I feel quite dizzy. It is like a cross between a menagerie and a circus out there with countless birds in the vicinity and dozens of them whizzing around between the plants and all the features we have dreamt up and constructed. As birds forage for food and dispute territorial rights, there is the sound of the combined fluttering of many tiny wings, a chorus of chattering, trilling and twittering interspersed with the odd alarm call and some sweet winter song in the background. Some of these birds have distinctive characters, markings or even unfortunate disfigurements which help us to identify them individually.

The more Peter and I watch our birds, the more we learn. And the more we learn the more we marvel at their beauty and the way they live their lives. I often ponder – do our birds now give us more pleasure than the plants in the garden? The answer is simple: the two interests are inseparable and generate equal joy for all.

THE
ROUND
GARDEN

*This summer nectar-garden attracts
thousands of insects, including bees,
butterflies and moths, which are hugely
beneficial to the garden ecosystem as well as
providing food for other creatures.*

Contrasting forms and gentle colours mark this close
community of cultivated plants, wildflowers and grasses.

T HE SAME SAD TALE of lost habitat, together with intensification of farming and countryside management, has affected the range and numbers of insects remaining in Britain. For instance, the survival of certain breeding colonies of butterflies is inextricably linked to the way downland and lowland pasture is grazed, and to the management of traditional hay meadows and woodlands. Mercifully, some of the modern agricultural crops seem to suit some species of bees – just as well for farmers because the bees are vital for the pollination of some major crops, such as oil-seed rape. All the same, some bee species have suffered as a result of foreign, imported broad-leaved plant species introduced into grassland. All these, plus many other contributory factors, have resulted in the fact that a quarter of our 254 bee species are now on the official list of endangered species. Five of our native butterfly species are now extinct and many are in serious decline and need all the help we gardeners can give them.

Huge numbers of useful insects are taken out of the food chain by chemicals purposely designed to eliminate so-called pests. Sometimes, however, it is the secondary, and unfortunate, effect of the chemicals that results in non-targeted species also being wiped out. The importance of creatures at the bottom of the food chain – the thousands of tiny insects and invertebrates we hardly notice – should never be underestimated. Many of these live below the soil surface and are vital to its health as well as that of other creatures – be it insect, amphibian, reptile or mammal – which prey on them, or with whom they may have a symbiotic association.

The subject of genetically modified crops rumbles on and I fear the present halt to procedures is only a temporary amnesty while the public are left to become complacent about the many political, social and environmental issues that need to be debated and resolved. Noone can predict the outcome of the growing of GM crops but some reports have suggested that the crops themselves (and the fact that chemicals are a mandatory part of crop production) could pose an additional hazard to wildlife. If insect-resistant GM crops are let loose in our environment, there will undoubtedly be a knock-on effect on the numbers of garden pest predators, such as ladybirds and lacewings, which may feed on the newly poisoned, yet still surviving aphids that the crop is designed to wipe out. Another real danger is the greater, more "efficient", destruction of weeds as a result of using herbicide-tolerant crops. Weeds are the natural diet for many creatures and for foraging herbivores and nectar-seeking insects this would be a disaster.

For mankind the bottom line is this: we need insects to pollinate many of our food crops, orchards, meadows, gardens, woods and hedgerows, and the implications are pretty grave if they are imperilled. Happily, it is the easiest thing in the world for gardeners to give a helping hand to boost the populations of many of these tiny miracle-makers. Without our network of wildlife-friendly gardens there would be considerably less chance of protecting Britain's diminishing numbers of insects. Butterflies, moths, bees, hoverflies, beetles and other insects are not only fascinating to watch, but join forces to turn vital cogs in the whole incredible ecological system. This is a system that we simply cannot allow to fragment if man and both his indigenous and imported flora and fauna are to co-exist on earth.

GARDEN CONSERVATION   There are many species that can benefit from our "manufactured" habitat, although there will always be those whose requirements remain too specific for the habitats our gardens can provide. For example, if we happen to garden immediately next to a large wood or conservation site, such as a site of special scientific interest (SSSI), we might seduce some of the rarer inhabitants to drop in to feed, but generally it is only about one third of the local butterfly species that one might expect to record in a garden. This may amount to about fifteen butterfly species, but moth species are likely to be much higher – perhaps several hundred!

With the current garden design epidemic of decking, concrete, glass and stainless steel, let alone exotics like banana trees, changing the face of the urban landscape, we must be thankful there are still many of us who want to retain the charm and old-world romance of the traditional "English" garden that wildlife so much enjoys. For a start, there are masses of beautiful wildflowers and fabulous garden plants laden with pollen and positively oozing nectar. It is the easiest thing in the world to choose and grow a few of the best plants. This will massively increase the insect food supply, with the reward of seeing a garden filled with the beauty and vitality of some of the most beautiful creatures in Britain.

THE WILDLIFE BRIEF   I decided to concentrate my collection of insect-friendly plants in a circular garden where I could take a close look at what was going on in the magical world of garden wildlife, and with bees and butterflies in particular. I needed to give prime consideration to the needs of butterflies because they are delicate creatures which appreciate a warm, sheltered place to feed, roost, mate and breed. I understand that, in their natural environment, woodland edges, sunny glades and wide, open rides suit most of them admirably. Although some may cling to the shade more than others, there are many that venture out into open grassland.

I designed the Round Garden by mimicking these "sunny glade" conditions and felt reasonably confident that my formula would also suit the other slightly less habitat-specific insects that I particularly wanted to invite to my insect commune. I tried to cater for the useful pollinating and pest-predating workforce that an aspiring organic grower particularly needs on their side when trying to tip the balance favourably between the creatures regarded as friend and those as foe in the garden.

THE DESIGN BRIEF

I chose a circular design for several reasons: firstly, the concentric circles of paths would enable us to stroll among the plants and closely observe them and their inter-relationship with the visiting insects at work on the feast laid before them. The geometric design had to be considered carefully as I wanted the dissecting paths to cause minimum disturbance to the overall rhythm of the planting. In fact, I foresaw the strong pattern becoming increasingly incidental to the overall blend of colours and the general haze of planting that I hoped would blend together in a painterly way.

Apart from it being an insect sanctuary, I wanted this garden to be extraordinary in a personal way. Circles are said to represent protection, safety and harmony so I assumed that as true for humans and wildlife alike, and made that my starting point. I placed a seasonally changing feature at the epicentre, to be encircled by mounded camomile rings – just hinting at an echo of an ancient henge, labyrinth or maze but without the physical or psychological complications.

This pastiche of fanciful notions formed my mental concept for this garden and I loosely incorporated them into the design. I wanted to encompass my interest in the magic and mystery of circles but without getting too spooked by invoking strange powers I might not understand. I was also drawn to the contemplative aspect of monastic gardens, although I have to admit that my garden feels as if it may have rather pagan overtones! I had an intuitive desire to create a special circular space rather than try to incorporate any informed association with religion, astronomy or meddling with the occult. Be that as it may, there are times when I can distinctly feel strange (but generally comforting) forces and energies.

THE CAMOMILE ENERGY CENTRE   There is no place in the garden to compare with the energy that exists in the centre where a luxurious carpet of aromatic camomile and thyme flourishes, fringed with wisps of airy, silvery-pink cloud grass. These same plants also carpet the two low, encircling, mounded rings which are broken in two places, rather like a small remnant of a maze or labyrinth. But my feature is not intended to confound, confuse, pay penance or have any particular allegorical associations. It is there to complete the calming process that begins when I progress round the paths in an anti-clockwise direction. Anti-clockwise feels good – it "unwinds" me. A mandala is a circular, spiritual space symbolizing the world and the universe. Maybe this was at the back of my mind when I began but I cannot claim the notion was at the forefront. However, within this central space I can feel the drawing force of earth's energies and at the same time imagine a prayer spiralling upwards to heaven. On a more mundane level, and weather depending, this is also an excellent spot for an afternoon nap with my whippets or a glass of whisky of an evening!

From this awesome place I have celebrated 17 Christmases and birthdays and 34 summer and winter solstices; the birth of my god-children; the new millennium; mourned the loss of several loved ones; witnessed the eclipse of the sun and the moon, and seen the Northern lights.

THE VARIABLE EPICENTRE   At the very epicentre of the inner camomile circle I can vary the central feature according to the seasons and occasionally for a special event, such as a gathering of friends for an evening shindig. In this case we might place a mobile wood-burner to warm ourselves and cook by as well as celebrate the element of fire. In spring and autumn I like to reveal the water that lies beneath the earth's surface so there is a tiny, shallow, central well which is usually brimming at these times. In summer the well is dry so I put a lid over it in the form of a sundial and honour the power of the sun. In deepest winter I weave a willow globe as a decorative centrepiece which looks most spectacular when frosted or iced with snow. It embodies a ball of cold, clean air. Thus all the elements of earth, air, fire and water are represented.

THE RINGS OF BORDERS   I wanted to create a space which, rippling outwards, would engulf me in flowering plants and grasses and make me feel as if I was strolling through the borders rather than gazing at them, as is more usual in gardens. In fact, I wanted a sort of stylized, meadow-like plant community that just happened to have an intersecting geometric pattern of paths (rather like a crop circle) and so I made two concentric circles of paths with three straight ones dissecting the beds into segments. The main axial path runs almost due north-south from the French windows of the main room in the house. I tapered the path to create a false perspective to make it look longer than it is.

This garden is a place where we can wander between the beds in quiet contemplation, touching, smelling and closely examining our sensational assembly of plants. I can study and wonder at their interrelationships, both colourwise and with the visiting insects we see at work among the flowers. I deliberately used crisp gravel for the paths that were visible from the main vantage point (the house and forecourt) but in other places I used bark as a softer (and much quieter) option for a path covering.

CURTAIN OR FRAME It struck me that what I was about to create could be compared with either a large stage set or a huge painting, depending on whether one stood within it or stood back to view it. Whichever way I scrutinized the setting, to complete the analogy I required either ample curtains or a substantial frame to match the proportions and to shelter, contain and embrace, both visually and ecologically. The success of a flower garden of insect food plants would be very considerably boosted by the close proximity of the enclosing, semi-natural habitats that I would use as a surround.

THE ENFOLDING HEDGES AND TREES To shelter the site I needed a 2m (6ft) rugosa hedge which would yield a wealth of pollen, nectar and hips while forming a tough, shielding barrier since both the plants and the butterflies would need protection in order to thrive. Three metres (ten yards) behind, and parallel with this, a wide hawthorn hedge would clearly define the northern arc of the circle and diffuse the prevailing south-westerly winds while offering excellent wildlife habitat. A little holly and ivy would augment its dual function and add to its appearance. The hedge height needed to be 2.2 m (7ft) at the tallest place in the middle and to taper to 1.3m (4ft), accentuating the circularity of the layout of the garden (the shelter distance is reckoned to be about four times the height of the hedge). My round garden was to be 35m (40yd) in diameter so my hedge would be an effective barrier against the winds that gust down into our valley.

To the south-west, the group of birches which form my nearby woodland garden would provide an additional wind-break. In just the same way, a dozen or so sheltering fruit trees around the perimeter of the garden would help shield and enfold the inner sanctuary. These trees (plums and damsons, and dessert, cooking and crab apples) would be pollinated by bees drawn to the Round Garden in spring and this would ensure a reliable crop of fruit each year.

HEDGEROWS Existing stretches of mature, boundary hedges to the east and west would complete the enclosure and greatly boost the supporting habitat there. As I have stressed, these British native hedgerows are immensely important to all the visiting and resident wildlife. There could be no finer foundation than our benevolent oak, with its accompanying ivy and underplanting of holly. For butterflies alone, the oak is the singular home for Purple Hairstreaks which live high up, feeding on aphid honeydew and laying eggs on the oak tips. There are also many moths among the 300 or so native insects that the oak can host. Migrant birds time their return to feed their nestlings with these caterpillars. The Holly Blue butterfly breeds on holly in the spring, laying her eggs just under the flowers, but is forced to use ivy for her August brood. Ivy comes up with the goods, pollen-wise and nectar-wise, late in the season when there is a diminishing food supply for lingering bees and late-season butterflies such as Peacocks, Red Admirals and Small Tortoiseshells. Brimstones hibernate in thickets of holly and ivy, cleverly disguised amongst the yellowing dead leaves. Christmas must be a generally fearful time for them, when hedgerows are raided for decoration, but not here at Sticky Wicket where such plants are sacrosanct for wildlife, regardless of celebration.

THE UBIQUITOUS NETTLE PATCH As a giant feeding-station, the nectar garden would serve the wildlife well but, when it comes to perpetuating their species, most insects, especially butterflies, need wild plants on which to lay eggs and provide food for their larvae when they emerge to search to satisfy their voracious appetites. Some insects are very specific in these requirements and will only use as few as one or, perhaps, two particular host plants. The plant that is singled out by the highest number of butterflies is, of course, the nettle. We all know how easy it is to grow nettles but for Red Admirals, Tortoiseshells and Peacocks to lay eggs, the plants must be in a sunny, sheltered site. Commas will accept the sort of partially shaded hedgerow site which many of us would be more willing to sacrifice than a prime, sunny spot held sacrosanct for our garden plants. It is hard luck that the full force of the feel-good factor of abandoning unusable or uncontrolled, over-shaded corners to wildlife doesn't always quite hit the spot! Never mind, there are always those early-hatching aphids, which are such well-timed fodder for the first hatching of ladybirds. These aphids will breed on nettles that colonize in the backwoods we are more readily prepared to consign to wildlife.

NEARBY GRASSLAND Many of our British butterflies live and breed in the sort of unimproved grassland that is increasingly eroded from the countryside. Flower-rich meadows are extremely rare, with 98 per cent having been destroyed. When we began to make the Round Garden we had already begun work on several grassland projects and hoped the Meadow Brown butterflies, Gatekeepers, and Common Blues we were beginning to attract would be drawn to the Round Garden if they needed extra sustenance.

The word "meadow" can conjure an image of almost infinite acres of grasses and wildflowers but this does not necessarily have to be so. I have meadows ranging from one acre to just 3m (10ft) square and every one of my grassland projects is uniquely valuable to the variety of creatures for which they provide a home. On the immediate fringes of the Round Garden, there are two small samples of the sort of semi-natural grassland habitats I have created on our land. Neither patch is more than 5sq m (5½sq yd) but I believe that an area even this size would certainly support a few breeding butterflies and moths, and countless other insects.

PLANTING BRIEF

Within this bountiful framework of woodland, hedgerow and grassland, the Round Garden was intended to be rich in herbs and other nectar plants, mixed with and softened among many varieties of ornamental grasses in a relaxed and naturalistic way. From within a sheltered, plant-festooned, willow-woven arbour at the top of the garden, we would sit peacefully and enjoy watching the wildlife, absorbing the gentle progression of colours and imbibing the cocktail of sweet and spicy herbal fragrances that would waft gently towards us from the scented and aromatic plants.

From the house and forecourt, the picture I wanted to paint was inspired by my having often viewed the original plot through a pane of rain-streaked glass in my kitchen window. The late-19th century neo-impressionists, such as Seurat and Pissarro, used dots of colour (pointillism) to create their impressionistic images; I decided I would use a similar, but more linear technique with mine. I would utilize many fine and upwardly aspiring plants and grasses to give me a trickle of vertical brush strokes mirroring the trickles of water that originally captured my imagination.

The impression I looked for differed again when viewing the garden from the camomile at the core of the design. From this standpoint it would feel more like being at the centre of a stage than viewing a picture. As far as possible, I hoped to make the kaleidoscope of gently blended colours link together, like those that appear as a slowly spinning top loses momentum and comes to rest. There would be yet another different perspective when walking round the garden and as each image becomes a backdrop for another. I decided the planting needed to be staged so as to be viewed in progression as I moved in the anti-clockwise direction I instinctively tended to take.

TIMING THE "FLORAL DANCE" There is a range of early-flowering nectar plants in the other gardens but, to meet the prime-time needs of the insects, the flowering event in the Round Garden would begin in May, peak in August and carry on until the end of October, when the season of insect activity wanes. I needed to keep the planting florally primed during the period when the greatest numbers of insects are creeping, scuttling or flying about. From mid-June onwards the volume of plant growth would swell and the complete floral picture would begin to form as the insect population built.

SELECTING TRULY UNMODIFIED PLANTS Where there is a choice, single forms of garden plants are far more useful to wildlife. I can't think of an exception, but there is bound to be at least one which will be stoutly defended by some knowledgeable and observant plantsman. Single flowers display their stamens prominently and very often the petals have conspicuous markings to further entice and guide the creatures that assist in pollination. When plant breeders select occasionally occurring sports and/or deliberately hybridize the plants to make double-flowered varieties, the whole *raison d'être* of the plant is altered or (in some cases) taken away. As far as I am concerned that blows away most of the pleasure of having the plant in my garden. How must a plant react when it has had its vital organs turned into a frivolity just to pleasure us humans? How disappointing and frustrating for the insects looking for a useful floral body part with which to interact. If a stamen is sacrificed and transposed into a comparatively dysfunctional petal, there is really no point in looking seductive! There is nothing to reward the pollinating insects, which would normally gather pollen and nectar in return for their services. Indeed, we do some very strange things to plants. Sometimes scent is sacrificed in the cause of altering or perfecting a colour or, worse still, to make a plant "dwarf" and thereby distort its proportions, often in a grotesque way.

TRADITIONAL COTTAGE-GARDEN PLANTS I first referred to Margery Fish (see Useful Books, page 205) for a wider selection of cottage-garden plants than either my mother or my grandfather had grown in their gardens. Aquilegias, phloxes, delphiniums, lupins and poppies were first to spring to mind when I thought back to the halcyon days when, as a "child-gardener", everything in the garden was simple and, yes, rosy. It is fruitless to try and categorize cottage-garden plants, herbs and wildflowers separately because they usually borrow some of each other's credentials. Country folk relied on the common sense and knowledge handed down through generations and most of their garden space would be taken up with edible plants and herbs. They probably had no need to prioritize wildlife-friendly plants; the need for premeditated conservation had yet to arrive. To make sure of pollination and to supplement their diet they or their neighbours probably kept honey-bees. I bore some of the folk history of artisan garden-making in mind during the gestation period between the conception and the delivery of my infant garden. I am by no means a compulsive collector of plants but I developed a penchant for geraniums and there are many varieties in this garden, as well as in each of the others.

CONSTRUCTION

Before any of my dreams could begin to become a reality there was some very serious groundwork to undertake. So, to begin at the beginning: it was 1988 when we began the daunting task of setting out and cultivating the 37m- (40yd-) diameter Round Garden.

I ran a line from the centre of my French windows to the appointed spot to the south and marked it. I then stuck a stout stake at the exact point in the middle and attached to it a 40m (43yd) length of string. Using this simple giant compass, I measured and marked out the concentric rings with ever-widening distances between them, like a ripple of water in the ocean of the existing rough, but very closely scalped, grass. I used farm-animal marker-dye to trace the exact pattern and gave myself a couple of weeks to try out the routes I had mapped to make sure they would work in a fluid and workable way as part of our daily beat around our property. After all, this was a pivotal point in the main passage to the most regularly visited parts of our land – the hen-run and the stockyard, on the eastern and south-western edges, respectively.

Once I had made the definitive adjustments, Peter and I began the gargantuan task of hand-digging, manuring and forming the beds. We removed the topsoil from the paths, where it was not needed, and added it to the beds to increase their height to

A desolate scene indeed! We certainly had to focus hard on our ultimate vision as we struggled with the layout and preparation of paths, borders and railway-sleeper steps during the cold winter of 1987.

provide better drainage and increase their potential for growing healthy plants. We double-dug each bed in order to bury the top layer of turf to a level where grasses and weeds would be devoid of light and so die off and decompose to make much-needed humus. The many tons of well-rotted farmyard manure (which we added) would help in this respect and put lost vitality back into the soil. In this part of our land, the ground had not been cultivated for many years but, even so, the quantity of our beautiful loamy topsoil above the subsoil varied considerably from place to place and we took this into account when redistributing the topsoil from the paths.

The drainage system had to be sensitively installed at the same time; it ran diagonally across the whole site beneath one of the dissecting paths, making it easy to locate and tap into in case we needed to access it in the future. By doing the work by hand we were able to avoid the unworkable quagmire that we found in the Frog Garden. Treating soil with utmost respect is fundamental to successful garden-making.

MAKING THE PATHS In my dreams I would like to have constructed the paths using a variety of materials, to form the intricate pattern of a knot garden. In that way I could have achieved the spirit of an elaborate Elizabethan creation without torturing plants to form symbolic and decorative interwoven designs. In the harsh reality of our finances, the circular and dissecting paths were constructed using a gloomy assortment of broken, recycled paving slabs, which we tendered for and bought at bargain price from the local council. We needed a low-cost, sound base to make sure the paths would take the wear and tear in the years ahead so we laid them in a random pattern but used the largest pieces in the centre of the path to carry the load. I reckoned that looking at yard upon yard of sub-standard crazy-paving would drive us to distraction and be a nightmare to maintain, so it was always our intention to splash-out and cover the dizzy-making base with gravel.

We used path gravel or "hogging" as a first coating because this rugged sand/stone mixture consolidates well, especially if rolled when damp and left for a few days to set. Later on, when all the preparations were complete and the first stage of the planting had begun, we invested in expensive 6mm (¼ in) gravel and I topped the surface of the inner paths to look smart and reflect the heat of the sun. This

Dreams came true just a few years on as the garden gradually matured and the carefully selected and orchestrated plants began to weave their spell-binding magic.

surface provides extra warmth for the plants and a place for the butterflies to bask and (I have been told) from which to draw minerals. The gravelled paths are fully exposed to the sun because the planting in this central area of the design is no more than half a metre (18in) tall. The planting height then gradually ascends towards the outer beds where the tallest nectar plants rise to about 2m (6ft) in places. Here the outer paths remained more rugged-looking with just the hogging and, for a while, I enjoyed the visual contrast of texture and the slight difference underfoot. After a few years, the harsh sound and the feel of the paths began to grate on my nerves. I knew just how bad it was when a visiting BBC *Gardener's World* film crew asked us to drag out our carpets to muffle the sound while they were trying to make a programme on the pleasures of butterfly gardening! By then the garden was maturing rapidly and we had quantities of woody prunings to shred, so I began to smother the paths on the outer ring with this recycled garden debris. This had the triple effect of suppressing the annoying growth of weeds and of giving me the softness and quietness I desired, as well as the ability to wildlife-watch with more stealth, so enabling me to get closer to the shyer species.

The new system also impacted on wildlife. The butterflies still had their warm, central, gravelled paths but on the outer circle, as the shredding decomposed, the bark paths became a perfect habitat for worms to work and subsequently became a first-class hunting ground for birds. OK, so they scratched the bark all over the place but what the hell – they were effectively mulching the edges of the beds and saving me the chore! Every year we top up the supply with an increasing quantity of shreddings.

We had made no futile investment in an underlay of horticultural fabric between the soil and the surface materials. No invasive, perennial weeds were likely to resurrect from the barren subsoil and this type of membrane does nothing to prevent weeds germinating on the surface of gravel or bark topping. The birds make a good job of "hoeing" the bark paths and keeping them reasonably free of weeds, but the gravel paths are much more labour-intensive. I share the workload between my worn fingers and bent back plus an occasional bout with a flame-thrower.

PLANTING

Bearing in mind the importance of my enclosing hedgerows, I added both woody and herbaceous native species to build on the range I had inherited in my splendid hedge.

Brambles join a bed of similarly rampant but valuable wildlife plants safely contained in their own jungle border and merging into the boundary hedgerow.

The beautiful butter-coloured Brimstone butterfly is just as choosy as Hairstreaks when it searches for a maternity unit; only purging buckthorn (chalky soil) or alder buckthorn (acid soil) will do. Neither buckthorns existed anywhere in my hedgerows so, having neutral soil, I added several plants of both species wherever I had a sunny enough aspect to satisfy the female Brimstone's exact habitat specifications. Thank heavens Brimstones are less picky with their adult diet than the one upon which they insist for their offspring – though thistles are their preferred nectar plant.

Not surprisingly, I did not have to plant extra brambles! I just had to tolerate and lightly control their prickly, rambling ways so that they could continue to be great providers of nectar and berries without our falling out with each other. Their nectar contains three sorts of sugar so I guess that makes them triply nourishing for insects. One of the best ways to control a thuggish plant is to pitch a few more bullies into the ring and I am lucky to have sufficient space to allow a battle-royal to rage in a few appointed spots. My contenders include rosebay willowherb and campion, the food plants for the Elephant Hawk-moth and the Campion moth, respectively.

In this stretch of hedgerow I have allowed in aromatic herbs such as mint, lemon balm and tansy, all of which act like hooligans in the garden borders but ooze nectar and, as a result, are a magnet for insects. Aromatic foliage can often act as an insect deterrent but perhaps the leaves have to be disturbed to trigger the release of the natural chemicals that have this effect. Mint beetles obviously haven't been told about it because these spectacular metallic-green insects devour mint leaves like locusts. As all gardeners know, mint has unparalleled powers of recovery, so it suffers no ill effect from playing host to a most intriguing insect.

EXPERIMENTAL PLANTING It was to be several years before I was able to acquire and propagate all the plants I needed to begin to bring the complex and ever-evolving planting design into fruition. But, in the meantime, I made an interesting start and used vegetables and colour-selected annuals as infill, rather like an under-coat for the paintwork. Somehow I needed to cover as much bare earth as possible to stifle the weed growth and minimize the erosion of soil and loss of water by evaporation. In this respect, hand weeding, rather than hoeing, was the order of the day (in fact, most days, to begin with). Carefully measured weed tolerance is just fine in mature borders but in the formative year or so of a newly composed planting I am a strict disciplinarian. This plant-gathering time presented a great opportunity to study a vast range of mostly perennial plants, including many herbs and grasses, and to begin to learn exactly how to mix, match and blend the colours. I use the word "begin" advisedly; there is an unlimited journey of discovery because the possibilities and permutations are endless.

INSECT-WORTHINESS During the process we also began to discover which were the prime nectar plants. It was particularly interesting to observe how the bees and butterflies became complacent about a favoured plant once they discovered a new one they liked better. For instance, the first year the Small Tortoiseshell butterflies flocked around my anise hyssop (*Agastache rugosa*) to such an extent that they caused me an abrupt "double take" because I thought for a moment I had mistakenly planted an orange plant among the subtle the purple, lavender and lilac combination I was composing! By the following year I had planted several varieties of scabious and the fickle Tortoiseshells forsook the anise hyssop almost completely. I was comforted to see that the bees remained true to their opinion that the plant is indeed nectar-worthy. It seems bees were easier to please.

EARLIEST NECTAR PLANTS The majority of the very earliest nectar-producing plants in my garden grow in my nearby woodland garden and in other sheltered

Reading across, from top left: *Echinacea purpurea* is a magnet for Tortoiseshell and several other butterfly species; a ladybird forages amongst the awns of the barley grass; spiky *Liatris spicata* tempts the Brimstone butterfly; alliums such as *A. sphaerocephalon* are favoured by bees and hoverflies; Mint beetles devour and help restrain the spread of mint; the Comma butterfly nectars on purple loosestrife; late-summer asters are a feast for late hatchings of Red Admirals; a Speckled Wood ventures onto *Angelica gigas*.

spots where snowdrops, hellebores, primroses, comfrey and pulmonarias are more suitably placed. I have very few bulbs in the Round Garden because they complicate the process of managing herbaceous plants and grasses, which need lifting and separating from time to time. Bulbs are wonderful for early nectar but I use them in places where they can remain undisturbed. However, some of these plants and bulbs stray into the perimeter of the Round Garden among the limited number of shrubs that grow in the outer circle. In natural habitats this could be compared to the more shaded edge of the woodland glade.

THE EARLY SCENE   There is a sprinkling of biennial, self-seeding honesty dotted through the outer borders and hopefully making a breeding-ground for the early-flying Orange Tip butterflies and leaving an infiltration of beautiful silvery seed-heads for winter. Dame's violet (*Hesperis matronalis*) is also useful to Orange Tips so I provide a very attractive pale mauve one which blends with my plant colours. *Allium hollandicum* 'Purple Sensation' matches well and grows willingly, the first of several I include for bees' delight. Aquilegias are one of the first plants to have stirred a deep passion in my heart and each year this emotion is rekindled when they appear in shades of mulberry, pink, mauve, purple and lavender-blue in almost the places I had in mind.

  Some plants have a will of their own and it is counter-productive to try and argue the case for a strict colour discipline. I used to try but no longer do. Soon the whole scene is dominated by shell-pink valerian which also grows mostly in the larger beds towards the outer ring. This is the real thing – *Valeriana officinalis* – with calming herbal properties and a soothing appearance. It is a native plant which stands about 1 to 1.2m (3 to 4ft) tall on strong stems (not to be confused with *Centranthus ruber*, the "wall" valerian, which is unrelated). Visitors often think it is a pink form of *Verbena bonariensis* and are understandably confused by the similarities of form. To a lesser degree it is also a "see-through" plant and it does have verbena-like flat heads. It differs in having an elusive scent which is usually pleasing but at times appears strangely disagreeable. Herbs and wildflowers are always full of mystery, which is probably why I love them, especially when they are as pretty and useful as valerian.

Early summer in the Round Garden and a haze of cloud grass fringes the camomile lawn. The multitude of nectar-rich plants generate a constant buzz and flutter as beneficial insects are drawn to our sunny, sheltered glade.

It continues to impress for weeks because, as the flowers fade, the fluffy seed-heads remain a modest feature for us, are of continued interest to insects and finches keenly eat the seeds. This valerian has fairly attractive foliage, is totally hardy, self-supporting, self-seeds willingly, transplants uncomplainingly, prefers damp ground but tolerates dryish conditions and will compete quite well in grass (its natural habitat). Sometimes it isn't necessary for plant-finders to travel to the ends of the earth to find a good plant; it can be right under your nose.

Towards the centre of my "sunny glade" *Allium cristophii* is among the few bulbs planted and is one of the earliest of the nectar-rich flowers. The starry globes are set in a silvery sea of grasses, including my beloved cloud grass. There is some dispute whether this annual grass is *Agrostis nebulosa* or *Aira elegantissima*. I sit on the botanical fence and just admire. Who minds? It is just exquisite and never more so than when glittering with dew or raindrops, which it holds like millions of tiny sparkling diamonds. In June its young flowers are silvery green, then become quite a feisty

pink during July before holding on in a more modest buff colour until about October. Foxtail barley grass (*Hordeum jubatum*) comes into action as the cloud grass is fading and, if dead-headed, flowers until November unless struck down by frost.

Scabious, marjoram, thyme and prunellas are very fine nectar providers. Marjoram, above all other plants, is beloved by the Gatekeepers, Meadow Browns and Common Blues, which are more often found in my meadows but breeze in to the Round Garden when nectar stocks begin to diminish a little in the grassland. I grow the finely foliaged, aromatic, silver-leafed *Artemisia canescens* for my own pleasure and for the ladybirds which very often inhabit it. By autumn, the innocent sounding (but somewhat over-domineering) *Festuca mariei* takes control of the inner ring. This large festuca has fine, grey-green, gently arching foliage and just a scattering of slender flowering stems that stand at twice the height of the foliage. But by autumn, small plants have gradually become dense tussocks; a wonderful habitat for insects but a bit overwhelming for its more frail bedfellows.

HARDY GERANIUMS Having disclaimed myself as a plantaholic I do seem to have amassed a fair collection of geraniums. All of my species and varieties are very tough and amenable, extremely attractive to bees and some have seeds which the finches eat with relish. I believe the phaeum types are best in both respects. *Geranium phaeum* 'Lily Lovell', for example, behaves true to form and has very lovely violet-coloured

Globes of *Allium cristophii* set amongst a silvery sea of early cloud grass. A week or two later the same grass assumes a shimmering pink glow.

flowers that are larger than those of my other phaeums, in shades of palest pink to deepest plummy maroon colours. *Geranium pratense* is dear to me because it is a wildflower of our meadows, which is where I confine the true species. This garden is a stud farm for some of the lovely chance progeny to further interbreed. Some very subtle-coloured descendants are emerging including my 'Blue Shimmer' (see Frog Garden) and others we will meet. *Geranium sylvaticum* is another native that I grow extensively, but it is white, and white plants are excluded from the Round Garden because they can be over-conspicuous. I just allow the violet-mauve, white-centred G. *s*. 'Mayflower' into this particular arena. The third native geranium species is *Geranium sanguineum*, whose purple-magenta colour fits perfectly with the scheme of colours at their most extreme range. *Geranium sanguineum* var. *striatum* has barely a trace of that colouring in its gentle, light pink flowers. The sanguineums have neat, finely divided foliage that often colours well in autumn. *Geranium maculatum* grows wild in moist meadows and woodland in North America. It has quite large, soft mauve flowers early in the season and then the plant sits good-naturedly tucked away, swallowed up in the exuberant growth of later-flowering perennials. *Geranium* 'Johnson's Blue' is the bluest of my collection, lacking the violet veining that tints some of the other purple-blues such as those of *Geranium ibericum*, G. *himalayense* and G. x *magnificum* which intensify in colour, ascending in that order. Amongst the redder-purple assortment, *Geranium* x *oxonianum* f. *thurstonianum* is a great rambling creature which means business; as an efficient, ground-covering individual it is best given space to get on with it. This way it will continue an extended flowering period as it progresses, arm over arm, to make new flowering growth on top of the original. Its flowers have oddly shaped, narrow, pointed, petals. My most intensively livid magenta is *Geranium psilostemon*, which glowers passionately with its dark eyes. *Geranium psilostemon* 'Bressingham Flair' is a blink or two less dynamic and G. *clarkei* 'Kashmir Purple' has none of that dazzling, day-glow element. Wide-eyed and innocent-looking, G.*c*. 'Kashmir White' is a stunner that likes to gaze at the sun and turns its head to do so. It is made the palest of pinks by the colour of the fine web of lilac veins on white petals. Both Kashmirs have a busy root system and a deceptively lively habit of gaining territory and smothering their neighbours.

Similarly tinged pink, *Geranium x cantabrigiense* 'Biokovo' is far less rampant and my favourite of the smaller macrorrhizum dynasty, having the aromatic foliage of its brethren but a much neater habit. *Geranium x cantabrigiense* is a magenta-pink and *G. macrorrhizum* 'Bevan's Variety' is a shade or two more intense, but neither of these become over-intrusive. The earliest geraniums start to flower in May and, with some mid-season dead-heading, most continue for three or four months.

COHERENT COLOUR   After a fragmented start to the essentially mid- to late-summer planting compositions in the larger beds, the full palette of colours eventually manifests; they begin to flow from soft, pastel colours at the northern segment near the house to become richer and deeper southwards, where the crimson, violet and magenta zone attract the most insects towards the height of their season. Like a water-colour painting, the lavender-blues and palest yellows are washed in from the Frog Garden to the south west while the pinks and reds fuse in from the Bird Garden to the south east. This expands the feeling of circularity to encompass all three of the gardens surrounding the house.

STRONG PINK BORDER, WITH RED COMPANIONS   The richest of pinks and maroons are arranged in the mixed border closest to the Bird Garden. The bed has a wealth of provision for wildlife; it includes fruit and seed-heads for birds but focuses mostly on insects, many of which will, in turn, become high-protein food for birds and other creatures in the food chain. This large bed contains *Malus* 'Wisley', which displays its sultry pink blossom against purple-tinged foliage and has huge, aubergine-coloured crab apples. Close by grows the complementary, claret-coloured *Berberis* 'Red Chief' with its dark berries and the needle-like thorns that help make it a safe roosting or nesting place for birds. Nearby, and suckering merrily into its neighbours, the good-natured, crimson-maroon rose 'Tuscany' makes a decorative thicket and tolerates the same-coloured *Knautia macedonica* thrusting its way among its stems and adding small, embossed, deep red dots to the larger, flat heads of the velvety rose. I clear just a few of the suckers to leave space for my annual opium

A close community of nectar-rich cottage-garden plants that include *Allium sphaerocephalon*, *Liatris spicata*, *Knautia macedonica*, nicotiana, our own *Eryngium* 'Bewitched' and an accidentally double opium poppy.

poppies, *Papaver somniferum*, which are nothing like as well able to compete where space is in dispute. Time spent in this necessary intervention is well worthwhile when it results in the unparalleled joy of managing to grow my exquisite fimbriated poppy, the colour of blackcurrant jam. I envy the seemingly ecstatic bees as they tumble about in the jungle of golden, pollen-dusted stamens.

How amazing to belong, and be essential to, a world of flowers and to be able to fly from one to another, lured in by their colours, scent, shapes and patterns – all the features which make them fascinating to us as mere onlookers. At the back of this group stands the tallest and the most productive of my nectar-yielding perennials, which is just about equal in popularity with buddleia in this respect. It has large, silky, dusky-purplish-pink flower-heads that are just slightly dome-shaped. Over 1.5m (5ft) in height, yet self-supporting, *Eupatorium purpureum* is truly magnificent looking. Even into deepest winter, its stately stems and seed-heads persist, the assembled plants looking like a diminutive, skeletal rainforest. It is

closely related to *Eupatorium cannabinum* or hemp agrimony – a wildflower belonging
in damp meadows.

THE BORDER BECOMES PALER ...   Set against a backdrop of the impressive grass,
Miscanthus sinensis malepartus, and the similar but slightly shorter M. *sinensis* 'Rotsilber',
together with fluffy pink *Filipendula rubra*, there is *Lupinus* 'My Castle', *Echinacea purpurea*,
Persicaria amplicaulis 'Atrosanguinea' and *Leonurus cardiaca*, which are all very well-
endowed with nectar. Admittedly, I rarely see a butterfly on the persicaria; the usual
pollinators are wasps and sometimes hoverflies, so I was astonished when I found a
Holly Blue nectaring on the red flower-spikes. Both bees and butterflies adore
echinacea, which attracts the Tortoiseshells, Red Admirals, Commas and even
Clouded Yellows – less often found in gardens as visiting migrants. They list
sideways, oddly, to expose their wings to the right angle to gain maximum heat from
the sun. As flight is their means of travelling great distances and escaping from
predators, they have to keep their wings in first-class working order.

I often wonder if insects recognize the herbal properties of plants like echinacea,
which is well-recognized for its ability to boost the immune system. Large

bumblebees have the strength to force open the jaws of the pink lupin with its evocative, peppery scent; a scent which transports me back in time to my grandfather's garden and my earliest memories of, and association with, gardens. There is a luscious, similarly coloured, pink opium poppy with a maroon blotch at its base helping to keep the purple-pink colours threading through the border. Sometimes I succeed in helping a crop of dark, purple-podded French beans to romp towards the back of the border and add a little *je ne sais quoi* to the composition. *Leonurus cardiaca*, or "motherwort", has an easy clue to its medicinal virtues in both the Latin and the folk name. It is a little-grown herb, probably because its subdued pink flower colour is so modest and because modern mothers seem to be strangely mistrustful of ancient "witchcraft" to ease the pain of childbirth, placing more confidence in modern drugs. However, I am devoted to it because it is an obliging, self-seeding, self-supporting "vertical" with an outstandingly long-lasting and impressive seed-head and strong, square, hollow stems that eventually become excellent insect breeding sites.

Two very special wildflowers grow in the bed nearby. Ragged Robin (*Lychnis flos-jovis*) is now as rare in the wild as it is abundant at Sticky Wicket. It seeds itself in a well-balanced matrix among *Achillea* 'Apfelblute' (formerly 'Apple Blossom') and *A. millefolium* 'Cerise Queen'. This interests me because these plants are naturally occurring bedfellows in meadows (damp ones) where ragged Robin cohabits with *Achillea millefolium*, or yarrow. Spiny restharrow (*Ononis spinosa*) is another very garden-worthy native plant. It prefers drier, chalky ground but defies the predicted science and copes well enough perched on one of the steeper edges of my winter-wet flower bed. It is covered in sprays of small, pink, pea-like flowers that make a decorative edging and please the bees at the same time.

There is an even softer pink planting close by with the paler pinks easing the way back to the mixture of pastel colours in front of the house where I wanted a minimal colour impact. *Lythrum salicaria* 'Blush' is a variety of our native loosestrife and has two-toned, pink flower spikes that help to graduate the flow. *Veronicastrum virginicum roseum* – a magnet for bees – is taller and more elegant with slender, pale-pink spires

The fluffy flower heads of *Filipendula rubra* 'Venusta' in the background and the pink astilbe to the fore make a soft background for the spikes and spires of *Lupinus* 'My Castle' beloved by bumblebees, *Lythrum* 'Blush' and the herb, motherwort.

that stand firm and imposing with rich, cinnamon-brown winter seed-heads.

I wanted a very pale pink umbelliferous flower to complement the veronicastrum and the grasses that accompany it. I chose coriander as a perfect companion. It is an annual herb that always seems to be in a hurry to flower and make seed rather than produce tasty foliage. I decided to let it have its way and I enjoy both seeing the results and eating the seeds instead of the leaves. Soapwort (*Saponaria officinalis*) is a herb with a sweet fragrance which attracts moths. I grow it in one of the smallest beds – partly as a ploy to contain it in a relatively small space. Beautiful it may be, but "thuggish" would be a civil word to describe the way it behaves in company. I would never want to be without it, but it is worth thinking long and hard before setting it loose in polite society. I have difficulty in restraining the pernicious root system from penetrating the neighbouring assembly which includes *Oenothera speciosa* 'Siskiyou', nestling into a soft haze of *Stipa tenuissima*. Only a little human intervention is required to sustain a meadow-like balance between the two because both are inveterate self-seeders. However, I tamper with the grass and thin the flowering stems from time to time to control the tangle of growth that can inhibit its ability to wave in the breeze.

MOTH APPEAL   As well as soapwort, moths are attracted to evening primroses. I wonder if pink ones work for them or is it the yellow colouring that is the criteria? There is still a whole world of night-life to discover including the mysterious world of bats which I sometimes see insect-hunting at dusk. I grow several varieties of honeysuckle on the perimeter of this garden because I believe moths particularly favour this plant and I can smell why. As I also adore it, there is certainly no hardship involved in allowing *Lonicera periclymenum* 'Belgica' to intertwine among mature shrubs such as *Escalonia* 'Apple Blossom', which also happens to be a good source of nectar. I cannot put a name to the nearby seedling hebe that arrived by chance just when I had given up the struggle to grow named varieties on the comparatively exposed site during the early years. This vagrant hebe is tough and surprisingly tolerant of my soggy soil conditions.

PALE PINK, PALE YELLOW AND PALE LAVENDER   These are by no means a fashionable mix of colours but they are an essential part of my planting strategy to accommodate all the plants in my brief, while achieving the gentle progression of colours I wanted. To make a butterfly and bee paradise I obviously needed to include several buddleias which I intended to grow in a range of colours to match each part of the circle. *Buddleia fallowiana* has grey foliage and the palest, rather ghostly lavender-mauve flower-spike, similar to B. 'Lochinch', but just a little more refined. I have two other plants in the same class which grow nearby. One, an uncertified delphinium, is slightly paler with greyish undertones and just the slightest hint of yellow. The individual flowers are delightfully uncrowded on stems which benefit from only a little necessary support. I love this plant dearly and call this delphinium 'Dodie' after the local lady who kindly gave it to me. It survives with absolutely no measures to control slugs, seems to come true from seed and, unlike other delphs I have tried to grow, it is a real trooper. I have an iris which, strangely enough, happens to have exactly the same elements in its colour make-up. I brought it with me from my last home and although its name has slipped my mind, its fabulous fragrance is totally unforgettable.

By some sort of magical chance interbreeding among my meadow geraniums,

Planting for wildlife need never be at the expense of aesthetics! The vertical form of veronica contrasts with soft, flowing barley grass; they are a perfect partnership in colour and both plants have value for the insect population.

Geranium 'Dove' emerged nearby and I soon adopted it and named it thus to reflect the gentleness of its subtle colouring (just a shade paler than the delphinium) and because it grows near *Aster* 'Ring Dove'. This tiny-flowered aster performs in autumn, when the geranium finally gives up after two rounds. The minute daisy flowers of the aster give it a hazy look – as if it is permanently surrounded in its own romantic autumn mist. *Calamintha nepeta* also looks as if it has partially materialized out of a morning mist, although in all probability one might hear this plant before seeing it! There are few plants which create such a buzz among bees of all sorts. Even in dense fog or darkness you could trace its whereabouts by the delicious minty aroma of its minuscule leaves. And should you, perchance, be groping about in the darkness, *Stachys byzantina* (syn. *S. lanata*) is also an interesting plant to encounter. Its common name, "lamb's ears", tells you it has the softest of foliage and although the flower stems look similarly textured, they are really unexpectedly harsh. I think it must be this feature which enables bumblebees to cling on to the pale lilac flowers when they

are braving out the summer rains. (They use eryngiums in the same way.) Stachys shares the ghostly and nectar-producing qualities with the calamintha.

PALE PINK MEETS PALE YELLOW   Maybe *Rosa* 'Lucetta' (syn. *R.* 'Ausemi') is not actually the palest of the David Austin roses but it is one of the healthiest I have met and this tall shrub is a good shape. The old-fashioned, cabbage-shaped flowers are deeply scented, not disproportionately over-large and have the grace to just about show their yellow stamens enough to make me feel they are not entirely dysfunctional for all wildlife. With regular dead-heading and the benefit of my top-grade garden compost, 'Lucetta''s flowering season lasts into October. They then look marvellous against the neighbouring miscanthus when it displays silky, pink, tassel-like flowers at this time. 'Lykkefund' is also a pink rose and there, apart from a similarly hearty constitution, the similarities end. It is a climbing rose, conveniently thornless, and has virtually no scent but is most prettily smothered in masses of small, loosely double blooms which have the same subtle yellow under-tones that somehow allow it to combine with the delphinium in the most pleasing but unlikely way. *Hemerocallis* 'Catherine Woodberry' helps link the colours because her soft pink flowers have a hint of yellow to remind her of her ancestry. Other yellows come from the pale *Oenothera odorata* whose spent flowers then conveniently fade to pink. This allows me to cue-in two of my favourite grasses; foxtail barley grass (described in Bird Garden) and *Calamagrostis brachytricha* whose squirrel tail plumes have a pink phase as well as a silver one. Fennel is a stronger yellow with no trace of any other colour but the ample helping of finely divided green foliage tones it down and allows it to be a wonderful mixer in a border where yellow appears. It is another herb which insects, including hoverflies, love to visit for nectar. I am happy to allow it to self-seed amongst all the plants in the group but now and again I dig up some of the older plants if they are in the way or I may just thin out the odd flowering stems (and live on a generous diet of well-flavoured fish and fennel tea for a day or two). This border relates to the western side of the Round Garden where there is a visual connection to the Frog Garden but the lavender-lilac-blue colouring

The Round Garden in the mid-90s as the character of the garden continued to evolve; at this stage, Mediterranean shrubs were still surviving the increasingly wet winters and annuals, such as nicotiana, featured more conspicuously.

intensifies as the planting progresses towards the southern zone at the top, where we sit looking back towards the house.

DEVELOPING THE PURPLE HAZE   There is a seat set in a metal-framed, willow-woven arbour which is home to a divinely scented, annual, bicoloured sweet pea, *Lathyrus odorata*. If there is a rare moment to spare, it is here that we sit, having a cup of tea and watching the butterflies on the plant groups in shades of lavender, mauve, violet and magenta which are picked up in the sweet pea and its accompanying *Clematis* 'Kermesina'. These colours are sometimes difficult to describe but their combined effect can be loosely termed "purple" and, looking up from the house to the top of the Round Garden, I now see the purple haze I envisaged in 1988.

THE UBIQUITOUS BUDDLEIAS   A sequence of buddleias is "top totty" for the insects that visit a butterfly garden. *Buddleia alternifolia* flowers ahead of the rest in June

and I have known it to be absolutely covered in early-arriving Painted Ladies. I prune most buddleias very hard to ensure they flower a little later and so are timed for late summer when most butterflies are present. I leave one or two unpruned for earlier insects but these are the vagabond plants that set seed around the nursery where it matters not one jot how woody, overgrown and uncouth-looking they become.

Back in the garden, I also grow the special *Buddleia* 'Beijing', given to me by a butterfly conservationist and plant collector friend who realized it flowers a whole month later than any we commonly grow here and is perfectly timed for the late-hatching residents or late-arriving migrants. Professor David Bellamy recognized the importance of the introduction of this plant and has been promoting it nationwide. Among a host of others, I love to see Commas nectaring on this buddleia and on the similarly coloured B. 'Lochinch', their orange colour picked up in the eye of each of the mauve florets. It is said that butterflies prefer mauve buddleias but I have never noticed them turn up their noses (or probosces) at any of the other coloured buddleias such as B. 'Nanho Purple', 'Nanho Blue' or 'Black Knight'.

THE "LINEAR LOOK" Starting with vervain, the plant that makes the least impact, I mention *Verbena officinalis* with a word of caution: its seeding habits can be tedious. I readily forgive it because it contains properties to staunch bleeding and cure infection – always handy – and prevent spells. (This may be a good precaution in a mystical space where any old witch could pass through unnoticed!) Vervain is a skinny individual with small leaves and very tiny pale lilac flowers at the tip of its slender stems. Little wonder it is not widely sought-after at garden centres but John Brookes used to tell us to use "not too much meat and add plenty of gravy" when selecting plants. How right he was: star plants need a more modest supporting cast. *Verbena hastata* is much taller with a slender, deeper-coloured, tapered flower-head. It has very greedy roots but at least they give good anchorage to the strong, self-supporting stems. *Teucrium hircanicum* is of medium height, and more floriferous, but still a quietly understated, pale violet spire. Bees like it but butterflies are indifferent. Anise hyssop (*Agastache foeniculum*) is a similar colour and texture and makes a slightly

Both my insects and I are especially attracted to the violet spectrum of plants. Among the assembled August-flowering plants there are various buddleias, monardas and phloxes, interspersed with *Verbena bonariensis*.

more substantial impact. It is a herb with a pleasing aniseed aroma and I sometimes put a few leaves in salad or dry a few for my homemade pot-pourri. Both bees and butterflies are attracted to the agastache's chunky flower spikes. It is not a long-lived perennial but easy to grow from seed.

Even more impressive are the taller spikes of *Liatris spicata*, or "gay feather" to address it more familiarly! The bright, purple-magenta spikes broaden at the top and the plant makes an impact which merits positioning it so it can, indeed, steal the show for a few weeks. The stage is then well set for the arrival of the ultimate adornment – the butterflies. Last year the liatris chiefly took the fancy of Brimstones and Clouded Yellows and the combination of plant and insects was simply mesmerizing.

Nepeta racemosa and the smaller N. x *faassenii* have spiked flower heads but the plant has a floppy manner of growth with a soft appearance that barely makes an impression on my linear-look objectives. However, both bees and butterflies love this plant and so do silver "Y" moths. These day-flying moths are wonderfully fluttery, grey-brown insects which visit a great range of plants but seem to highly favour blue flowers such as nepeta. Where there is limited space for *Nepeta* 'Six Hills Giant' to sprawl, I grow N. x *faassenii*. Although this plant is shorter and neater, it is less robust; over the years I believe many have perished on account of my soggy winter soil conditions. I believe *Nepeta* 'Souvenir d'André Chaudron' eventually met the same fate, although in its early years it seemed unstoppable as it ran amok through the newly dug borders with its more upright, soft, lavender-blue flower stems.

Astilbe 'Purple Lance' is a fine, tall plant with just the visual impact I seek. I have to mulch it well to help it to weather the dry spells in summer. I suppose the flower-heads are more of a plume than a spire or spike, but they enhance the effect I try to achieve as a 21st-century-garden "impressionist". If I have one grievance with astilbes it is this: their dead-heads are very fine but they occur too early in the year. I am ready and waiting for brown flowers after September but before that they look like a premature death, which has a depressing effect on the rest of the planting. Sometimes I stick it out but other times the twitchy secateur fingers become uncontrollable and I cheer myself up for the instant – but deprive the winter garden of a valued member for several months ahead.

The tallest of this sequence of spires is *Lythrum salicaria*, known as purple loosestrife: a colourful wildflower often found on river banks. The flowers, which

are the same magenta/purple colour as the liatris, draw in scores of bees and
butterflies. I find it is Brimstones and Commas which like it the most, but they
certainly find more secretive places to roost. A predator could spot them a mile off
and I do have a rather large and healthy population of birds! Even when I am
ferreting about in the borders, I never find them loitering in odd places on dull days.
They must disguise themselves well while they hang about waiting for a sunny
moment to fly. I don't suppose they know how brilliant and beautiful they look
against the vibrant flower colour but perhaps they realize they are highly
conspicuous when feeding. I have planted one or two garden cultivars, such as
Lythrum virgatum 'Dropmore Purple' and L. salicaria 'Firecandle', in my time but some
skulduggery seems to have occurred. As a result I can detect some minimal colour
variations in the ensuing generations but I cannot vouch for the pedigree of the
offspring. I might be accused of allowing lythrum a little too much freedom of
occupation in the garden but I also value this plant for its fine, upstanding, skeletal
winter form. In spite of its tendency to seed itself rather liberally, I leave it standing
until February or March and have months of pleasure admiring the tawny stems and
seed-heads, especially with the grassy foliage of Miscanthus sinensis 'Gracillimus'
arching gracefully among them. Both plants gleam in the rain and on frosty
mornings they look outstanding when hoary-edged with white.

ROUND FLOWER-HEADS FOR CONTRAST I am often asked what my impressive,
long-flowering, bee-attracting alliums are. There are looks of incredulity when I
reply, "They are leeks.". I love to mix edible plants into the borders, especially when
they look so fine and function so well as a wildlife attractor. The decorative effect of
leeks is superbly complementary to Salvia sclarea var. turkestanica, or clary sage in herbal
parlance. They share the same mixture of almost indefinable pallid pink and ashen-
mauve colouring, although their shape and form are totally contrasting. The salvia
seeds can be soaked in water to make a soothing eyewash – therefore quite a
pertinent companion to an onion. It certainly is a "sight for sore eyes" – as they say
– although the aroma is an acquired taste. Bergamot is another herb that bees
frequent and butterflies sometimes visit. I grow a variety called Monarda 'Blue
Stocking', which is actually a strong magenta colour. It has quite strange "mop-
heads" with long, arched flower tubes. Its seed-heads last for months and look
particularly impressive when iced with frost. Salsify is a wonderfully decorative

vegetable; so much so I seldom eat it. It is related to *Tragopogon pratensis*, known as goat's beard and also Jack-go-to-bed-at-noon. Like its wild yellow relative, salsify's soft, round, lilac flowers close up at noon but the extra-large dandelion-clock seed-heads and even the pointed, closed heads lend a distinct touch of drama.

SCABIOUS TYPES   Of all my ace nectar plants, I think scabious make the most perfectly enchanting platform for butterflies to display their beauty as they delicately sip the sugary juices. Large-flowered varieties such as *Scabiosa caucasica* are certainly very decorative but all the charming floral details exist in the smaller, wild species and it is these that I prefer to grow. They also happen to survive much better in my damp, clay soil. *Scabiosa columbaria* is very branched with masses of small, lavender-blue flowers that are often covered in a crowd of predominantly Small Tortoiseshell butterflies which also like the devil's-bit scabious (*Succisa pratensis*). This wildflower loves to grow in damp meadows or on chalk so perhaps it is this versatility that helps it to excel as a garden plant. The stems are less branched than the former scabious and the pin-head flowers a little deeper-coloured. Devil's-bit is the specific food plant of the rare Marsh Fritillary, but the chances of one visiting are fairly slim in most gardens, mine included. They need a traditionally managed woodland environment where their caterpillar food plant, violets, can proliferate. However, the usual garden butterflies and the bees will be just as happy as I am with the devil's bit. Common knapweed (*Centaurea nigra*) is another admirable wildlife-attracting wildflower that will enthusiastically adapt to garden conditions and I have selected and propagated some very fine specimens from those growing in my meadow. The colours and forms can be variable and I have singled out the later-flowering ones with the most exaggerated rays and the richest colours, from mauve to magenta. This has pleased a wide range of butterflies as well as bees, hoverflies and Burnet Moths. The garden knapweed (*Centaurea montana*) flowers earlier in the year and is also a good nectar plant. I have pink, blue and purple forms; all pretty-looking and all pretty mildew-ridden by mid-summer. They crowd themselves out with volumes of over-exuberant growth but I would rather forgive that trait than have to coax the reluctant

I love to integrate herbs and edible plants in my borders. Leeks are irresistible to bees and hoverflies, have long lasting, decorative flowers and seed-heads, and make handsome bedfellows for the clary sage (*Salvia sclarea* 'Turkestanica')

or faint-hearted one. Both native and garden knapweeds benefit from having the faded flower stems cut to the base to stimulate growth of fresh ones.

POTENTIALLY POTENT   The mauve-to-plum mix of colours of the lovely *Papaver somniferum*, far from having a soporific effect on bees, as the Latin name implies, sends them into a pollen-foraging frenzy! Growing "opium" could be said to put a little controversy into the planting associations. However, there are no dodgy substances in the seeds – they are quite safe to use for bread topping. Like many herbs, true opium (the garden one is not used in commercial production of the drug) is a valuable panacea in small doses, but becomes a dangerously addictive drug when abused. Nature probably provides us with most of the remedies we need to heal ourselves but we unfailingly upset the balance of power and abuse the gifts. (Imagine what havoc could result from modern genetic manipulation if the results are as unpredictable as some scientists suggest. Supposing important, undiscovered healing properties were to be lost in the process or as a result of unintended hybridization between GM and non-GM plants? And what if toxic properties were to manifest in an unforeseen way? "Scary" is the popular word to describe what I feel about the way this technology is being railroaded upon the environment before our plants and their potential powers are fully scientifically explored and recorded.)

FLATTISH HEADS   The elegant, see-through plant, *Verbena bonariensis*, is another superlative, late-flowering nectar plant. Its flower-heads make an ideal podium for butterflies including the stunning Painted Ladies whose pinkish-orange, patterned underwings are such a perfect study. Lovable little bumblebees also pose delightfully on the purple verbena, which appears to have been purposefully designed to display its pollinators at work. *Achillea millefolium* 'Lilac Queen' is dear to me because it is a close cousin to the grassland wildflower, yarrow. In spite of its name, it is distinctly pink but intermingles smoothly with another of my more flat-headed plants, *Phlox paniculata* 'Franz Schubert'. This is a good plant of medium height and bears flowers with a gentle merging of mauve-pink and white. It is floriferous to the point of embarrassment when trying to compose compositions where no one plant is over-dominant. I relieve the situation by prematurely dead-heading a proportion of the stems. The thinned clumps look more graciously elegant and the apparently cruelly treated stems then fully recover and flower again later, thus keeping the layered sequence going longer than it would otherwise. The same methods apply to *Phlox paniculata* 'Border Gem', whose fiery magenta colouring can be altogether a bit too show-stopping in a solid mass. I have another taller, unnamed and wilder-looking phlox that I much prefer to the aforementioned pair. This wildling's flowers are smaller, lilac-coloured and both the individual florets and the whole flower-heads are less cluttered and more neatly spaced than the hybrids. Because of its wilder provenance, I would like to be able to report that the insects prefer it to the modern hybrids but this is not apparent: rather the reverse, in fact.

Daisy flowers are also individually flat but, in the case of my asters, for example, are arranged in sprays. Asters are essential late-nectar stores for butterflies and I have two which I recommend for their beauty and disease-resistance. *Aster* 'September Charm' is a dark cerise-magenta which Red Admirals are glad to find at the end of the season. *Aster* 'Little Carlow' is violet-blue, extremely elegant and more valued by bees than butterflies. I would like to be able to champion 'Little Carlow' as an ace candidate for the wildlife garden because, as a garden-worthy plant, it is in a class above any other aster I have grown.

WILLIAM'S GROUP The rose 'William Lobb' is a very beautiful dusky purple and crimson rose but has little to offer wildlife. However, it is a great treat for me and in amongst it there is a truly valuable collection of nectar plants, so I have singled out this group for special recommendation and will describe William's sequence of alluring bed-fellows. The honesty is first to flower, followed by our own star, the fabulous *Lupinus* 'Witchet'. 'Witchet' arrived as a seedling resulting from a cross between some old-fashioned lupins I grew from seed from an old cottage garden in Kent. Similar to L. 'Thundercloud', it is a thunderous purple, struck with the deep crimson flashes of its keel petals. *Cirsium rivulare* 'Atropurpureum's crimson, thistle-like flowers make a sumptuous place to hang out and feed if you are a bee. It begins to flower in May and if the faded stems are cut down, this plant will flower for months on end – even into December. Despite the rivulare bit, it grows in a range of conditions, provided it feels so inclined. I gather it can be a bit temperamental but so far it hasn't shown its teeth in my gardens. Corncockle, a wildflower now unhappily banished from cornfields, seems happy enough in my "border sanctuary". If I am lucky and the scattered seed germinates in the right place, it forms an impressive duet with the hardy *Salvia* 'Purple Rain' whose aspiring stems

Although the moss rose 'William Lobb' is beautiful and beguiling, it has no obvious attraction for wildlife. However, *Linaria purpurea* and *Lupinus* 'Witchet' (in the background) amply make up for the shortfall.

adds a desirable vertical element. The aster, well-named 'September Charm', flowers last of all just as the rugosa rosehips are ripening as a dual attraction for wildlife. I have great admiration for the mixture of tough rugosa roses that grow at the back of the border in question. The most highly scented and deepest crimson-coloured is 'Roseraie de l'Haye', which is semi-double with good hips, but there are also some more humble, single-flowered rugosas which the bees prefer. They all flower for ages, especially if dead-headed. Masses of insects visit for pollen and nectar and, when the hips form, there is food for birds, Red Admirals and field mice – and Pam Lewis, who also likes to nibble the vitamin C-rich flesh.

WEAVERS Leaving the last border with the bold clumps of nectar plants, you come to a small bed with a matrix of nectar plants weaving in among each other – more like the wildflowers of the meadow. *Knautia macedonica* has pretty, scabious-like flowers that grow in profusion on branching stems. Its colour range extends from deep crimson to pastel pink and mauve. They are constantly attended by wildlife, including bees, butterflies and then greenfinches, which feast greedily on the seeds. I have to restrain a little of the exuberance of the knautia, thinning out the oldest and tallest stems to persuade it not to overpower its bedfellows, in particular the less branching purple eryngium and the silvery-maroon *Allium sphaerocephalon*. The similar shape and "needlepoint" texture of this teasel-like pair makes it easy for the bumblebees to keep a firm grip and I find they often hang in there during rainstorms. Apart from the wildlife "underworld" that surrounds them, they make a sensational planting combination! The eryngium is seemingly unnamed because it developed as a reversion from a variegated form called 'Calypso', which seems to have disappeared from the current edition of the Plantfinder. The only clue to its parentage is that it looks like *Eryngium planum*, but the colour is more intensely purple so I have taken the liberty of naming it E. 'Bewitched'. Understandably my green-leafed plant, having escaped the restraints on its health relating to the variegation, seems much happier *au naturel*.

Oregano is a herb I often use in cooking and pot-pourri and is one of the top-of-the-range nectar plants. *Origanum laevigatum* 'Hopley's' is one of the tallest, finest-looking and richest coloured purple. O. l. 'Herrenhausen' is another fine form with flatter heads of a similar colour. *Origanum vulgare* 'Compactum' is a neat and obliging edging plant with a dense covering of mid-pink flowers on very short stems. For all their garden-worthiness, bees and butterflies barely recognize the superiority of these superb varieties and seem not to make any distinction or preference as they also forage for nectar amongst my inferior, mongrel seedlings which serve them just as well.

WILD WEAVERS   I often allow volunteer wildflowers or invite them in without knowing whether they will be a well-ordered guest or if they will give me a hard time. I have yet to discover whether it was wise or foolhardy to introduce tufted vetch, *Vicia cracca*, one of the loveliest, later-flowering vetches which tempts some of the meadow butterflies and moths from the meadow to the garden. The flowers combine blue, purple and pink colouring which makes them a good "mixer" as they clamber amongst plants in that colour zone. Common vetch, *Vicia sativa*, has bright pink flowers more sparsely arranged amongst the similarly fine, pinnate foliage. This vetch is earlier flowering and is a great favourite with bees. A word of caution! – the related bush vetch, *Vicia sepium*, is the vetch from hell in the garden. It is almost impossible to control or eradicate and barely redeems itself, appearance-wise, with its coarser foliage and dull flowers.

Unlike the vetches, common fumitory (*Fumaria officinalis*) has no tendrils to help it hitch a lift among its rivals in its plant community but it manages to lounge about among, or on top of, other plants. It appears in odd places where there is bare or disturbed soil so, although it was an attractive feature of the young Round Garden, fumitory has found it more difficult to keep its place as the garden planting has matured. I have found it sadly non-negotiable in this respect but I am fond of this curious little character and intend to keep trying ways to make it content. It is more than happy with conditions in my poly-tunnel so at least I have a dependable seed source. Apparently it is self-pollinating because insects ignore its ample nectar supply. I wonder what that is all about? Wild plants seldom waste resources. An extra element of mystery now creeps into the nectar garden . . .

GRASSES With all the intensity of the flowering plants I have shown, it would be easy to lose sight of the fact that the plants are mixed with grasses to remind me of my beloved meadows. There is a wealth of ornamental grasses to choose from and I have tried out many of them. Lyme grass (*Leymus arenarius*) was one of the first to be planted after I discovered it was a great favourite with Gertrude Jekyll. She must have been an intrepid lady to use a plant with a reputation for its powers to anchor its roots in sand dunes. In my early enthusiasm, I barely registered just how much regular digging would be required to thin it and restrain its threshold. I suppose Miss Jekyll had an army of gardeners to help but if the load falls on one person, it needs to land on a strong one, full of grit and determination. I waver as I try to decide if I should put myself through the same trials again, even when I see those grand, glaucous-blue blades at their most sensational in high summer. *Elymus magellanicus*, or even the finer, clumpier *Festuca mariei*, might be a better choice in a similar situation. The winter effect of any of these is modest and by the end of the year they tend to succumb to a certain amount of fungal attack, which disfigures rather than debilitates them.

WINTER GRASSES Most of my other varied grasses constitute a superb element of my Round Garden in winter. In fact, they create a whole fantastic winter scene of their own, as most of the other plants retreat into dormancy, leaving only a handful of perennials with fine, long-standing stems with seed-heads. It takes that special, low winter light and a touch of rain to reveal fully the wonder and range of the colours so often lumped together and dismissed as "buff" – even by those who claim to appreciate it. Look carefully at the leaf blades and you can see the colours of sand from the Sahara and spices from the Indies, as well as the browns, yellow-ochres and grass-greens of our British landscape in winter. I have mentioned some of the grasses but I have made no reference to one of the most exciting I know: *Miscanthus sinensis* 'Morning Light'. It seldom flowers, which means that there are no stiff flower stems to impair the way it moves in the wind, like a horse's flowing mane or a stormy sea, depending on one's mood and imagination. Its fountain of foliage has added winter colours of russet reds, which fire up and glow when diffused with winter light. Before the drama that surrounds it in winter, 'Morning Light' stands serene and gracious with its fine, silvery-green, arching leaves. It is one of the shorter miscanthus with a slightly less brutish root system than others, making it very user-friendly, especially in a smaller garden.

Pennisetum alopecuroides has strong, clumps of pleasant but plain green foliage, about 60cm (2ft) high. It begins to flower in September and its outstanding "bottle brush" flowers endure until the New Year, having run the gauntlet of silver, pinkish, greenish, and then straw, colouring. Agrostis curvula, or African lovegrass, is finer in details of foliage and flower and, although it is less show-stopping, I very much admire its graceful, arching form, which makes an impression for about ten months of the year. I have to thin it radically if it is to share space with other plants so I remove old plants and allow new seedlings to take their place. Grasses are wind-pollinated and although they have no nectar for insects to feed on, they are good habitat providers for hibernating insects or their overwintering larvae. The spent foliage is often tough and enduring as a nesting material for birds, reason enough to consider grasses a useful addition to the wildlife garden.

NATURAL BALANCE   Like annual plants, many insects die at the end of the season and leave it to their few surviving relatives to frantically produce fresh generations as soon as the weather starts to warm up in spring. Other insects hibernate or leave a new generation to overwinter as eggs or in their larval forms. As far as gardeners are concerned, there are friends and foes among them but for the carnivorous creatures that depend on them, all are welcome fodder. I hold the belief that the broader the range of insects I encourage, the more likely the chance of achieving a happy balance where there will not be a disproportionate or overwhelming number of pest species. So far my faith has been rewarded and nowadays I seldom have to intervene and squash anything. I must confess that it took time for me to be able to say this because – remember – I began my garden on a barren site and the system only began to kick in when the garden began to mature and I had less need to interfere with the soil and the plants once they were established.

THE SEASONALITY   With the range of grasses and seed-heads left intact, this garden can look most inspiring, especially on frosty mornings. The winter tracery lasts until mid-February when we gradually clear the brittle remains and "adjust the choreography" of planting in preparation for the next season of dance. Meanwhile, the birds have the opportunity to feed on seeds and insects, and field mice and voles thrive in the protection of the hitherto uncleared herbaceous aftermath. When the time comes to prepare the garden for spring and summer, we wait for dry weather before treading on the beds to cut down the remains of the winter scene and tackle the weeding, lifting, splitting and rearranging perennials. We meticulously avoid compacting the soil and damaging its structure or harming the vital soil-life.

HABITAT BOOSTERS

It is possible to buy artificial nests for bumblebees and masonry bees, and I have tried the latter with some success. In principle, bumblebees like to use holes at the base of a hedge in a shady, sheltered south-facing spot, so I have tried to oblige

them with a variety of materials, such as piles of air-bricks and half-buried, overturned, clay flower-pots to give them a well disguised and protected "front door". The rest they can do themselves if they approve my outline planning regulations. Sometimes these things work out as intended and pretty often they don't. I am often compensated and amused when a field mouse or some other creature bags the site for nesting and I am repeatedly confounded when the chosen or alternative creature makes a nest just a few feet or even inches away from my well-thought-out "eco-feature". Nature always has the last – and in this case, I suspect, the loudest – laugh!

As in all my other gardens, I tuck bundles of hollow stems of varied diameter under shrubs that I am unlikely to disturb for a while. Admittedly I find the evidence of recent occupation more often than I find the actual resident, but that is probably because some other creature has eaten it and that is what it is all about; one species feeding on another in the complex chain which God or Nature masterminded. As gardeners, we have to cross our fingers and hope it all pans out in our favour as well as for the asylum-seekers we harbour. I am convinced my various "habitat boosters" were as great an asset in the juvenile garden as they are now, when the garden is fully fledged. In the Round Garden, as in other places, there are small piles of stones, logs and hollow stems tucked away wherever they can be discreetly placed. I always save the hollow stems of herbaceous plants such as *Filipendula rubra*, *Eupatorium purpureum*, the angelicas, and motherwort. I tie them in bundles and stack them in odd places, sometimes horizontally, sometimes vertically, some placed on the earth and some laid between branches of dense shrubs, such as berberis and escalonia. Our sundial has a circular groove for holding a shallow volume of water, ideal as an insects' "bar", if I can remember to fill it regularly. Mostly they prefer to visit the pond but it is worth considering their needs and fun to watch when they respond to my offerings.

SEDUM RY *Sedum spectabile* is a plant that shares star rating with butterflies and bees and failing to mention it so far may seem like an obvious omission. In fact, this has been deliberate because I have given them special prominence in the garden. I have

A woven-willow globe takes precedence amidst a circle of *Festuca mareii*. The seats and woven-willow arbour are fully revealed at the top of the Round Garden.

clumps of sedum in the various parts of the garden borders and have watched how the insects, butterflies in particular, migrate around the circle seeking the warmest place to feed. I recently decided to give them what I hope will be their hearts' desire and concentrate this special delicacy in a sunny, almost south-facing, feature position. I have built a small flint stone bank to aid the drainage and to reduce the amount and availability of our loamy, nutrient-rich soil which has overfed them in the past; too rich a diet has caused them to grow over-lush and hefty. Hefty plants are then more prone to collapse and I believe they suffer more with fungal problems affecting the stems. Rotting stems cause disarray amongst the winter dead-heads and deep sadness for the gardener who values the winter garden as I do. I hope all these problems will be resolved and that the sedums will share the space congenially with my mongrel oreganos which I remove from places where there is less scope for allowing and appreciating their promiscuous habits.

One good reason to leave seed-heads intact in winter! Having attracted and fed an abundance of butterflies and bees in summer, the snow-capped sedums have a moment of unsurpassed winter glory as they enfold the sedumry bench.

IN CONCLUSION

There are many other good nectar plants besides the ones I have listed, including annuals such as candytuft, white alyssum, certain marigolds, mignonette, lobelia, heliotrope, single dahlias and many more. I am sure everyone can tell a different tale of the preferences that their garden population of butterflies has demonstrated. My Round Garden is constantly evolving to take on board our discoveries, both in terms of wildlife value and experimental planting compositions. It is a victory when a border turns out to be a key "crowd-pleaser" – be it a crowd of bees, butterflies, hoverflies, moths, birds or human onlookers.

In the daytime we can often hear the collective buzz and watch the gentle flutter of insects in this paradise. The most favoured plants literally "rock and roll" with wildlife. At night the moths and bats have the arena to themselves, although I confess I bear testament to very little of the shady night-life, except for the odd evenings when I have the energy to creep out and listen to the owls and the other mysterious sounds of the night; mostly I am too weary after a day's work which frequently begins at dawn.

I must admit that the Round Garden has taxed my physical and creative resources even while it has been a fantastic experience and experiment. Commonsense tells me I was over-ambitious in choosing rather too large a site for a sensible, normal person to manage as a hobby. Be that as it may, the concept could be very easily scaled down to just a few choice plants that I would – or will – take with me to the retirement home, madhouse or workhouse, depending on what the future holds!

THE
WHITE
GARDEN

With its naturalistic design and planting, this garden combines fruit, berries, perennials and grasses with ecological features to create habitats for all creatures great and small.

The maturing white border provides lessons both in the subtleties of colour and in providing for the creatures the flowers were specially selected to support.

I DOUBT IF THERE IS ANY PROBLEM persuading fellow gardeners of the joys of making their gardens attractive to birds, bees, butterflies and other positively beneficial creatures, but not all the larger mammals are ideal visitors in the garden and some can be disruptive and destructive – especially in small gardens. But who would wish to turn away a dormouse or a hedgehog?

Mice, voles and shrews can hardly be classified as "beneficial" to the garden, but a reasonably large country garden can accommodate their nibbling habits with little harm to plants once they are mature. These small mammals provide food for others in the chain; for some owls, for instance, voles are the main ingredient in their diet. It is this food chain that must be considered, and we must be especially aware of the importance of insects and invertebrates in it, both above and below the soil. Foxes will prey on almost anything they can catch, so they easily earn a living in both urban and rural gardens. Some people welcome their company though others are not amused. I find that stoats, weasels and hares are comparatively rarely found in gardens and those I have seen have been too shy to hang about for long. I expect much depends on the proximity of the garden to their more natural habitat. To be realistic, while "gardening in tune with nature" is essentially about encouraging and enjoying beneficial wildlife, it also involves negotiating with the creatures whose presence may sometimes disturb the order we seek to create.

Having been involved with the conservation of grassland for many years, I seize any opportunity I find to restore or create areas of meadow, whether they be a few yards square or several acres in size. In Britain, 98 per cent of species-rich grassland has been destroyed since the war and that devastation has resulted in lost habitat for dependent flora and fauna alike. Our natural woodland has similarly suffered, 50 per cent of it destroyed in that same period. It is almost impossible to replace such priceless habitat, and hard to imagine how gardeners can begin to make up for the irresponsible actions of our predecessors. However, we can certainly help in a small way – even with the tiniest patches of simulated woodland and meadow patches, and this was my intention in my proposed White Garden.

THE WOODLAND EDGE In the countryside some of the best wildlife habitat exists where woodland or hedgerow start to merge into open grassland (the "ecotone" in modern parlance) and the more gradual the transition, the better. On farmland this often amounts to field edges – at their most valuable when a generous margin is left between crops or pasture and the dividing or boundary hedgerow. If the hedgerow is broad and tall, with mature trees, then so much the better; there is a special bonus if there is mature, broad-leaved woodland adjoining. If such woodland is well-managed and sections of the under-storey are coppiced on a traditional ten-to-fifteen year system of rotation, the ecosystem continually improves, as the richest diversity of wildlife is supported. Wildlife can benefit from the best of all worlds where a choice of shaded places, dappled light and sunny spots offers shelter and protection for a wide range of creatures. At the same time, these assorted conditions support the growth and survival of a diversity of essential native plants on which these creatures depend. Some such individuals rely on just a single plant species for their survival. This is often the case with butterflies, such as the Hairstreaks, Fritillaries and certain Blues; no host plant in a suitable environment = no butterfly. It is as simple and sad as that.

THE SAD REALITY Unfortunately the paradigm of countryside management I have described for woodland, for example, is more or less non-existent where intensive agricultural practice maximizes the use of every square inch of ground and woods are often managed simply for the commercial growth and extraction of timber. Farm hedgerows, if they are lucky enough to survive being grubbed up to extend field acreages, are generally brutally flailed within an inch of their lives – very often at nesting time when birds are in occupation or later when they are relying on hedgerow berries for winter fodder. Field crops are grown cheek by jowl against the mutilated hedges and both are treated to a cocktail of chemicals as spray-drift often clobbers the non-targeted hedgerow species and their interdependent wildlife. So serious has the effect on the environment become that, albeit late in the day, there are government incentives to encourage farmers to care for their hedges and leave wide field margins. Sadly, the positive impact of such sustainable management seems to be fairly limited. I see little evidence of conservation – or even plain common-sense – filtering through in parts of my own county. In fact, rather the reverse is occurring where field edges are deliberately sprayed with herbicide and hedges battered and shattered during the period when birds are nesting.

THE GOOD NEWS However, although ignorance, lack of legislation, the economic climate or other reasons may prevent some landowners from caring for the environment, there are wonderful conservation organizations and also some farmers, particularly the organic growers, who manage their land in a highly sympathetic and sustainable way. Gardeners like myself can join with them through our smaller conservation efforts. We can help by very simply mimicking the desirable "ecotone principles" in our gardens. In effect we do this when we plant a combination of native and garden plants to make a smooth and progressive change from shady woodland to dappled glades to sunny open borders and then lawns. Amazingly, we can achieve this in a surprisingly small space. With two or three trees, an under-storey of a few shrubs that emerge to form the backdrop for a border of nectar-rich cottage-garden plants and herbs and a lawn, or preferably a patch of meadow close by, we have simulated the type of habitat that will provide a safe haven for a wealth of creatures which will, in turn, benefit our gardens. Threading in a few British native plants as well as choosing trees and shrubs with fruits and berries adds to the wealth of our bequest. If sympathetically – and preferably organically – managed, our garden habit can be a jewel for at least some of the wildlife displaced from the ever more hostile countryside.

THE DESIGN BRIEF

The white wilderness I had in mind was to be the last part of our two acres of garden to be designed and cultivated. My aim was to use this area to mimic the woodland edge (or ecotone) habitat and also to create a half-acre wildflower meadow. After the constraints that are an inevitable part of planting and managing our Round Garden with its formal, geometric pattern, I felt the urge to make our final garden space one of comparative freedom and with a greater sense of open space and interrelationship with our surroundings. However, the White Garden was barely a twinkle in the eye until 1990 when we planted the first trees to establish a framework for a garden in which we could extend our interest in combining garden planting with native plants and grasses. We wanted this garden to appear to melt imperceptibly into the background as it merged with our hedgerows, meadow, smallholding, neighbouring farmland and the wider landscape beyond. It was part of our original aim to make sure our garden project would blend unobtrusively, rather than intrude conspicuously, on the bucolic charm of the Blackmore Vale countryside. Here, on the higher point of our land we could view the widened horizons with views extending to Dorset's famous Bulbarrow Hill.

To help strengthen the defences against potential marauders, one of the very first things we did in 1987 was to widen the northern boundary of the small-holding by making a small band of woodland, with additional oaks, ash and beech. Although commonly found in the countryside, beech is not a British native tree. It supports only a few insects but the masts are valuable food for tits, chaffinches, bramblings, greater-spotted woodpeckers and nuthatches. We introduced three poplars: the black poplar (*Populus nigra*) would hopefully become home to the Poplar Hawk-moth; the grey poplar (*Populus x canescens*) was included to look beautiful and match others in our local landscape, and *Populus balsamifera* would waft its most delicious, balmy scent downwind across our land.

We underplanted the new trees with hazel and field maple. Near the front woodland edge we added cherry plum, wild crab apple, wild pear and damson, which all have thorny stems, and wild cherry with guelder rose and wayfaring tree in between with wild honeysuckle intertwining among them. The hazel would be coppiced about every 12 years to let light in and regenerate the growth of plants on the woodland floor. Once the light levels had begun to shade out the nettles, we would introduce the local English bluebells we had been given by our neighbour and which we were multiplying in nursery beds.

This part of our land is at the edge of the smallholding and has a substantial bank and ditch, which is the territory of badgers. We hoped they would be content to stay there rather than disturb our garden and, in fact, we have seen very little of them in recent years, the only evidence being the removal of ground-based wasp nests. It is strange, considering their diet can include about 250 worms per night, that we see so few signs of disruption from their foraging. With our extra scrub planting, we crossed our fingers and hoped to increase the chances that dormice would travel along the hedgerows of the neighbouring farmland and connect to this little oasis of coppiced woodland habitat. Foxes come and go, and for two consecutive years we had a resident vixen who reared an enchanting litter of cubs in the White Garden. Rabbits are more permanent inhabitants and, with some extra protection for young plants, we managed an acceptable level of co-existence while our whippets were young and agile hunters and before our cats became geriatric and disinclined to stalk them.

GARDEN STYLE I decided on an informal style – a far cry from the more traditional concept of the "white garden". There are many famous formal white gardens, none better than Vita Sackville-West's beautiful garden at Sissinghurst. At Sticky Wicket our starting point was quite different. My planting would not be so strictly design-led nor correspondingly subject to the constraints of formality. I wanted to encourage spontaneity, interfere as little as possible and to have a steady programme of development that would eventually allow more of a "white wilderness" to evolve as the garden matured. I wanted a "garden for all seasons" that would generate yet more wildlife habitat and be robust enough to support some of the larger, furry creatures; a garden in which I could constantly learn from the experience of trying to sketch a fine line between a reasonably acceptable level of order and escalating chaos. In order for the garden to bring joy to humans as well as providing a haven for some larger wildlife, there would be an inevitable conflict of interest and a need for compromise. In short, I wanted to discover the parameters of garden anarchy! It is disingenuous to suggest that managing wild gardens is an effortless task, but I was convinced it would be far less stressful than trying to maintain the necessary order required by conventional borders.

THE PLAN   My plan was a very simple cross-banding of approximately 65m- (70yd-) long grass paths leading to the five essential elements: the hen-run gate by "Africa House" – a sort of gazebo for hens; our shepherd's hut, which acts as a summerhouse; the two entrances to the meadow and the one that secretly disappears into the utility area, compost and recycling bay – the "engine room" of our organic garden management scheme. The grass paths would vary in width, creating an imperceptible false perspective at some points and facilitating extra open space, for a picnic or other such gathering.

SHELTER, SCREENING, SAFETY AND SCALE   These were the first things to consider. I wanted the site to be protected from the elements and there were less lovely parts of the smallholding which I needed to screen. I had to take care to do this without blotting out any of the cherished views across the countryside. Peter and I also had to make sure the hen-run was safe from foxes and the garden safe from horses and goats, which meant that electric fencing would be necessary to reinforce the security. For my overall concept to work, I tried to judge the scale of the allotted areas and the perspective of design. I wanted to make the garden seem as extensive and yet as mysterious as possible and, at the same time, I had to decide where and how to make the gentle transition from shady wooded places to sunny open borders or grassland.

DOMESTIC WHITE ANIMALS   It may be said that I forced the design issue somewhat unduly by choosing white animals as "living statuary". I admit that doves (and their white dovecote) were certainly intended to be a feature here. They may interbreed to gain a few odd colours but they are genetically principally white, so that was acceptable. But there are also white animals in the pens and paddocks that are within or close to the garden. Some of our bantams have dodgy origins and come in assorted colours, but our first choice was to acquire and help conserve an old English breed – the Light Sussex – which happens to be white with black markings. The snow geese were rescued from an uncertain fate and the breed is nearly always white, so the choice was made for us there. Only one of our four ducks is white but she is certainly the most conspicuous. Saanan goats – also white – are good milkers, lovely characters and I have kept them for years. The "white" horses? Well, I have always favoured grey horses and again my association with them goes back many years "pre-Wicket". My case rests on sentimental grounds. I must admit, I do get a great thrill out of seeing my white pets in close proximity to the white planting! There is also the fact that both the white plants and animals contribute towards the gentle ambience of morning mistiness and the contrastingly eerie evening atmosphere which I wanted to intensify. At least I resisted the notion of having a white peacock; that would have been one pretentious step too far for a wildlife gardener and smallholder!

PLANTING BRIEF

My brief, as always, was to choose hardy stalwarts to provide pollen, nectar, seeds, fruit, berries, nuts or form protective wildlife habitat. The habitat element was intended to be a particular strength in this garden. As ever, I would arrange all my plants so as to draw attention to their natural beauty but here there was to be a somewhat wilder approach compared to the planting associations in the more disciplined domain of the previous gardens. I wanted to make a rambling and romantic garden where wafting fragrances filled the air and where there was a strong winter effect from coloured stems or from those that were otherwise effective in their winter nakedness. I decided to up the stakes on the conservation of wildflowers and mingle a plethora of them among their only slightly more exotic bedfellows. In this wilder garden I wanted to experiment with growing grasses, both ornamental and native, in a way that would take "naturalism" to a new level. Both grasses and wildflowers in the borders, mixed with garden plants, would prepare a visually gentle passage to those in a nearby garden meadow or "flowery mead", as I ambitiously perceived it would one day be.

My selected plants would hopefully cater for insects, birds, foxes, field mice and any other creatures that might care to live among them. I admit to hoping the badgers would continue to stay in their nearby hedgerows away from the garden and that deer would not wander in, but in the event of their occupation, the matured garden would hopefully be robust enough for all to co-exist. Rabbits are an inevitable part of country life and I braced myself for negotiation and probably a little conflict in this wilder setting. This garden was for "all creatures great and small" and that involved a different level of tolerance from previous gardens, where rabbits had been discouraged by our dogs or held at bay by rabbit-proof fencing. I am not opposed to the idea of shooting the odd rabbit for the pot, but in principle I didn't want to have to fight over this garden or to assert undue control over it. I wanted to nudge things along in a pragmatic way, as I believed this was how it should be with a "wilderness" garden.

WHITE-FLOWERED GARDEN PLANTS In selecting my white-flowered trees and shrubs, I was delighted to discover what an extensive and pertinent range was available to me. Most fruit-, hip- and berry-bearing plants have white flowers and many have the bonus of autumn colour, so we would be able to see an exciting colour transformation happening as summer faded and both foliage and berries would begin to light up the landscape. To add to this and for winter delight I could include trees and shrubs with coloured, patterned or spectacularly thorny stems. As usual, I yearned for a sequence of scented plants at all points of the garden. The criteria were very easy to meet. There is a preponderance of white forms of garden plants, including deliciously scented ones. There are dozens of white wildflowers which can be pleasingly integrated with the relaxed style of planting I favour, so I was spoiled for choice. I kept strictly on course and resisted any temptation to stray into selecting exotic or unusual plants for the sake of "plantsmanship" or, heaven forbid, "plant one-up-manship."

I had a lot to learn about the vagaries of the plant colour we loosely term "white". I began to divide my plants into those with hints and undertones of pink, cream, yellow, green or blue and also the rather understated russet and bronze tints. The subtle colour influences can be induced by the colour of the surrounding foliage of the plant, its bracts, stem buds, stamen, central eye or the underside or veins of petals. I discovered that very few plants are actually pure white but some are whiter than others, and can make the tinted ones look rather dirty if the placing is ill-considered. Naturally these observations went hand-in-glove with discovering which of my selected wildlife-friendly plants were to be most valuable and also which ones would be sturdy and reasonably rabbit-resistant.

CONSTRUCTION

For a harmonious coexistence between gardener and garden wildlife, it helps if parameters are set either physically or at least in one's mind. I did not want to show zero tolerance to any creature but I had misgivings about one or two of those in the vicinity and I needed to set out my strategy with regard to creating exclusion zones.

WILDLIFE DEFENCES Fortunately we have no problem with deer and therefore no need to try to fence them out. Badgers seldom bother us but I know they can be a bit disruptive, especially if their chosen route is made in any way inaccessible to them. Where badgers are in residence I think it wise to give in and design the garden around their regularly used tracks because they become extremely belligerent when obstacles are placed to exclude or divert them. Peter and I have mixed feelings about foxes because, although we love to see them, and they help thin the rabbit population, there is always the terrible fear they will penetrate our defences and massacre our poultry and waterfowl. To separate fox from fowl, we constructed a 1.8m (6ft) fence with a strand of electric wire top and bottom. The bottom one was just 15cm (6in) away from the base of the wire netting and this netting was also laid along the ground for 30cm (12in) to further thwart the attempts of any animal trying to dig its way in.

A similar fence, but just 1m (3¼ft) high would have been necessary if we had been determined to exclude rabbits from all of the gardens, but the costs involved and the amount of maintenance required meant that this was not even a consideration. To include the White Garden we would have needed to cater for the comings and goings of badgers, including special gates so that they had access and, in my experience, this never fails to rub them up the wrong way and incites sabotage.

MOLES, MICE, VOLES AND EGG-STEALERS Of course, moles cannot be fenced out and, in my opinion, life is too short to devote the time required to try to trap them or to play games with the windmills, upturned bottles, garlic or moth-balls intended to repel them or drive them at least as far as the property next door! I just spread the big heaps of mole-hill soil where they pop up, or use some for potting compost, and I try to comfort myself that they help keep the ground aerated in winter. Admittedly I get more than a little "aerated" myself when I consider the vast number of earthworms they devour. Worms are most efficient and valuable conditioners of soil and we need their input. When mole damage is just too rife and conspicuous, Peter, blessed with the patience of Jove and the persistence of a saint, would sometimes stalk and shoot them when he saw fresh soil erupting as they worked their four-hourly tunnelling shifts. That solved the problem for just the amount of time it takes for another mole to take the place of the dead one. Naturally we would rather put up with them than even for one moment consider poisoning or gassing them. Goodness knows how many other creatures could become the innocent victims of such draconian measures.

Shrews, mice and voles may annoyingly nibble a few plants and bulbs but they are food for owls and other predators. I catch only a fleeting glimpse of them, but I often find rather enchanting little nests in both likely and improbable places. Field mice include worms and snails in their diet so, as with so many of these mammals, there are pros and cons for the gardener to evaluate, who sometimes eradicates friends along with foes. Hedgehogs consume slugs, caterpillars and also insect larvae, some of which are pests to the gardener and some of which, such as beetles, are an asset. They also eat birds' eggs and chicks and, I am told, will even kill snakes. On balance, hedgehogs are a friend to the gardener and are fascinating animals to have visit our gardens, where they can at least be temporarily safe from the hazards of the traffic that accounts for a large percentage of their high mortality rate.

Stoats, weasels and grey squirrels are fascinating to watch but they also steal birds' eggs. Stoats compensate for their destructiveness by catching rats, which definitely need to be controlled, and rabbits, which become more manageable when their numbers are reduced. Owls and hawks will, in turn, take the stoats as well as weasels, which are Britain's smallest carnivores and half the size of a stoat. Weasels prey on mice, voles, and occasionally even a rabbit. The harsh reality of nature's system has to be faced and it can be tough.

Grey squirrels, cute-looking as they may be, are the most persistent, up-front and provocative in their hedgerow-raiding activities. They also vandalize trees with their bark-stripping habits. Being aliens to this country they have no natural predators to balance the numbers. All these predatory mammals are a law unto themselves and there is no practical physical barrier to prohibit them so we just have to take them on board if they choose to drop in or become resident. The only way nesting song-birds can avoid such predators is by finding a dense, well-camouflaged site, which is difficult for invaders to penetrate.

There are mixed feelings among ecologists regarding interference with other predators, such as crows, magpies and sparrowhawks. The latter are protected but the former two can be controlled with a gun or, in the case of magpies (if their numbers are excessive), using live bait, in the form of one of their own kind, to lure them into a Larsen trap. After witnessing a lethal raid on a precious thrush's nest, I was not unduly disturbed when our neighbour culled either the culprit or at least one or two of his relations.

PROGRAMME OF WORK Having faced the fact that trials and tribulations exist with certain wildlife, I will now re-focus on the pleasures of attracting more benevolent creatures desperately needing the protection and food our gardens can offer.

I was in no hurry to complete this garden so it was planted in three logical phases, starting in 1990. We set out the design by mowing the intended pattern in the long grass of what was still rough pasture, Peter swiftly wielding the machinery once I had set out the simple design in the morning dew. We very carefully positioned and then planted the considered framework of trees, including cherries, crab apples, rowans and hawthorns. I had in mind a small fruit forest where the bounty would be shared by all the inhabitants, human or otherwise. We also planted two groups of nine birches to form small, wooded places dissected by bark paths.

The trees were generously mulched with two or three inches of wood peelings, securely protected with spiral guards against rabbit damage and further protected by a wide surround of rails and stock wire. This defence would keep them safe while both our goats and horses continued to graze the remaining grassland during the two years we would allow for the trees to begin to mature. I prefer to plant small trees and wait for them to grow healthily, at their own pace, rather than planting large trees, which can struggle rather feebly unless mollycoddled and consistently irrigated. I used the interim time to propagate some of the shrubs and most of the perennials I had in mind for future planting.

SPRING 1992 Once the trees were well established, our stock were permanently banished from the site as we set out the rest of the design once more – this time for real. In spring we began the process of double-digging and manuring the borders and then dealing with the first flushes of weed growth, allowing a whole summer to pass before we began to plant into the cleaned and conditioned soil. As ever, our border preparations were thorough and time allowed for repeated applications of garden compost and manure. We were soon to be handsomely repaid by the rapid and healthy growth of the plants and the minimal need to water them.

Where grassy paths were intended, we persuaded the existing pasture turf to be a little more lawn-like simply by a summer regime of occasional light rolling and regular mowing. We also designated a 60 by 6m (70 by 7yd) area of long grass to be converted from rough pasture to "garden meadow", where wildflowers and selected garden plants would hopefully grow side by side. This garden meadow

would form the fringe between the White Garden and the "pukka" wildflower hay-meadow we hoped one day to create still further beyond.

AUTUMN 1992 — THE SHRUB PLANTING   I planted an under-storey of shrubs beneath some of the trees and a framework of shrubs for the mixed borders in the more open spaces nearby. Once more, the new plants were treated to a thick mulch of pulverized bark from our local timber growers. But how were the rabbits to know the plants had not been provided to cater for their appetites? At first all the plants had to be individually protected with wire or plastic mesh surrounds; we used beige-coloured clematis netting, which looked reasonably unobtrusive. Rabbits seem particularly attracted to new plants set into bare ground. When the novelty had worn off and the plants were well grown, the protection was removed while we apprehensively watched and waited to appraise their activities. Meanwhile, we erected the white wooden dovecote; we started with just two pairs of doves and now have around thirty.

SPRING 1993 — THE HERBACEOUS PLANTS   I began to introduce some of the herbaceous plants, including ornamental grasses which would complement the tints and tones of the flowers and foliage of the shrubs, and help to provide ground cover and, of course, sustenance for wildlife. Once more we had to try and outwit the rabbits or simply give up attempting to grow the plants they found most irresistible. They have a frustrating and unreasonable way of changing their preferences just when you think you have the measure of their appetites.

The struggle to persuade wildflowers to grow in the over-fertile soil of the garden meadow led me to an experiment; I tried killing off the existing turf by smothering it with plastic before setting some small plants and re-seeding. Unfortunately, this proved a hopeless idea as the same grasses and weeds returned with a vengeance. I had to keep digging them out, along with their clods of topsoil, until the nutrient level started to abate; it took several years before I could coax the wildflowers to establish themselves. I also sowed yellow rattle, a semi-parasitic native plant, to help

We mowed wide grassy paths to form the template of the very simple design needed to accommodate domestic fowl and doves. Having previously planted about forty strategically sited trees, we began to prepare and plant the borders around them.

suppress the growth of the grasses. Gradually I began to naturalize a few suitably competitive garden plants, such as hardy geraniums, and after several years, my romantic notion of the "flowery mead" began to take shape.

AUTUMN 1993 – THE SHEPHERD'S HUT AND SHEEPFOLD By now we had foxes breeding in the hedgerows and regularly visiting the garden with their cubs. We needed a sheltered place to observe our charming guests and Peter resolved to find a suitable building. He took himself off to the Great Dorset Steam Fair, struck a deal with a colourful local character, and returned the proud owner of a shepherd's hut; the perfect choice of shelter for our location and the general ambience of this outer garden. (Shepherds originally lived in these mobile, corrugated iron shacks at lambing time; the huts would be towed to the distant fields or downs so the shepherd could be on hand to attend his flock.) "Haycombe One" – as ours was called – was towed into place at the furthest end of the garden, adjoining the meadow.

Our hut, honourably retired from lambing service, is now both a wildlife hide and a resting spot, and a place to display information about wildlife gardening for our visitors. In winter it provides exactly the right temperature for butterflies and

lacewings to hibernate. We have recently watched a young stoat playfully popping in and out of the undercarriage; foxes, too, sometimes shelter between the huge metal wheels in the 60cm- (2ft-) deep space below the hut. While it may be perfect heaven for the stoats and foxes, it is highly disconcerting for our domestic fowl in the run immediately beside the wildlife squat. A line of electric fence has so far dissuaded the foxes from carrying out a deadly raid. We play with fire when we try to divide such tempting prey from their natural predators. Fortunately, our hens roost high in our alder trees and the more vulnerable ducks and geese have a reasonably large pond for refuge in the event of attack.

The design for our "sheepfold" was inspired by one of Gordon Beningfield's paintings. Gordon was an exceptional artist and conservationist who loved Dorset and often chose shepherd's huts as a subject for his work. One such painting portrays a straw-bale sheepfold enclosure next to a hut. I re-interpreted this with a willow-woven "sheepfold" beside our hut and within the nearby, recently planted birch copse. We used ash poles for stakes and then wove long wands of willow in a diagonal pattern to complete a semi-circular shape. There is a break in the structure to allow access and make a tempting entrance to the meadow. The sheepfold is underplanted with a combination of white woodland plants and grasses, which compliment the white bark of the birches.

AUTUMN 1997 After five years of trying to achieve my heart's desire with the strip of garden meadow, I finally grasped the problem of the extreme fertility of our soil. The battle to suppress the vigorous grasses and creeping buttercup proved much harder than the removal of the odd dock or nettle – also indicating the fertile nature of my rich loam. After several experiments, I realized a more radical approach would be required if Peter and I were to tackle the next half-acre area we had in mind.

In September 1997 we made a dramatic departure from our rule of hand-digging only and excavated the site with a JCB. We removed hundreds of tons of topsoil to reveal an infertile subsoil much more conducive to growing wildflowers. With the removal of the turf went the layer of Yorkshire fog grass, creeping buttercup and

The "woodland-edge" habitat (to the left) and the garden-meadow grassland habitat (to the right) flank the path to the former shepherd's hut that serves as a wildlife hide and information centre for our visitors.

white clover, which had hampered our previous grassland restoration programmes.

This huge ecological disruption would never have been contemplated had we not been utterly convinced that the ends would justify the means. The combination of the flower-rich grassland with the nearby woodland, hedgerow and garden habitat would offer extended opportunities for an even wider range of wildlife to flourish. A friend and conservationist had advised me and offered some locally sourced wildflower seed from his own project nearby, so that with this priceless gift we would also be able to make a significant contribution to the conservation of the grassland flora (and the associated wildlife) of our part of Dorset. (I have described this venture in my first book, *Making Wildflower Meadows*.)

Not wanting to part with the displaced topsoil, we built a feature known as "Mount Wicket" with the spoil from the excavation. This upwardly extended the grazing area for our goats, which had been systematically robbed as the garden encroached on their territory. This turned out to be just the place for voles to live and (unfortunately for them) to become, in their turn, the favoured food for the owls we hear all around our property. The rich soil is conducive to the growth of a luxuriant crop of nettles and with a little extra management from us – cutting about three-quarters of them down in June to regenerate fresh growth – they provide a perfect and well-used maternity unit for caterpillars of the Peacock, Red Admiral and Small Tortoiseshell butterflies.

PLANTING

To make the flowering period of the garden as extensive as possible, we celebrate the arrival of the New Year with hellebores and carpets of bulbs in the borders, the birch woodland and especially in the garden meadow. One of the most stimulating sounds is that of the early bumblebees trying to squeeze themselves into the flowers of *Helleborus foetidus*. When I hear that buzz and see snowdrops and narcissi forging their way upwards, I know the earth is stirring and it is time for me to increase my gardening activities. I keep the floral momentum going with trees, shrubs and herbaceous plants that flower in a measured sequence until late October with late-flowering asters and Japanese anemones, together with late-flowering shrubs such as *Clerodendron trichotomum* var. *fargesii*. Thus there continues a succession of hips and berries for more or less twelve months of the year.

SHARING THE PRODUCE   The 17th-century essayist, Joseph Addison, wrote, "I value my garden more for birds than for cherries and very frankly give them fruit for their song". What fine sentiments! I keep repeating this when a consistently charitable attitude is needed at raspberry, gooseberry and black-, red- and white-currant time, when I would be grateful if they would sometimes share the pickings with me just a little more charitably. To be fair, they do leave me a very reasonable share of delicious, raspberry-like Japanese wineberries. Do I imagine it or are white-fruited alpine strawberries even more flavoursome than the red ones? They seem to taste as if they have had the cream added and the birds have gradually learnt to recognize them for the delicacy they are. I could possibly build a fruit cage to protect my portion of the fruit but it would have to be 100 per cent sound and solid to eliminate any risk of having birds trapped in floppy netting. I would rather take my chance and accept a more meagre ration than be responsible for such a catastrophe. I can hardly complain since I introduced most of the plants with the deliberate intention of providing for wildlife; my reward is the endless hours of pleasure in watching and hearing the results. And what a result we are having!

TREES WITH FRUIT OR BERRIES   The wild cherry (Prunus avium) is ideal in a wild garden setting, as its large leaves produce a shaded canopy. It often suckers rather annoyingly and is a greedy beast for a small garden, but I was fortunate to be able to allow my group of three plenty of room to spread and form a mini-wooded environment for flora and fauna. The blackbirds cherry-pick before the fruits are ripe enough for us to eat so we seldom even notice their rapid disappearance. My most popular bird-attracting garden tree is Malus hupehensis with its bright red, cherry-sized crab-apples. In spring its clusters of white, almond-scented blossoms are visited by hundreds of eager honey-bees. The bees are just as keen on the hawthorn (Crataegus crus-galli) and there is a very audible buzz from the direction of my trio which stand at the edge of the garden meadow. Like the malus, it has stunning autumn colour, is simply covered in berries and has a very fine winter shape with the substantial thorns that give it its name. The rowan (Sorbus aucuparia) is a comparatively slender, white-flowered tree and its large clusters of orange berries are usually eaten almost as soon as they ripen in August. I think rowans are happiest in drier conditions but mine survives well enough to contribute to the "fruits of the forest" and stimulate my curiosity in the folk-law aspect of this magical tree. The wild pear (Pyrus communis) has fruits with too sharp and dry a flavour for our palates, but they are totally acceptable to the wasps and birds that are not so discerning. The medlar (*Mespilus germanica*) is a small, white-flowered tree with a unique character; well-spaced, spreading branches with strange-looking fruits with olive-brown russeted skin and a peculiar "orifice" at the base. Who eats it? Well, once it is thoroughly over-ripe – or "bletted" – I make a sort of jam which has been pronounced "unusual" by polite friends; I think the birds eventually eat the remainder if other, more favoured fruits have been devoured by mid-winter.

MULTI-ATTRIBUTED SHRUBS Among the shrubs, the shiny black berries of both *Amelanchier lamarckii* and *Aronia melanocarpa* are usually amongst the first to be eaten and then the autumn foliage of both plants is exceptional. *Amelanchier*, or June berry commonly, has berries which are a special treat for thrushes and blackcaps – two of our favourite songbirds. The evergreen *Sarcococca confusa* has red/black berries that

they don't seem to be a particular magnet for birds. I grow it more for the heady delights of its wafting winter perfume. On the other hand, birds very soon devour the white berries of *Cornus alba* 'Elegantissima'. This plant is certainly a "good act" with its green-and-white splashed leaves, white berries and its vibrant, bright red winter stem. It is more than happy to grow in a soggy part of the border where many other plants would struggle to survive the wet winters.

With other eye-catching winter stems in mind, I grow two forms of rubus, which prefer drier ground and need plenty of space to spread. Most rubus are hard to confine and although well suited to a wilderness garden, they could be troublesome in a more genteel and confined space. I am very taken with the cool, purple-tinged, white-grey bloom of the winter stem of *Rubus biflorus*. It can look agreeably weird in a certain light. I slow down its relentless advance by planting it in grass and then tackling the ensuing chaos in late winter, when I am almost certain to find the remains of a nest towards the centre of the clump. *Rubus phoenicolasius*, the Japanese wine-berry I mentioned earlier, has contrastingly warm-looking stems with a multitude of tiny red bristles, giving the younger stems an astonishing, incandescent appearance when backlit by winter sunlight.

The extraordinary raspberry-pink and orange fruits of the spindles are four-lobed seed capsules. They are not an immediate pull for wildlife but, although they are inconspicuous in summer, they certainly declare their identity and become human crowd-pleasers in autumn. In fact, all who encounter *Euonymus planipes* are simply bowled over by the large, flamboyant berries and the fiery autumn foliage. Winged spindle (*Euonymus alatus*) competes for attention with its vivid autumn foliage, but has only small purple and red fruits. Particularly pronounced, corky, winged stems are an additional characteristic of this plant and of its rather attractive compact form, *Euonymus alatus* 'Compactus'. *Euonymus europaeus* 'Red Cascade' has smart green stems, the foliage is slightly less spectacular colour-wise and it has smaller fruits than *E. planipes* but has a very pleasing shape (as its name suggests) and I find it easier to integrate into the mixed borders. The wild spindle (*Euonymus europaeus*) adds extra colour to a rich hedgerow collection of red, white and blue-black hips and berries.

A range of hips and berries and autumn foliage of shrubs give the White Garden a dramatic seasonal colour transformation. As summer fades, *Euonymus alatus* 'Compactus' and the even more flamboyant *E. planipes* have their moment of glory.

Of my 16 varieties of cotoneaster in the whole two-acre garden, most are red berried and all have flowers that are very sought after by bees. Forms of *Cotoneaster horizontalis* have berries that are the early favourite with the birds and others seem to be eaten in a fairly predictable order through the season. *Cotoneaster x watereri* 'John Waterer', at the other extreme, is the tallest shrub (or small tree) and the mass of berries are usually left until after Christmas. *Cotoneaster bullatus* arrived as a self-seeded volunteer and I welcome it for its blood-red berries and harlequin autumn colour.

The grey-leaved sea buckthorn, *Hippophae rhamnoides*, is well laden with succulent orange berries and has the added benefit of being armed with substantial thorns. Most years see the berries stripped by visiting fieldfares or redwings on their migratory passage. The same raiders often return for the C. x w. 'John Waterer' berries. Lovely as it is to see the migrants, I feel very sorry for the resident blackbirds which seem to have jealously guarded the plant for many weeks.

THICKETS AND THORNY PLANTS FOR HABITAT   A wildlife wilderness needs thickets to give cover and, design-wise, to add to the sense that all is not quite revealed, accessible or entirely controlled. I try to enter the mind of a hedgehog, slow-worm, bird or a mouse and think what, for them, would represent a safe, protected environment. For instance, tuckering down or nesting in – or beneath – a tangle of unclipped evergreen privet, a thorny pyracantha or a hawthorn hedge bottom would seem like a snug, safe and private little kingdom.

Tangled thickets are also excellent warm roosts for birds in winter and offer secret hideouts to nest in spring. *Stephanandra incisa* is one such thicket-forming shrub. Its stems grow arm over arm, forming a very dense, medium-height shrub with an arching habitat. It has clusters of tiny, rather insignificant white flowers and crinkly leaves that turn into a rather sophisticated mosaic of autumn colour. As the leaves fall, its shiny, tan, zigzag stems are revealed and the skeleton becomes a major player in the winter garden. Its relative, *Stephanandra tanakae*, has similar flowers, fine golden autumn colour and notable impressive stems in winter, but its form is far less complex and it is taller and more open-branched. Both varieties do well in sun or

From shady woodland and thorny thickets to open meadowland this garden is intended as a sanctuary for all creatures great and small. Domestic fowl are provided with their own featured accommodation!

shade. Seldom do plants make a more congested mass of stems than *Viburnum opulus* 'Compactum' but all this activity seems to be at the expense of berry-production.

Only a foolhardy marauder or one with a death wish would meddle with my large semi-arching tangle of barberry (*Berberis vulgaris*) so I expect any pair of birds that reserve that pitch for nesting are among the safest of families in the garden. This wild plant has useful herbal attributes, including edible berries which birds ignore. Now that it has an irretrievable bramble interwoven with it, life is even safer for wildlife yet rather testing for a gardener. *Rosa grandiflora* adds to the affray; it is a suckering species rose, which also has a great ability to harbour weeds in its root system. I forgive all as I tussle with its nettles because it is so beautiful and so healthy, and such little trouble otherwise. It has quite large, single, creamy-white flowers with the conspicuous stamens that I love to see in a rose. By forging its way among other shrubs, it gives them the benefit of added thorny security while gifting yet other plants the apparent addition of unfamiliar blooms; a rather amusing spoof.

EVERGREENS Our native holly (*Ilex aquifolium*) and butcher's broom (*Ruscus aculeatus*) both bear red berries and have prickly leaves so they are useful to wildlife for both food and protected habitat. Wild privet (*Ligustrum vulgare*) has no prickly defense but has black berries and is the nectar and food plant for the impressive Privet Hawk-moth. I include these three plants at the edge of both my small woodlands and in the boundary hedge. Conifers do not provide much food for birds but they are certainly used as snug places to roost. I am not keen on any of the conspicuously shaped conifers but I do grow a few Scots pines (*Pinus sylvestris*) for a couple of reasons. Firstly, there are mature pines growing in my neighbour's garden and I wanted to make the connection with the local landscape. Secondly, they are very attractive to many tits, including coal tits and long-tailed tits, and to the tiniest of our native birds – the goldcrest.

Of the non-native evergreens, laurel (*Prunus laurocerasus*) and bay laurel (*Laurus nobilis*) can provide useful nesting habitat, have white flowers that are attractive to bees and bear shiny black berries, but the plants are just too lumbering and solid-looking for my liking. I can tolerate the darker green Portuguese laurel (*Prunus lusitanica*) or *Prunus laurocerasus* 'Otto Luyken' which has a more forgiving form and serves wildlife equally well. I leave room for thickets of evergreens such as shrubby loniceras, just as I have in the Bird Garden, and underplant one or two of my trees with box (*Buxus sempervirens*) that is allowed to grow in its natural form. Prickly pyracanthas boost both the armoured, evergreen framework and the pollen, nectar and berry supply. *Pyracantha atalantioides* is my favourite because both the flowers and the orange berries have a delicacy and subtlety lacking in some of the modern varieties.

ROSEHIPS I grow several white-flowered climbing roses that are prickly and hip-bearing. Among these, 'Bobbie James' is one of the most beautiful and vigorous and yet it is 'Seagull', now having scaled a Scots pine, that receives the most admiration for both flower, foliage and prettier hips. 'Wickwar', with sea-green foliage and the most orange of all the hips, has reached high into the cherry trees and cascades downwards. The shrubby *Rosa sericea* subsp. *omiensis* f. *pteracantha* has unusual flagon-shaped hips and looks totally fierce and unapproachable with its huge, blood-red, young thorns and its gnarly old brown ones. In fact its bark is worse than its bite when it comes to the pruning, which is necessary to encourage the blood-red thorns. It is another white-flowered, hip-producing shrub rose, *Rosa* 'Pleine de

Grace', that is the most ferocious in this respect. I take revenge and chop her exceedingly vicious prunings into 60-90cm (2-3ft) lengths to make an impenetrable lid to one of my eco-heaps. (And then I go indoors and treat my wounds!) All these aggressive plants help confound and repel the enemies of nesting birds. Thorny habitat provides a considerable safety factor when it comes to nesting. What a bonus if those plants can offer food as well as protection and, at the same time, dazzle us with their beauty and fill the air with perfume.

SCENTED PLANTS   Among my scented shrubs, the fragrance of philadelphus exemplifies to me all that is magical about the summer garden. I have three favourites: *Philadelphus microphyllus*, which has delicate, slightly arching stems with small leaves and masses of sweetly scented flowers and P. 'Beauclerk', which is contrastingly bold structure-wise and has impressive, open, back–to-back flowers with a sumptuous scent. My third choice is the more unusual *Philadelphus delavayi* which falls somewhere between the two in its form and has a purple blotch at the centre of its pretty, richly fragrant flowers. I am not usually impressed with the over-sized, waxy flowers of magnolias, especially after the inevitable frost damage which gives them that unattractive brown edge. But *Magnolia wilsonii* is in a different league. Its pure white, waxy, pendulous flowers hang gracefully, revealing prominent red stamens and drawing one to sample the heavenly citrus fragrance. They flower later in the year, avoiding any treacherous cold spring snaps.

Choisya ternata is always good value for its ability to produce a long succession of orange-blossom-like, scented flowers and to have reliable evergreen and aromatic foliage. *Clerodendrum trichotomum* var. *fargesii* also has scented flowers and aromatic foliage but it is a bitter-sweet combination because, while the August-flowering blooms are pleasantly fragrant, the faintly purple-tinged leaves, when touched or bruised, have an abrasive bitterness. I rather admire it for this quirk and for its fascinating and totally unique berries, which are surrounded by red calyces and vary from sage green to jade blue. I cannot claim that these shrubs are particularly valuable to wildlife but they make the wildlife gardener very happy in her work!

Among my fragrant herbaceous plants, *Phlox paniculata* 'White Admiral' and *Lupinus* 'Noble Maiden' make amends to nectar-seeking insects. The lupin is a great attraction for bumblebees and its white flowers, which are greenish-yellow in bud, have a strong, evocative, peppery scent. Butterflies are among other insects that visit the pure white scented flowers of the phlox, which begins to flower as the lupin fades. In spring, sweet white violets are there for bees and for certain butterfly larvae – should I eventually be so lucky as to have fritillaries breeding at Sticky Wicket.

OTHER HERBACEOUS PLANTS   Other outstanding plants for nectar include *Echinacea purpurea* 'White Swan', *Sedum spectabile* 'Iceberg' and, to a lesser extent *Lysimachia clethroides*. I am surprised that butterflies also nectar on *Anaphalis margaritacea*; it is so dry looking with nothing oozing to be seen. One of my favourite plants is the elegant *Veronicastrum virginicum* f. *alba*, a classy plant with tall, slender spires that attract a buzz of bees. The seed-heads last well and the stately effect goes on for months into winter. The silvery, globe-shaped flowers of *Echinops* 'Nivalis' are another draw for bumblebees and the seed-heads also last for several weeks. *Chamerion* (syn. *Epilobium*) *angustifolium* 'Album' is a striking form of our native rosebay willowherb. If all goes to plan, it will hopefully support the larvae of the spectacular Elephant

Hawkmoth. Although it rarely sets seed, this willowherb spreads its root system just as fast as its pink relation so it needs to be positioned where it can be allowed space to do so. Admired by humans more than wildlife, the delicately pink-tinged *Gillenia trifoliata* has such a mass covering of flowers that it is often mistaken for a shrub. Of the lower-growing, ground-covering plants, *Pulmonaria* 'Sissinghurst White' is one of the first to flower in readiness for the early bees that eagerly congregate round its snow-white flowers. There are several white species and varieties of geraniums including *Geranium phaeum* 'Album', *G. sylvaticum* 'Album', *G. sanguineum* 'Album', *G. pratense* 'Album', *G. robertianum* 'Album' and *G. r* 'Celtic White', which are directly descended from our wild crane's-bills. This makes a very satisfying native-to-garden plant cross-over in a wilderness garden. Tall clumps of the white-flowered form of goat's rue (*Galega officinalis* 'Alba') and both *Tanacetum balsamita* and feverfew (*T. parthenium*), with their clusters of daisy flowers, were among the original herbs I wove into the borders. Edible herbs included asparagus, white chives and parsley, which, together with the fruits, provided plenty for a browser like me.

GRASSES I mingled ornamental grasses into the herbaceous layer of planting. The grasses help to make the transition to the "garden meadow" and in turn to the traditional hay-meadow beyond. I have always loved grasses and now that they have become fashionable, there are more and more available from nurseries. I am particularly attracted to those closely related to our own native grasses. Garden forms of molinias, carex and deschampsias are very much at home in our garden and the true British native species can be found growing in ancient grassland not far from here. *Molinia caerulea* 'Moorhexe' is descended from our native purple moorgrass with a linear form similar to its parent and dark, pencil-slim flower spikes like exclamation marks. *Deschampsia cespitosa*, our silvery flowered, native hair grass, has cultivars with both bronze and straw-coloured flowers. In addition to the true species, I grow *Deschampsia cespitosa* 'Bronze Veil' and *D.c.* 'Golden Veil' and relate their subtle colours and hazy, misty form to the definitive flower colours and the specific mood of the borders.

Although there are many scented white-flowered shrubs, there are comparatively few fragrant herbaceous plants. *Lupinus* 'Noble Maiden' is an exception, as is *Phlox* 'White Admiral', waiting in the wings to waft its distinctive perfume into the warm summer air.

The field mice and other small furry creatures certainly don't seem to care one bit about the colours or origins of the grasses. I find many of the tussocks have all manner of snug little homes where they have used the softer of the leaf blades to make nests. Birds seem to find the tougher blades of some ornamental grasses to be very enduring nesting material. Insects move into the dense centres of the tufts and tussocks, and I am convinced that grasses earn their place in a wildlife garden. But there is one in particular that I would be unable to resist even if this were not the case. To me, life would be poor indeed without the joy of seeing the golden, oaten flowers and seed-heads of *Stipa gigantea*. Even though it hates my cold, wet winter soil, such is the spellbinding beauty of this grass that I was prepared to make an exception to my non-mollycoddling policy and lift my three young clumps to overwinter in the poly-tunnel for the first year or so until they were well grown and began to be established.

Miscanthuses are imported from North America but we have the moist and fertile conditions they need to thrive here. *Miscanthus sinensis* 'Silberfeder', one of the tallest,

demands plenty of space to make an impact. It has a particularly spectacular winter effect when windblown hither and yon. As with other miscanthus, it produces a soft rustling sound that gives it extra-charismatic garden-worthiness.

BULBS   Once I had studied the colour and characteristics of the plants and monitored the measure of success I could achieve with the herbaceous plant and grass selection, and once the volume of stocks had increased, I started to arrange them into more permanent positions within the framework of the now satisfactorily maturing trees and shrubs. Only then did I gradually start to introduce bulbs.

Most bulbs have a white form but in spite of this I have not been very adventurous with my selection. I am content with drifts of snowdrops, snowflakes, anemones, white narcissus and Star-of-Bethlehem, all of which naturalize easily and provide a sequence of early pollen and nectar for bees and other insects when they hatch or emerge from hibernation. This is the perfect garden for narcissus and snowdrops, which are generally eschewed by creatures foraging for vegetarian food. My assortment of bulbs has so far survived the appetites and annoying habits of the rabbits and squirrels, but the wet winter ground has proved more of an adversary. Of the crocuses I have tried to grow, C. tommasinianus (though not white) is the only one with the tenacity to spread with any conviction. My personal collection of old varieties of narcissus thrive in the borders and the grass of the garden meadow. I love the intoxicating scent of the later-flowering pheasant's eye varieties, especially N. 'Sinopel', with its green-edged corona (instead of the usual cadmium-red one).

The emergence of the first snowdrops is one of the highlights of the gardening calendar. What a perfect bulb for a white wilderness – a flower that is equally at home in woodland, grassland or border. I have collected about half-a-dozen excellent varieties of snowdrops but I have no wish to add many more and become a galloping galanthophile. Our wild Galanthus nivalis is exquisite as it is, without being altered in any way, but the taller, more full-bodied varieties, such as G. elwesii or G. 'Atkinsii', make more of an impact where they have to struggle to peep through the petticoats of shrubby plants or penetrate a dense mat of ground cover.

Beneath the trees and amongst the shrubs, a summer haze of British native and ornamental grasses intermingles with wildflowers and hardy herbaceous plants to create tussocky habitat for insects and small mammals.

WILDFLOWERS IN THE BORDERS A great proportion of the wildflowers we see in the countryside are white. There are also some unusual white forms of wildflowers which I feel honour-bound to nurture. I have white forms of ragged Robin, campion, foxglove, greater knapweed, devil's-bit scabious, self-heal and bugle, most from local sources. All these plants provide vital sustenance for wildlife in exactly the same way as do their coloured relatives. I grow them in both meadows and borders and one or two in the woodland or at its edge. I love to see bumblebees nectaring on the beautiful flowers of white deadnettle (*Lamium* sp.). It has an efficient running root system, so I grow it where it can spread without interfering with other less robust plants.

WILD WHITE UMBELS I can effortlessly indulge my fascination with umbelliferous plants, as there are several natives growing more than willingly in this garden. The exception is pignut, a grassland wildflower that grows in profusion in our cemetery but, for reasons unknown, has so far steadfastly refused to germinate anywhere on my land. This confounds my attempts to help provide habitat for and conserve the Chimney-sweeper moth, which depends on this one species for its survival. Cow parsley and hogweed, my childhood passions, moved in from the hedgerows and are welcome in places but I diligently control the spread of seed to prevent an overwhelming invasion. Of course, the alien giant hogweed is strictly banned. Hemlock and hemlock water dropwort have tried to seduce me with their attractive, nectar-laden umbels, but I have been strong-minded in removing them, two of the most deadly poisonous of our native plants. Corky-fruited water dropwort (a wildflower located in south-west England) is socially acceptable in this respect, being non-toxic, and looks handsome in both the meadow (where it belongs) and in the border, where it has also made itself at home. As it fades in midsummer, along comes the beautiful and beguiling wild carrot which is without exception my favourite plant – umbelliferous or otherwise. It is very attractive to insects, in particular soldier beetles. Wild angelica flowers at about the same time and draws many insects to its nectar bar; a biennial with a preference for wet ground, it has no trouble finding places to seed and re-seed.

Of all the white umbelliferous flowers, the humble wild carrot is the favourite of the soldier beetle, and myself. This exquisite plant thrives in the border or in grass although its capricious nature can sometimes be difficult to manage.

OTHER WHITE WAIFS The starry stitchworts, greater and lesser, grow on hedge banks and grassland respectively but I have allowed, or in some cases encouraged, them to grow near shrubs where they can clamber enchantingly through their lower branches. White mignonette (*Reseda alba*) seeds where it will and if it feels so inclined. I would like to be able to place the pretty spires where they could intermingle attractively with the herbaceous garden plants but they always choose odd and awkward places – usually too close to the border edge. This mignonette has a delicious smell of nectar and is an ace bee-plant so I let it have its way. Ox-eye daisies tend to overwhelm other less lusty plants in the borders. I love them and welcome them but by the end of the summer they have overstepped the mark, so I thin them and plant the extras in the garden meadow, thereby gaining more flower-power for the many species of insects that visit this simple but appealing plant.

CLIMBERS AND TWINERS Among the many woody and herbaceous species in the hedgerow, hedge bindweed, old man's beard, bryony and hop twine or clamber over some sections where the hedge is tall and wide enough to withstand bearing an extra layer of vegetation. The white trumpet flowers of bindweed are every bit as beautiful as the much-cherished morning glories, but it is difficult to appreciate this when they invade the garden borders. Since being filled with wonder by the sight of my first Convolvulus Hawk-moth, I have been probably a little too forgiving of bindweed in some parts of the garden but it can do little harm in a healthy native hedge where the moth can visit and possibly breed on the foliage. Old man's beard, with its translucent, fluffy seed-heads, is also good-looking but possibly even more to be feared as it can become very insistent if allowed free rein. I love bryony for its heart-shaped leaves and strings of red berries, but it is a poisonous plant that must be controlled near stock – and children should be controlled near the bryony!

WILD FLOWERS IN THE LAWNS AND MEADOW The wildflowers that colonize lawns (whether we want them to or not) and those that grow in summer meadows do so because of the way we manage the grass. They almost always do best on poor, infertile soils where there is the minimum competition from vigorous grasses. Some

No place in the garden can compare with the beauty and joys of the New Hay Meadow in June. Clary is the perfect living statue to enhance the pastoral setting.

wildflowers, such as self-heal, medick, dandelion, plantain, daisies, cat's ear, clover, speedwell and trefoil, are well adapted to survive regular beheading by the mower. My land is highly fertile and lies very wet in winter so I struggle to increase the diversity of flowering plants. Daisies grow best in the drier parts and creeping buttercup is in its element. I have begun to overcome this problem by building up some of the paths with rubble to form a cambered track, which is far more wildflower-friendly and I can begin to realize a white, daisy-strewn grass path, which many conventional gardeners regard with disdain. Beside the grass track is my stretch of "garden meadow" and at the juncture between mown and uncut grass I can guarantee to find blackbirds foraging.

The first flowers to light up the meadows are cowslips, bugle, lady's smock, sorrel, ragged Robin, yellow rattle, trefoils and ox-eye daisies, which are soon joined by the golden flower-heads of rough hawk-bit. Corky-fruited water dropwort, which is special to our area and soil type, joins in the throng. Insects breed and increase dramatically during summer and from June onwards. Peter and I sometimes pause for tea and a nap in the meadow, lulled by the "song" of bush crickets and grasshoppers, and the buzz and drone of bees and other insects on the wing. Wildflowers, such as knapweed, betony, yarrow, sneezewort, fleabane, wild carrot and devil's-bit scabious, flower through mid- to late summer, roughly in that sequence. They are all wonderful wildlife plants and the meadow is a constant hive of activity and a total joy to behold.

BIRCH COPSE Our two tiny woodland areas each consist of a few birches and two or three Scots pines that are closely planted within about three yards of each other. To achieve a multi-stemmed effect with the birches, we planted the saplings in groups of two or three. Sometimes it worked and in other cases some trees eventually proved unequal to the contest for survival. If I had been a little more patient and prepared to demonstrate my faith in the coppicing system, I could have planted single trees and then cut them to the base after a few years. They would then, in theory, regenerate with naturally occurring multi-stems.

Even a tiny birch copse, such as ours, makes significant woodland habitat for wildlife. The under-storey of white-flowered scented shrubs, herbaceous plants and bulbs offers a sequence of seasonal attractions in addition to the white-barked trunks.

After the oak (294 species supported) and willow (266), the birch supports the next highest number of species of interdependent fauna. Many birds depend on the insects and caterpillars found in these trees, which are constantly visited – particularly by tits and finches. Families of long-tailed tits are frequent visitors and goldcrests are occasional but delightful ones, which are probably also attracted by the pines (93 species). They are even tinier than the wrens, which also hunt for food in these trees. Birches have rather greedy roots but they are light-leafed and provide an ideal dappled canopy for both native and garden plants. I also chose birches for their splendid white trunks, a striking addition to the winter garden.

The shrubby under-storey is comprised of *Cornus mas*, hollies, cotoneasters, sarcococca and skimmia, which all provide berries, and the last two the bonus of winter and spring fragrance. The herbaceous layer includes a matrix of white forms of ground-covering plants such as early-flowering pulmonarias, lamium, lily-of-the-valley and vincas which supply food for the first bees to emerge. The slightly taller *Helleborus orientalis* (white forms) soon follow and then there are geraniums, Solomon's seal, foxgloves and white forms of campanulas, such as *Campanula latiloba*, *C. lactiflora* and *C. persifolia* to follow. I so love the special summer sound-effects made

by large bumblebees in an apparent tight squeeze in a foxglove flower! *Silene fimbriata* is an unusual and self-sustaining plant whose delicate appearance belies its tenacity.

My previously listed sequences of bulbs perform from spring snowdrops to autumn colchicums. All these plants and bulbs have to fight for their domain in a tangle of honeysuckle and ivy. I rarely have to weed but I do have to be a firm referee. Two plants I was unwise enough to throw into the mêlée were variegated ground-elder (what on earth did I expect?) and woodruff. The latter is a native plant with attractive foliage which is aromatic when cut and dried like hay. It is a competent, galloping ground coverer and will grow in the driest and shadiest of woodland conditions, but it is just too efficient to mingle with a mixed community of plants and it out-competes all its rivals for space.

The proximity of the birch copses to the shrubs and herbaceous plants in the adjacent mixed borders simulates the woodland-edge habitat found in the countryside and again, in conservationist's language, forms the "ecotone zone" where one sort of habitat eases into another. This woodland-edge habitat has the benefit of shelter and gradually increasing light levels. For instance, we often find Speckled Wood butterflies, a woodland species, sunning themselves on shrubs on the southern outskirts of this part of the garden.

SPECIFIC HABITAT BOOSTERS

Mature woodland trees shed debris in the form of leaf litter, twigs and damaged branches, which fall to the ground and feed the fungi, flora and fauna of the woodland floor. It takes years before the trees are mature enough for the system to provide for the opportunist range of life that relies on such an element of apparent disaster. The wildlife gardener often has to improvise to speed up the procedure of habitat creation.

WOODEN STRUCTURES   We have various log-piles around the garden and save some weird and wonderfully shaped branches to make interesting-looking, sculptural arrangements. Dead leaves tend to gather around the larger heaps and add insulation. Some of our configurations of materials have been occupied by hedgehogs or other creatures which seek places to hibernate, hide out or breed. We use wood from a variety of tree species and this helps attract a wide range of fungi

We have positioned varied "eco-heaps" of logs and stones to provide valuable breeding, sheltering, hiding and hibernation sites for insects, reptiles, amphibians and small mammals. Some, like this stag-beetle pile (below), have been customized for specific creatures with their particular requirements.

and insects as the wood biodegrades. Our arrangements of logs are formed into interesting features and attract a wide range of fungi and insects as the materials biodegrade. Some of the logs have been set in the ground (about 45cm/18in deep) to encourage the endangered stag-beetles whose habitat is being seriously eroded.

In the White Garden, our log edging helps to define the woodland paths and retain the chunky bark chippings we use for a dry, weed-free surface. These lengths of wood are just lightly set in the soil and I am always amazed at the mass of insect life which soon colonize the area around them. Log piles are becoming increasingly scarce in our countryside as intensive agriculture requires ever-larger fields and as traditional woodland management has declined.

STONE STRUCTURES Dry-stone walls are also very user-friendly to a great range of wildlife. Unfortunately, there are very few local stone walls in our area of Dorset. We didn't have the resources to build any seriously large walls but we constructed several small "eco-heaps" (as I call them) using recycled flint, limestone and air-bricks from a local demolition job. To increase the biodiversity, some of these features were built in fully exposed, sunny sites and some on the shady woodland edges. Incorporating some logs and turf helped to boost the wildlife-friendliness and to encourage native plants to colonize. There are built-in cavities of various sizes to provide (hopefully) habitat for a range of creatures from insects to reptiles and small mammals – including field mice and hedgehogs. We particularly hope to accommodate slow-worms and toads (good garden pest predators) as well as masonry bees and bumblebees (both excellent pollinators), who like to nest in holes. The latter sometimes move into redundant mouse-holes.

OTHER MATERIALS Apart from wood and stone, there are many materials which, when laid on soil, provide opportunities for creatures to make their homes. If we peer under a sheet of corrugated tin or almost any upturned vessel, we can be certain to find holes and tunnels and sometimes the poor creature which hitherto regarded the dark lid as a bastion of surreptitious and safe habitat. Lengths of plastic, ceramic or metal pipe or tough tubes of cardboard, are used both for passages or underpasses, for living quarters and for storing food. Old boots, whether lodged into a hedge, set into the ground, or thrown casually into any vegetation where they may be overgrown (or even just parked by the back door) are more than likely to be occupied by nesting birds or mice. Each year I look forward to peering into my ever-increasing line-up of boots (such are modern manufacturing methods, they are constantly discarded but not wasted!) while old-fashioned kettles are a classic nesting place for robins.

BIRD- AND BAT-BOXES As well as all the artificial and semi-natural habitat we try to create we also put up a few extra bird- and bat-boxes. Our hedgerows are old and valuable but not so ancient as to provide really deep, safe nesting places for some of the wildlife we would like to attract: woodpeckers, owls, dormice and bats, for instance. In spite of being a protected species, bats are one of our most threatened creatures and need all the help we can give them. In fact, apart from putting up bat-boxes, safeguarding their chosen roosting sites, and encouraging insect life, there is little the amateur can do. In the event of any problems the public must consult the relevant authorities (see page 204). Bats are very sensitive to the smell of humans and their chemicals, so untreated wood must be used for bat-boxes and it is best to buy them from specialist suppliers. Bats appreciate several boxes in close proximity – perhaps three or four around one tree trunk and this increases the chance of attracting them to the garden. Even so, it may take several years and, although we see bats on the wing, I am not convinced we have a result from our fairly recent efforts.

Owl-boxes can be bought custom-made for a particular species of owl. We have erected a large, elongated box type for the tawny owls we know to be resident and a very large "chalet-style" home for the barn owls we hope will take up residence. We were advised to place the barn owl lodgings in a mature oak which overlooks their hunting ground of open grassland on two sides. Our own barn is modern and unlikely to be suitable for owls but it is well used by nesting swallows and wrens. On the east-facing outside wall Peter has built "terraced accommodation" for sparrows, which like communal nesting facilities.

IN CONCLUSION

Over the years, I have been thrilled and amazed as I have carefully observed the visiting wildlife. I have studied both the ecological details and colour discrepancies of a large range of white plants, both woody and herbaceous, and it has been fascinating to see how they interrelate with each other and with the wildlife they support. I shall now allow this garden to be further relaxed and become an even less controlled wilderness. I am not going to harass the borders into containing any plants which are not lion-hearted enough to compete without my mothering and nagging. The less disruption that I cause, the better it is for wildlife. Native plants are of more value to wildlife than most garden plants so, more than ever, I want to learn how to live in peace with my "weeds" and just direct them a little when they take advantage of my leniency. Of course, it may all become so chaotic that one day I could lose my credibility as a gardener and garden-maker, but I can feel satisfied that Peter and I have left few stones unturned in our determination and homespun efforts to help conserve wildlife and wild plants. Certainly, we have valued every minute of the journey along the sometimes smooth and sometimes rocky path of our garden-making during our eighteen years at Sticky Wicket.

GARDEN MANAGEMENT

*This chapter outlines the key points in
managing a garden to be in "tune with nature".
In other words, how to strike a balance
between our own needs and those of the
different forms of wildlife, large and small,
that we must recognize and support.*

A generous mulch of home-made compost helps to
prevent the need to water, except in extreme conditions.

FUNDAMENTAL REQUISITES for plants are the same as those for humans and animals so these are the guidelines I use for my holistic system of management: a safe environment with enough space, fresh air and light; protection from extreme elements; a well-balanced diet with sufficient uncontaminated water; appropriate hygiene standards and a stress-free treatment with understanding. (This automatically rules out being hit with chemicals or being genetically modified.)

At Sticky Wicket, this amounts to creating the right balance of shelter and shade to safeguard the diversity of plants I have selected to suit my soil type. Young plants receive special attention and protection. We grow plants that will attract beneficial wildlife, such as pest predators, and create suitable habitat for these creatures to feed and breed. Likewise, we include plants that benefit others and help ward off disease.

We do not use chemical fertilizers, herbicides, pesticides or fungicides. Neither do we use peat or peat-based potting composts; we recycle all the by-products from our gardening activities to make our own. Keeping surface water and watercourses uncontaminated, conserving rainwater and soil moisture, and using tap water thriftily, are an important part of our system of management and this goes hand-in-glove with the way we value and care for our soil.

Correctly managed and well-conditioned soil is the foundation for the well-being of the garden so we nurture our soil and treat our land with great respect. The healthy soil then supplies the plants with all the nutrients they need to grow and the stamina to resist disease.

"Be gentle with our earth", we are urged, "and tread lightly upon it". And so we do; both literally and figuratively. We keep off wet, bare earth to avoid compaction and leave it alone when frozen because the soil structure could be harmed. In fact, we try not to tamper with it more than necessary. Incorporating humus will improve the structure, condition, function, nutrient content and vitality of all types of soil and we do this by regularly mulching with homemade compost and, rather than digging it in, we allow the worms to do the work for us.

With the prediction that global warming will create potentially hazardous climate change, gardeners are going to have to work harder at soil-care if our plants are to

Compost heaps in the making are a great resource for wildlife and the resulting product is every bit as valuable. We feed and condition the soil to ensure the plants are robust and disease resistant.

survive the anticipated conditions brought about by this. We already have to deal with prolonged spells of drought and abnormally wet winters. To give our plants the best chance, we have always invested freely in thorough planting preparation and aftercare, which has so far paid handsome dividends. Surface mulching with humus has reduced the impact of major fluctuations in our clay/loam soil structure, but the same is true for every soil type.

COMPOSTING AND FEEDING

A healthy compost heap is composed of a balance of dry, carbon-rich materials and moist, nitrogen-rich materials. There must also be the right balance of air and moisture. A thriving compost heap never smells and materials speedily biodegrade to provide nutrient-rich humus for the garden. Rather than using chemical fertilizers, home-produced compost is a far superior, natural and more environmentally friendly way to nourish the soil and, at the same time, condition it. By composting garden and household vegetable debris we can make a vital contribution to the health of the environment by reducing the load on land-fill sites.

We take great care not to position any compost-making unit where any resulting concentrated effluent can run directly into, and pollute, nearby ground water and watercourses, or leach unwanted nutrients into our wildflower meadows.

Compost heaps can be a valuable source of food and warmth for wildlife. Our heaps are visited by scores of birds, especially in winter when, as well as foraging for a share of my worker-worms, they will also gather to bask in the warmth generated by the invisible army of bacteria and fungi working on the first stages of decomposition. We have to be cautious when moving or turning compost because there is a very real chance we may find a toad lurking there. We also need to take great care not to disturb hedgehogs, which may welcome the drier corners of this habitat for hibernation or breeding. Slow-worms are attracted to compost conditions, which are perfect breeding places for them, where they can rely on the ready food supply of slugs doing what slugs are so well designed to do – processing and disposing of vegetation. Grass snakes sometimes hide and breed in the warmth of the decomposing compost. Admittedly rats are an occasional problem, forcing us to set humane traps.

The advantage of all these tunnelling creatures is that they keep the heaps brilliantly aerated. In this respect there is a plus side to having moles (generally disadvantageous in that they eat massive numbers of the red worms that greatly assist in breaking down the materials). Unless we were to build or buy an efficient, custom-made, vermin-proof compost container, excluding moles is not an option for us. My garden is a gift to wildlife so by imprisoning the compost to exclude moles, I would also deny access to creatures for which a compost heap is a terrific resource for food and habitat. Our recycling system supports beneficial wildlife from tiny organisms to quite large ones! We sometimes have visiting or resident foxes inspecting the heaps for worms, beetles and other tasty morsels.

We create conditions where mixed plant debris can biodegrade efficiently and therefore speedily. When our formula is right, the compost will heat up to about 60 degrees C (140 degrees F) and the first stages of this aerobic decomposition will be rapid. The larger the heap, and the more materials added at one time, the hotter it is likely to get.

NOTE: I am fortunate in having plenty of space to make compost in well-organized heaps on the ground but in a small garden it may be more efficient, tidier and possibly more hygienic to use custom-made containers, where heat and moisture can be more easily regulated and vermin excluded.

OUR COMPOST HEAP RECIPE

DRY (CARBON-RICH) INGREDIENTS These include non-woody hedge clippings, ripped up or crumpled paper and cardboard (not glossy or coloured), straw, wood chippings and some autumn leaves and stalky debris.

WET (NITROGEN-RICH) INGREDIENTS These include lawn clippings, herbaceous excess and dead-headings, suitable weeds, kitchen vegetable waste and some windfall fruit.

ACTIVATORS Comfrey and nettles are excellent compost activators but we take care to add the leaves and flowering stems before they make ripe seeds. We grow comfrey close to the compost area for easy access and regular application. (There are compost activators you can buy from garden centres but make sure they contain only organic substances.)

We are fortunate to have farmyard and stable manure which we add in layers. It is a wonderful bonus to the process and the end-product of composting.

Urine, human or animal, will activate the process of decomposition. If you do not have farm stock or horses, it only requires a little imagination! (Cottage gardeners used to refer to the useful application of "night water"!)

Method
- Include mature stems of herbaceous plants (for example, asters), haulms of peas and beans or clematis stems at the bottom of a new heap to make an airy base (but you may need to chop up very long or thick stems).
- Build the heap up in varied layers of ingredients and avoid an excess of any single material at one time.
- Turn the compost from time to time, mixing the ingredients from sides to middle and letting in air as the layers rise.
- Try to regulate conditions to prevent the compost getting too sodden or dried out but if the ingredients are well balanced and well mixed this is not usually a problem.
- A waterproof covering reduces the amount of nutrients likely to be washed away in winter but needs to be folded back to allow summer rain to moisten the decomposing ingredients.
- It helps if the top of the heap is rounded in winter to deflect excess rainfall and if it has a central depression in summer to capture any summer rain.

Results

After the bacteria and fungi have done their work, the heap cools as worms and other invertebrates continue to process the materials during the anaerobic phase. Within a year the components are transformed into a dark brown, reasonably crumbly, odourless, soil conditioner. A healthy compost heap never smells (ours does only if we have just added a excess of decaying brassica leaves – and then only for a short while.

We use the finest crumbs of this organic matter as potting compost and distribute chunkier material on the borders and vegetable garden as a moisture-retaining mulch and as a soil conditioner, which supplies all the vital, natural nutrients the plants require.

We grow certain crops, such as potatoes, pumpkins and courgettes, on the maturing heaps. Although they rob the compost of a small proportion of their nutrients, they smother any germinating weed seedlings and help the compost to break down during the summer period.

Useful tips

- Do add an occasional forkful of mature compost and/or soil to a fresh heap; it inoculates it with helpful bacteria and fungi.
- Do add chicken and bird droppings as they have a high nitrogen content – we add an occasional bucketful to further stimulate the process of decomposition.
- Do watch out for creatures such as hedgehogs, toads and slow-worms when forking over the heaps.
- Do not add too many grass cuttings: lawn-mowing-overload is the main cause of unhealthy, slimy compost heaps that are slow to break down and start to smell. If there is too high a proportion of grass cuttings at any one moment, mixing in a little straw, dead leaves or paper will keep some airways functioning.
- Do not add too many autumn leaves (especially large, tough ones such as chestnut and plane) as they can "constipate" the procedure. If there is a disproportionate quantity of autumn leaves to dispose of, it is best to stack some of them separately, or place them in bags, where they can be left for a year to break down into valuable leaf-mould.
- Do not include any cooked material or egg shells which might encourage vermin to open heaps.

- Do not include citrus fruit as it can deter worms – we avoid over-burdening the heap with too many skins
- Do not allow weed seeds or roots of pernicious weeds such as bindweed or ground elder. These may survive the digestive process of the decomposing heap and come back to haunt you.
- Do not add faeces of carnivorous pets, such as dogs and cats, to the compost heap.
- Do not site compost heaps close to watercourses; they are an environmental hazard.

ADDITIONAL FEEDING

Well-made compost usually contains all the nutrients a plant needs, although some nitrogen may be leached away if the heap gets too wet. It is sometimes necessary to supplement greedy fruit and vegetable crops or boost the diet of the juvenile, ailing or geriatric plants. An organic fertilizer such as pelleted chicken manure or liquid seaweed would be appropriate but a home-made brew of comfrey and nettle does the trick for most of our plants, with perhaps a dose of Epsom salts if any look a bit jaundiced. I daresay I shall one day be forced to comply with EU regulations controlling the application of any such home-made concoctions, and be required to invest in some expensive product that has been costly and energy-consuming to manufacture and probably prepared and packaged thousands of air miles away. Yarrow, which is so excellent in the composting system, can be used as an infusion containing copper for any plant needing a remedial boost. Our poultry-run pond for ducks and geese becomes fouled with their droppings but our roses thrive on the barrow-loads of watery slurry that we spread during the clearance operations.

MULCHING

This is important for soil improvement, weed suppression and moisture retention, and also provides extra wildlife habitat. Mulches can be sympathetic with nature or, by their own "nature", at odds with our best intentions as concerned conservationists. There are various environmental considerations: composted bark and mushroom compost (which may contain chemicals) need to be well processed or they can be damaging to some plants; gravel is a useful mulch but its extraction drains the dwindling earth's resources; coconut by-products involve many air miles of travel which add to atmospheric pollution.

Old carpet, cardboard and newspapers and magazines have their uses where they can be acceptably disguised but coloured, glossy paper must be rejected because it contains heavy metals that are detrimental to the environment. There are biodegradable fleece or jute mats which are excellent, but the expense and limited lifespan is a consideration. Some of the manufactured horticultural fabrics are acceptable, durable, mould to the soil surface and can be cut to size with clean edges which do not fray. However, woven polypropylene is a nightmare in this respect; when the cut edges are exposed, its strands get caught up in implements, and it can be a formidable environmental hazard to any creature that gets tangled up in it.

Well-rotted farmyard manure and leaf-mould are natural, cheap and effective and there is nothing to beat well-made, homemade compost, which incorporates a wide mixture of components including the aforementioned. We spread most of the compost in spring when the plants are beginning to burst into life and when the ground is moist and preferably warming up, and we avoid such operations when the ground is frozen or waterlogged or later on, when it is dried out. A covering of about 5-8cm (2-3in) is adequate in most places but we set a few barrow-loads in heaps in parts of the borders where a reserve is needed for particularly hungry plants or for soil that needs extra conditioning.

We are careful not to let deep layers of compost smother the base of woody stems (including roses) or put deep layers touching tree trunks as this can cause damage. We apply only the thinnest of layers of the most crumbly materials in places where annual plants are sown or expected to set seed. Generous layers of mulch are helpful to prevent annual weeds becoming a recurring issue. A little of this fine compost is spared for top-dressing odd areas of lawn which need repair and encouragement. We save some compost for topping up during the summer – preferably immediately after a shower. We avoid compost near our meadows or flowering lawns, which need infertile soil. With wildlife in mind, we leave most of our leaf litter and windfalls in situ unless they foul paths or smother grass; it is nature's way of returning organic matter to the soil and the worms help to incorporate this seasonal gift.

I wonder what the ruling will be on placing banana skins near roses? They are full of useful minerals including calcium, magnesium, sulphur, phosphates, sodium and silica; much too good to waste! I even make use of horse hair and at moulting time I spread mats of it around the garden, hoping the soil and plants will benefit from the trace elements it contains.

RECYCLING PRUNINGS

Nothing is ever wasted at Sticky Wicket and, provided it is healthy, every pruned branch, stick or stem is put to use in either a decorative or functional way. With plant welfare in mind, we tackle "the 3Ds" first – removing dead, damaged or diseased material. We prune with the well-being of our wildlife as important a priority as the health and appearance of the plants. When push comes to shove with tricky decisions about the timeliness of a pruning operation, we put the welfare of the wildlife first and are exceptionally careful with hedge-trimming. I ask myself what I am specifically trying to achieve with the pruning. Do I need to control the plant to a manageable size or shape to keep the planting proportions or emphasize a feature of my design? Is it necessary to prune in order to thin, thicken or regenerate stem growth, to stimulate the formation of flower or fruit or to heighten the foliage effect? It isn't a compulsory procedure for every plant every year! Once I have decided my strategy and completed the task, I consider ways to recycle the prunings and benefit nature at the same time.

We prune nearly all our shrubs in winter before birds start to nest, aiming to complete by the end of February but with week one in March an absolute deadline. Walls and hedges and other prime nesting sites are dealt with as a pruning priority and any building repairs (or decoration) also have to be dealt with outside the nesting period. Whatever the conventional wisdom, unless we can be one hundred per cent certain a shrub is unoccupied, summer pruning does not begin until August when the birds have finished nesting.

Substantial branches of pruned or coppiced wood are used for fencing, furniture, eco-heaps or firewood. With

Every part of every plant is returned to the soil one way or another. Recycling is a serious activity at Sticky Wicket but it has its frivolous side!

the single, whippy stems of hazel, willow or cornus prunings, we weave various features for wildlife and use some for simple, woven plant supports. Our "retired" hazel and willow-woven items, along with thorny prunings, are threaded back into our hedgerows to reinforce and shield nesting sites.

We do not use ash for plant supports because some climbing plants recoil from and mysteriously refuse to cling to its wood. Twiggy stems of hazel and hornbeam are useful for supporting plants or laying over bare ground where seeds are sown. I find they help deter cats and at the same time create a microclimate for germinating seedlings.

Some prunings, including prickly ones, are deliberately left in tidy piles in discreet places around the garden. While they are intact and as they later begin to rot, they offer more habitats for the chain of creatures which play an immensely useful and integrated part in the garden ecosystem.

Where possible, fallen wood is allowed to decompose naturally and thus provide welcome habitat for all sorts of creatures. Twenty per cent of Britain's 22,400 insect species are associated with dead wood and moribund trees, according to the RHS. The dead branches that remain on trees are often used for song posts or look-out points for birds so, from the wildlife point of view, they are a bonus.

If we have seriously diseased wood, which might compromise the health of other plants, I burn it in an incinerator and use the potash-rich wood ash, which must be applied immediately or, if stored, kept in a dry place to prevent the nutrient content being rapidly leached away when wet.

My remaining leftover woody debris is shredded and the chunkiest of the resulting wood chips used directly as a path covering and moisture-retaining mulch while the finer grade material is added to the compost heap.

Shredded evergreen material is harmful to worms, so I separate it from the rest and avoid using it as an ingredient of the compost heap.

MANAGING HERBACEOUS BORDERS

The herbaceous parts of my mixed borders contain plants that are extremely useful to wildlife, not only for the pollen and nectar but also for seed-heads and extra habitat. Over-zealous dead-heading and tidying "for tidiness' sake" could remove this bonus resource and make the border far less hospitable to wildlife. Therefore I clear my borders in easy stages between October and March. My "hands off" system is compassionate to the hibernating or active insects and insect larvae, and the birds and small mammals that feed on them. It helps protect my plants, allows the worms to do their stirring work of incorporating decaying vegetation into the soil, and also supplies sporadic and varied materials for my compost heap. On a personal note, we are left with a winter scene that is especially magical on frosty mornings, has plenty of wildlife activity to entertain us and results in less back strain than a massive autumn assault would.

SUMMER PROGRAMME   We dead-head herbaceous plants where the process of doing so will prolong the flowering period or generate a second flush but leave those, such as eupatorium, sedum and lythrum, which flower just once and have fine, upstanding, winter seed-heads that are both handsome and good for wildlife. We remove the seed-heads of some seriously invasive plants, such as saponaria, that we need to restrain. Hefty, arching or fallen stems that interfere with neighbouring plants can be a problem so we thin or remove the most tiresome. Some herbaceous plants – persicaria is an example – soon become unsightly and break down into a slimy condition as their flowers fade, so we use them for compost before they become increasingly unpleasant to look at and handle.

AUTUMN/WINTER PROGRAMME   Week by week in autumn and early winter, I gradually cut down any such faded herbaceous plants once they have nothing left to offer except their tattered remains for recycling.

Rigid, hollow stems provide useful wildlife habitat for insects; I tie these stems in bundles and place them – some vertically and some horizontally – in hedges, among shrubs or in wilderness areas. Less durable and insect-worthy stems are used in compost making (as described).

While vulnerable wildlife retreats or hibernates, late winter is a reasonably safe time to strim some of the areas requiring otherwise back-breaking trimming down.

It is important to prioritize parts of the borders that have vulnerable shoots or spring bulbs emerging among the herbaceous plants.

SPRING PROGRAMME   Ornamental grasses are left undisturbed until late March when they are either trimmed down or combed out depending on the needs of the variety. There is competition for the resulting debris which is either left in situ as a self-mulching material or, if excessive, divided between the compost heap and the wildlife "eco-heaps" for insect life or bird nesting supplies.

Some plants may require restraint or rejuvenation so we lift and divide the plants and replant with pieces of hale and hearty young growth from the edges of the clump. Now is the time to put twiggy hazel stems in place to help prop up the very few herbaceous plants we grow that lack the backbone to be self-supporting.

MANAGING WEEDS

Once we begin to see merit in plants that we perceive as undesirable "weeds", a different light is shone on our battle to restrict our resident native flora in order to enable our introduced garden species to retain their allotted space or to self-seed in bare ground. I take into account the need for discipline but, where practicable I am a little lenient with weeds. British wildflowers are best for British wildlife and crucial for the survival of many species but are unfortunately constantly persecuted in gardens and on farmland. Although I am diligent in controlling weed competition around young plants, I gradually allow certain weeds a restricted place in the border, particularly if they look pretty and offer a suitable colour match to the planting.

However, when it comes to the business of either arbitrating the advance of inoffensive weeds or controlling the invasion of the aggressive ones, identifying species, and understanding their nature, mode of growth and methods of propagation, allows the gardener to stay ahead of the game. Most weeds arrive by seed which may pop, ping, spiral earthwards or just drop fairly locally beside its parent. Some may be spread in bird droppings or even by ants or hitch a lift by clinging to the fur or feather of animals. Other seeds are airborne by virtue of parachute or winged devices or travel even more widely as they float on the wind or on water. The mature plant may rely on an insidious system of self-perpetuation; with creeping roots and stems below the ground or creeping stems and runners above the ground. Roots can be deeply penetrating and stubborn or grow sneakily sideways. Canny as they are, native plants may confound or frustrate us with their combination of survival techniques!

Weeds can adapt their size and even change shape to fit surroundings (however hostile), survive drought, disease or damage and defend themselves with stinging mechanisms, prickly armour or poison. They can produce multiples of thousands of seeds; with a life cycle of seven weeks chickweed, for example, can produce 15,000 million plants a year. No wonder the old adage suggests the conservative estimate that "one year's seeding means seven years' weeding"! Frustrating as all this is for a gardener, I cannot help but admire the doggedness of native plants.

It is six of one and half-a-dozen of another when weighing up the benefits and disadvantages of weeds. On the one hand, they provide for beneficial wildlife and even for the plants we like to grow; on the other, they can overwhelm our garden plants and some can harbour pest insects and diseases. At least I can begin to call the shots and, while I am strict with those that must not become ungovernable, I can be tolerant of those that offer a clear advantage to associated plants and wildlife.

A POSITIVE SIDE TO WEEDS   Most weeds have special benefits for the wildlife I hope to attract and can expect to find in my garden: dead nettles, thistles, willowherbs and groundsel are examples and I believe all to have their uses.

Plant cover is important to prevent bare soil baking in hot sun and killing soil life. Weeds are natural ground-cover so, as with all garden "pests", the idea is to control their numbers but not obliterate the ones that have their uses.

Many weeds, such as nettle, colt's-foot and dandelion have herbal virtues from which the garden, my animals and I can benefit. Some weeds – probably more than we think – are edible. They are not all ideally suited to our palate but bittercress, chickweed and young dandelion leaves are very passable in a mixed salad and are highly nutritious. I cook nettles, greater plantain and ground-elder leaves, often mixed with other greens or added to soup.

Some plants have leaves that are a particular asset to, and speed up, the composting process. Nettle, dock, yarrow, dandelion and comfrey have very penetrating or deep tap roots and draw up valuable soil minerals. If the leaves are added to the compost heap, even more enrichment can be speedily returned to our soil and then to our plants.

There are leguminous weeds, such as clover, trefoils and vetches, which manufacture nitrogen in their root nodules and enrich our soil; a bit of a quandary in meadows where they are good for wildlife but can impede the development of other wildflowers; good news in the vegetable garden where nitrogen is useful for crop production.

If a weed is, by definition, a plant out of place, then I certainly have no objection to primroses, campion, sorrel, stitchwort and wild carrot – among many others that take up residence in my garden.

In the spirit of the traditional cottage gardener, I "harvest" our unwanted weeds and recycle them to fuel my compost or feed to the hens to produce eggs or to our goats to turn into milk. I find such natural cycles are most satisfying and offer me very constructive ways to approach what could otherwise be perceived as a chore!

TROUBLE SHOOTING FOR WEEDS

Here are a few issues that require special treatment:

SEED SPREAD Preventing the spread of weed seed is my first line of defence, so we try to stay ahead of the game and restrict germination with layers of mulch. With problem invaders, such as willowherb, we remove the plant or its flower stems before the seeds ripen. We are especially diligent with bittercress, annual meadow grass and chickweed which mature and produce offspring in the blink of an eyelid.

If we fail to deal with the plant before the seed ripens, we grasp and capture the unruly seed-heads (particularly those with an explosive or aeronautical nature) in a black plastic bag, seal it and leave them to decompose a little before disposing of the contents. When approaching and handling fluffy, ripe, seed-heads such as willowherb, it helps to do so after dew or rainfall temporarily cripples the aeronautical mechanisms or to dampen them deliberately to momentarily harness them to their stems and prevent them taking to the air when disturbed.

VEGETATIVE INVASION Brambles are excellent for wildlife but bad for our health and temper when they grow in the borders. Between August and September, we cut them back to prevent them from literally "dropping in" from the hedgerows and their root-forming tips (stolons) from anchoring themselves to begin a new dynasty of plants in unwanted places.

Plants with creeping roots are a menace; creeping thistle is wonderful for butterflies but a torment for farmers and gardeners. I bear this little ditty in mind, and try to act on it:

> "Stub a thistle in May, it will be back next day,
> Stub a thistle in June, it will be back soon,
> Stub a thistle in July, it will surely die."

If we have a problem with underground stems (rhizomes) of couch and ground elder, we smother them with a light-excluding material that is durable enough to be left in place for at least a year (the time it takes to kill them off).

Some weeds, such as ground ivy, creeping buttercup and cinquefoil, have creeping stems (runners) that allow the weed to gain territory when your back is turned, at an alarming rate. We try to dig them out in time to prevent them from advancing.

These, and many other weeds, are often easier to remove at the time when they are throwing most energy into stem growth, and there is a temporary armistice in their determination to anchor their roots in the soil.

Our efficient composting system (see above) ensures that neither "undigested" root remains (nor weed seeds) re-inoculate the soil.

ALTERNATIVE METHODS

Turnips are said to deal with a ground-elder infestation, if grown among it, and marigolds, particularly *Tagetes minuta*, also control this unpopular weed as well as discouraging horsetail and ground ivy. I have had some success with a method whereby you cut the growth of perennial weeds, having allowed them to grow until about to flower, and then lay them thickly on the surface of their own roots. For some reason, and in some cases, it seems to debilitate them.

Flame throwers are useful weed deterrents for certain places, such as paths, but we find we have to persevere with repeated treatments, especially with the highly resistant annual meadow grass. Insects can accidentally frazzle in the inferno so I keep a keen look out for ladybirds and other innocents.

The use of herbicides is understandably condemned by the Soil Association because of the side-effects on soil health and certain creatures (including humans). It clearly makes sense to eliminate unnecessary risk and avoid using them.

POTENTIALLY HAZARDOUS WEEDS One or two weeds are poisonous and I am resolute in preventing the spread of those that might cause a problem in the wider environment: for example, ragwort and hemlock water dropwort could spread onto neighbouring farms.

Alien species can threaten our native wildflowers so I take a responsible stand and assiduously deal with plants such as Himalayan balsam, Japanese knotweed and giant hogweed if any stray my way.

A few weeds can carry pests and diseases that occasionally transfer to crops and ornamentals. I remove every seedling of rape that germinates from bought-in bird seed. There is no way of knowing and no certification to suggest whether or not they are GM-contaminated and I adhere to the precautionary principle and fight tooth and nail to keep my land GM-free until the safety of such plants is proven.

RECYCLING WEEDS All the inhabitants at Sticky Wicket have to work for their living! This is a cottage garden in essence and our poultry plays an important part in our garden recycling system. They delight to scratch about among the weeds which we dump among the alders and willows. "Civilized" weeds are sacrosanct for our well-ordered compost heap but "uncivilized" ones, with indestructible seeds or pernicious roots, can be reliably dealt with by our chicken army. Few weeds survive in the run, but the ones that do succeed do little harm and are welcome. Weeds, such as bitter-cress and annual meadow grass, can sometimes survive the composting process but not once they have been through the gut of a chicken.

Nettles, docks, buttercups and excessive mint are hard to discard without root re-growth coming back to harass us but it doesn't matter much in here. Delicious, organically produced eggs become the by-product of unwanted or surplus vegetation. The year-round eggs supply feeds family and friends handsomely. By-product eggshells are baked dry, ground up and fed back to the hens as grit, which they need for healthy digestion and efficient egg-production. Some crushed shell is scattered on our vegetable garden to add calcium where brassicas are grown and we might also try using them to discourage slugs – if we had an unsolved problem!

When our duck pond is refreshed, water is spread onto parts of the garden, complete with its sludgy, high-nutrient content. When hen sheds (and dovecote) are cleaned out, the "guano" is added to the compost heap to enrich its nutrient value and help to activate the process of decomposition.

Quite a return on a few pesky weeds!

KEEPING PLANTS HEALTHY

It obviously makes sense to match our choice of plants to soil type and conditions, exposure to wind and sun, and extremes of heat and cold and, in this respect, native plants are easiest to evaluate and accommodate. Drainage is the easiest thing to change if needs must and, although it was necessary for us to deal with some of our ill-drained sites, we have conceded to the nature of our clay-based, loam-topped soil. Our soil pH is neutral, varying slightly across the acres but allowing us a choice of a wide range of native and garden plants. Trying to alter the conditions we are dealt, especially the soil pH is generally far too much of an uphill struggle to be worth attempting.

I bear in mind that most of the garden plants we grow come from far-away places where conditions may be vastly different from our own, so it makes sense to research their origin in order to cater for (or pamper to) their needs. If our climate is to change as dramatically as scientists predict, some doors may close and others may open when it comes to plant choice. I put my money on our British native plants being best able to survive and I seriously hope that, for all our sakes, this will be the case. The highly speculative wisdom of the spread of European imported wildflower species will be sorely tested and debated when such impostors are put to the test. Non-native varieties may have crucial differences, such as flowering times and susceptibility to disease, and even slight differences may be the make or break criteria for survival.

I am fascinated by the sustainable communities of plants where there is a truce in the combat for the supremacy of particularly boisterous species. I study and admire the system in ancient meadows and woodland where an equilibrium exists and, in an optimistic way, I try to emulate this finely tuned type of matrix planting in parts of the garden. I look for plants that will thrive, with roughly matched dynamism, in the conditions I can offer and then I pitch the contenders into contest. I would rather strong-arm a thug than nurture a wimp, but it is as well to recognize the parameters!

AVOIDING PLANT PROBLEMS   I choose both native and garden plants that will eagerly accept our soil type and conditions and the available degree of sunlight and shelter. A study of the natural habitats of our county is fascinating and helpful and, to encourage wildlife, I mimic these natural habitats, such as wetland, grassland, woodland and the ecotones where one habitat meets another.

I use many British native plants, local to my county, and mingle some of them with introduced garden plants. Native or garden plants with fruit, berry, seed, pollen, nectar and larval food plants are a life-line for wildlife. I grow wildflowers from locally sourced seed or buy it from reputable seed merchants that guarantee the seed is of British provenance, not from imported British forms grown abroad.

I try to place garden plants in conditions similar to that of the natural environment of their country of origin.

Discovering how to select and encourage plants to live compatibly in a plant community helps me work towards achieving equilibrium between species. I find it helpful to select ornamental border plants that are reasonably well-matched in terms of gusto for community border life.

Plants are pretty wise at choosing the right place to put themselves so I seldom refuse a volunteer. I generally leave self-seeded plants in place unless very much at odds with my vision for the border or seriously invading another plant's space.

Annuals, the opportunists of the plant world, rapidly make seed to ensure their perpetuation; I try to pre-empt such activities with unwanted species and create suitable conditions for those I would like in their place.

It is important to recognize the pace and tenacity of the spread of ground-covering plants and only introduce the most uncompromising squatters (such as lamium, periwinkle, woodruff and comfrey) where their job is exclusively to exclude other vegetation.

I avoid plants known to be susceptible to disease and avoid monocultures of plant species (such as roses) as this may provoke vulnerability to disease.

COMPANION PLANTING

Although I have excluded our vegetable garden from the main chapters of this book, I grow some edible plants in my flower gardens, too. It is worth noting here that our food crops are organically grown and, while we are not aspiring to be entirely self-sufficient, we have a fair supply of fresh, chemical-free and GM-free vegetables all year round. Nothing compares to the flavour, freshness and overall wholesomeness of organically reared home-grown vegetables so they justify any amount of extra commitment – even digging by moonlight!

Apparently there is insufficient scientific evidence to support ancient folk law and some of the theories of companion planting, but common knowledge and common-sense have underpinned traditional garden husbandry since man began to cultivate land for crops. Certainly there are many plants that have herbal attributes which help us to avoid using environmentally harmful chemicals. Such herbs are usually also excellent nectar plants and will attract pollinating insects that are so vital to the formation of seeds nuts, fruits and berries. Companion planting is dismissed by some sceptics as "old wives' tales". Maybe; but the old wives had a special wisdom and many of their beliefs and practices survived and are applied today, particularly in herbal medicine and biodynamic methods.

I daresay organic growers ("new wives") of the 21st century may have to revise their know-how to cope with the superbugs which have developed since modern chemicals forced Mother Nature to retaliate against the heavy-handed assault she has so far been dealt. I hold on to my firm faith in nature and, because I never underestimate the power and potency of certain plants (or old wives!), I look forward to broadening my knowledge of natural husbandry; my amateur efforts barely scratch the surface of the fascinating principles of biodynamic husbandry, which take organic gardening to a heightened level. Meanwhile, I revel in the delights of mixing and matching my companions with my selected colours in the four gardens I have described. In my vegetable garden I grow hot-coloured companion plants to attract pollinating and pest-predating insects, or sometimes act as a lure to draw pests away from the crops.

GOOD COMPANIONS FOR VEGETABLES AND ORNAMENTALS Many companion plants happen to come in the lively range of red, orange and strong yellow colours, which I eschew in most of my borders and prefer to confine to my vegetable garden. Red and other odd-coloured vegetables suffer fewer pest attacks because they are naturally camouflaged and less recognizable.

The edible red and gold orache act as an attractive, annual, weed-suppressing cover-crop while they grow as seedlings among the rows of veg. We thin (and eat) most of them but leave some to mature before making seeds for the next generation and plenty for the birds. Our tawny-red sunflowers attract bees to help pollinate our scarlet runner beans, which thread their way around them and later offer seeds for our birds. I include additional strong or hot-coloured plants, such as golden rod, rudbeckias, heleniums and fiery crocosmias, which are pollen and nectar-rich and then seed-laden in autumn. Seed-heads are left until February for the birds, which deal with any over-wintering pest insects.

Some herbs, such as the dye plants anthemis tinctoria and woad, and others, such as fennel, achillea and agrimony, have strong yellow colouring and join my throng of plants which have dual benefits to wildlife and organic vegetable production.

Amongst the vegetables I grow a riot of hot-coloured companion plants, including fennel, to attract useful predatory insects and pollinators, such as hoverflies, which help to control pest insects.

Achillea is a good example; it is a good nectar plant with useful seed-heads and its root secretions activate disease resistance in nearby plants. Foxgloves and camomile also stimulate healthy growth of other plants and nettles can profit plants – especially fruit – in the same way.

Plants contain all sorts of natural chemicals to attract pollinators or repel predators away from themselves or their neighbours. For instance, aromatic plants such as tansy and mint contain substances which repel certain insects. Nasturtiums lure Cabbage White caterpillars and black-fly away from brassicas, repel white-fly and woolly aphids, attract hoverflies, are edible and full of vitamin C and iron, and have antiseptic properties. A pretty impressive CV, which can only be eclipsed by the merits of evening primrose. This is well known for its long list of medicinal properties, plus it has edible flower buds and roots and is evening scented to entice night-flying moths. African marigolds are said to emit substances that kill harmful nematodes in soil and are said to be best mates for potatoes and tomatoes.

Caterpillars and aphids edge away from garlic, which can be planted near susceptible plants or applied topically as a liquid dilution. Both garlic and chives have a reputation for their ability to help protect roses from black spot and I am almost convinced the leeks in my borders have the same aptitude.

There are mixed opinions as to the legitimacy of the assertion that caper spurge deters moles. I wonder if it is purely circumstantial that I find relatively little mole activity in my vegetable garden where this herb grows freely.

PEST CONTROL Chemicals spell disaster to wildlife and must be avoided, so we manage the garden to pre-empt problems from pest, disease or over-bearing weed problems. Encouraging beneficial wildlife helps turn the contest between pest and predator in our favour. We actually need a few of the pest insects to encourage a healthy population of the necessary predators. Less than one per cent of Britain's 22,400 insect species are pests!

If there is an acutely disruptive imbalance I have, on very few occasions, used "applied" biological control in the form of nematodes for pest insects, such as vine weevils and slugs. Naturally-occurring biological control is cheaper and more fun. Birds, bats, hedgehogs, frogs and toads, beetles, ladybirds, lacewings, hoverflies, slow-worms, centipedes and wasps are there to help. Positive thinking also helps; we regard our small number of aphids as "bird and ladybird food" – then they barely bother us! There is always the finger-and-thumb or heavy-boot technique for any particularly disagreeable little blighters.

DISEASE CONTROL   It seems that most plants get sick because we invite them to live in inhospitable conditions, so that plight is the first thing to avoid or relieve. Growth-stressed, or otherwise unthrifty, plants are more susceptible to, and less able to deal with secondary problems, such as pest invasion or fungal attack.

My first line of defence is to watch out for pointers: changes in colour are often the first clue and can indicate that physiological problems, such as drought, water-logging, wind-rock and scorching or nutrient deficiency, may be the cause. If it is a bacterial or viral infection I don't know of any effective weapons to treat contaminated plants. Fungal infections are often too far gone to remedy unless identified and treated with great expediency. Certain fungicides – such as sulphur and Bordeaux powder – are permitted by the Soil Association but we never use them as, all too often, products certified as "safe" are withdrawn from the shelves.

We prefer to cut out the affected parts of the plant and give them the TLC needed to help them recover. Mostly they do. If the problem is widespread, I believe it unlikely that chemicals will successfully control a runaway disease. My plants either eventually survive the problem or they don't – c'est la vie. With contagious diseases such as potato-blight, fire-blight and some viruses, we are scrupulous in removing and burning all affected plant material immediately.

PROPHYLACTIC AND ORGANIC TREATMENT   The three Ds – damaged, diseased or dead wood – are removed and incinerated if contagious. It is vital to disinfect secateurs after cutting into diseased wood but ideally the pruning cuts should be made well below the infected stem or branch so that the tools remain uncontaminated and the plant will recover from a healthy growing point.

Lacewing and ladybird houses provide additional habitat for these hugely beneficial aphid predators.

Morning glory (Ipomea sp.) and poached egg flower (Limnanthes douglasii) are among favourite plants for hoverflies, whose larvae have a voracious appetite for aphid larvae.

We feed and encourage the birds such as tits, which help control pest insects, robins, which eat vine weevil larvae, and thrushes, which hammer away at the snail population. Frogs and toads hop about in pursuit of slugs while hedgehogs and slow-worms are also useful predators.

The use of slug pellets is obviously out of the question and is thankfully unnecessary in our garden. Only rarely have I needed to use commercially produced nematodes as an additional biological control for abnormally increased populations of slugs in the vegetable garden or for infestations of vine weevil amongst the ornamentals.

A rather more tangible method is to capture the enemy. I do my own share of predation and go out at night and squash a few undesirables (such as the aforementioned). I sometimes trap slugs in citrus fruit skins and vine weevils in rolls of corrugated paper. I find beer traps attract other boozy creatures that I have no wish to drown. Slugs find it hard to resist an up-turned bucket that has contained a bran and milk mixture so they offer me a transparent clue to making a trap with these ingredients. Soot, crushed egg shells and coffee grounds are also recommended for slug control.

I keep meaning to try using moth-balls to deter carrot-fly, but sowing them thinly with spring onions alongside works fairly well in disguising the scent which attracts this pest insect and this is a more natural form of deception.

Natural pest and disease deterrents made from plants and materials, such as horsetail, rhubarb, elder, garlic, tobacco, soap and soda, were tools available to our ancestors and no doubt served them well. Although the use of home-made concoctions is now outside the EU law, I doubt if such an embargo is enforceable.

MANAGING HEDGES

Species-rich hedgerows with British native plants are superb for wildlife and, whether they are regularly trimmed or allowed to grow tall, they serve an abundance of different creatures in different ways. The thicker the hedge the better, and an A-shape grows most successfully, but the most important thing is that they are not interfered with between March and August when birds are nesting. It is an offence under Section 1 of the 1981 Wildlife and Countryside Act to intentionally take, damage or destroy the nest of any wild bird while it is in use or being built so I cannot imagine why it is within the law and yet outside the limits of common-sense to even consider cutting native hedgerows between March and August. Birds sing to claim their domain so when I hear them in full voice in February, I make sure all my hedgerow management is very soon up to speed for at least the next six months. In fact, I wouldn't touch them until late December when nearly all the berries have disappeared and the insects have had plenty of time to breed on the leaves. Some of our stretches of hedgerow are cut and laid, or even coppiced, to thicken them up and keep them rejuvenated but this is only likely to happen every ten years or so. Other parts of our hedgerow are trimmed by hand or mechanically depending on the sensitivity of their nature or position.

It is a bit more difficult to be as decisive with garden hedges that are also used for habitat and, depending on choice of species, may also provide food for wildlife, but need to be shaped and controlled if they are to fulfil their structural or decorative function. Just one false snip and the cover can be totally blown for a nesting bird even if no harm appears to have been done, so I carefully consider the nature of each of my garden hedges. The hornbeam hedge that shelters my vegetable garden is a well-used haven where birds regularly nest in the gnarled framework beneath the annual growth it produces in a year. Fortunately for the birds I allow it to remain untouched until August.

My mixed box (Buxus sempervirens) and privet (Lonicera nitida) hedge is also routinely used as a nesting place and I am faced with a dilemma when it makes a massive amount of bushy growth and needs cutting in prime-time May and June. The exterior fuzz of young shoots augment the natural wildlife cover of the woody interior but cause the hedge to become an increasingly shapeless feature of the design of the garden. I must either accept the disordered appearance, and give such hedges an annual winter chop (which can be a bit savage for some species) or lightly trim those with the absolute regularity required to keep the profile as unaltered as possible.

My approach with hedges depends on the species of plant, the probability of its occupation by vulnerable wildlife and whether or not I can very discreetly peer into the branches and detect any occupied sites. While gardening in summer months I leave a wide birth around any known nesting sites.

HEDGEROWS   I have my own special procedure when it comes to boundary hedgerow management.

During December and January I cut out sticks for peas and any whippy hazel stems I may need for weaving or plant supports. Ash usually makes vigorous growth and the stems are excellent for shredding so the most substantial branches are harvested for this along with the shorter but twiggier field maple and other non-thorny, woody stems with some substance.

Major stems of thorny hawthorn and blackthorn are cut out and set aside in small heaps until the work is complete. The remainder of the hedge is then cut with a hand-held, or tractor-mounted, mechanical hedge cutter. The thorny stems are afterwards threaded back into any gaps in the hedge and some are flattened onto the hedge top where spring growth soon forges through this extra lid of protective covering. This considerably reinforces the hedge's natural defences against predators such as magpies and squirrels and is also effective against human intruders forcing an entrance or domestic pets or stock making an escape. Badger and fox runs are easy to spot and I avoid blocking their passage. As the cut branches gradually biodegrade, they enhance the habitat for insects and fungi and their remains mulch the hedge bottom.

During the summer, long wandering stems of brambles begin their quest to stray into new territory. After the August bird-nesting watershed, I trim and re-trim these where it is necessary to keep them at bay and to encourage fruiting stems for the following year.

If parts of our hedge are to be cut and laid, we also do this in the midwinter period although it is less likely the re-formed hedge will be used for nesting in the first year of its resurgence. Cutting and laying is a traditional countryside practice that involves severing about nine-tenths of the hedgerow trunk or stem and laying it more or less horizontally with just this fraction of its woody lifeline attached. New and vigorous growth occurs along the length of the recumbent wood and large gaps in the hedge can thus be filled.

It may appear to be a radical attack, but the benefits are soon realized and improve and prolong the life of the hedge. If it is well-managed in subsequent years, and trimmed annually to an A-shape, the wondrously rejuvenated hedge will thrive and thicken and its potential for harbouring wildlife will be many times greater than one that is skinny or gappy.

The practice of coppicing a hedgerow (cutting the stems to within a few inches of the base) may appear even more extreme, but is another way of rejuvenating and thickening a hedge, provided it is reasonably healthy and was not too gappy in the first place.

GARDEN HEDGES From May until the end of July, I keep formally shaped and dynamically growing hedges, such as privet, regularly but very lightly trimmed to maintain some order whilst minimizing the risk of exposing nesting sites close to the surface of the thatch of growth. I re-discipline the shape in August and September, allowing plenty of time for the soft regrowth to harden up properly before winter.

I leave less formally shaped and open-branched ornamental hedges, such as philadelphus or forsythia, untouched until after nesting time unless the odd wayward stem can be trimmed with the total certainty that no harm can be done to the resident wildlife.

My living, willow-woven hedge is rewoven during the winter when I conceal my "retired" woven bird features (feeding globes and roosters) among the network of newly threaded stems for extra wildlife cover. The next generation of long wands of new growth are left to grow freely during the summer.

In selected parts of my hedges I weave dense, living, leafy domes by bending and weaving the flexible young stems of hedging plants, such as hazel, willow, cornus and snowberry. If I have sussed out an appropriate place, I am seldom disappointed when, come the autumn, I check for evidence that some of our birds have nested there.

I trim the sides of my hornbeam hedge in August and trim the lengthy top-growth back hard in winter, saving the substantial twiggy stems from the prunings for brushwood for plant supports and tightly bundling the remainder to make additional habitat boosters.

MANAGING GRASSLAND

For the organic and wildlife gardener, the rules of grassland management are very much at odds with the sort of lawn care now the norm in conventional gardens. Our aim is to reduce the fertility level and restrain the over-zealous growth of grass in order to encourage the wildflowers to gain a stronghold. This may be an anathema to some gardeners, who may perceive such broad-leaved plants as "weeds" when they occur in the grass they are trying very hard to encourage, but at Sticky Wicket we see a grassy space as a place where at least some of our much-persecuted wildflowers, and associated wildlife, can be given respite from the environmental maltreatment which is sadly a part of the production of many a "bowling green" lawn.

A chemical-free grass sward is an excellent breeding ground for invertebrates and in turn becomes feeding ground for the birds that forage for these worms, grubs and bugs. We certainly have stretches of luxuriant, verdant lawns but ours are self-fed with the content of white clover that volunteers to grow there and which manufactures natural nitrogen, leaving us with no need, and certainly no desire, to use chemicals.

We have successfully created opportunities for growing wildflowers in damp clay and on nutrient-deprived chalk and rubble and gravel mounds and most of these grassland projects are just a few meters square. We have even succeeded in meeting the ultimate challenge of growing wildflowers in our rich loam of the garden but success did not come without a considerable amount of remedial work.

These grassland patches are cut between one and four times a year depending on the requirements of individual systems. Our one-and-a-half acres of lowland clay meadows are annually cut for hay using traditional methods but with extra proviso that the timing of any such cutting operations are carefully geared to the well-being of the wildflowers and to the welfare of the various associated wildlife. We use a "patchwork" system whereby different sections are cut at different times according to the best interests of both flora and fauna.

The reduced number of mowing operations involved in our overall grassland management has the additional benefit that it lessens the volume of noise pollution and fuel emissions generated from our four to five acres. The cut meadow-grass and lawn mowings are variously either recycled via the composting system, used as a green mulch or fed to our poultry or goats and "returned" to us in the form of eggs and milk.

MANAGING LAWNS

In line with organic principles and for the protection of wildlife, our lawns and grass paths are obviously chemical-free.

With wildlife in mind, we allow, or indeed encourage, mowable wildflowers (or weeds) such as white clover, selfheal, daisies and trefoil, to grow in the grass. To protect insects and help minimize the effects of drought, we never mow our lawns too closely. Where the ground is very compacted I might aerate the turf with a fork in spring or autumn. Where there are muddy patches or there is undue wear, I reinforce with gravelly soil – recycled from our path-weeding operations.

Once a year I re-define all the lawn edges with a spade or half-moon edger. I use these off-cuts of turf to repair subsidence in the lawn or grass paths or where they are mole-damaged.

I harvest wildflower seed throughout the summer and sprinkle the turf with this after their final cut in autumn. I add extra grass seed where I need to cater for the wear and tear on the well-worn routes.

As far as possible I keep off the lawns in winter when they are very wet or frosted.

Some areas are spared the mower blades for some weeks during the summer so that the low-growing flowers can hold their heads a little higher and bloom for longer, as a gift to wildlife.

Our mixtures of fine-leaved, native grasses are less competitive than ryegrass which is great for rugby pitches but would be far too headstrong in this situation and must be avoided where wildflowers are the priority.

Prior to mowing, I painstakingly check the longer grass of flowering lawns for hedgehogs, frogs, toads and newts ahead of the lawn mower or strimmer.

Sometimes I am delighted to find ant hills forming in longer grass. I am careful to avoid scalping them and allow them to eventually form a raised wildflower micro-environment and provide food for green woodpeckers.

MANAGING WILDFLOWER MEADOWS

For the sake of both wildflowers and wildlife, we cut our meadows section by section in a "patchwork" system between July and October. Over-fertile places are targeted first to help reduce the vigour of course grasses. We avoid cutting the more flowery patches until the plants have set seed and thousands of insects have benefited from the nectar-rich plants.

We leave the cut grass in swaths for a couple of days for creepy-crawlies to creep and crawl to safety and for wildflower seeds to shed or be harvested. Careful removal of hay, or cut grass or debris, will avoid a build-up of excess fertility from decomposing vegetation. We leave designated areas uncut and undisturbed for wildlife but the size and position of these is varied from year to year to avoid encouraging coarse grasses or scrub regeneration.

Fertilizers, especially chemical ones, are the enemy of wildflowers so we avoid using any and hope that none will leach onto our land from boundary watercourses.

MANAGING PONDS

It is essential to try and create a balanced environment with the right management and appropriate choice of plant material. As with meadows, excessive nutrients, especially those that are chemical-based, are likely to cause problems, creating similarly excessive or unwanted vegetation. Ponds with too few plants, especially oxygenating ones, will have problems with excess algae (plants with fine filaments that restrict the growth of other plants), which can turn the water green and reduce the oxygen levels crucial to the health of pond water and pond-life. A submersible pump helps to aerate the water while water snails help balance the weed growth.

We have to be aware of and bear in mind the struggle for supremacy between species of aquatic plants and the similar battle for survival between aquatic creatures. We also have to understand that the interrelationship between aquatic flora and fauna can amount to a fragile coexistence. Minimum interference is recommended so that a natural balance can develop, but garden ponds seldom reach an equilibrium that pleases all parties concerned, including the gardener.

If interfere we must, there is never an ideal time to do so as far as wildlife are concerned, but the period between August and October is said to be the most acceptable. When it comes to keeping the pond topped up, rainwater is much healthier than tap water and, in spite of the atmospheric pollutants it picks up, it is hopefully less chemically enhanced than most tap water. Spring-fed ponds are a pure source but might induce mineral-rich water, the cause of blanketweed, which smothers other plants until the oxygenating plants consume the minerals.

I have selected mostly native plants in the hope that they will form a reasonably stable community and encourage pond-life, such as water snails and tadpoles; these consume decaying plant matter and algal growth. Water temperature affects pond-life as well and the idea, as with most other environments, is to avoid extremes. Warm water encourages algae. Deeper water at the centre of the pond helps to regulate temperature fluctuations, as does controlling the amount of plant cover.

We mow our meadows between July and October using a patchwork system of cutting, targeting the most fertile grassy areas first and leaving flower-rich patches to set seed and provide for wildlife.

POND CARE PROGRAMME

Unless absolutely essential we resist the temptation to interfere with the wildlife ponds. If absolutely necessary, we wade in and remove excess vegetation between August and October; underwater plants also require some light for photosynthesis, so we need to see fair play between submerged, floating and emergent plants.

We leave the cleared vegetation beside the pond for two or three days so accidentally displaced creatures can escape before debris is removed to the compost heap. During this time we turn and inspect the debris because some of the weird and wonderful pond-dwellers get trapped among the plants or blanketweed and need to be released back into the water. I am cautious when handling diving beetles and water-boatmen, however, which can deal a mean nip!

We try to relieve the pond of at least some of the fallen autumn leaves to prevent oxygen being removed as they decompose.

February and March is courting and mating time for frogs, with toads usually a couple of weeks behind. They like privacy, so this is the time to steer clear of the pond edge, and just watch and listen from a polite distance.

We take great care when mowing or strimming near the pond, ensuring all visible creatures are chased away and no grass is dropped into the pond to compound the debris situation.

In summer we try to channel in as much rain water as possible to keep the water refreshed and the level constant.

If we do need to use tap water we trickle it in gently to avoid disturbing the mud or sprinkle it on to help with aeration and lower the water temperature.

Movement of water via winter excess rainfall removes salts and toxic materials.

We wrap netting around our submersible pump to prevent blanketweed blocking its filter and mechanism, and we bring the whole apparatus in before the frogs start to hibernate in the deep water in winter.

POND TROUBLE-SHOOTING

- If the pond is heavily frozen over in winter, keep an airway open to allow accumulated gases to escape lest they poison the wildlife. A pond-heater is a good way to keep an opening without trauma to the wildlife but a simple bowl of hot water can be used instead.
- If aphids become a problem on pond plants, I am advised that hosing these insects

into the water provides a snack for the pond creatures and is a positive resolution to the problem.

- Use barley straw to help control blanketweed (but EU regulations may present future obstructions to the way we mange our water). Organically grown straw would be preferable to conventional, potentially contaminated straw.
- If you find a luxuriant green lid of duckweed, gently sift some out with a net or rake (we feed ours to our ducks). It will inevitably re-grow but regular thinning allows at least a little necessary light to penetrate the water and reach the submerged plants.

PROPAGATION

I need to propagate a certain number of plants to keep the garden revitalized or to experiment with new ones grown from seed. Rather than have too many plants imprisoned in pots, I find seeds, cuttings and bare-rooted plantlets are a more environmentally sensitive way to share plants with other gardeners.

Large-scale removal of peat from bogs is annihilating our most precious habitats. Centuries of peat formation have been sacrificed to supply the horticultural trade. Fortunately, enlightened gardeners can now buy peat alternatives or use homemade compost. I insist on using organic, peat-free compost for both sowing and potting on in spite of the fact that seed germination is a bit erratic with some products. Some wildflower seeds prefer to grow in molehill soil, but this inevitably contains other seeds which may need to be weeded out.

SEED-SAVING AND SOWING   I harvest seed when it is ripe, in dry weather. As a general rule of thumb, most seeds are ripe when they are hard, dark-coloured and part fairly willingly from their seed-head or capsule.

Seed-heads are then dried in paper bags in the poly tunnel or kitchen. The seed is cleanly separated from the husks and overwintered in paper envelopes placed in waterproof containers in the fridge.

Some seed must be sown when freshly harvested even though the seeds may not germinate until the following spring (or even longer after sowing).

For seeds that are slow to germinate, a covering of grit or vermiculite (for surface-sown seeds needing light to germinate) helps to keep growing conditions healthy.

I sow very few spring-grown plants until the natural growing season begins in March, so only a tiny minority need to be "nannied" in an electrically heated propagating unit. Hundreds of seedlings volunteer in the gravel paths and we carefully lift these and pot all we need.

I try to follow the principles of sowing seed and transplanting plants with the waxing rather than waning moon, out of respect for the fact that the lunar rhythms of the earth's magnetic field affect plant growth, but it is difficult enough keeping up to date with the work, let alone conceding to further limitations.

HERBACEOUS PLANTS   I lift and divide herbaceous plants in spring when the weather starts to warm up and there are signs of growth. I use only the most virile, healthy pieces of plant material in the minimum-sized pot needed to comfortably contain the required length and volume of roots. For these plants I use the most friable of my home-produced compost, topped up with just an inch of so of the more sterile commercial product to minimize weed germination.

I have some shaded benches for juvenile or recently potted plants that need respite from bright sunshine.

I allow about an inch of space at the top of the pots for efficient use of water.

I re-use pots and seed trays, disinfecting any which have traces of diseased plants or very stale soil.

Any woody cuttings I need are done by a friend, Rose Dennison, as she succeeds where I fail.

IN CONCLUSION

Our five acres of garden and meadows undeniably require hard work and dedication. I am not about to claim that everything in the garden is always rosy but I do know for sure that the balance of nature generally swings in our favour. Rabbits, for instance, do very little to endear themselves to us but the unlucky few that end up in a pot make a wholesome dinner. We do suffer the effects of certain fungal diseases, which can blight the look of some of the plants, but in fact most of them survive.

We lose more plants as a result of the increasing wet winters than for any other reason, so we just have to make do with the ones that can cope. Slugs, snails and aphids are the least of our problems and although I get a bit miffed when the mice eat my vegetable seeds, I lose very little sleep over the effects of pests on our plants.

I admit to sometimes feeling a little overwhelmed by certain of the pesky and persistent weeds that I try hard to love and tolerate. But that slight pressure and a few creaking bones are a very small price to pay for living in a flourishing wildlife paradise which is delightfully easy on the eye and which provides essential food for both body and soul.

Our garden flourishes because we work in tune with nature and respect and nurture the soil. Our methods enable us to garden without the use of any chemical fertilizers or pest control, make full use of our weeds and prunings, minimize the need to water and to live in peace and harmony with our wildlife.

USEFUL ADDRESSES

Emorsgate Seeds
Limes Farm, Tilney All Saints
King's Lynn, Norfolk PE34 4RT
01553 829028
(specifies county of origin)
www.wildseeds.co.uk

Suffolk Herbs
Monks Farm, Coggeshall Road
Kelvedon, Colchester, Essex CO5 9PG
01376 572456
www.suffolkherbs.com

G. and J.E. Peacock
Kingsfield Conservation Nursery
Broadenham Lane, Winsham
Chard, Somerset TA20 4JF
01460 30070

Green Farm Plants
Bury Court, Bentley
Farnham, Surrey GU10 5LZ
01420 23202

Nori and Sandra Pope
Hadspen Garden and Nursery
Castle Cary, Somerset BA7 7NG
01749 813707
www.hadspengarden.co.uk

Ian and Angela Winfield
Snape Cottage
Chaffeymoor Hill, Bourton, Dorset
01747 840330
www.snapestakes.com

Knoll Gardens
Hampreston, Wimborne
Dorset BH21 7ND
01202 873931
www.knollgardens.co.uk

The Woodland Trust
Autumn Park, Dysart Road
Grantham, Lincolnshire NG31 6LL
01476 581111
www.woodland-trust.org.uk

Butterfly Conservation
Manor Yard, East Lulworth,
Wareham, Dorset BH20 5QP
0870 7744309
www.butterfly-conservation.org

Bat Conservation Trust
Unit 2, 15 Cloisters House
8 Battersea Park Road, London SW8 4BG
020 7627 2629
www.bats.org.uk

The Mammal Society
2B Inchworth Street, London SW11 3EP
020 7350 2200
www.abdn.ac.uk

Royal Entomological Society
41 Queens Gate, London SW7 4HU
020 7584 8361
www.royensoc.co.uk

Royal Society for the Protection of Birds
The Lodge, Sandy,
Bedfordshire SG19 2DL
01767 680551
www.rspb.org.uk/

The British Trust for Ornithology
The Nunnery, Thetford, Norfolk, P24 2PU
01842 750050
www.bto.org/

C. J. Wildbird Foods
The Rea, Upton Magna
Shrewsbury SY4 4UR
01743 709545 and 0800 731 2820
www.birdfood.co.uk

Flora-For-Fauna
c/o The Natural History Museum,
Cromwell Road, South Kensington,
London SW7 5BD
020 7942 5000
Postcode Plants Database: www.nhm.ac.uk/
science/projects/fff/Tech.htm

The Wildlife Trusts
The Kiln, Waterside, Mather Road,
Newark NG24 1WT
0870 036 7711

Royal Horticultural Society
Vincent Square, London SW1P 2PE
020 7834 4333

Plantlife International
14 Rollestone Street, Salisbury
Wilts SP1 1DX
01722 372730
www.plantlife.org.uk

The Centre for Alternative Technology
Machynlleth, Powys, SY20 9AZ
01654 702400
www.cat.org.uk

The Henry Doubleday Research Association
Ryton Organic Gardens, Ryton on Dunsmore
Coventry, CV8 3LG
024 7630 3517
www.hdra.org.uk

The Soil Association
40-56 Victoria Street, Bristol BS1 6BY
www.soilassociation.org

USEFUL BOOKS

Chris Baines, *How to Make A Wildlife
Garden*, Frances Lincoln Ltd, 2000
Ron Wilson, *Gardening for Wildlife*,
Capall Bann Publishing, 1997
Robert Burton, *New Birdfeeder Handbook*
(RSPB), Dorling Kindersley, 2000
Peter Harper, *The Natural Garden Book*,
Gaia Books Limited, 1994
Charlie Ryrie, *The 'Daily Telegraph' Wildlife
Gardening*, Cassell Illustrated, 2003
Anna Kruger (Editor), *HDRA:
Encyclopedia of Organic Gardening*,
Dorling Kindersley, 2005
Pauline Pears and Sue Stickland,
*Organic Gardening (RHS Encyclopedia and
Practical Gardening)*, Mitchell Beazley,
1999
Bob Flowerdew, *Bob Flowerdew's Organic
Bible*, Kyle Cathie Ltd, 2003

INDEX

Numbers in *italic* refer to
illustrations and captions

achillea 111, 122, 189, 190
African lovegrass 127
alliums 102, 104, 105, 107, 108,
   119, 120, 124
amelanchier 150
angelica 67, *67*, 70, 102, 129, 160
anise hyssop 102, 117-18
apples 79-80
aquatic wildlife *see* Frog Garden;
   ponds
aquilegia 104
artemisia 106
aster 102, 114, 123, 148
astilbe 118

bats 45-6, 113, 168
bees, butterflies and moths 9, 39,
   62, 70, 135, 148, 149, 154,
      156, 157, 166, 167
   see also Round Garden
berberis 60, 80, 108, 129, 153
birch 143, 164-5, *164*
Bird Garden 10, 11, 15, 48-85
birds 9, 33, 46-7, 135, 137, 143,
   149, 150, 151, 152, 154, 158,
      164-5, 168, 174, 192, 193
   bird food and feeders 53, 74,
      75-6, 78-84
   bird- and bat-boxes 71, 72,
      168
   bird-baths 56-7, 74-5, 76
   see also Bird Garden
borders 12-13, 20, 36-43, 54,
   91-2, 108-28, 155-60
   management 180-2
boundary planting *see* hedgerows
brambles 59, 101, *101*, 184, 194
buckthorn 100-1, 152
buddleia 43, 113, 116-17, *117*
bulbs 39, 104, 105, 159, 165

calamintha 114
camomile lawn 91, 104, 171
campanula 38, 165
campion 69, 101, 160
chaenomeles 62
cherry trees 22, 59-60, 137, 149
choisya 155
clematis 37, 38, 116
cloud grass 104, 105-6, 107
comfrey 36, 175
companion planting 188-90
compost 172, 173-7
conifers 154
coriander 112
cornus 23, 36, 62-3, 151, 165
cosmos 60, 64
cotoneaster 39, 41, 62, 69, *69*,
   152, 165
cottage-garden plants 96
crab apple 59, 108, 137, 149

deschampsia 38, 41, 157
domestic animals 139, 147, 148
dry-stone walls 28, 167

echinacea 102, 110, 156
elder 58, 61, 165-6, 185
eryngium 71, 108, 115, 124-5
eupatorium 70, 109-10, 129,
   181
evening primrose 39, 112, 113,
   115, 190
evergreens 62, 154

farming practices 8, 18, 50, 88,
   135
feeding plants 173
fennel 39, *39*, 115, 189, 190
fertilizers/herbicides/pesticides
   18, 50, 84, 88, 135, 172, 185,
   198
festuca 106, 126, 129
foxglove 43, 160, 165

foxtail barley grass 12, 64, *64*,
   67, 102, 106, 113, 115
Frog Garden 10, 11, 15, 16-47
frogs and toads 167, 174
   see also Frog Garden
fruits and berries 59-60, 61-3,
   69, 93, 149-52, 153, 154-5

garden management 170-203
geranium 34, 38, 57, 70, 106-8,
   113-14, 157
GM (genetically modified)
   plants 12, 84, 88, 122, 186
grasses 23, 41, 64, 67, 105-6,
   110, 115, 126-7, 140, 157-8,
   181-2
grassland management 10,
   196-8
ground-cover planting 36, 157,
   165, 183, 188

habitat boosters 43-7, 71-82,
   128-30, 166-8
hazel 61, 137
hedgehogs 45, 142, 166, 174
hedgerows 50, 53-4, 58-9, 93,
   135
   management 194-5
hedges 20-1, 92-3, 193
   management 193-4, 195-6
hellebore 148, 165
herbaceous plants 38, 145, 155-
   7, 202
   see also borders
herbs 12, 38, 39-40, 101, 111,
   112, 115, 117-18, 119, 125,
   157
holly 93, 154, 165
honeysuckles 43, *43*, 55, 62, 63,
   113, 137
hops 39
hosta 46
house walls 54-5, 68-9

ACKNOWLEDGMENTS

Without Peter's love, strength and ingenuity, Sticky Wicket garden would be merely a castle in the air and if it had not been for the support of our family and friends we would have been unable to realize so many of our dreams and aspirations.

Our love and eternal thanks to: our outstanding project team – Emma Munday, Mark Smith and Marcus Lewis; our skilled gardening team – Fizz Lewis and Shane Seaman; Rose Dennison, Theodora Scutt and Ginny Bulman who have propagated so many of our plants; the multi-talented Ed Brooks for a memorable year as a student here and James Duell, Josefina Prieto and Catalina Phillips, who also studied with us, loved the garden and made unique contributions; our very special friends Lorely and Mike Brimson, Nori and Sandra Pope, John and Margaret Sutor, Ian and Angela Whinfield, and David and Marion Brookes for their phenomenal inspiration, love and support.

We could never have survived and opened the garden to the public for sixteen years without the unfailing help and love of my mother, Pauline Wilkes, my aunt and uncle, Pam and Alan Bartlett, my cousin Louise Skett, and our dear Lillian White, who must have baked more than a thousand cakes. Our thanks to Jill Pearce, May and Goff Corke, Carol Wilson, Brian and Sylvia Dicker and other helpers from Butterfly Conservation, plus many others who have volunteered their services for the NGS and other charity open days. But for the praise and encouragement of faithful garden visitors and friends, including Clive Farrell, Dennis and Peggy Seaward, Nigel and Lesley Slight, Sue and Hanna Smithies, and John and Lizzie Leach, we might have faltered over the years.

I thank my genius friend Andrew Lawson for his brilliant photographs of the garden, spanning sixteen years, and Susan Berry for her encouragement and help with this book. I also thank Alison and Ruth Martin, who assisted me with my writing and, along with all those I have mentioned, held my hand through the harrowing time of Peter's illness and in the dark days since his death in June 2004.